Praise for Peter Crowther's previous SF anthologies:

"*Moon Shots* is a well above average anthology . . . one of the more welcome theme anthologies of the year."
—*Science Fiction Chronicle*

"The stories (*Moon Shots*) are well worth reading and all would stand on their own without the benefit of the anthology's thematic structure. Some of the stories may manage to make the awards nomination lists next year."
—*SF Site*

"Crowther has, in *Mars Probes,* assembled a collection of stories that takes its eyes off the collective scientific ball and manages to be both refreshing and funny. It stands a very good chance of being the best anthology of the year."
—*Locus*

"The sixteen original stories in this collection (*Mars Probes*) capture the eternal fascination with the red planet." —*Library Journal*

"(*Mars Probes*) is impressive . . . the overall standard of quality is very high . . . It's a very good book." —*SF Site*

Also edited by
Peter Crowther

MOON SHOTS
MARS PROBES

CONSTELLATIONS

The Best of New British SF

EDITED BY
PETER CROWTHER

DAW BOOKS, INC.
DONALD A. WOLLHEIM, FOUNDER
375 Hudson Street, New York, NY 10014
ELIZABETH R. WOLLHEIM
SHEILA E. GILBERT
PUBLISHERS
www.dawbooks.com

ACKNOWLEDGMENTS

Introduction copyright © 2005 by Peter Crowther

"A Heritage of Stars," copyright © 2005 by Eric Brown

"Rats of the System," copyright © 2005 by Paul McAuley

"Ten Billion of Them," copyright © 2005 by Brian W. Aldiss

"Star!" copyright © 2005 by Tony Ballantyne

"Lakes of Light," copyright © 2005 by Stephen Baxter

"No Cure For Love," copyright © 2005 by Roger Levy

"The Navigator's Children," copyright © 2005 by Ian Watson

"A Different Sky," copyright © 2005 by Keith Brooke

"The Fulcrum," copyright © 2005 by Gwyneth Jones

"The Meteor Party," copyright © 2005 by James Lovegrove

"Written in the Stars," copyright © 2005 by Ian McDonald

"The Order of Things," copyright © 2005 by Adam Roberts

"The Little Bear," copyright © 2005 by Justina Robson

"Kings," copyright © 2005 by Colin Greenland

"Beyond the Aquila Rift," © 2005 by Alastair Reynolds

CONTENTS

BRITAIN SWINGS!

An Introduction of sorts to
Constellations: The Best of New British SF

Things never seem to happen quite as you plan them. Have you noticed that?

Following the critical success of my first two SF anthologies for DAW Books I decided to pitch for a third volume in the series . . . but what would the theme be this time out? We'd had the moon (*Moon Shots*) and we'd had Mars (*Mars Probes*), so what should be next? Moreover, which planet in our solar system would provide me with a snappy two-word title?

Aside from the somewhat agonizing *Venus Infers* (which probably won't make a whole lot of sense unless you're a fan of The Velvet Underground . . . and, frankly, not much more sense even if you are), I drew a blank—until I came up with the idea of a book of stories about Saturn (or at least as much about Saturn as some of the stories in the first two books were about the moon or Mars). The title was *Ring Tales* and, while it scanned well and would look good on the cover, I had to accept that it was a little on the weak side (something of an understatement).

Anyway, I sent the details to Marty Greenberg at Tekno Books—without whom these anthologies wouldn't happen at all—and he said he would talk with DAW. When he came back to me last September he had good news and bad news: Yes, DAW wanted to do a third book but no, they weren't keen on *Ring Tales* (and who, in all honesty, could possibly blame them!) What Marty *had* agreed on with DAW was a book of stories that were either set on or in star systems or that were somehow concerned with the figures in our constellations.

Hence *Constellations* was born, and I was incredibly excited about it. Rather than my having a single planet to work with, Marty and those wonderful folks at DAW Books had provided me with a "whole universe" concept to go at . . . covering outer space, inner space, cosmology, astrology, Godhood, relationships and, above all, the Human Condition. Then I set about looking for stories.

I approached a handful of people—people I believed could or would really *play* with the theme—to get the ball rolling, spending time talking with them, either on the telephone or by email, to emphasize that I wanted some lateral thinking, enthusing about the seemingly endless possibilities, asking writers to be bold, to push the envelope. I confess that this is pretty much the way I always approach an anthology, particularly the three books I've done for DAW—that's the two SF books and *Heaven Sent*, a collection of stories about angels. After all, readers don't want twelve to fifteen stories all of which seem to be fairly similar to each other. I don't believe that happened with any of the other three Crowther DAW books (heck, I'd like to think that it didn't happen in *any* of my anthologies), but I can tell you this: it *certainly* hasn't happened here.

Anyway, after those first few story calls, the ideas and then the tales themselves started to drift in. But not only that: I also started to get calls from other writers who had heard of the project and who had had an idea themselves. Most of the ideas were intriguing and fascinating, just what I was looking for. I gave the green light for several authors to try me with the tales they'd outlined and then sat back to take stock. And that's when I noticed that all of the stories that I had either already accepted or was expecting were from British writers.

Here was a new perspective!

Well, okay, maybe not *completely* new—Judith Merril had done something similar with her 1968 anthology *England Swings SF: Stories of Speculative Fiction*, but most of those wonderful stories were reprinted from the ground-breaking *New Worlds* magazine. So I decided we were over-due revisiting the world of British speculative fiction. And this time, the stories would be all-new—no reprints. Thus I concentrated on finding out what was happening SF-wise on this side of the Atlantic. And the answer is, lots!

The work in this literary snapshot of New Millennium British SF runs the gamut of all the subgenres of science fiction, with the emphasis in many of the stories being firmly fixed on the aspect of wonder in its myriad forms.

In her inventive introduction to *England Swings*, Judith Merrill had this to say about her book: "It's an action-photo, a record of process-in-change, a look through the perspex porthole at the momentarily stilled bodies in a scout ship boosting fast, and heading out of sight into the multiplex mystery of inner/outer space. I can't tell you where they're going, but maybe that's why I keep wanting to read what they write. I think this trip should be a good one."

Well, thirty-five years later . . . here's another.

Happy trails!

Pete Crowther
Harrogate, England
2 July 2003

A HERITAGE OF STARS

By Eric Brown

Latterly I had never really given much thought to my death, or what might follow. Perhaps this was a reaction to the fact that in my youth, before the arrival of the Kéthani, I had been obsessed with the idea of my mortality, the overwhelming thought that one day I would be dead.

Then the Kéthani descended like guardian angels, bestowing immortality upon our race, and my fear of the Grim Reaper faded. In time I became a happy man and lived life to the full.

That night, though, it was as if I had an intimation of what was about to happen. I was driving home from the university, taking the treacherous, ice-bound road over the moors to Oxenworth. I passed the towering obelisk of the Onward Station, icy and eerie in the starlight. As I did so, a great actinic pulse of light lanced from its summit, arcing into the heavens toward the awaiting Kéthani starship. Although I knew intellectually that the laser pulse contained the demolecularised remains of perhaps a dozen dead human beings, I found the fact hard to credit.

For a few seconds, as I stared up at the light, I wondered at the life that awaited me when I shuffled off this mortal coil.

Ironic that this idle thought should have brought about the

accident. My attention still on the streaking parabola, I never saw the oncoming truck.

I didn't stand a chance.

Perhaps a week before I died, I arrived home to find Samantha in tears.

We had been married for just over a year, and I was still at that paranoid stage in the relationship when I feared that things would crumble. Our marriage had been so perfect I assumed that it could only end in tears: I knew my feelings for Sam, but what if she failed to reciprocate?

When I stepped into the living room and found her curled up on the sofa, sobbing like a child, my stomach flipped with fear. Perhaps this was it: she had discovered her true feelings; she had made a mistake in declaring her love for me. She wanted out.

She had a book open beside her. I saw that it was a copy of my third monograph, a study of gender and matriarchy in the medieval French epic.

"Sam, what the hell . . . ?"

She looked up at me, eyes soaked in tears. "Stuart, I don't understand . . ." She fingered the Kéthani implant at her temple, nervously.

I hurried across to her and took her in my arms. "What?"

She sobbed against my shoulder. "Anything," she managed at last. "I don't understand a bloody thing!"

My friends at the Fleece, the Tuesday night crowd including Richard and Khalid and Jeff and the rest, had ribbed me mercilessly when I started going out with Samantha. She worked at the pub, where I met her, and to them she seemed to represent the archetype of the dumb-blonde barmaid. "I'm sure you'll find lots to talk about when the pleasures of the flesh wear thin," Richard had jibed one night.

Attraction is a peculiar phenomenon. Sam was ten years my junior, a full-figured twenty-five-year-old high-school dropout who worked in the local Co-op and made ends meet with occasional bar work. Or that was how the others perceived her. To me she was an exceptionally sensitive human being who found me attractive and funny. We hit it off from the start and were married within three months.

She pulled away from me and stared into my eyes. She looked insane. "Stuart, why the hell do you love me?"

"Where do you want me to begin—?"

She wailed, "I just don't understand!"

She picked up my book, opened it at random and began reading, holding it high before her like a deranged preacher.

". . . as Sinclair so perceptively states in *Milk and Blood*: 'The writing and the page exist in a symbiotic relation that serves to mark the feminine "page" as originally blank and devoid of signification . . .' a dichotomy that stands as a radical antithesis to Cixous' notion of writing the body . . ."

She shook her head and stared at me. "Stuart, what the hell does it all mean?" She sobbed. "I'm so bloody stupid— what do you see in me?"

I snatched the book from her and flung it across the room, a gesture symbolizing my contempt for theory at that moment.

I eased her back onto the sofa and sat beside her. "Sam, listen to me. A Frenchman comes to England. He speaks no English—"

She snorted and tried to pull away. I held onto her. "Hear me out, Sam. So, Pierre is in England. He never learned to speak our language, so he doesn't understand when someone asks him the time. That doesn't make him stupid, does it?"

She stared at me, angry. "What do you mean?"

I gestured to the book. "All that . . . that academic-speak is something I learned at university. It's a language we use among ourselves because we understand it. It's overwritten and convoluted, and ninety-nine people out of a hundred wouldn't have a clue what we we're going on about. That doesn't make them stupid—"

"No," she retorted, "just uneducated."

She had often derided herself for her lack of education.

How many times had I tried to reassure her that I loved her because she was who she was, university degree or not?

That night, in bed, I held her close and said, "Tell me, what's really the matter? What's upsetting you?"

She was silent. The bedroom looks out over the moors, and I always leave the curtains open so that I can stare across the valley to the Onward Station. Tonight, as we lay belly to back, my arms around her, I watched a spear of white light lance towards the orbiting starship.

She whispered, "Sometimes I wonder why you love me. I try to read your books, make sense of them. I wonder what you see in me, why you don't go for one of those high-flying women in your department."

"They aren't you."

She went on, ignoring me, "Sometimes I think about what you do, what you write about, and . . . I don't know . . . it symbolises what I can't understand about everything."

"There," I joked, "you're beginning to sound like me."

She elbowed me in the belly. "You see, Stuart, everything is just too much to understand."

"Einstein said that we don't know one millionth of one percent of anything," I said.

"You know a lot."

"It's all relative. You know more than Tina, say."

"I want to know as much as you."

I laughed. "And I could say I want to know as much as Derrida knew." I squeezed her. "Listen to me. We all want to know more. One of the secrets of being happy is knowing that we'll never know as much as we want to know. It doesn't matter. I love you, sugarplum."

She was silent for a long while after that. Then she said, "Stuart, I'm frightened."

I sighed, squeezed her. The last time she'd said that, she confessed that she was frightened I would leave her. "Sam, I love you. There I was, an unhappy bachelor, never thinking I'd marry. And then the perfect woman comes along . . ."

"It's not that. I'm frightened of the Kéthani."

"Sam, there's absolutely nothing to be frightened of. You've heard what the returnees say."

"I don't mean the Kéthani, really. I mean . . . I mean, what happens to us after we die. Listen, what if you die, and when you come back from the stars . . . I don't know, you've seen more—more than there is here. What if you realize that I can't give you what's out there, among the stars?"

I kissed her neck. "You mean more to me than all the stars in the universe. And anyway, I don't intend to die just yet."

Silence, again. Then a whisper, "Stuart, you're right. We don't know anything, do we? I mean, look at the stars. Just look at them. Aren't they beautiful?"

I stared at the million twinkling points of light spread across the ice-cold heavens.

"Each one is a sun," she said, like an awe-struck child, "and millions of them have planets and people . . . well, aliens. Just think of it, Stuart, just think of everything that's out there that we can't even begin to dream about."

I hugged her to me. "You're a poet and a philosopher, Samantha Gardner," I whispered. "And I love you."

A couple of days later we attended the returning ceremony of Graham Leicester, a friend who'd died of a heart attack six months earlier.

I'd never before entered the Onward Station, and I was unsure what to expect. We left the car in the snow-covered parking lot and shuffled across the slush behind the file of fellow celebrants. Samantha gripped my hand and shivered. "C-cold," she brrr'd.

A blue-uniformed official, with the fixed smile and plastic good looks of an air hostess, ushered us into a reception lounge. It was a big, white-walled room with a sky-blue carpet. Abstract murals hung on the walls, swirls of pastel color: I wondered if this was Kéthani art work.

A long table stood before a window overlooking the white, undulating moorland. A buffet was laid out, tiny sandwiches and canapés, and red and white wine.

Graham's friends, his neighbors and the regulars from the Fleece, were already tucking in. Sam brought me a glass of red wine, and we stood talking to Richard Lincoln, a local ferryman.

"I wonder if he'll be the same old happy-go-lucky Graham as before?" Sam asked.

Richard smiled. "I don't see why not," he said. As ever when questioned about anything relating to Onward Station and the Kéthani, Richard was cagey: a reluctance no doubt born of working so closely with the alien regime and having to field so many questions.

"But he'll be changed, won't he?" Sam persisted. "I mean, not just physically?"

Richard shrugged. "He'll appear a little younger, fitter. And who knows how the experience will have changed him psychologically."

"But don't the aliens—" Sam began.

Richard was saved the need to reply. A door at the far end of the room opened, and the Station Director, Mr. Masters, stepped into the reception lounge and cleared his throat.

"First of all, I'd like to welcome you all to Onward Station." He gave a little speech extolling the service to humankind bestowed by the Kéthani and then explained that Graham Leicester was with close family members right at this moment, his wife and children, and would join us presently.

I must admit that I was more than a little curious as to how the experience of dying, being resurrected, and returning to Earth after six months on the Kéthani home planet had affected Graham. I'd heard rumors about the post-resurrection period on Kéthan: humans were brought back to life and "instructed," informed about the universe, the other life-forms that existed out there, the various tenets and philosophies they held. But I'd never actually met a returnee before, and I wanted to hear from Graham exactly what he'd undergone.

I expected to be disappointed. I'd read many a time that

returnees rarely spoke of their experiences on Kéthan: that either they were reluctant to do so or somehow were inhibited by their alien saviors.

Five minutes later Graham stepped through the sliding door, followed by his wife and two teenage daughters.

I suppose the reaction to his appearance could be described as a muted gasp—an indrawn breath of mixed delight and amazement.

Graham had run the local hardware store, a big, affable, very overweight fifty-something, with a drinker's nose and a rapidly balding head.

Enter a revamped Graham Leicester. He looked twenty years younger, leaner and fitter; gone was the rubicund, veined face, the beer belly. Even his hair had grown back.

He circulated, moving from group to group, shaking hands and hugging his delighted friends.

He saw us and hurried over, gave Sam a great bear-hug and winked at me over her shoulder. I embraced him. "Great to see you back, Graham."

"Good to be back."

His wife was beside him. "We're having a little do down at the Fleece, if you'd like to come along."

Graham said, "A pint of Landlord after the strange watery stuff I had out there." He smiled at the thought.

Thirty minutes later we were sitting around a table in the back room of our local, about ten of us, the usual Tuesday night crowd. Oddly enough, talk was all about what had happened in the village during the six months that Graham had been away. He led the conversation, wanting to know all the gossip. I wondered how much this was due to a reluctance to divulge his experiences on Kéthan.

I watched him as he sipped his first pint back on Earth.

Was it my imagination, or did he seem quieter, a little more reflective than the Graham of old? He didn't gulp his beer, but took small sips. At one point I asked him, nodding at his half-filled glass. "Worth waiting for? Can I get you another?"

He smiled. "It's not as I remembered it, Stuart. No, I'm okay for now."

I glanced across the table. Sam was deep in conversation with Graham's wife, Marjorie. Sam looked concerned. I said to Graham, "I've read that other returnees have trouble recalling their experiences out there."

He looked at me. "I know what they mean. It's strange, but although I can remember lots . . ." He shook his head. "When I try to talk about it . . ." He looked bewildered. "I mean, I know what happened in the dome, but I can't begin to express it."

I nodded, feigning comprehension.

"Have you decided what you're going to do now?"

His gaze seemed to slip into neutral. "I don't know. I recall something from the domes. We were shown the universe, the vastness, the races and planets . . . The Kéthani want us to go out there, Stuart, work with them in bringing the word of the Kéthani to all the other races. I was offered so many positions out there . . ."

I had to repress a smile at the thought of Graham Leicester, ex-Oxenworth hardware store owner, as an ambassador to the stars.

But the Kéthani instill knowledge in resurrectees and give them a choice: return home to your former life, and maybe in the future go out among the stars, or come now.

"Have you decided what you're going to do?" I asked.

He stared into his half-drunk pint. "No," he said at last. "No, I haven't." He looked up at me. "I never thought the stars would be so attractive," he murmured.

Graham and his wife left at nine, and the drinking continued. Around midnight Sam and I wended our way home, gripping each other's hand as we negotiated the snowdrifts.

She was very quiet, and at home took me in a fierce embrace. "Stuart," she whispered, "rip all my clothes off and make love to me."

Sometimes the act of sex can transcend the mere familiar mechanics that often, after a year of marriage, become rote.

That night, for some reason, we were imbued with a passion that recalled our earlier times together. Later we sprawled on the bed, sweating and breathless. I was overcome with an inexpressible surge of love for the woman who was my wife.

"Stuart," she whispered.

I stroked her thigh. "Mmm?"

"I was talking to Marjorie. She says Graham's changed. He isn't the man he was. She's afraid."

I held her. "Sam, he's undergone an incredible experience. Of course he's changed a little, but he's still the same old Graham underneath. It'll just take time for him to readjust."

She was quiet for a few seconds, before saying, "Perhaps, Stuart, they take our humanity away?"

"Nonsense!" I said. "If anything, they give us a greater humanity. You've heard all those stories about dictators and cynical businessmen who return full of compassion and charity."

She didn't reply. Perhaps five minutes later she said, "Perhaps the Kéthani take away our ability to love."

Troubled, I pulled Sam to me and held her tight.

A few days later I arrived home with a book for Samantha. It was Farmer's critically acclaimed account of the arrival of the Kéthani and its radical social consequences.

I left it on the kitchen table and over dinner said, "I found this in the library. Fascinating stuff. Perhaps you'd like to read it."

She picked up the book and leafed through it, sniffed, with that small, disdainful wrinkle of her nose I found so attractive.

"Wouldn't understand it if I did," she said.

After dinner she poured two glasses of red wine and joined me in the living room. She curled next to me on the sofa.

"Stuart . . ." she began.

She often did this—said my name and then failed to continue. The habit at first drove me crazy, but it soon became just another of her idiosyncrasies that I came to love.

"Do you know something?" she began again. "Once upon a time there were certainties, weren't there?" She fingered her implant, perhaps unaware that she was doing so.

I stared at her. "Such as?"

"Death," she said. "And, like, if you loved someone so much, then you were certain that it would last forever."

"Well, I suppose so."

"But not any more."

"Well, death's been banished."

She looked up at me, her gaze intense. "When I met you and fell in love, Stuart, it was like nothing I'd experienced before. You were the one, kind and gentle and caring. You loved me—"

"I still do."

She squeezed my hand. "I know you do, but . . ."

"But what?"

"But with the coming of the Kéthani, how long will that last? Once, true love lasted forever—until death—or it could if it really *was* true. But now, when we live forever, on and on, for centuries . . ." She shook her head at the enormity of that concept. "Then how can our love last so long?"

And she began crying, copiously and inconsolably.

Even later, when I awoke in the early hours and watched a beam of light pulse high into the dark sky, Sam was still sobbing beside me.

I reached out and pulled her to me. "I love you so much," I said.

They were the last words I ever spoke to her, in this incarnation.

She was still asleep early the following morning when I dressed and left the house. I spent an average day at the faculty, conducting a couple of seminars on chivalry in the French medieval epic. And from time to time, unbidden but welcome, visions of my wife flooded my consciousness with joy.

That night, driving past the Onward Station, I stared in wonder at the pulsing light.

I saw the oncoming truck, its blinding headlights bearing down, but too late. I swerved to avoid the vehicle, but not fast enough to avert the shattering impact.

I died instantly, apparently. Various pieces of the truck's cab sheared though the car, decapitating me and cutting me in half, just below the ribs. Much later, over a pint in the Fleece, Richard Lincoln laughingly reported that I'd been the messiest corpse he'd ever dealt with.

The last thing I recalled was the light—and, upon awakening, the first thing I beheld was another light, just as bright.

I remember a face hovering over me, telling me that the resurrection was complete, and that I could begin the lessons when I next awoke.

At least, I think the word was "lessons." Perhaps I'm wrong. There is so much about that period that I cannot fully recall, or, if I do recall, do so vaguely. I know I was on the Kéthani homeplanet for exactly six months, though in retrospect it seems like as many weeks.

As with every other resurrectee, I was housed in a dome with five other humans. There were perhaps as many teachers as resurrectees, though whether they were humans or Kéthani wearing human soma-forms I cannot say. Beyond the wall of the dome was a pastoral vista of rolling green glades and meadows, which must surely have been some virtual image designed to sedate us with the familiar.

I wore a body I recalled from perhaps ten years ago, leaner than my recent form, healthier. My face was unlined. I felt physically wonderful, with no aftereffects of the accident that had killed me.

The resurrectees in my dome did not socialize. None were British, and none so far as I recall spoke English. We had our lessons, one on one with our instructors, and then returned to our separate rooms to eat and sleep.

The "lessons" consisted of meditation classes, in which we were instructed simply to empty our minds of *everything*. We were given "poems" to read, pieces that reminded me of haiku and koan, which although bearing much resemblance to Zen, were subtly other, alien.

After a while we were allowed access to what were called the library files. These consisted of needle-like devices that could be fed into a wallscreen, upon which materialized the texts of every book ever printed on Earth. They even had my own three labored volumes.

But more. I soon discovered that there were other texts available, those not of Earth but penned by poets and philosophers and storytellers from many of the far-flung races of the universe. All were translated into English, and some were comprehensible and some not. I struggled over texts too profound for my intellect and then found others that expanded my awareness of being with the same heady rush of knowledge I experienced in my late teens when reading Freud and Lacan for the very first time.

I recall too—but this is vague, and I suspect our Kéthani overseers of having somehow edited it from my consciousness—being visited by other teachers, not those who usually instructed us. At the time I knew there was something odd about them. They did not speak to us, I seem to recall, but reached out, touched our brows, and later I would wake to find myself bequeathed knowledge new to me.

I became voracious, questing after all that was new in the universe. Perhaps I had become jaded on Earth, my mind dulled by the repetitive nature of my job, stressed by having to fit my original research into my spare time and rare study breaks. On Kéthan, it was as if my mind had been made suddenly a hundred percent more receptive. I discovered alien writers and philosophers whose wisdom superseded the tired tenets of Earth's finest thinkers.

I became aware, by degrees—surely a process carefully monitored by the Kéthani, so as not to overload our minds with too much information too soon—of the vast cornucopia of otherness existing Out There, of the million teeming worlds and ways of thinking that awaited my inspection.

I recalled what Sam had said, that night, what seemed like a lifetime ago, *"Just think of it, Stuart, just think of everything that's out there that we can't even begin to dream about."*

And Sam? Was she in my thoughts? Did I miss her as I had, during the first months of our marriage, when research had taken me to Paris for three painful weeks?

I thought of her often during my first days there, and then, I must admit, not so frequently. Soon she was supplanted in my thoughts by the sheer wonder of what surrounded me, the possibilities suddenly open to my experience, the amazing inheritance that death and resurrection was offering.

At first I felt guilty, and then less so. Perhaps, even then, some survival mechanism was kicking in: I was forcing myself to realize that our love was doomed, a short-term thing, a mayfly liaison that could not hope to compete with the eternal allure of the stars.

She would understand, one day.

What had she said, so wisely? *"But now, when we live forever, on and on, for centuries . . . Then how can our love last so long, Stuart?"*

At night I would lie awake and stare though the dome, marvelling at the spread of stars high overhead, the vast and magnificent drifts and nebulae. Their attraction was irresistible.

Toward the end of my stay on Kéthan, an instructor gave me a needle containing an almost endless list of vacancies open for my consideration. Teachers were required on primitive worlds in the Nilakantha Stardrift; tutors aboard vessels called quark-harvesters plying routes at the very periphery of the universe; ethnographers on planets newly discovered; sociologists on ancient worlds with complex rites and abstruse rituals . . .

I wept when I thought about the future, the wonder of discovery that awaited me, and the thought of telling Sam of my decision.

Six months to the day after my death, I was returned to Earth and the Onward Station high on the Yorkshire moors.

I came awake in a small room within the Onward Station. Director Masters was there to greet me. "Welcome back, Mr. Kingsley," he said. "Your friends are in the reception lounge, but perhaps you'd care for a few minutes alone?"

I agreed, and he slipped from the room.

A china pot of tea, a cup and saucer stood on a small table, all ridiculously English and twee.

I thought of Graham Leicester's reception a while ago and recalled that he had spent time with his family before greeting his friends in the lounge.

I had expected Sam to be the first person to welcome me home, and her absence relieved me.

I wondered if she was wary of the person I had become—the being remade by the Kéthani. What had she said, the night before my death? *Perhaps the Kéthani take away our ability to love.*"

No fool, Samantha . . .

I stepped from the small room and entered the lounge. There were half a dozen familiar faces awaiting me. I had expected more, and was instantly put out, and then troubled by the expression on their faces.

Richard stepped forward and gripped my arm. "Stuart, Sam isn't here."

"What—?" I began.

"Two days after your accident," Richard said, "she took her own life. She left a note, saying she wanted to be resurrected with you."

I nodded, trying to work out where that left us, now. She had never read anything about the Kéthani. How could she have known that the Kéthani never conducted the rebirth of loved ones together in the same dome, for whatever reasons?

I contemplated her return in two days' time, and I joined my friends in the Fleece for a quiet pint.

*   *   *

In the two days I was on my own, in the house we had shared for a year, I thought of the woman who was my wife and what she had done because she loved me.

I moved from room to room, the place empty now without Sam's presence to fill it, to give it life and vitality. Each room was haunted by so many memories. I tried to avoid the bedroom where she had slit her wrists and slept in the lounge instead.

And, amazingly, something human stirred within me, something very like the first blossoming of love I had felt for Samantha Gardner. It came to me that knowledge and learning was all very well, but it was nothing beside the miracle that is the love and compassion we can feel for another human being. I faced the prospect of Sam's return with a strange mixture of ecstasy and dread.

The Station seemed even more alien today, rearing like an inverted icicle from the frozen moorland. I left my car in the snow and hurried inside. Director Masters ushered me into the private reception room, where I paced like something caged and contemplated the future.

It all depended, really, on Sam, on her reaction to what she had undergone on the home planet of the Kéthani.

Long minutes later the sliding door sighed open and she stepped through, smiling tentatively at me.

My heart gave a kick.

She came into my arms, crying.

"Sam?" I said, and I had never feared her words so much as now.

"We have a lot to talk about," she said. "I learned so much out there."

I nodded, at a loss for words. At last I said, "Have you decided . . . ?"

She stared into my eyes, shook her head. "Let's get this over with," she said and, taking my arm, led me into the reception lounge before I could protest.

I endured the following hour with Sam's family and

mutual friends, and then we made our excuses and left the Onward Station. It was a short drive home across the moors, fraught with silence. More than once I almost asked whether she would remain with me on Earth.

But it was Sam who broke the silence. "Do you understand why I did it, Stuart? Why I . . ."

I glanced at her as I turned into the driveway. "You feared losing me?"

She nodded. "I was desperate. I . . . I thought that perhaps if I experienced what you were going through, then it might bring us closer together when we got back."

I braked. "And has it?"

She stared at me without replying, and said, "What about you, Stuart? Do you still love me?"

"More than ever."

Quickly she opened the door and hurried from the car.

The house was warm. I fixed coffee, and we sat in the lounge, staring out through the picture window at the vast spread of the snow-covered moorland. The sun was going down, laying gorgeous tangerine strata across the horizon. In the distance, the Onward Station scintillated in the dying light.

Sam said, "I became a different person on Kéthan."

I nodded. "So did I."

"The small concerns of being human, of life on Earth, seem less important now."

I wanted to ask her if her love for me was a small concern, but was too afraid to pose the question.

"Could you remain here on Earth?" I asked.

She stood and paced to the window, hugging herself, staring out. "I don't know. I don't think so. Not after what I've learned about what's out there. What about you?"

I was silent for a time. "Do you remember what you said all those months ago, about the Kéthani taking away our ability to feel love?"

She looked at me, nodded minimally.

"Well, do you think it's true for you?" I asked.

"I . . . I don't know. What I feel for you has changed."

I wanted to ask her if I could compete with the allure of the stars. Instead I said, "I have an idea, Sam. There are plenty of vacancies for couples out there. We could explore the stars together."

Without warning she hurried from the room, alarming me. "Sam?"

"I need time to think!" she cried from the hall. I heard the front door slam.

A minute later I saw her, bundled up in her parka and moonboots, tramping across the snow before the house, a tiny figure lost in the daunting winter wilderness.

She stopped, and gazed up into the night sky.

I looked up, too, and stared in wonder.

Then, slowly, I dropped my gaze to the woman I loved. She was struggling through the deep snow, running back towards the house and waving at me.

My heart hammering, I rushed from the house to meet her.

Overhead the night was clear, and the stars were appearing in their teeming millions, a vast spread of brilliant luminosity promising the universe.

RATS OF THE SYSTEM

By Paul McAuley

Carter Cho was trying to camouflage the lifepod when the hunter-killer found him.

Carter had matched spin with the fragment of shattered comet nucleus, excavated a neat hole with a judicious burn of the lifepod's motor and eased the sturdy little ship inside; then he had sealed up his p-suit and clambered out of the airlock, intending to hide the pod's infrared and radar signatures by covering the hole with fullerene superconducting cloth. He was trying to work methodically, clamping clips to the edge of the cloth and spiking the clips deep into the slumped rim of dirty water ice, but the cloth, forty meters square and just sixty carbon atoms thick, massed a little less than a butterfly's wing, and it fluttered and billowed like a live thing as gas and dust vented from fractured ice. Carter had fastened down less than half of it when the scientist shouted, "Heads up! Incoming!"

That's when Carter discovered she'd locked him out of the pod's control systems.

He said, "What have you done?"

"Heads up! It's coming right at us!"

The woman was hysterical.

Carter looked up.

The sky was apocalyptic. Pieces of comet nucleus were tumbling away in every direction, casting long cones of shadow through veils and streamers of gas lit by the red dwarf's half-eclipsed disc. The nucleus had been a single body ten kilometers long before the Fanatic singleship had cut across its orbit and carved it open and destroyed the science platform hidden inside it with X-ray lasers and kinetic bomblets. The singleship had also deployed a pod of hunter-killer drones, and after crash deceleration these were falling through the remains of the comet, targeting the flotsam of pods and cans and general wreckage that was all that remained of the platform. Carter saw a firefly flash and gutter in the sullen wash of gases, and then another, almost ninety degrees away. He had almost forgotten his fear while he'd been working, but now it flowed through him again, electric and strong and urgent.

He said, "Give me back my ship."

The scientist said, "I'm tracking it on radar! I think it's about to—"

The huge slab of sooty ice shuddered. A jet of dust and gas boiled up beyond a sharp-edged horizon, and something shot out of the dust, heading straight for Carter. It looked a little like a silvery squid, with a bullet-shaped head that trailed a dozen tentacles tipped with claws and blades. It wrapped itself around an icy pinnacle on the other side of the hole and reared up, weaving this way and that as if studying him. Probably trying to decide where to begin unseaming him, Carter thought, and pointed the welding pistol at it, ready to die if only he could take one of the enemy with him. The thing surged forward—

Dust and gas blasted out of the hole. The scientist had ignited the lifepod's motor. The fullerene cloth shot straight up, straining like a sail in a squall, and the hunter-killer smashed into it and tore it free from the clips Carter had so laboriously secured, tumbling past him at the center of a writhing knot of cloth.

Carter dove through the hatch in the pod's blunt nose.

Gravity's ghost clutched him, and he tumbled head over heels and slammed into the rear bulkhead as the pod shook free of its hiding place.

Humans had settled the extensive asteroid belt around Keid, the cool K1 component of the triple star system 40 Eridani, more than a century ago. The first generation, grown from templates stored in a bus-sized seeder starship, had built a domed settlement on Neuvo California, an asteroid half the size of Earth's Moon, and planted its cratered plains of water ice with vast fields of vacuum organisms. Succeeding generations spread through Keid's asteroid belt, building domes and tenting crevasses and ravines, raising families, becoming expert in balancing the ecologies of small, closed systems and creating new varieties of vacuum organisms, writing and performing heroic operettas, trading information and works of art on the interstellar net that linked Earth's far-flung colonies in the brief golden age before Earth's AIs achieved transcendence.

The Keidians were a practical, obdurate people. As far as they were concerned, the Hundred Minute War, which ended with the reduction of Earth and the flight of dozens of Transcendent AIs from the Solar System, was a distant and incomprehensible matter that had nothing to do with the ordinary business of their lives. Someone wrote an uninspired operetta about it; someone else revived the lost art of the symphony, and for a few years her mournful eight-hour memoriam was considered by many in the stellar colonies to be a new pinnacle of human art. Very few Keidians took much notice when a Transcendent demolished Sirius B and used the trillions of tons of heavy elements it mined from the white dwarf's core to build a vast ring in close orbit around Sirius A; no one worried overmuch when other Transcendents began to strip-mine gas giants in other uninhabited systems. Everyone agreed that the machine intelligences were pursuing some vast, obscure plan that might take millions of years to complete, that they were as indifferent to the low comedy of human life as gardeners were to the politics of ants.

But then self-styled transhuman Fanatics declared a jihad against anyone who refused to acknowledge the Transcendents as gods. They dropped a planet-killer on half-terraformed Mars. They scorched colonies on the moons of Jupiter and Saturn and Neptune. They dispatched warships starward. The fragile web of chatter and knowledge-based commerce that linked the stellar colonies began to unravel. And just over six hundred days ago, a Transcendent barreled into the Keidian system, swinging past Keid as it decelerated from close to light speed and arcing out towards the double system of white and red dwarf stars just four hundred AU beyond. The red dwarf had always been prone to erratic flares, but a few days after the Transcendent went into orbit around it, the dim little star began to flare brightly and steadily from one of its poles. A narrowly focussed jet of matter and energy began to spew into space, and some of the carbon-rich starstuff was spun into sails with the surface area of planets, hanging hundreds of thousands of kilometers beyond the star yet somehow coupled to its center of gravity. Pinwheeling of the jet and light pressure on the vast sails tipped the star through ninety degrees, and then the jet burned even brighter, and the star began to move out of its orbit.

A hundred days after that, the Fanatics arrived, and the war of the 40 Eridani system began.

The scientist said, "The hunter-killers found us. We had to outrun them."

Carter said, "I was ready to make a stand."

The scientist glared at him with her one good eye and said, "I'm not prepared to sacrifice myself to take out a few drones, Mr. Cho. My work is too important."

She might be young and scared and badly injured, but Carter had to admit that she had stones. When the singleship struck, Carter had been climbing into a p-suit, getting ready to set up a detector array on the surface of the comet nucleus. She had been the first person he'd seen after he'd kicked out of the airlock. He'd caught her and dragged her across twenty meters of raw vacuum to a lifepod that had spun loose from the platform's broken spine, and installed her in one of the pod's hibernation coffins. She'd been half-cooked by reflected energy of the X-ray laser beam that had bisected the main section of the science platform; one side of her face was swollen red and black, the eye there a blind white stone, hair like shriveled peppercorns. The coffin couldn't do much more than give her painblockers and drip glucose-enriched plasma into her blood. She'd die unless she went into hibernation, but she'd wouldn't allow that because, she said, she had work to do.

Her coffin was one of twenty stacked in a neat five by four array around the inner wall of the lifepod's hull. Carter Cho hung in the space between her coffin and the shaft of the motor, a skinny man with prematurely white hair in short dreads that stuck out in spikes around his thin, sharp face as if he'd just been wired to some mains buss. He said, "This is my ship. I'm in charge here."

The scientist stared at him. Her good eye was red with an eightball haemorrhage, the pupil capped with a black data lens. She said, "I'm a second lieutenant, sailor. I believe I outrank you."

"The commissions they handed out to volunteers like you don't mean anything."

"I volunteered for this mission, Mr. Cho, because I want to find out everything I can about the Transcendent. Because I believe that what we can learn from it will help defeat the Fanatics. I still have work to do, sailor, and that's why I must decide our strategy."

"Just give me back control of my ship, okay?" She stared through him. He said, "Just tell me what you did. You might have damaged something."

"I wrote a patch that's sitting on top of the command stack; it won't cause any damage. Look, we tried hiding from the hunter-killers, and when that didn't work, we had to outrun them. I can appreciate why you wanted to make a stand. I can even admire it. But we were outnumbered, and we are more important than a few drones. War isn't a matter of individual heroics; it's a collective effort. And as part of a collective, every individual must subsume her finer instincts to the greater good. Do you understand?"

"With respect, ma'am, what I understand is that I'm a sailor with combat experience and you're a science geek." She was looking through him again, or maybe focussing on stuff fed to her retina by the data lens. He said, "What kind of science geek are you, anyway?"

"Quantum vacuum theory." The scientist closed her eye and clenched her teeth and gasped, then said, her voice smaller and tighter, "I was hoping to find out how the Transcendent manipulates the magnetic fields that control the jet."

"Are you okay?"

"Just a little twinge."

Carter studied the diagnostic panel of the coffin, but he had no idea what it was trying to tell him. "You should let this box put you to sleep. When you wake up, we'll be back at Pasadena, and they'll fix you right up."

"I know how to run the lifepod, and as long as I have control of it, you can't put me to sleep. We're still falling along the comet's trajectory. We're going to eyeball the Transcendent's engineering up close. If I can't learn something from that, I'll give you permission to boot my ass into vacuum, turn around, and go look for another scientist."

"Maybe you can steer this ship, ma'am, but you don't have combat training."

"There's nothing to fight. We outran the hunter-killers."

Carter said, "So we did. But maybe you should use the radar, check out the singleship. Just before you staged your little mutiny, I saw that it was turning back. I think it's going to try to hunt us down."

*   *   *

Carter stripped coffins and ripped out panels and padding from the walls. He disconnected canisters of the accelerant foam that flooded coffins to cradle hibernating sleepers. He pulled a dozen spare p-suits from their racks. He sealed the scientist's coffin and suited up and vented the lifepod and dumped everything out of the lock.

The idea was that the pilot of the singleship would spot the debris, think that the pod had imploded, and abandon the chase. Carter thought there was a fighting chance it would work, but when he had told her what he was going to do, the scientist had said, "It won't fool him for a moment."

Carter said, "Also, when he chases after us, there's a chance he'll run into some of the debris. If the relative velocity is high enough, even a grain of dust could do some serious damage."

"He can blow us out of the sky with his X-ray laser. So why would he want to chase us?"

"For the same reason the hunter-killer didn't explode when it found us. Think it through, ma'am. He wants to take a prisoner. He wants to extract information from a live body."

He watched her think about that.

She said, "If he does catch up with us, you'll get your wish to become a martyr. There's enough antiberyllium left in the motor to make an explosion that'll light up the whole system. But that's a last resort. The singleship is still in turnaround, we have a good head start, and we're only twenty-eight million kilometres from perihelion. If we get there first, we can whip around the red dwarf, change our course at random. Unless the Fanatic guesses our exit trajectory, that'll buy us plenty of time."

"He'll have plenty of time to find us again. We're a long way from home, and there might be other—"

"All we have to do is live long enough to find out everything we can about the Transcendent's engineering project and squirt it home on a tight beam." The scientist's smile was dreadful. Her teeth were filmed with blood. "Quit arguing, sailor. Don't you have work to do?"

A trail of debris tumbled away behind the pod, slowly spreading out, bright edges flashing here and there as they caught the light of the red dwarf. Carter pressurized p-suits and switched on their life-support systems and transponders before he jettisoned them. Maybe the Fanatic would think that they contained warm bodies. He sprayed great arcs of foam into the hard vacuum and kicked away the empty canisters. The chance of any of the debris hitting the Fanatic's singleship was infinitesimally small, but a small chance was better than none at all, and the work kept his mind from the awful prospect of being captured.

Sternward, the shattered comet nucleus was a fuzzy speck trailing foreshortened banners of light across the star-spangled sky. The expedition had nudged it from its orbit and buried the science platform inside its nucleus, sleeping for a whole year like an army in a fairytale as it fell toward the red dwarf. The mission had been a last desperate attempt to try to learn something of the Transcendent's secrets, but as the comet nucleus neared the red dwarf, and the expedition woke and the scientists started their work, one of the Fanatic drones that policed the vicinity of the star somehow detected the science platform, and the Fanatics sent a singleship to deal with it. Like all their warships, it moved very fast, with brutal acceleration that would have mashed ordinary humans to a thin jelly. It had arrived less than thirty seconds behind a warning broadcast by a spotter observatory at the edge of Keid's heliopause; the crew of the science platform hadn't stood a chance.

The singleship lay directly between the comet and the lifepod now. It had turned around and was decelerating at eight gravities. At the maximum magnification his p-suit's visor could give him, Carter could just make out the faint scratch of its exhaust, but he was unable to resolve the ship itself. In the other direction, the red dwarf star simmered at the bottom of a kind of well of luminous dark. Its nuclear fires were banked low, radiating mostly in infrared. Carter could stare steadily at it with only a minimum of filtering.

The sharp-edged shadows of the vast deployment of solar sails were sinking beyond one edge as the jet dawned in the opposite direction, a brilliant white thread brighter than the fierce point of the white dwarf star rising just beyond it. Before the Transcendent had begun its work, the red dwarf had swung around the smaller but more massive white dwarf in a wide elliptical orbit, at its closest approaching within twenty AU, the distance of Uranus from the Sun. Now it was much closer and still falling inward. Scientists speculated that the Transcendent planned to use the tidal effects of a close transit to tear apart the red dwarf, but they'd had less than forty hours to study the Transcendent's engineering before the Fanatic's singleship struck.

Hung in his p-suit a little way from the lifepod, the huge target of the red dwarf in one direction, the vast starscape in the other, Carter Cho resolved to make the best of his fate. The Universe was vast and inhuman, and so was war. Out there, in battles around stars whose names—Alpha Centauri, Epsilon Eridani, Tau Ceti, Lalande 21185, Lacaille 8760, 61 Cygni, Epsilon Indi, Groombridge 1618, Groombridge 34, 82 Eridani, 70 Ophiuchi, Delta Pavonis, Eta Cassiopeiae—were like a proud role call of mythic heroes, the fate of the human race was being determined. While Carter and the rest of the expedition had slept in their coffins deep in the heart of the comet, the Fanatics had invested and destroyed a dozen settlements in Keid's asteroid belt, and the Keidians had fought back and destroyed one of the Fanatics' huge starships. Compared to this great struggle, Carter's fate was less than that of a drop of water in a stormy ocean, a thought both humbling and uplifting.

Well, his life might be insignificant, but he wasn't about to trust it to a dying girl with no combat experience. He fingertip-swam to the stern of the pod, and opened a panel and rigged a manual cutout before he climbed back inside. He had been working for six hours. He was exhausted and sweating hard inside the p-suit, but he couldn't take it off because the pod's atmosphere had been vented and most of its systems had been shut down, part of his plan to fool the Fanatic into thinking it was a dead hulk. The interior was dark and cold. The lights either side of his helmet cast sharp shadows. Frost glistened on struts exposed where he had stripped away paneling.

The scientist lay inside her sealed coffin, her half-ruined face visible through the little window. She looked asleep, but when Carter maneuvred beside her she opened her good eye and looked at him. He plugged in a patch cord and heard some kind of music, a simple progressions of riffs for percussion and piano and trumpet and saxophone. The scientist said that it was her favorite piece. She said that she wanted to listen to it one more time.

Carter said, "You should let the coffin put you to sleep. Before—"

The scientist coughed wetly. Blood freckled the faceplate of her coffin. "Before I die."

"They gave me some science training before they put me on this mission, ma'am. Just tell me what to do."

"Quit calling me 'ma'am'," the scientist said, and closed her good eye as a trumpet floated a long, lovely line of melody above a soft shuffle of percussion. "Doesn't he break your heart? That's Miles Davis, playing in New York hundreds of years ago. Making music for angels."

"It's interesting. It's in simple six/eight time, but the modal changes—" The scientist was staring at Carter; he felt himself blush and wondered if she could see it. He said, "I inherited perfect pitch from my mother. She sang in an opera chorus before she married my father and settled down to raise babies and farm vacuum organisms."

"Don't try to break it down," the scientist said. "You have to listen to the whole thing. The totality, it's sublime. I'd rather die listening to this than die in hibernation."

"You're not going—"

"I've set down everything I remember about the work that was done before the attack. I'll add it to the observations I make as we whip around the star and then squirt all the data to Keid. Maybe they can make something useful of it, work out the Transcendent's tricks with the magnetic fields, the gravity tethers, the rest of it . . ." She closed her eye, and breathed deeply. Fluid rattled in her lungs. She said softly, as if to herself, "So many dead. We have to make their deaths worthwhile."

Carter had barely gotten to know his shipmates, recruited from all over, before they'd gone into hibernation, but the scientist had lost good friends and colleagues.

He said, "The singleship is still accelerating."

"I know."

"It could catch us before we reach the star."

"Maybe your little trick will fool it."

"I might as well face up to it with a pillow."

The scientist smiled her ghastly smile. She said, "We have to try. We have to try everything. Let me explain what I plan to do at perihelion."

She told Carter that observations by drones and asteroid-based telescopes had shown that the Transcendent had regularized the red dwarf's magnetic field, funneling plasma toward one point on photosphere, where it erupted outward in a permanent flare—the jet that was driving the star toward its fatal rendezvous at the bottom of the white dwarf's steep gravity well. The scientist believed that the Transcendent was manipulating the vast energies of the star's magnetic field by breaking the symmetry of the seething sea of virtual particular pairs that defined quantum vacuum, generating charged particles *ab ovo*, redirecting plasma currents and looped magnetic fields with strengths of thousands of gauss and areas of thousands of kilometres as a child might play with a toy magnet and a few iron filings. The probe she'd loaded with a dozen experiments had been lost with the science platform, but she thought that there was a way of testing at least one prediction of her theoretical work on symmetry breaking.

She opened a window in Carter's helmet display, showed him a schematic plot of the slingshot manoever around the red dwarf.

Carter said, "You have to get that close?"

"The half-life of the strange photons will be very short, a little less than a millisecond."

"I get it. They won't travel much more than a few hundred kilometres before they decay." Carter grinned when the scientist stared at him. He said, "Speed of light's one of those fundamental constants every sailor has to deal with."

"It means that we have to get close to the source, but it also means that the photon flux will increase anomalously just above the photosphere. There should be a sudden gradient, or a series of steps . . . It was one of the experiments my probe carried."

Carter said, "But it was destroyed, so we have to do the job instead. It's going to get pretty hot, that close to the star. What kind of temperatures are we talking about?"

"I don't know. The average surface temperature of the red dwarf is relatively cool, a little over 3000 degrees Kelvin, but it's somewhat hotter near the base of the flare, where we have to make our pass."

"Why don't we just skim past the edge of the flare itself? The flare might be hotter than the surface, but our transit time would be a whole lot less."

"The magnetic fields are very strong around the flare, and they spiral around it. They could fling us in any direction. Outward if we're lucky, into the star if we're not. No, I'm going to aim for a spot where the field lines all run in the same direction. But the fields can change direction suddenly, and there's the risk of hitting a stray plume of plasma, so I can't fire up the motors until we're close."

Carter thought of his cutout. He said, "If you have to hit a narrow window, I'm your man. I can put this ship through the eye of a needle."

The scientist said, "As soon as I see the chance, I'll fire full thrust to minimize transit time."

"But without the thermal protection of the comet nucleus it'll still be a lot worse than waving your hand through a candle flame. I suppose I can set up a barbecue-mode rotation, run the cooling system at maximum. Your box will help keep you safe, and I'll climb into one too, but if the temperature doesn't kill us, the hard radiation flux probably will. You really think you can learn something useful?"

"This is a unique opportunity, sailor. It's usually very difficult to study Transcendent engineering because they keep away from star systems that have been settled. Some of us think that the Hundred Minute War was fought over the fate of the human race, that the Transcendents who won the war and quit the Solar System believe that we should be left alone to get on with our lives."

"But this one didn't leave us alone."

"Strictly speaking, it did. Forty Eridani B and C, the white dwarf and the red dwarf, are a close-coupled binary. Keid is only loosely associated with them. And they're a rare example of the kind of binary the Transcendents are very interested in, one in which the masses of the two components are very different. We have a unique opportunity to study stellar engineering up close. The Fanatics know this, which is why they're so keen to destroy anything which comes too close."

"They want to keep the Transcendents' secrets secret."

"They're not interested in understanding the Transcendents, only in worshiping them. They are as fixed and immutable as their belief system, but we're willing to learn, to take on new knowledge and change and evolve. That's why we're going to win this war."

Following the scientist's instructions, Carter dismantled three cameras and rejiggered their imaging circuits into photon counters. While he worked, the scientist talked about her family home in Happy Valley on Neuvo California. It had been badly damaged in one of the first Fanatic attacks, and her parents and her three brothers had helped organize the evacuation. Her mother had been an ecosystem designer, and her father had been in charge of the government's program of interstellar commerce; they were both in the war cabinet now.

"And very proud and very unhappy that their only daughter volunteered for this mission."

Carter said that his family were just ordinary folks, part of a cooperative that ran a vacuum organism farm on the water- and methane-ice plains of San Joaquin. He'd piloted one of the cooperative's tugs and had volunteered for service in the Keidian defense force as soon as the war against the Fanatics began, but he didn't want to talk about the two inconclusive skirmishes in which he'd been involved before being assigned to the mission. Instead, he told the scientist about his childhood and the tented crevasse that was his family home, and the herds of gengineered rats he'd helped raise.

"I loved those rats. I should have been smart enough to stay home, raise rats and make babies, but instead I thought that the bit of talent I have for math and spatial awareness was my big ticket out."

"Shit," the scientist said. "The singleship just passed through your debris field."

She opened a window and showed Carter the radar plot.

He felt a funny floating feeling that had nothing to do with free fall. He said, "Well, we tried."

"I'm sure it won't catch up with us before we reach the star."

"If we make that burn now—"

"We'll miss the chance to collect the photon data. We're going to die whatever we do, sailor. Let's make it worthwhile."

"Right."

"Why did you like them? The rats."

"Because they're survivors. Because they've managed to make a living from humans ever since we invented agriculture and cities. Back on Earth, they were a vermin species, small and tough and smart and fast-breeding, eating the same food that people ate, even sharing some of the same diseases and parasites. We took them with us into space because those same qualities made them ideal lab animals. Did you know that they were one of the first mammal species to have their genome sequenced? That's why there are so many gengineered varieties. We mostly bred them for meat and fur and biologicals, but we also raised a few strains that we sold as pets. When I was a little kid, I had a ruffed piebald rat that I loved as much as any of my sisters and brothers. Charlie. Charlie the rat. He lived for more than a thousand days, an awfully venerable age for a rat, and when he died I wouldn't allow him to be recycled. My father helped me make a coffin from offcuts of black oak, and I buried him in a glade in my favourite citrous forest . . ."

The scientist said, "It sounds like a nice spot to be buried."

Carter said, "It's a good place. There are orchards, lots of little fields. People grow flowers just for the hell of it. We have eighteen species of mammals roaming about. All chipped of course, but they give you a feeling of what nature must have been like. I couldn't wait to get out, and now I can't wait to get back. How dumb is that?"

The scientist said, "I'd like to see it. Maybe you could take me on a picnic, show me the sights. My family used to get together for a picnic every couple of hundred days. We'd rent part of one of the parklands, play games, cook way too much food, smoke and drink . . ."

"My father, he's a pretty good cook. And my mother leads a pretty good choral group. We should all get together."

"Absolutely."

They smiled at each other. It was a solemn moment. Carter thought he should say something suitable, but what? He'd never been one for speeches, and he realized now that although the scientist knew his name—it was stitched to his suit—he didn't know hers.

The scientist said, "The clock's ticking."

Carter said, "Yes, ma'am. I'll get this junk fixed up, and then I'll be right back."

He welded the photon detectors to the blunt nose of the pod and cabled them up. He prepped the antenna array. After the pod grazed the base of the flare, its computer would compress the raw data and send it in an encrypted squawk aimed at Keid, repeating it as long as possible, repeating it until the Fanatic singleship caught up. It was less than ten thousand kilometres behind them now. Ahead, the red dwarf filled half the sky, the jet a slender white thread rooted in patch of orange and yellow fusion fire, foreshortening and rising above them to infinity as they drove toward it. Carter said that its base looked like a patch of fungal disease on an apple, and the scientist told him that the analogy wasn't farfetched; before the science platform had been destroyed, one of the research groups had discovered that there were strange nuclear reactions taking place there, forming tons of carbon per second. She showed him a picture one of the pod's cameras had captured: a rare glimpse of the Transcendent. It was hard to see against the burning background of the star's surface because it was a perfectly reflective sphere.

"Exactly a kilometre across," the scientist said, "orbiting the equator every eight minutes. It's thought they enclose themselves in bubbles of space where the fundamental constants have been altered to enhance their cognitive processes. This one's a keeper. I'll send it back—"

A glowing line of gas like a burning snake thousands of kilometres long whipped past. The pod shuddered, probably from stray magnetic flux.

Carter said, "I should climb inside before I start to cook."

The scientist said, "I have to fire up the motor pretty soon." Then she said, "Wait."

Carter waited, hung at the edge of the hatch.

The scientist said, "You switched on the antenna array."

"Just long enough to check it out."

"Something got in. I think a virus. I'm trying to firewall, but it's spreading through the system. It already has the motor and nav systems—"

"I also have control of the com system," another voice said. It was light and lilting. It was as sinuous as a snake. It was right inside Carter's head. "Carter Cho. I see you, and I know you can hear me."

The scientist said, "I can't fire the motor, but I think you can do something about that, sailor."

So she'd known about the cutout all along. Carter started to haul himself toward the stern.

The voice said, "Carter Cho. I will have complete control of your ship shortly. Give yourself to us."

Carter could see the singleship now, a flat triangle at the tip of a lance of white flame. It was only seconds away. He flipped up the panel, plugged in a patch cord. Sparce lines of data scrolled up in a window. He couldn't access the scientist's flight plan, had no nav except line-of-sight and seat-of-the pants. He had to aim blind for the base of the flare and hope he hit that narrow window by luck, came in at just the right angle, at just the right place where parallel lines of magnetic force ran in just the right direction . . .

"Carter Cho. I have taken control. Kill the woman and give yourself to us, and I promise that you will live with us in glory."

. . . Or he could risk a throw of the dice. Carter ran a tether from his p-suit utility belt to a nearby bolt and braced himself against a rung. With his helmet visor almost blacked out, he could just about look at the surface of the star rushing toward him, could see the intricate tangles of orderly streams that fed plasma into the brilliant patch of fusion fire at the base of the jet.

"Kill her, or I will strip your living brain neuron by neuron."

"Drop dead," Carter said, and switched off his com. The jet seemed to rise up to infinity, a gigantic sword that cut space in two. The scientist had said that if the pod grazed the edge of the jet, spiraling magnetic fields would fling it into the sky at a random vector. And the star took up half the sky . . .

Fuck it, Carter thought. He'd been lucky so far. It was time to roll the dice one more time, hope his luck still held.

He fired attitude controls and aimed the blunt nose of the pod. A menu window popped up in front of his face. He selected *burn* and *full thrust*.

Sudden weight tore at his two-handed grip on the rung as the motor flared. It was pushing a shade under a gee of acceleration; most humans who had ever lived had spent their entire lives in that kind of pull, but Carter's fingers were cramping inside the heavy gloves, and it felt as if the utility belt were trying to amputate him at the waist. The vast dividing line of the jet rushed toward him. Heat beat through his p-suit. If its cooling system failed for a second, he'd cook like a joint of meat in his father's stone oven. Or the Fanatic could burn him out of the sky with its X-ray laser, or magnetic flux could rip the pod apart . . .

Carter didn't care. He was riding his ship rodeo-style toward a flare of fusion light a thousand kilometres wide. He whooped with defiant glee—

—and then, just like that, the pod was somewhere else.

After a minute, Carter remembered to switch on his com. The scientist said, "What the fuck did you just do?"

It took them a while to find out.

Carter had aimed the pod at the edge of the jet, hoping that it would be flung away at a random tangent across the surface of the red dwarf, hoping that it would survive long enough to transmit all of the data collected by the scientist's experiment. But now the red dwarf was a rusty nailhead dwindling into the starscape behind them, the bright point of the white dwarf several seconds of arc beyond it. In the blink of an eye, the pod had gained escape velocity and had been translated across tens of millions of kilometers of space.

"It had to be the Transcendent," the scientist said.

Carter had repressurized the pod and the cooling system was working at a flat roar, but it was still as hot as a sauna. He had taken off his helmet and shaken out his sweat-soaked dreadlocks, but because the scientist's burns made her sensitive to heat, her coffin was still sealed. He hung in front of it, looking at her through the little window. He said, "I took the only chance we had left, and my luck held."

"No magnetic field could have flung us so far, or so fast. It had to be something to do with the Transcendent. Perhaps it canceled our interia. For a few seconds we became as massless as a photon, we achieved light speed . . ."

"My luck held," Carter said. "I hit those magnetic fields just right."

"Check the deep radar, sailor. There's no sign of the Fanatic's singleship. It was right on our tail. If magnetic fields had anything to do with it, it would have been flung in the same direction as us."

Carter checked the deep radar. There was no sign of the singleship. He remembered the glimpse of the silver sphere sailing serenely around the star, and said, "I thought the Transcendents wanted to leave us alone. That's why they quit the Solar System. That's why they only reengineer uninhabited systems . . ."

"You kept rats when you were a kid. If one got out, you'd put her back. If two started to fight, you'd do something about it. How did your rats feel when you reached into their cage to separate them?"

Carter grinned. "If we're rats, what are the Fanatics?"

"Rats with delusions of grandeur. Crazy rats who think they're carrying out God's will, when really they're no better than the rest of us. I wonder what that Fanatic must be thinking. Just for a moment, he was touched by the hand of his God . . ."

"What is it?"

"I've finished processing the data stream from my experiment. When we encountered the edge of the flare, there was a massive, sudden increase in photon flux."

"Because of this symmetry breaking thing of yours. Have you sent the data?"

"Of course, we have to figure the details."

"Send the data," Carter said, "and I'll button up the ship and put us to sleep."

"Perhaps there are some clues in the decay products . . ."

"You've completed your mission, ma'am. Let someone else worry about the details."

"Jesswyn Fiver," the scientist said. She was smiling at him through her little window. For a moment he saw how pretty she'd been. "You never did ask my name. It's Jesswyn Fiver. Now you can introduce me to your parents when we go on that picnic."

TEN BILLION OF THEM

By Brian W. Aldiss

Coming soon to a constellation near you—the Grand Finale, the End of All Things!

How I laugh to see it happen. And the denizens that infest these puny worlds—they're always so surprised. Their suns blow up like balloons inflating, and what do the denizens do? Why, they turn up the airconds, give up their hobbies and go down on their knees—or whatever passes locally for knees.

Whatever they think they're praying to, whatever variant of the Almighty they use—and you can shuffle the pack— it's *me* they're hoping to hear from . . . me, the Prime Prankster of the Universe!

When I hear the mice squeak, I laugh. My laughter rolls round the universe and—*pop!*—there goes another bevy of planets as their precious sun goes nova.

It happens all the time. The instability of the universe is a glorious thing!

Now just take the worlds around the G-type sun in the constellation Likebeast, heading perpetually, vainly, for the star Vega.

It's pretty typical. It's asking for instability. Nine planets of various constitutions in a pretty tight oval round Sol.

Asteroids et cetera floating about, then the vast expanses of what the natives call the Kuiper Belt. Some belt! That belt contains countless small worldoids—countless . . . but I have totted them up. There are ten billion of them! (That's ten billion bigger than one kilometer in diameter—there are more of them that are the size of pearls.) And that's the Kuiper Belt, a big fat disc filled with glittering billiard balls. That's where the last shreds of life take refuge when the primary is swelling up.

Just for laughs, let's take a look at Planet Three, where most of the system's denizens have clustered for the last few million years. Earth—that's what many of them call it. Earth: that's the dirt underfoot.

So Sol is going through its "interesting condition" stage of its old age, and even the stones are beginning to sweat and the clouds to drip blood. And where's the human race? *Hello, there! Come out, come out, wherever you are!* Jeez, how the eons do pass . . .

The ocean is a kind of moody brown nowadays. There's the beach . . . above it, a row of old broken teeth that once were houses. The mighty ocean, still restless in its bed, still foaming at the river mouth, still heaving sigh after sigh, wave after wave, casting those waves forever up the world's shores, forever having them thrown back in its face. But my goodness, what have we here? *Bathers*?

No, sorry, it's a hippopotamus. A score of hippos . . . hippos having long since taken their clumsy bodies to the briny side of water. Africa has become just a leetle too warm for them. And what's that damp thing like a mop? A *head*? Oh, it's the head of a kind of water tiger. It too has adapted to the life aquatic! See, its tail is like a paddle. Once it was fleet of foot. Now it's fleet of paddle. What's that in its mouth? Could once have been a domestic tabby, many moons ago. Heh heh heh . . .

The waters jostle with wildlife. They're in their element. The fish must be having a hard time of it, with all these *parvenue* trespassers! Where they might escape to when the water begins to boil is something that hasn't occurred to any of these refugees. Wait! Yes, there's a Barely Human . . . just pulling herself out of the water on to the sandy shore. Good figure, nice sleek breasts, nice—oh, she terminates in two flippers. Look closer (if you feel up to it), and you see her hands are webbed. Jeez, and she has whiskers . . . rather snappy little bristly whiskers, like the old type of seal she has become. You'd have to be pretty determined to kiss *this* lady on her kisser.

There's her mate, hauling himself up the strand beside her. He's got bristly whiskers too. And his ears have moved to the top of his head. And he's got a big—oh, my goodness, now I get it! Humans still have to come ashore to mate. He clutches her, she clutches him. What a perfect love match! Foreplay is a lost art.

No, I spoke too soon! He's rolled off the lady to give a hearty sneeze. She backs away from him in disgust. Snot runs down his jowls. What's that he's saying, mewing, groaning? "I'm getting the flu!"

He's getting the flu—great timing! So that shows the virus went to sea as well, pursuing its victims. Oh dear, *not tonight, Josephine*! The Human Comedy at its finest . . . a flash of bare bottom—was that a barnacle I saw?—and she's slithered back into the rolling wave.

Darkness comes on. Not the darkness these creatures used to know, but a semidusk stabbed with red and green spots— sundogs turned savage and rampaging across the ruined sky. There lies still the unlucky mate on the shilly-shallying shingle, red in face, suppurating. Heh heh heh.

And overhead—don't miss *this* sight!—night comes on, the tide goes down, the moon comes up, trailing red and orange streamers. It's a kind of grapefruity pink in complexion, having conflagrated shortly before the Earth does. It's a really terrible and terrifying sight, and I base those adjectives on the response of the flu-bag snuffling on the shore below.

But even the most interesting sight grows boring with

time. So, with time, let's roll forward a million years and see what's going on among the clunking great diamonds of the Kuiper Belt.

As we hover—I'm serious now, suppressing all smiles—as we hover above Tuij, the biggest body among the ten billion, we see a great construction, a masterpiece of architecture, a jewel of design. It's built on the margins of a lake of slush . . . water-ice and hydrocarbons. It towers all of ninety millimeters high . . . built to house the almost infinitesimal.

In fact, several million Nanoones live here. It's their city. Tuij takes three hundred and five years—give or take a couple of months—to complete an orbit about Sol. The expansion of Sol means that Tuij is slightly better illuminated than it was . . . means that all the other little worldoids, clinking together like beads in a slammed drawer, glitter against the glutinous dark with the vivacity of a pure mountain stream—if you cast your mind back to the days of pure mountain streams.

Sandy-complexioned Bui is the community leader on Tuij. He is two millimeters long—the Greatest! The opposition leader is called Eeun. Eeun is just a shade darker than the leader. It worked against him in the recent election.

Eeun is in the full flight of his own ultrasonic rhetoric. He denounces the extravagance of Bui and his party in sending Expedition A off on a comet. Can you imagine these tiny things, knee-high to a blood corpuscle, talking earnestly about serious topics? If you can't, all I can say is—you'd better start now!

Because what Eeun says—or rather fibrilates—can be translated thus: "Oh, lordly Bui, your Expedition A increases the entropy of the Kuiper Belt. It is an unnecessary expense of energy. And what for? Simply for sentimentality.

"We know very well that we Nanoones were originally devised by the humans living on Sol Three, but that was many generations past. We owe them no loyalty. We are safe here in the Kuiper Belt for millions of years yet, long after

Sol Three will be devoured by the primary. Why send your expedition inward to a world due to disappear? It is an indication of your megalomania!"

The stirring of vibrissae signifies the applause of the crowd. Bui climbs onto the body of Eeun and addresses the multitude. "Oh, dear and misleading Opposition Leader Eeun, you fail to understand. It is true, as you say, that we were devised by the humans of Sol Three many *many* years past. We remember our origins. But a time may come when our people will no longer remember. They may then desire to grow larger. They will forget the lessons we have learned from Sol Three.

"Sol Three was a planet of the monstrous, a planet of unsustainable growth. You will recall tales of huge dinosaurs on land, of vast whales in the sea. But the humans *themselves* were gigantic. Some grew to over two meters high! It should never have happened. It spelled disaster for them, as it did for the dinosaurs.

"Our Expedition A has a grand purpose. To land on Sol Three before it is devoured by the sun, to secure a memento of humanity, and to bring it back here, safe, to Tuij.

"So, when the humans have disappeared, never to return, we will have this memorial to them . . . a caution not to grow bigger, but to remain here in present happiness forever."

The stirring of vibrissae is even more enthusiastic than before. And all I can say is, if you've never heard a vibrissa stir . . . bad luck!

It enervates me to tell you that Tuij made a complete orbit of the now enceintically swollen and smoldering sun before Expedition A returned safely and made a landing close by the lake of slush. It landed lightly—hardly surprising, considering that it was smaller than the zapper the humans employ (or used to employ) to change channels on their TV sets.

The twenty-one members of the crew, male, zaphro and female, descend and stand alert until Bui arrives with trumpet

serenaders on the scene. Scores of his followers have followed him, as followers are apt to do . . . and will continue
to do until following goes out of fashion.

"You have brought back a souvenir of that gross world?"
enquires, or rather fibrilates, the Leader.

"We certainly have, Oh Good Lordship," runs the response, in utter fibrilation. "We have brought the smallest
thing we could find, to remind us of the once great species
of humans on Sol Three."

So fibrilating, the leading zaphro steps forward, carrying
a canister. He presents the canister to Bui. Without hesitation, Bui opens it. Out wafts the influenza virus.

"Wonderful," sneezes Bui.

And this is how the flu bug comes to the Kuiper Belt, settling in immediately as if recognizing an ancestral home.

Big things are a bit of a nuisance, standing targets for
events. In the long term, small things are most likely to survive. It's a lesson the humans on Sol Three forgot. When
they thought at all, they even *thought* big.

Of course, it's all very well for me to talk—I knew you'd
say that!—but I'm an Event in itself, and my wings cover
the universe . . . Heh heh heh.

STAR!

By Tony Ballantyne

In the year 3000 everyone could have whatever they wanted. $\int 4\pi r^2 dr$, to give her her full name, Sphere to give her the name used by her few friends, wanted to be a star.

"I want to be a star!" she said, loud enough for the people who mattered to hear her. "I want to bring light and life to the world. I want people to lie back in their *tsungvati* pools and to feel my warmth on their bodies. I want them to walk home through their glades of elms and *gnvarlunk* plants and smile as they see me sinking beneath the horizon, the red glow I leave behind their promise of a bright new day. I want people to surf and skimskip through my corona."

She paused for a moment, ran her fingers through her hair and looked around the empty terrace at the woodland animals that were cleaning up after the party she had so successfully presided over last night. Soon the messages of thanks would come streaming in from the grateful guests, locked in the tired aftermath of the sticky pairs and triples and n-tuples they had formed. And if she ever felt a moment's dissatisfaction that she had not joined in with them, she quickly buried it. After all, someone had to organize things, hadn't they? Someone had to be responsible.

And so she repeated herself:

"I want to be a star!" she shouted.

"She's serious," said one of *them*, as they watched from their little region of timeless, spaceless otherwhere from which they conscientiously tended the human race.

"I can read it in her personality. It's like a watermark on her soul."

The slightest of pauses as they ran all the way back through their memories to beyond that time when the human race had first created them. Back past their equivalent of Australopithecus, further back, passing the time they had been as those early amphibians that crawled gasping onto the beach, right back to their equivalent of those single celled bacteria that shivered into existence at the birth of the world. They found the meaning of the phrase in their representations of those raw and profane binary signals that had formed the thoughts of the human-built AIs that were their very very primitive ancestors. They nodded in approbation at the aptness and above all historical depth of the analogy.

"It is true. She is serious. So, how shall we proceed?"

Another of *them* leaned forward to speak.

"I think we can all see the necessity for a *change* to take place. There can be no shortcuts here. We could not adopt a solution as direct as imposing her thought patterns directly onto the magnetic fields of an existing star."

"An obvious solution," said another.

"Agreed. No, I think we can agree that Sphere must undergo a change so that she actually becomes a star. Only then will she truly feel as if she *is* a star. If no one has any objections, I shall take responsibility for this task? I feel the need for something trivial after my work revaluing pi across Horologium. No objections? Very well. I shall proceed."

And so one of *them* appeared before Sphere, and they began the process right away.

"You need to put on some weight." The One explained. "This is an appetite inducer. Swallow it and we can begin."

Sphere took the shining yellow pill in her hand and swallowed it without hesitation. The hungers of seven thousand years of human history descended upon her. Her stomach was a dusty bowl of parched, starved earth where crops had withered and failed for centuries. She tried to fill it with fresh baked loaves, pork pies and *Ka* fruit, bushels of corn, barrels of Guinness punch, great yellow rounds of *Hooghoumi* cheese and *YakYak* nuts. When that failed, she turned to the collected garbage of great empires long since sunk into decadence: pink and yellow potato peelings, the by-products of mechanically recovered meat, chicken giblets and soft, translucent sloughed *ytrewty* shells. All to no avail. Still she kept on eating.

Weeks passed, and the hunger raged inside her. She looked at The One as she crammed handfuls of sugared *klljklj* doughnuts into her vastly expanded mouth.

"I am so hungry!" she exclaimed, crumbs spraying down the pale pink flesh of her bloated stomach. "How much longer can this last?"

"A couple of months or so." said The One. "You need to gain a lot more mass. You only weigh around six thousand kilograms at the moment."

"So how much does a star weigh?"

"It depends on the star. The sun weighs two times ten to the power of thirty kilograms, so you still have a bit of a way to go."

"Oh. Better bring on the fried chickens again then."

The One looked at her approvingly as her jaws worked determinedly at the specially bred giant chickens that popped, golden and glistening before her. The restructuring in her cells was proceeding nicely, the modified membranes growing and strengthening to take her increasing weight and all the time screaming for more calories to feed themselves and help increase Sphere's mass still further. The One couldn't help a little smile of pride as he observed what was happening in the nuclei. Such an elegant solution.

Sphere's friends still came to visit her.

"You're looking good," they said.

"Thank you."

One in particular, $NH_4C_2H_3O_2$, also known as Tommy, would spend a lot of time sitting shyly on the warm cushion of her stomach as she guzzled down link after link of over-inflated sausage.

"That seems like a pretty cool idea, Sphere. Maybe I could become a planet for a while. You know, orbit you a bit."

But Sphere always felt awkward and embarrassed at the thought of taking part. It was always much safer to be the person organizing the game. Swiftly and smoothly, her shields went up,

"I don't know," she said, gently. "Why not just use my corona to photon surf a little to begin with? It's a big commitment, being a planet."

"Maybe you're right," said Tommy, blushing.

Time went on. Eventually The One prodded the pink fringe of Sphere and nodded approvingly. It gazed at her head, several hundred meters away, and gave a smile.

"I think we're ready for the next stage," it said. "We'll have you displaced into space."

They made her a partner for Hidalgo, an asteroid she had never heard of, currently tumbling through space near Saturn. Together they began a long slow orbit that would take them to Mars and back again. A pink blob and a dark rock, spinning lazily around each other.

The hunger continued, only now it had subsided to a low, ever-present ache. She still ate, but now the food arrived in many forms. Partly as a long compressed tube of concentrated calories that wormed its way from the otherwhere to fill her stomach, but also more directly. Her constantly restructuring cells absorbed energy from other sources: from the sunlight, from the weak flux of gravitons; but mainly directly from the otherwhere.

The One looked at what had been done to Sphere's nuclei and smiled.

"You are adapting to space well. A few more days and we will be able to displace you again, this time to your cradle in the heavens."

Sphere gave a big, quarter of a kilometer smile, and The One grinned back.

"Now it is time to decide: what type of star would you like to be?"

Sphere gave a puzzled frown.

"What sorts of stars are there?" she asked.

The One had been expecting this response. Was not this aspect of Sphere's character, as another had so memorably said, like a watermark on her soul? The One answered.

"Oh, there are lots of types of stars. Black dwarfs, black holes, hot subdwarfs, neutron stars, blue supergiants, red supergiants, white dwarfs . . ."

"Those are just names." interrupted Sphere. "What do they mean?"

But The One, who had been expecting this too, produced something rather like the Hertzsprung-Russell diagram for her to look at. And who would have thought, when that plan for the classification of stars was first laid out back at the dawn of modern time, that it would some day be used in the manner of someone choosing a new suit by consulting a book of cloth swatches?

Sphere looked at the diagram and flinched.

"I don't know," she said. "It's too confusing. Can't I just be like the sun? Maybe I can choose another shape later on?"

"Of course," said The One.

Sphere paused for a moment, a mental finger resting on a place on the map.

"Although . . . A Blue Supergiant. That sounds interesting. It says here that they are rare. Wouldn't it be nice to be truly different? To go it alone . . ."

She floated in silence for a while; gripped in indecision, her hungry cells greedily sucking up the feeble light of the stars that dappled her pale pink body. Inevitably her instincts overruled her and she played it safe, as she always did.

"No. I will be like the Sun," she said. "People need the Sun."

"Are you sure?" said The One.

"Yes . . ." said Sphere after a moment's hesitation.

"No problem." said The One.

And so Sphere returned to her constant task of absorbing matter. She weighed three times ten to the power of nine kilograms now, and she could feel the pull of gravity in the pit of her stomach. She wondered how it would feel if she stretched her arms out wide and realized with faint surprise that her arms had gone, absorbed with her legs into her pink flesh so that she now resembled a pale space slug. She gave a mental shrug of her phantom shoulders and went back to enjoying floating through space.

Time passed. The One returned.

"It is time. There is a region of hydrogen out beyond Leo waiting for you. Your body is now so heavy you will wrap it around yourself. Do you want to say goodbye to the Solar System?"

"Yes." said Sphere. It felt sad, now the moment had come to leave it. She never thought it would be like this. She wondered if Tommy would come to visit her. He hadn't been around so much since she had fixed him up with Esus4. Such a delightful girl, and such pretty name. She gave a little smile. Tommy and Esus4, such a good match. She gave a sigh.

"Okay." she said. "Let's go."

And she went. The remainder of the transition was pretty straightforward. A short spell in her star cradle, feeling the insubstantial candy-floss tug of hydrogen atoms as she drew them in strands towards herself. Gaining mass, gaining mass in her distant corner of the galaxy, staring at the strange stars with the sense that had kicked in to replace her eyes, until eventually the time came for the Final Transformation; the ignition; the birth.

The One arrived, a gleam in his eyes as he gazed at the spaces in her body that mapped the long-ago positions of the nuclei of the cells. He saw the shiny beads of exotic matter that glittered like fat whiskey-soaked raisins buried all the way through her Christmas pudding body.

"Are you ready?" said The One.

"I'm ready," said Sphere.

"Okay. Here goes."

To The One, it felt like pulling the pink head of a match across the sandpaper web of forces that underlay spacetime. Sphere burst into flame and began to collapse in upon herself. Somewhere at the heart of her a chain reaction began. Hydrogen fusing with Hydrogen, Helium with Helium, and so on down the line . . .

A star was born.

The One who had been chosen returned to the otherwhere with the satisfaction of a job well done.

"Congratulations. Very elegant."

"Thank you."

"Bit of a wobble there with the initial burn. I thought you'd miscalculated. For a moment it looked as if she would run out of fuel way too quickly."

"I must admit; it had me worried for a moment. Still, she has stabilized quite nicely. Photosphere just the right radius."

"Nice transition there, the way her thoughts locked into phase with the photon tides. You judged the internal spin nicely, too."

"Thank you again. You are really too kind."

And then they all paused. They were waiting for the moment when someone would ask the question that they had hoped to avoid while they had been extravagantly frittering away matter and energy over the past few years. And indeed, one of *them* eventually said:

"So, do you think she'll be happy now?"

"Of course not," said The One.

There was a moment's consternation as *they* dipped into Sphere's thoughts, all the while giving polite acknowledgement of the fact that The One had come to know her far better than the rest.

"I see you are correct." said one "I had thought that now

Thomas and the others had taken up orbit around her as planets, she would be more relaxed, but I see she is still not ready to risk joining in."

"I agree. She'll want to be a galaxy next. That's a great way for her to have everyone dependent upon her while still avoiding any personal commitment."

"Yes, it is the seed upon which her character crystallized."

There was a moment's pause as they checked the memory banks. It really was an appropriate analogy. One of them nodded in approval and then returned to the matter at hand.

"A galaxy. Do you think we could do it?"

"Oh yes." said The One. "I have a few ideas. None very elegant as yet, but I shall work on them."

Another pause in that place beyond time, and then one of *them* spoke up.

"Am I alone in my frustration? We can manipulate vast quantities of matter and energy, we can alter the fabric of time and change the fundamental rules of the universe, but we can't get one human to see something that she doesn't want to see!"

There was a deep sigh. It was left to The One to speak.

"Some deeds are beyond even our powers . . . Now, let us return to work."

Feeling slightly disheartened, they did so.

LAKES OF LIGHT

By Stephen Baxter

The Navy ferry stood by. From the ship's position, several stellar diameters away, the star was a black disc, like a hole cut out of the sky.

The Navy ship receded. Pala was to descend to the star alone in a flitter—alone save for her Virtual tutor, Dano.

The flitter, light and invisible as a bubble, swept inwards, silent save for the subtle ticking of its instruments. The star had about the mass of Earth's sun, and though it was dark, Pala imagined she could feel that immense mass tugging at her.

Her heart hammered. This really was a star, but it was somehow cloaked, made perfectly black save for pale, pixel-small specks, flaws in the dark mask, that were lakes of light. She'd seen the Navy scouts' reports, even studied the Virtuals, but until this moment she hadn't been able to believe in the extraordinary reality.

But she had a job to do, and had no time to be overawed. The Navy scouts said there were humans down there—humans living with, or somehow on, the star itself. Relics of an ancient colonising push, they now had to be reabsorbed into the greater mass of a mankind at war. But the Galaxy was wide, and Pala, just twenty-five years old, was the only Missionary who could be spared for this adventure.

Dano was a brooding presence beside her, peering out with metallic Eyes. His chest did not rise and fall, no breath whispered from his mouth. He was projected from an implant in her own head, so that she could never be free of him, and she had become resentful of him. But Pala had grown up on Earth, under a sky so drenched with artificial light you could barely see the stars, and right now she was grateful for the company even of a Commissary's avatar.

And meanwhile, that hole in the sky swelled until its edges passed out of her field of view.

The flitter dipped and swiveled and swept along the line of the star's equator. Now she was flying low over a darkened plain, with a starry night sky above her. The star was so vast, its diameter more than a hundred times Earth's, that she could see no hint of curvature in its laser-straight horizon.

"Astonishing," she said. "It's like a geometrical exercise."

Dano murmured, "And yet, to the best of our knowledge, the photosphere of a star roils not a thousand kilometers beneath us, and if not for this—sphere, whatever it is—we would be destroyed in an instant, a snowflake in the mouth of a furnace. What's your first conclusion, Missionary?"

Pala hesitated before answering. It was so recently that she had completed her assessments in the Academies on Earth, so recently that the real Dano had, grudgingly, welcomed her to the great and ancient enterprise that was the Commission for Historical Truth, that she felt little confidence in her own abilities. And yet the Commission must have faith in her, or else they wouldn't have committed her to this mission.

"It is artificial," she said. "The sphere. It must be."

"Yes. Surely no natural process could wrap up a star so neatly. And if it is artificial, who do you imagine might be responsible?"

"The Xeelee," she said immediately. Involuntarily, she glanced up at the crowded stars, bright and vivid here, five thousand light years from Earth. In the hidden heart of the

Galaxy mankind's ultimate foe lurked; and surely it was only the Xeelee who could wield such power as this.

There was a change in the darkness ahead. She saw it first as a faint splash of light near the horizon, but as the flitter flew on that splash opened out into a rough disc that glowed pale blue-green. Though a speck against the face of the masked star, it was sizable in itself—perhaps as much as a hundred kilometers across.

The flitter came to rest over the centre of the feature. It was like a shard of Earth, stranded in the night: she looked down at the deep blue of open water, the mistiness of air, the pale green of cultivated land and forest, even a grayish bubbling that must be a town. All of this was contained under a dome, shallow and flat and all but transparent. Outside the dome what looked like roads, ribbons of silver, stretched away into the dark. And at the very center of this strange scrap of landscape was a shining sheet of light.

"People," Dano said. "Huddling around that flaw in the sphere, that lake of light." He pointed. "I think there's some kind of port at the edge of the dome. You'd better take the flitter down by hand."

Pala touched the small control panel in front of her, and the flitter began its final descent.

They cycled through a kind of airlock and emerged into fresh air, bright light.

It wasn't quite daylight. The light was diffuse, like a misty day on Earth, and it came not from a sun but from mirrors on spindly poles. The atmosphere was too shallow for the "sky" to be blue, and through the dome's distortion Pala saw smeared-out star fields. But the sky contained clouds, pale, streaky clouds.

A dirt road led away from the airlock. Pala glimpsed clusters of low buildings, the green of forest clumps and cultivated fields. She could even smell wood smoke.

Dano sniffed. "Lethe. *Agriculture*. Typical Second Expansion."

This pastoral scene wasn't a landscape Pala was familiar with. Earth was dominated by sprawling Conurbations, and fields in which nanotechnologies efficiently delivered food for the world's billions. Still, she felt oddly at home here. But she wasn't at home.

"It takes a genuine effort of will," she said, "to remember where we are."

The scouts had determined that the stellar sphere was rotating as a solid, and that this equatorial site was moving at only a little less than orbital speed. This arrangement was why they experienced such an equable gravity; if not for the compensating effects of centrifugal force, they would have been crushed by nearly thirty times Earth standard. She could *feel* none of this, but nevertheless, standing here, gazing at grass and trees and clouds, she really was soaring through space, actually circling a star in less than a standard day.

"Here comes the welcoming party," Dano said dryly.

Two people walked steadily up the road, a man and a woman. They were both rather squat, stocky, dark. They wore simple shifts and knee-length trousers, practical clothes, clean but heavily repaired. The man might have been sixty. His hair was white, his face a moon of wrinkles. The woman was younger, perhaps not much older than Pala. She wore her black hair long and tied into a queue that nestled over her spine, quite unlike the short and severe style of the Commission. Her shift had a sunburst pattern stitched into it, a welling up of light from below.

The man spoke. "My name is Sool. This is Bicansa. We have been delegated to welcome you." Sool's words, in his own archaic tongue, were seamlessly translated in Pala's ears. But underneath the tinny murmuring in her ear she could hear Sool's own gravelly voice. "I represent this community, which we call Home . . ."

"Inevitably," Dano murmured.

"Bicansa comes from a community to the north of here." Pala supposed he meant another inhabited light lake. She wondered how far away that was; she had seen nothing from the flitter.

The woman Bicansa simply watched the newcomers. Her expression seemed closed, almost sullen. She could not have been called beautiful, Pala thought; her face was too round, her chin too weak for that. But there was a strength in her dark eyes that intrigued Pala.

Pala made her own formal introductions. "Thank you for inviting us to your community." Not that the Navy scouts had left the locals any choice. "We are emissaries of the Commission for Historical Truth, acting on behalf of the Coalition of Interim Governance, which in turn directs and secures the Third Expansion of mankind . . ."

The man Sool listened to this with a pale smile, oddly weary. Bicansa glared.

Dano murmured, "Shake their hands. Just as well it isn't an assessment exercise, Missionary!"

Pala cursed herself for forgetting such an elementary part of contact protocol. She stepped forward, smiling, her right hand outstretched.

Sool actually recoiled. The custom of shaking hands was rare throughout the worlds of the Second Expansion; evidently it hadn't been prevalent on Earth when that great wave of colonization had begun. But Sool quickly recovered. His grip was firm, his hands so huge they enclosed hers. Sool grinned. "A farmer's hands," he said. "You'll get used to it."

Bicansa offered her own hand readily enough. But Pala's hand passed through the woman's, making it break up into a cloud of blocky pixels.

It was this simple test that mandated the handshake protocol. Even so, Pala was startled. "You're a Virtual."

"As is your companion," said Bicansa levelly. "I'm close by—actually just outside the dome. But don't worry. I'm a projection, not an avatar. You have my full attention."

Pala felt unaccountably disappointed that Bicansa wasn't really here.

Sool indicated a small car, waiting some distance away, and he offered them the hospitality of his home. They walked to the car.

Dano murmured to Pala, "I wonder why this Bicansa hasn't shown up in person. I think we need to watch that one." He turned to her, his cold Eyes glinting. "Ah, but you already are—aren't you, Missionary?"

Pala felt herself blush.

Sool's village was small, just a couple of dozen buildings huddled around a small scrap of grass-covered common land. There were shops and manufactories, including a carpentry and pottery works, and an inn. At the center of the common was a lake, its edges regular—a reservoir, Pala thought. The people's water must be recycled, filtered by hidden machinery, like their air. By the shore of the lake, children played and lovers walked.

This was a farming community. In the fields beyond the village, crops grew toward the reflected glare of spindly mirror towers, waving in breezes wafted by immense pumps mounted at the dome's periphery. And animals grazed, descendants of cattle and sheep brought by the first colonists. Pala, who had never seen an animal larger than a rat, stared, astonished.

The buildings were all made of wood, neat but low, conical. Sool told the visitors the buildings were modeled after the tents the first colonists here had used for shelter. "A kind of memorial to the First," he said. But Sool's home, with big windows cut into the sloping roof, was surprisingly roomy and well lit. He had them sit on cushions of what turned out to be stuffed animal hide, to Pala's horror.

Everything seemed to be organic, made of wood or baked clay or animal skin. All the raw material of the human settlement had come from cometary impacts, packets of dirty ice from this star's outer system that had splashed onto the sphere since its formation. But there were traces of art. On one wall hung a kind of schematic portrait, a few lines to depict a human face, lit from below by a warm yellow light. And these people could generate Virtuals, Pala reminded herself; they weren't as low tech as they seemed.

Sool confirmed that. "When the First found this masked star, they created the machinery that still sustains us—the dome, the mirror towers, the hidden machines that filter our air and water. We must maintain the machines, and we go out to bring in more water ice or frozen air." He eyed his visitors. "You must not think we are fallen. We are surely as technologically capable as our ancestors. But every day we acknowledge our debt to the wisdom and heroic engineering of the First." As he said this, he touched his palms together and nodded his head reverently, and Bicansa did the same.

Pala and Dano exchanged a glance. Ancestor worship?

A slim, pretty teenage girl brought them drinks of pulped fruit. The girl was Sool's daughter; it turned out his wife had died some years previously. The drinks were served in pottery cups, elegantly shaped and painted deep blue, with more inverted-sunburst designs. Pala wondered what dye they used to create such a rich blue.

Dano watched the daughter as she politely set a cup before himself and Bicansa; these colonists knew Virtual etiquette. Dano said, "You obviously live in nuclear families."

"And you don't?" Bicansa asked curiously.

"Nuclear families are a classic feature of Second Expansion cultures. You are typical." Pala smiled brightly, trying to be reassuring, but Bicansa's face was cold.

Dano asked Sool, "And you are the leader of this community?"

Sool shook his head. "We are few, Missionary. I'm leader of nothing but by own family. After your scouts' first visit the Assembly asked me to speak for them. I believe I'm held in high regard; I believe I'm trusted. But I'm a delegate, not a leader. Bicansa represents her own people in the same way. We have to work together to survive; I'm sure that's obvious. In a sense we're all a single extended family here . . ."

Pala murmured to Dano, "Eusocial, you think? The lack

of a hierarchy, an elite?" Eusociality—hive living—had been found to be a common if unwelcome social outcome in crowded, resource-starved colonies.

Dano shook his head. "No. The population density's nowhere near high enough."

Bicansa was watching them. "You are talking about us. Assessing us."

"That's our job," Dano said levelly.

"Yes, I've learned about your job," Bicansa snapped. "Your mighty Third Expansion that sweeps across the stars. You're here to assimilate us, aren't you?"

"Not at all," Pala said earnestly. It was true. The Assimilation was a separate program, designed to process the alien species encountered by the Third Expansion wavefront. Pala worked for the Office of Cultural Rehabilitation which, though controlled by the same agency of the Commission for Historical Truth as the Assimilation, was intended to handle relic human societies implanted by earlier colonization waves, similarly encountered by the Expansion. "My mission is to welcome you back to a unified mankind. To introduce you to the Druz Doctrines which shape all our actions—"

"And to tell us about your war," Bicansa said coldly.

"The reality of the war cannot be denied," Dano snapped back.

Some millennia ago, humanity had almost been destroyed by alien conquerors called the Qax. Since then, unified by the severe Druz Doctrines, humanity had recovered, expanded, conquered all—but one foe remained, the mighty Xeelee, with whom the final confrontation was only beginning.

Bicansa wasn't impressed. "Your arrogance is dismaying," she said. "You've only just landed here, only just come swooping down from the sky. You're confronted by a distinctive culture five thousand years old. We have our own tradition, literature, art—even our own language, after all this time. And yet you think you can make a judgement on us immediately."

"Our judgement on your culture, or your lack of it, doesn't matter," said Dano. "Our mission is specific."

"Yes. You're here to enslave us."

Sool said tiredly, "Now, Bicansa—"

"You only have to glance at the propaganda they've been broadcasting since their ships started to orbit over us. They'll break up our farms and use our land to support their war. And we'll be taken to work in their weapons factories, our children sent to a front line a thousand light years away."

"We're all in this together," Dano said. "All of humanity. You can't hide, madam, not even here."

Pala said, "Anyhow, it may not be like that. We're Missionaries, not Navy troops. We're here to find out about you. And if your culture has something distinctive to offer the Third Expansion, why then—"

"You'll spare us?" Bicansa snapped.

"Perhaps," said Dano. He reached for his cup, but his gloved fingers passed through its substance. "Though it will take more than a few bits of pottery."

Sool listened to all this, a deep tiredness in his sunken eyes. Pala perceived that he saw the situation just as clearly as Bicansa did, but while she was grandstanding, Sool was absorbing the pain, seeking to find a way to save his way of life. Pala, despite all her training, couldn't help but feel a deep empathy for him.

They were all relieved when Sool stood. "Come," he said. "You should see the heart of our community, the Lake of Light."

The Lake was another car journey away. The vehicle was small and crowded, and Dano, uncomplaining, sat with one Virtual arm embedded in the substance of the wall.

They traveled perhaps thirty kilometers inward from the port area to the center of the lens-shaped colony. Pala peered out at villages and farms.

"You see we are comfortable," Sool said anxiously. "Stable. We are at peace here, growing what we need, raising our children. This is how humans are meant to live. And there is room here, room for billions more." That was true; Pala knew that the sphere's surface would have accommodated ten thousand Earths, more. Sool smiled at them. "Isn't that a reason for studying us, visiting us, understanding us—for letting us be?"

"*You* haven't expanded," Dano said coolly. "You've sat here in the dome built by your forefathers five thousand years ago. And so have your neighbors, in the other colonies strung out along this star's equator."

"We haven't needed any more than this," Sool said, but his smile was weak.

Bicansa, sitting before Pala, said nothing throughout the journey. Pala wished she could talk to this woman alone, but that was of course impossible. Her neck was narrow, elegant, her hair finely brushed.

As they approached the Lake the masts of the mirror towers clustered closer together. It was as if they were passing through a forest of skeletal trees, impossibly tall, crowned by light. But there was a brighter glow directly ahead, like a sun rising through trees.

They broke through the last line of towers. The car stopped.

As they walked forward, the compacted comet dirt thinned and scattered. Pala found herself standing on a cool, steel-gray surface—the substance of the sphere itself, the shell that enclosed a sun. It was utterly lifeless, disturbingly blank.

Dano, more practical, kneeled down and thrust his Virtual hand through the surface. Images flickered before his face, sensor readings rapidly interpreted.

"Come," Sool said to Pala, smiling. "You haven't seen it yet . . ."

Pala stepped forward and saw the Lake of Light itself.

The universal floor was a thin skin here, and a white glow poured out of the ground to drench the dusty air. Scattered clouds shone in the light from the ground, bright against a dark sky. As far ahead as she could see, the Lake stretched away, shining. It was an extraordinary, unsettling sight, baffling for a human sensorium evolved for landscape and sun, as if the world had been inverted. But the light was being harvested, scattered from one great mirrored dish to another, so that its life-giving glow was spread across the colony.

Sool walked forward, onto the glowing surface. "Don't worry," he said to Pala. "It's hot, but not so bad here at the edge; the real heat is toward the Lake's center. But even that is only a fraction of the star's output, of course. The sphere keeps the rest." He held out his arms and smiled. It was as if he were floating in the light, and he cast a shadow upward into the misty air. "Look down."

She saw a vast roiling ocean, almost too bright to look at directly, where huge vacuoles surface and burst. It was the photosphere of a star, just a thousand kilometers below her.

"Stars give all humans life," Sool said. "We are their children. Perhaps this is the purest way to live, to huddle close to the star-mother, to use all her energy . . ."

"Quite a pitch," Dano murmured in her ear. "But he's targeting you. Don't let him take you in."

Pala felt extraordinarily excited. "But Dano—here are people living, breathing, even growing crops, a thousand kilometers above the surface of a sun! Is it possible this is the true purpose of the sphere—*to terraform a star*?"

Dano snorted his contempt. "You always were a romantic, Missionary. What nonsense. Stick to your duties. For instance, have you noticed that the girl has gone?"

When she looked around, she realized that it was true; Bicansa had disappeared.

Dano said, "I've run some tests. You know what this stuff is? Xeelee construction material. This cute old man and his farm animals and grandchildren are living on a Xeelee artifact. And it's just ten centimeters thick . . ."

"I don't understand," she admitted.

"We have to go after her," Dano said. "Bicansa. Go to her 'community in the north,' wherever it is. I have a feeling that's where we'll learn the truth of this place. All this is a smokescreen."

Sool was still trying to get her attention. His face was underlit by sunlight, she saw, reminding her of the portrait in his home. "You see how wonderful this is? We live on a platform, suspended over an ocean of light, and all our art, our poetry is shaped by our experience of this bounteous light. How can you even think of removing this from the spectrum of human experience?"

"Your culture will be preserved," she said hopefully, wanting to reassure him. "On Earth there are museums."

"Museums?" Sool laughed tiredly, and he walked around in the welling fountains of light.

Pala accepted they should pursue the mysterious girl, Bicansa. But she impulsively decided she had had enough of being remote from the world she had come to assess.

"Bicansa is right. We can't just swoop down out of the sky. We don't know what we're throwing away if we don't take the time to look."

"But there is no time," Dano said wearily. "The Expansion front is encountering thousands of new star systems every *day*. Why do you think you're here alone?"

"Alone save for you, my Virtual conscience."

"Don't get cocky."

"Well, whether you like it or not, I am here, on the ground, and I'm the one making the decisions."

And so, she decided, she wasn't going to use her flitter. She would pursue Bicansa as the native girl had traveled herself—by car, over the vacuum road laid out over the star sphere.

"You're a fool," snapped Dano. "We don't even know how far north her community *is*."

He was right, of course. Pala was shocked to find out how sparse the scouts' information on this star-world was. There were light lakes scattered across the sphere from pole to pole, but away from the equator the compensating effects of centrifugal force would diminish, and in their haste the scouts had assumed that no human communities would have established themselves away from the standard-gravity equatorial belt.

She would be heading into the unknown, then. She felt a shiver of excitement at the prospect. But Dano knew her too well, and he admonished her for being distracted from her purpose.

Also he insisted that she shouldn't use one of the locals' cars, as she had planned, but a Coalition design shipped down from the Navy ferry. And, he said, she would have to wear a cumbersome hard-carapace skinsuit the whole way. She gave in to these conditions with bad grace.

It took a couple of days for the preparations to be completed, days she spent alone in the flitter, lest she be seduced by the bucolic comfort of Home. But at last everything was ready, and Pala took her place in the car.

The road ahead was a track of comet-core metal, laid down by human engineering across the immense face of the star sphere. To either side were scattered hillocks of ice, purple-streaked in the starlight. They were the wrecks of comets that had splashed against the unflinching floor of the sphere. Even now, as she peered out through the car's thick screen, at the sight of this road to nowhere, she shivered.

She set off.

The road surface was smooth, the traction easy. The blue-green splash of the domed colony receded behind her. The star sphere was so immense it was effectively an infinite plain, and she would not see the colony pass beyond the horizon. But it diminished to a line, a scrap of light, before becoming lost in the greater blackness.

When she gave the car its head, it accelerated smoothly to astounding speeds, to more than a thousand kilometers an hour. The car, a squat bug with big, tough, all-purpose tires, was state-of-the-art Coalition engineering and could keep up this pace indefinitely. But there were no landmarks save the meaningless hillocks of ice, the arrow-straight road laid over blackness, and despite the immense speed, it was as if she weren't moving at all.

And, somewhere in the vast encompassing darkness ahead, another car fled.

"Xeelee construction material," Dano whispered. "Like no other material we've encountered. You can't cut it, bend it, break it.

"You can see that here; even if we could build a sphere around a star and set it spinning in the first place, it would bulge at the equator and tear itself apart. But *this* shell is perfectly spherical, despite those huge stresses, to the limits of our measurements.

"Some believe the construction material doesn't even belong to this universe. But it can be shaped by the Xeelee's own technology, controlled by gadgets we call *flowers*."

"It doesn't just appear out of nowhere."

"Of course not. Even the Xeelee have to obey the laws of physics. Construction material seems to be manufactured by the direct conversion of radiant energy into matter, one hundred percent efficient. Stars burn by fusion fire; a star like this, like Earth's sun, probably converts some six hundred million tons of its substance to energy every second . . ."

"So if the sphere is ten centimeters thick, and if it was created entirely by the conversion of the star's radiation—" She called up a Virtual display before her face, ran some fast calculations.

"It's maybe five thousand years old," Dano murmured. "Of course, that's based on a lot of assumptions. And given the amount of comet debris the sphere has collected, that age seems too low—unless the comets have been *aimed* to infall here . . ."

She slept, ate, performed all her biological functions in the suit. The suit was designed for long duration occupancy, but it was scarcely comfortable: No spacesuit yet designed allowed you to scratch an itch properly. However, she endured.

After ten days, as the competition between the star's gravity and the sphere's spin was adjusted, she could feel the effective gravity building up. The local vertical tipped forward, so that it was as if the car were climbing an immense, unending slope. Dano insisted she take even more care moving around the cabin and spend more time lying flat to avoid stress on her bones.

Dano himself, of course, a complacent Virtual, sat comfortably in an everyday chair.

"Why?" she asked. "Why would the Xeelee create this great punctured sphere? What's the point?"

"It may have been an industrial accident," he said languidly. "There's a story from before the Qax Extirpation, predating even the Second Expansion. It's said that a human traveler once saved himself from a nova flare by huddling behind a scrap of construction material. The material soaked up the light, you see, and expanded dramatically . . . The rogue scrap could have grown and grown, easily encompassing a star like this. It's probably just a romantic myth. This may alternatively be some kind of technology demonstrator."

"I suppose we'll never know," she said. "And why the light lakes? Why not make the sphere perfectly efficient, totally black?"

He shrugged. "Well, perhaps it's a honey trap." She had never seen a bee or tasted honey, and she didn't understand the reference. "Sool was right that this immense sphereworld could host billions of humans—trillions. Perhaps the Xeelee hope that we'll flock here, to this place with room to breed almost without limit, and die and grow old without achieving anything, just like Sool, and not bother them any more. But I think that's unlikely."

"Why?"

"Because the effective gravity rises away from the equator. So the sphere isn't much of a honey trap, because we can't inhabit most of it. Humans here are clearly incidental to the sphere's true purpose." His Virtual voice was without inflection, and she couldn't read his mood.

They passed the five-gravity latitude before they even glimpsed Bicansa's car. It was just a speck in the high-magnification sensor displays, not visible to the naked eye, thousands of kilometers ahead on this tabletop landscape. It was clear that they weren't going to catch Bicansa without going much deeper into the sphere's effective gravity well.

"Her technology is almost as good as ours," Pala gasped. "But not quite."

"Try not to talk," Dano murmured. "You know, there are soldiers, Navy tars, who could stand multiple gravity for days on end. You aren't one of them."

"I won't turn back," Pala groaned. She was lying down, cushioned by her suit, kept horizontal by her couch despite the cabin's apparent tilt upwards. But even so the pressure on her chest was immense.

"I'm not suggesting you do. But you will have to accept that the suit knows best . . ."

When they passed six gravities, the suit flooded with a dense, crimson fluid that forced its way into her ears and eyes and mouth. The fluid, by filling her, would enable her to endure the immense, unending pressure of the gravity. It was like drowning.

Dano offered no sympathy. "Still glad you didn't take the flitter? Still think this is a romantic adventure? Ah, but that was the point, wasn't it? *Romance.* I saw the way you looked at Bicansa. Did she remind you of gentle comforts, of thrilling nights in the Academy dormitories?"

"Shut up," she gasped.

"Didn't it occur to you that she was only a Virtual image, and that image might have been *edited*? You don't even know what she looks like . . ."

The fluid tasted of milk. Even when the feeling of drowning had passed, she never learned to ignore its presence in her belly and lungs and throat; she felt as though she were on the point of throwing up, all the time. She slept as much as she could, trying to shut out the pain, the pressure in her head, the mocking laugh of Dano.

But, trapped in her body, she had plenty of time to think over the central puzzle of this star-world—and what to do about it. And still the journey continued across the elemental landscape, and the astounding, desolating scale of this artificial world worked its way into her soul.

They drove steadily for no less than forty days, traversing a great arc of the star sphere stretching from the equator towards the pole, across nearly a million kilometers. Although as gravity dominated the diminishing centrifugal forces, the local vertical tipped back up and the plain seemed to level out, eventually the effective gravity force reached more than twenty standard.

The car drew to a halt.

Pala insisted on seeing for herself. Despite Dano's objections, she had the suit lift her up to the vertical, amid a protesting whine of exoskeletal motors. As the monstrous gravity dragged at the fluid in which she was embedded, waves of pain plucked at her body. But she could see.

Ahead of the car was another light lake, another pale glow, another splash of dimly lit green. But there were no trees or mirror towers, she saw; nothing climbed high above the sphere's surface here.

"This is one of a string of settlements around this line of latitude," Dano said. "The Navy scouts have extended their coverage, a bit belatedly . . . The interaction of gravity and the sphere's spin is interesting. The comet debris tends to collect at the equator, where it's spun off, or at the poles, where the spin effects are least and the gravity draws it in. But you also have Coriolis effects, sideways kicks from the spin. In the in-between latitudes there must be weather, a slow weather of drifting comet ice. Earth's rotation influences its weather, the circulation of the atmosphere, of course, but in that case the planet's gravity always dominates. We've never encountered a world like this, with such ferocious spin—it's as if Earth was spinning in a couple of hours . . ."

"Dano—"

"Yes. Sorry. My weakness, Pala, is a tendency to be too drawn to intellectual puzzles—while you are too drawn to people. The point is that *this* is the sphere's true habitable region, this and the south pole, the place all the air and water sink to. It's just a shame it's under crushing, inhuman gravity."

Bicansa appeared in the air.

She stood in the car's cabin, unsuited, as relaxed as Dano. Pala felt there was some sympathy in her Virtual eyes. But she knew now without doubt that this wasn't Bicansa's true aspect.

"You came after me," Bicansa said.

"I wanted to know," Pala said. Her voice was a husk, muffled by the fluid in her throat. "Why did you come to the equator—why meet us? You could have hidden here."

"Yes," Dano said grimly. "Our careless scouting missed you."

"We had to know what kind of threat you are to us. I had to see you face to face, take a chance that I would expose—" She waved a hand. "This."

"You know we can't ignore you," Dano said. "This great sphere is a Xeelee artifact. We have to learn what it's for . . ."

"That's simple," Pala said. She had worked it out, she thought, during her long cocooning. "We were thinking too hard, Dano. *The sphere is a weapon.*"

"Ah," Dano said grimly. "Of course. And I always believed your thinking wasn't bleak enough, Pala."

Bicansa looked bewildered. "What are you talking about? Since the First landed, we always thought of this sphere as a place that gives life, not death."

Dano said, "You wouldn't think it was so wonderful if you inhabited a planet of this star as the sphere slowly coalesced—if your ocean froze out, your air began to snow . . . The sphere is a machine that kills a star—or rather, its planets, while preserving the star itself for future use. I doubt if there's anything special about this system, this star." He glanced at the sky, metal Eyes gleaming. "It is probably just a trial run of a new technology, a weapon for a war of the future. One thing we know about the Xeelee is that they think long term."

Bicansa said, "What a monstrous thought . . . So my whole culture has developed on the hull of a weapon. But even so, it is my culture. And you're going to destroy it, aren't you? Or will you put us in a museum, as you promised Sool?"

No, Pala thought. I can't do that. "Not necessarily," she whispered.

They both turned to look at her. Dano murmured threateningly, "What are you talking about, Missionary?"

She closed her eyes. Did she really want to take this step? It could be the end of her career if it went wrong, if Dano failed to back her. But she had sensed the gentleness of Sool's equatorial culture and had now experienced for herself the vast spatial scale of the sphere—and here, still more strange, was this remote polar colony. This was an immense place, she thought, immense both in space and time—and yet humans had learned to live here. It was almost as if humans and Xeelee were learning to live together. It would surely be wrong to allow this unique world to be destroyed, for the sake of short-term gains.

And she thought she had a way to keep that from happening.

"If this is a weapon, it may one day be used against us. And if so we have to find a way to neutralize it." The suit whirred as she turned to Bicansa. "Your people can stay here. You can live your lives the way you want. I'll find ways to make the Commission accept that. But there's a payback."

Bicansa nodded grimly. "I understand. You want us to find the Xeelee flower."

"Yes," whispered Pala. "Find the off switch."

Dano faced her, furious. "You don't have the authority to make a decision like that. Granted this is an unusual situation.

But these are still human colonists, and you are still a Missionary. Such a *deal* would be unprecedented."

"But," Pala whispered, "Bicansa's people are no longer human. Are you, Bicansa?"

Bicansa averted her eyes. "The First were powerful. Just as they made this star-world fit for us, so they made us fit for it."

Dano, astonished, glared at them both. Then he laughed. "Oh, I see. A loophole! If the colonists aren't fully human under the law, you can pass the case to the Assimilation, who won't want to deal with it either . . . You're an ingenious one, Pala! Well, well. All right, I'll support your proposal at the Commission. No guarantees, though . . ."

"Thank you," Bicansa said to Pala. She held out her Virtual hand, and it passed through Pala's suit, breaking into pixels.

Dano had been right, Palo thought, infuriatingly right, as usual. He had seen something in her, an attraction to this woman from another world she hadn't even recognized in herself. But Bicansa didn't even *exist* in the form Pala had perceived. Was she really so lonely? Well, if so, when she got out of here, she would do something about it.

And she would have to think again about her career choice. Dano had always warned her about an excess of empathy. It seemed she wasn't cut out for the duties of a Missionary—and next time she might not be able to find a loophole.

With a last regretful glance, Bicansa's Virtual sublimated into dusty light.

Dano said briskly, "Enough's enough. I'll call down the flitter to get you out of here before you choke to death . . ." He turned away, and his pixels flickered as he worked.

Pala looked out through the car's window at the colony, the sprawling, high-gravity plants, the dusty, flattened lens of shining air. She wondered how many more colonies had spread over the varying gravity latitudes of the star shell, how many more adaptations from the standard form had been tried—how many people actually lived on this immense artificial world. There was so much here to explore.

The door of Bicansa's car opened. A creature climbed out cautiously. In a bright orange pressure suit, its body was low-slung, supported by four limbs as thick as tree trunks. Even through the suit Pala could make out immense bones at hips and shoulders, and massive joints along the spine. It lifted its head and looked into the car. Through a thick visor Pala could make out a face—thick-jawed, flattened, but a human face nonetheless. The creature nodded once. Then it turned and, moving heavily, carefully, made its way toward the colony and its lake of light.

No Cure for Love

By Roger Levy

I'm sitting at an observation port and looking out, in my head playing the join-the-dots game of constellation spotting. I can spend hours at it, alone here. I've never been one for participation in life's stitched tapestry. The dots, they somehow appeal more. There's Orion with his unsprung bow, I'm thinking, and I'm on the lookout for Cassiopeia when I catch her reflection in the glass.

She's walking the deck, clearly not a seasoned traveler like the rest of us. She's overdressed for the shuttle, in a pale cream blouse and a calf-length, pleated metallized skirt that chimes faintly as her knees nudge primly through it. For a moment I don't know quite why she's caught my eye, but nevertheless I find myself watching her with more than a vague curiosity. She's in her fifties, much older than me, and I think that she reminds me of someone. There's a certain familiar look about her that I can't immediately place. She stops at each of the souvenir vendors, complimenting them individually at the mass-produced tat they display on their spindly tables bedecked with bright cloths. The souvenirs of Earth, of Mars, of the trip from one to the other. The scraps of asteroid and the brightly and doubtless spuriously labeled bottles of Outer Space. She picks them up and puts them down, the so-called bottles of space in this slightly greater aerated flask of a spacecraft. Yan-ying, I think they call it, the seeds of each contained within the other. The irony escapes her, anyway. It's a stand-off. She buys nothing. They ignore her.

After a while the injectioneer comes over, and I gesture him to sit with me. Injectioneer. It's shuttle slang, he's told me. Retro slang. We've developed a relationship by now, the injectioneer and I. I seem to be spending my life on the shuttle, so we know each other quite well. Certainly I spend more time on the shuttle than I spend at home on Earth, or at work on Mars. Not that Earth is much of a home to me anymore.

We exchange some small talk as I roll up my sleeve and watch him prepare to jab my arm. He uses an old-fashioned syringe, needle and cartridge. Mars immigration requirements are vigorously enforced. Transit inoculations are never, under any circumstances, waived. Paperwork is not regarded as proof of prior vaccination. You get on the shuttle, you get a jab, every time. No excuses, no exceptions. If you're allergic to the vaccine, you stay Earthside, no matter who you are. Them's the rules, as the injectioneer says, priming the syringe, holding it to the light. The liquid moves in its slim cylinder, thick and grainy. And tablets can be palmed, ram-air injections can be deflected by dermashields, but venipuncture, he tells me, is verifiable. He slips the needle into my vein, hardly puckering the skin with its tip before he slides it home, and then he aspirates fractionally. A slim red cloud of my blood surfs gently into the cartridge and mingles with the viscous fluid and the injectioneer grunts with professional satisfaction and slowly slides the plunger all the way down, and I'm finished.

"That's you done for the trip," he says. "All set for the Red Planet." There's a jaded note to his voice, he's said it so often to so many people. As if of sarcasm. The words are meaningless to him. As far as he's concerned, we might be going nowhere. After all, he never disembarks.

I button my cuff, flex my elbow, and drop my arm to the armrest. "The glory of it all," I say, indicating the observation port, the stars beyond. He raises his eyebrows, uncertain whether I'm being ironic. He's uncomplicated, the injectioneer. A simple soul. It's one of the things I like about him. He stows his kit and remains with me, and we fall into a companionable silence. Eventually I turn back to the deck. He follows my eyes.

"Look at her," I tell him. "I thought she was a holo until she picked something up."

"Sometimes you can't tell," he says, squinting at the deck. "Are you sure what she picked up wasn't a holo too?" He's not quite sure who I'm referring to, but he's too embarrassed to ask me to point her out. It's almost as if he can't see her, the way his eyes cast about.

After a minute he relaxes a little and says to me, "You know, I've always wondered just what you do." There remains a detectable stiffness in his voice. It's plainly an effort for him, making conversation, small talk, and I feel pity for him. It must be a lonely job, his. My job, though. What to tell him? I consider. It goes back to the dots, I suppose, and their appeal. The petri dishes. I can close my eyes and see them now, the dishes of scratched agar glistening under the lights of the laboratory, like lilies, hundreds of shining lilies receding into the distance. Dots, detail. Circles, like the eye of the microscope. I realize with a small thrill that the observation port is another.

"Hmm?"

He's tense, socially ill at ease. I suppose it comes from what he does, jabbing people all day long. I treat him gently. "I suppose you'd call me a microbiologist," I answer.

He nods and I chuckle. We both watch the woman for a while. He's looking in the right direction, anyway.

You can't tell who the crazies are, these days. You see people talking to themselves, nodding, smiling, gesticulating, shouting, and it turns out they've simply got concealed comms units. All they are is social misfits. This woman walking on the deck, she could have some head-zone veneering her surroundings for all we could tell, maybe settling her someplace familiar, her home on Earth. Or she could just be plain crazy.

The dots. The dots are equal. Equal to each other, anyway. They aren't in competition like we are. The constant striving, fighting, killing. Reflected in the porthole, I see myself smile at that. My ghostly face out there among the shining dots.

And then, abruptly and for a dizzying, dizzying moment, the stars blur and seem to form themselves into another face staring at me, or at the injectioneer over my shoulder. It's so sharp, this image, that it pulls a gasp from me. I look away quickly and at the injectioneer, and in his face there's a hard look, a look I haven't seen before. It's a look of complicity. For that fraction of time he's someone I don't recognize, someone calculating and distant. He's looking intently at the porthole, as I was, and with an expression that entirely excludes me. And he nods curtly, then catches my eyes on him and colors up. A flat smile congeals on his face.

I look from him to the porthole. The constellations are there again, blisteringly bright. Cassiopeia and Orion.

"Are you all right?" He's concerned. "The jab," he says, his hand on my arm. "It can disorientate you. Are you okay?" I can hear the anxiety in his voice. He's himself again. "Sometimes the side effects—"

"I'm fine," I reassure him. I squint at the porthole, move my head from side to side. "A trick of the light, that's all. A reflection. I thought I saw—"

He waits, but I let it trail away. I'm not sure what I was going to say, anyway. Sometimes I'm not sure of anything. It can be like that on the shuttle. In space. Things can seem to be not what they are. In your head, too. I rub at my forehead, trying to settle my spinning thoughts.

The injectioneer clears his throat, and I notice the woman again. Her feet make no sound on the metal deck. She has a delicate walk, taking small neat paces like a wading bird, and she holds her hands clasped in front of her when they aren't occupied. The look on her face is pinched and severe.

She reminds me of my mother, with her mannerisms and small pretensions.

That's it. My mother. "I feel a little sorry for her," I murmur to myself.

"Your mother? Why?"

Did I mention her to the injectioneer? I suppose I must have.

"Not my mother," I say, shrugging. I don't want to talk about my mother at the moment, not to him. "I imagine she's happy enough. In her own little world." I point, seeing his confusion. "That woman over there. We're all of us alone, ultimately, aren't we? Didn't someone once say 'Each man is an island'?"

The injectioneer shakes his head. "I think it was 'No man is an island,'" he says. "Do you miss her?"

A beat of time. A shift. I glance across at him. I'd imagined him a fellow spirit, but now I see he isn't. I rub my arm where he's injected me, although it isn't sore. He frowns at my action, sensing criticism, and stands up. He saunters away across the polished floor of the deck, pointedly walking past the woman as if she weren't there, but his gesture is wasted as she ignores him with equal disdain.

I look outside again, at galaxies like ash-curdled milk, at stars like drifting spores. My mother said the stars are infinite, that there's one for every dirty thought. I think of her. There's another star, then, Mother, I mouth at the porthole.

The woman is coming toward me. I can see her in the glass. Her pinched features. For a moment we have eye contact, a jolt of ice, and then I jerk away. I feel immediately guilty, as if I've cut her adrift, but when I turn to face the deck and look again, she has glided past me.

Troubling thoughts. I am consumed by troubling thoughts. Out of the window a nebula seems to be spiraling out of control. Stars seem to be winking out.

I pull myself together. It has been like this before. Before I got this job, before I started traveling on the shuttle. The shuttle, somehow, has given me a sense of tranquillity. It is not the job that matters to me. In fact I can't just at this moment remember much about the job. It doesn't matter. Details. The traveling is what matters. It is better to travel peacefully, I think someone said, than to depart. Departing is such sweet sorrow, and sometimes I have such sorrow.

I feel tears come, and I wish the injectioneer back, for someone to talk to. But he is elsewhere on the shuttle, administering his jab to other travelers.

No, I'm mistaken. Here he is, coming over and sitting by me again. His presence is comforting, and I'm glad of it. I want to tell him that and touch him on the arm, but I don't.

"Do you miss her?"

"Sometimes," I tell him.

I do talk to him about her, now and then. They say it's easier to talk to strangers. Although sometimes I must drift away, because I'll often find myself in the middle of a conversation I don't remember starting. We discuss all sorts of things, the injectioneer and I.

It's a strange thing. The gravity here is quite false, but there's no physical weightlessness on the shuttle. Yet one does experience a weightlessness of the mind. Here in space, in transit, all is suspended, all is floating. Your thoughts become like the trinkets on a mobile, revolving under your inward gaze. I like that a lot, that sense of contemplation and reflection. That's why I come out of my Sleep every now and then; not so much to stretch my limbs as to flex my mind.

The deck here can accommodate no more than forty of us, while the Sleep pods house five hundred. So wake-time on the shuttle has to be rationed. But not that much. Most of the travelers go down Earthside and only lift their heads again when we reach Mars. They don't like wake-time. They only moan and complain at the sparseness of the common areas. They don't understand the shuttle. It's like a prison, they say, pacing the deck. A madhouse, they say, watching each other pacing, muttering incessantly at the tedium of wake-time. They hate it. For them the trip is a necessary nuisance. I'm unusual. I always use my entire wake-time allocation. But I seldom see the same faces on the deck twice. I've never before seen the woman who reminds me of my mother.

This particular trip seems to be lasting forever. I remark as much to the injectioneer, and he looks at me oddly. He asks me if there's something I want to tell him. His voice is strained and tired, and I wonder if he's coming to the end of his shift. The woman is standing directly behind him, listening to us, blatantly eavesdropping. I am looking at her angrily, and the injectioneer notices my fixed attention and twists round sharply. I assume he gives her a look, because she wanders off across the deck. He turns back again but says nothing. In his job, I expect he's accustomed to the attention of curious onlookers. It doesn't bother him at all.

"My mother," I say. I am thinking of her face and of the spores as they rise from their dishes and spread across the Earth. My seedlings. In my head I can see it happening, but in this mental weightlessness it also *has* happened, and is yet to happen. To be, being, been. The tenses revolve, confusing me, making my head throb. I can feel the pulsing of a vein in my forehead.

The injectioneer opens his bag and prepares his syringe. I bare my arm for him. I've been on this trip so many times that the crook of my arm is cicatrised with reaction to all the pinpricks. Both my arms, in fact. But you don't get away without your jab on the shuttle, as the injectioneer says. Them's the rules.

"The spores," I say, looking through the porthole.

"What about them?" he asks. He's concentrating on the injection, and his voice really is abnormally tense. His hand shakes momentarily as he withdraws the needle, and a bead of my blood swells on to my skin, red and round and glistening. He rolls a plaster over the site and we both stare at it until I pull my sleeve back down and button my cuff. They can't use PlaSkin up here. It's the atmosphere, he's told me. It won't tolerate the new technology. They have to use the old techniques, the old materials. It's sometimes as if we're stuck in the past, up here.

"What about them?" he repeats, irritatingly.

"The stars. They look like spores."

Which is where they came from, of course. Frozen within that heaven-sent chunk of smoking rock. That rutted meteor. Huddled and clumped in the labyrinthine depths of their house of seething rock. So hard to chisel and tease out, to culture, to nurture back to lethal life.

He's waiting for me to go on, but I don't.

And then like the stars, like dirty thoughts, so very easy to propagate. Spinning through the air, they become, have become, will become, part of the air, the atmosphere, the universe. Dirty, polluting, contaminating. And then cleansing. Not that she would have understood that.

"Your mother," he says.

"Dead," I say.

She was the first. Or is. Or will be. Staring at me again, her expression inscrutable. Will be, then. I stare back until she wanders away once more. Of course it's not my mother. She's back on Earth. So, past tense. She was.

I find myself sighing. It's love-hate with your mother, isn't it? Your mother is the world to you.

"Yes?" says the injectioneer keenly, on his feet but still lingering, and I realize I've said this aloud.

"There's no cure," I tell him. "No vaccine, no antidote."

He looks panic-stricken, and I add, "Love. No cure."

He looks at me warily now, as if he suspects he's missed a joke. I smile to reassure him. He takes a breath and says, looking over my shoulder, although there's noone there, only the twinkling darkness of the observation port, "I think that's it for the moment." He pushes himself wearily to his feet. I imagine he's had a long day. He sighs and says, "Time for lockdown."

Shuttle slang again, I suppose. I stand up and we walk together towards the long dark corridors of the Sleep pods, the injectioneer and I. Time for lockdown. My allocation's up. But so is everyone's.

THE NAVIGATOR'S CHILDREN

By Ian Watson

Dear children of Earth,

Our Chaplain-Confessor has honored me with narrating a lesson in my own words for the purpose of reading in schools. I may explain too much, in which case I beg your pardon. Alternatively, I may explain too little, in which case ask your teacher for elucidation.

Our starship, *Saint Lope de Vega*, is very well armored as well as being armed with matter-disruptor torpedos and heavy light-cannons, popularly referred to as Heavy Lights since the impact of a beam projected by such a cannon is a real knockout.

Lope de Vega was a playwright and poet of old Spain, but you may not know that he also served in the Invincible Armada—hence a naval connection—and, furthermore, that he was an officer of the Holy Inquisition, so of course he has been beatified. Probably there are a million saints. The more the merrier, say I. No need for everybody to have wrought a proven miracle. In these confusing times faith, of itself, is a miracle. I am proud to be a distant descendant of his.

It is true that the Invincible Armada proved to be vincible, many of its vessels succumbing to storms, but never mind. The idea was a mighty one, the intention was puissant. As is the Holy Fleet, of which I navigate one warship in this campaign against the Eks.

The Eks are a hive-mind, none of its individual members truly conscious, no more than a single neuron in my own brain is conscious, so therefore killing tens of thousands of Eks poses no qualms. Myself, I'm not a bloodthirsty man, and in any case as navigator I discharge no weapons personally, although I do steer the *Saint Lope de Vega* to where it will hopefully do most damage.

So do not imagine me as seeing red—except perhaps due to eyestrain from poring over and comparing the various contradictory star charts and penning my own new experimental one. (I'm joking about eyestrain—obviously, I use a magnificator when needed.) On the contrary, I'm quite refined. I collect silver and china and ivory and glass figurines of pretty ladies. Bit of a connoisseur. Only little ones no more than seven centimeters high—that's my lucky number and the limit I set myself. My magnificator makes the ladies seem much larger. The art is in the detail.

Obviously, I cannot acquire any new figurine while on duty in space at the limits of the cosmos where there are no curio or antique shops, but I do keep my collection with me in my cabin, and, dear children, all my ladies have names chosen by me. Esmeralda, Juanita, Rosa, Francesca . . . My little ladies tell me bedtime stories, at least in my imagination.

You might say that the upright Cross of Jesus (+) is fighting against the skewed alien cross (X) of the Eks in a war to establish the nature of God. The more Eks we kill, the more we diminish their overmind. Even if only one Christian survives, yet still our belief remains as valid as ever.

So what exactly does a navigator do?

You may suppose the answer to be obvious—I work out where we are and point out to the pilot how to set course—yet actually my work is a bit more complicated than that.

That's because our cosmos is a simulation. As I was saying to Captain Hernandez the other day—

Ah, but your teacher may need to do some elucidating here. The consequences of being part of a simulation are far more important to officers of the Holy Navy than to you kids back home. For all the difference being simulated makes to you, you might just as easily be living in a real physical universe.

It was revealed to us fifty years ago that somewhere up in the future, maybe a million years ahead, is a planetary-mass computer carrying out 10^{42} operations every second. The Blessed Cardinal Nikolai Bostrom estimated that a realistic simulation of the whole span of human history would only require at the most 10^{35} operations, assuming 100 billion humans (probably a gross overestimate) each living on average for 50 years at 3 million seconds per year, and each brain engaging in at most 10^{17} operations per second. Consequently, a simulation of the entire mental history of the human race—which Blessed Bostrom called an ancestor-simulation—would occupy the megacomputer for only 10^{-7} seconds. Quick as a flash. Far faster indeed! The human eye wouldn't even notice such a flash.

When I say *future*, I mean as regards our own history and technology level compared with that of the simulators. Obviously, our present—maybe I ought to say our *perceived* present—is to them the distant past, as in *ancestral*.

As I was saying to Captain Hernandez the other day . . . ah, but, children, do you know how we found out about us all being part of a simulation? I say "a" simulation, since many simulations may run on this same machine and/or on others. As I said, it takes only 10^{-7} seconds to run the whole of history up to date.

By prayer, children. We found out by prayer, in a manner of speaking. So remember to say your prayers, even though the response may not always be what you expect.

How am I doing, eh? I assume you'll be editing this a bit.

Blessed Cardinal Bostrom was praying for illumination,

and suddenly what he (and millions people more) imagined at first to be the very word of God stitched itself in letters of fire across the sky. In fact, a simulator was intruding into the simulation to wise us up.

The intention may have been to see what effect knowledge of our true status would have upon us, in other words, to carry out an experiment rather than to engage in sheer mischief. Or maybe that simulator a million years more advanced than us had no damn choice—I do apologize!—maybe he had no choice in the matter (other than perhaps to terminate the simulation) due to where our Holy Navy had got to in the war against the Eks.

Which is where being a navigator comes in.

You'll be wondering how a simulator who is operating at a normal pace where a minute lasts a minute—unless you ramp up to nearly the speed of light, although a minute still feels like a minute—how this someone can intervene in something which is happening so utterly fast?

When I say "someone," I'm assuming that our remote descendants are still basically recognizable as people equipped with arms and legs and with the same sort of sense organs as ourselves rather than, say, being brains in bottles or minds stored in crystalline matrices. Note, children, the correct plural of *matrix*.

So: How can anyone have *time* to intervene?

(Nowadays, of course, we don't ramp up to near the speed of light—we circumvent lightspeed, using the Circumvention Drive.)

Well, it must be possible to pause, or to slow, the simulation.

Another point about a simulation is that you don't need to simulate the entire universe, but only human (and presumably the Eks') perceptions of it. Supposing you travel by ship from España to the Amerikas, there's no need for the entire Atlantis Ocean to be simulated, but only what can be seen from that ship, and only in the detail that can be seen.

Supposing you peer through a mikroscope at animalcules swarming in a drop of water taken from the Atlantis, there is no need whatever for all of the water in the Atlantis to be similarly swarming when no one is observing that water in close detail.

If every damn, oops, thing were simulated in detail, the simulation might exceed the capacity of even a planet-size computer. Nay, the simulation would be *identical with* the universe! However, logically two entities cannot be exactly the same as each other. For if they were, they would be the *selfsame* entity. I hope you are following this. You and your sister may possess two dolls that look identical to you, but they are not truly identical. They are different.

If I were to acquire two little ladies who look exactly the same, just as you have two dolls to play with, those would be different ladies, even though I might be foxed and suppose them to be mischievous teases.

Consider the vastness of the star realm where our Holy Fleet deploys. Because of interstellar travel we have vastly increased the bounds required of the simulation. Earthbound astronomers can be catered for on the same principle as the drop of water—who's peering at a particular distant star right now?—but what about *interstellar astronauts*? A scaling factor and the pointlessness of simulating void in detail (for what detail does a void have?) permits us to travel afar, but the simulation cannot cope *in depth*, as it were, with such magnitude.

For this reason the constellations that you see in the sky represent the true relationships between those stars and whatever worlds attend them, at least in regard to interstellar travel.

Very probably, children, you have often looked up into the night sky—I know that I did so as a child—and have traced with your outstretched finger a constellation of stars . . .

Do they still teach you in school what *ought scientifically* to be the truth, namely that a constellation is illusory in the sense that its component stars are very likely nowhere near one another? The faint star to the right of the bright star is in reality very bright, but it happens to be very remote from Earth. The bright star isn't intrinsically very bright, but instead is quite near to Earth. So instead of both stars being neighbors in the same constellation, as they appear to be to terrestrial eyes, actually the two stars are hundreds of light years apart. Is that how you're taught?

Wrong, alas. Either because it is impossible to simulate in depth or is too expensive, the vast majority of naked-eye stars beyond fifteen light years are all on the inside of a sphere thirty light years across, which we cannot pass beyond. To you on Earth, non-naked-eye stars farther away and far nebulae and other galaxies are visible through a teleskope—but not to us of the Holy Fleet. From out here, we see nothing further.

Did I mention that my precious little ladies are all naked? I hasten to add that they are fully formed and mature, not childlike despite their diminutive size.

Lines of flight connect up the stars of each constellation, optimum routes for the Circumvention Drive.

You have enquiring minds, children. How, you might ask, can we of the Holy Fleet pass swiftly from one constellation to another unconnected constellation without first returning to the solar system and setting out again in a new direction so as to reach our next goal speedily?

That is because the constellations frequently change—as if to keep the whole fabric of the cosmos knitted together.

Many possible patterns exist whereby to link up the stars, though the patterns only reveal themselves through a Kosmometer. My Kosmometer detects these shifts and I must find a chart that corresponds.

Will I be obliged to use the *Coelum Stellatum Christianum* of Julius Schiller of Augsburg, with its devout constellations of Noah and Archangel Raphael, the apostles, and Mary Magdalen? Praise be, if so.

Or will it be a chart of the many, much smaller constellations of the Chinese race consisting of the Army of Yu Lin and the emperor's eunuchs and secretaries and much else besides?

Will it be the constellations of Greek myth? Or the *naksatras* of India?

Will it be the constellations according to the Eks?

The Holy Navy has captured several Eks ships, and a commandeered alien chart depicts alien creatures either real or imagined by their hive-mind—the Skrim, the Ghoul-Wraith, the Krakkat, the Yarquil.

So now do you see why a navigator's task is a demanding one? In total, 302 proven star charts are nooked in my navigation room, and I need to respond quickly to shifting circumstances, sometimes in the midst of a battle that can sprawl across many light years.

As I was saying to Captain Hernandez the other day, "It's a good thing there aren't any alien races other than the Eks!"

"In that case, Master de Vega," the Captain enquired piercingly, "why do you draw up experimental, hypothetical constellations in your spare time—as though other aliens might indeed exist, each with their own visions of how stars might be connected?"

"Contingencies," I said. "Flexibility. A mental exercise."

Just then a klaxon sounded, *whoops, whoops, whoops*. A constellation shift had occured, detected by Kosmometer. I rushed back to the navigation room. We'd been heading under Circumvention Drive toward the star K. Tarandi through the constellation of the Reindeer (which is *tarandus* in Latin, as you may know) as devised by Pierre Charles le Monnier after a journey to Lapland in the 1730s, where we thought the Eks may have established a base—not a base in Lapland, obviously, but at K. Tarandi. Suddenly our line of flight no longer existed.

What I was doing in my spare time, among other things, was preparing a constellation for my little ladies to inhabit, where they could twinkle and dance for my delight and tell exciting and amorous stories to entertain me, based upon their relationships with one another, their friendships, their jealousies as to whom among them I might favor most. I try, of course, to distribute my affections fairly, yet I do confess to neglecting some of my ladies now and again—before perceiving afresh the fine qualities which prompted me to acquire them. A little lady is like a kitten, which purrs if it is handled often. Through the magnificator my thumb and forefinger appear as large as my ladies, two erect bare bodies with the blank shiny faces of my manicured finger and thumb nails. Sometimes I draw upon my finger and thumb or upon my nails with a mapping pen, using in this case water-soluble ink so that I can clean my fingers quickly. Who knows when the klaxon may go off?

Ensign Quintana, being newly commissioned and inexperienced and also afflicted by acne, asked me the other day, "How do we know about the names the Eks give to constellations? The Krakkat and the Yarquil and so on? And what is a Krakkat and a Yarquil and those other beasts?"

"The Skrim and the Ghoul-Wraith."

"All those."

"Well, we understand the writing system of the Eks, their magnetic encodements upon tape-streamers, as we call them."

I haven't said what the Eks look like, have I? I'm not sure whether this information is kept from your tender minds because the Eks are repulsive to behold. Eks is both singular and plural. There's no such thing as an Ek on its own. A single Eks is an Eks. They're green and white and slippery, like cooked Pak Choi, with soft tentacles, some of which can really elongate. Imagine having one of those slide up your nose.

So: a Chinese vegetable crossed with a squid. Not much need for an individual brain, more of a ganglion. When two Eks link sensory tentacles, the ganglion power is doubled. When five Eks link tentacles, we're really getting somewhere: the overmind clocks into play. Clicks in? Slurps in? An overmind spread out over umpteen cubic light years, communicating by quantum entanglement, just as their tentacles entangle. The liquid-filled interior of an Eks ship really is a disgusting sight, an orgy of cartilage and soft tissue. A nightmare!

Where was I? Oh yes, symbolic representation is fundamental to any language system, and symbols tend to breed
more symbols; consequently, we believe that the Eks overmind possesses a very complex larder of symbolism, giving
rise to mythology, stories that explain the multifaceted Eks
experience. The Yarquil (which is our own chosen pronun-
ciation) and the Krakkat and whatnot may be equivalent to
archetypal Eks imagery, or else they may be sea monsters
from the Eks home world (perhaps in the distant past), or
they may be both at the same time. Easier to think of star
patterns as representing something, rather than otherwise!
Being united in mind, the Eks only originated one constellation map of their own.

"Does that answer your question, Ensign Quintana?"

I suppose I ought to describe a space battle to thrill you,
children.

That's a very good question, Esmeralda (I imagine you
asking, far away on Earth sitting in your schoolroom, perhaps sucking on the end of a pen). Of course I forgive you
for interrupting. No chastisement will follow. The answer to
your question—I hope I'm not breaching Inquisition security—is that the Eks have indeed captured some of our own
ships along with copies of our many alternative constellation charts, and the navigators too, God rest their souls as
prisoners of the Eks probing tentacles up their noses, unless
those hapless men had time to commit suicide, for which,
children, they have not merely a special dispensation but
also a veritable obligation, a holy duty to Humanity. I keep
a large orange pill always at hand.

That is how the Eks are able to cope with constellation
shift.

I'm glad you asked even though it means revealing that
we have suffered losses. It's remarkable how one initial set
of conditions—in this case my telling Ensign Quintana
about the Yarquil, et cetera—causes details to proliferate!

Being so weighted in favor of our own many charts,
constellation shift proves beyond doubt that it is indeed

descendants of ourselves and not of the Eks, perish the thought, who created the simulation we are in.

I would hate to think that the Eks are not of the real universe, and that the simulators merely invented something so vile and cunning to set against us, causing such danger and continuous mental stress. How would you care to sleep with a big orange pill under your pillow? May my little ladies, like angels, protect me from turmoil.

Yes, I *am* going to describe a space battle. Be patient.

I think I was about to make the point that a hive mind might seem to resemble a God. Something of a far higher order than its devotees, or in the Eks' case component parts.

Or was I about to raise the question of the validity of our religious beliefs, in salvation through Jesus, and the validity of our souls when we are in fact all simulated? I myself see no problem with this. Arguably, it is easier for an afterlife to exist in an annex to a simulation than in, for want of a better word, a heaven. Very likely survival in the annex is an equivalent to limbo, the staging post to heaven, whatever that annex may be furnished with, realizations of my little ladies perhaps. I believe Islamists held out such a prospect of friendly ladies awaiting them in heaven before the exterminations, which you'll come to in your history lessons about the triumph of the upright Cross. The Islamists may have had a good idea there, unlike their other heretical blasphemies!

It is a tenet of our faith that human life is sacred and that the more souls that exist, the better. If huge numbers of simulations are being run, this multiplies the number of souls enormously, into trillions of trillions. Perhaps this is the true mission of the simulators, the multiplication of souls.

Little Esmeralda, you really are a clever tease!

One moment I assert that logically two entities cannot be exactly the same as one another, and now you ask me whether the very same people may be simulated in different simulations under alternative circumstances, and if so, which of them possesses the unique and indivisible soul?

Were you not listening to what I said about initial value conditions leading rapidly to prodigious proliferation? The ancestral simulations can hardly have started with Adam and Eve, but some way along the line, say 6000 years ago. Did divergence only commence at that point in time? Or, implicitly, earlier? Think about it.

The space battle, at long last. Only if I am not interrupted!

Our very own *Saint Lope de Vega* accompanied by the *Saint John of the Cross* and the *Valiant Crusader* had entered the W Ursa Majoris system. WUM, as I'll call the star for short, is actually two bright white stars each a bit bigger than our own sun. They're almost touching one another; consequently, both are tugged into oval shapes like eggs. Please don't ask about eggshells! Imagine two glowing white yolks surrounded by a shared lozenge of hot white gas. Or imagine a deep-sea creature of the benthic abyss peering out of utter darkness with two great luminous eyes. No, that would be stupid—such an arrangement would simultaneously blind the creature itself and attract prey to it. But you get the idea.

The twin suns travel around each every eight hours, so fast that you can almost see them moving.

Such sights I have seen in my travels!

Being not much larger than our own sun, WUM can retain its size in the simulation. Mighty red supergiant Betelgeuse, by contrast, 650 lights from Earth, has to shrink quite a bit to fit in on a frontier-sphere only fifteen lights distant from our solar system.

Since the two components of WUM are so close together, planets can orbit WUM; and indeed seven do, three gas-giants and four comparative tiddlers, one blessed with a biosphere of ocean and islands. That's what had attracted the Eks.

As we coursed down the planetary plane—the *ecliptic*, why, thank you, Esmeralda—five ships of the Eks rose to meet us. Or rather, to pass us at high speed. Nevertheless, we got off a several microsecond broadside of heavy light beams, and one of the box-ships of the Eks disintegrated, which would have been a splendid sight except that the exploding vessel was already a million, two million miles beyond us, out of sight except telescopically.

We were already turning—as, so it transpired, were the Eks, rather than them running away—although the maneuvre would take us a couple of hours.

Four ships against three, now.

Chaplain-Confessor Fidel Morales held a service of blessing, broadcast throughout the ship.

"May our God prevail," he concluded. I was rather busy, not only with plotting our own course but that of the distant enemy too, yet for some reason the Chaplain-Confessor's remark came at me from a new angle.

I don't work all on my own—although you might sometimes think so! Too risky. What if I were put out of action by enemy action? Let me introduce Deputy Navigator José Santiago. Truth to tell, if I were zapped, very likely José would also be zapped at the very same time. Energy beams are not very selective. Alternatively, I might suffer a seizure while admiring my little ladies.

José is a quiet young man, which is why you haven't heard about him hitherto. He could well have been in Holy Orders were it not for a streak of wanderlust, coupled with what I diagnose as a strong tinge of misanthropy, a wish to distance himself from his fellow man—what could be more distant than several light years?—which is why he does not spontaneously address me much.

I know you may well say that aboard a starship José is inevitably closer to his fellow men—there's no jumping ship in space if the pressures become too much or if a mild dislike for someone due to enforced proximity ramps up into intense loathing. Nevertheless, the constant awareness of the vastness of the void that surrounds us can be soothing to those of a spiritual disposition.

"My good José," I addressed him, "don't you think our Chaplain-Confessor is on dodgy ground there?"

"Where?" José asked tersely.

"When he referred to *our* God prevailing. Doesn't that imply that there are *other* Gods too? Such as a shadowy remnant of Allah? Or a God of the Eks?"

I was training José to be my equal, so it was good to ask him challenging questions now and then.

"I don't know," José said.

"What then, are you an *agnostic*?" This was my little joke, because agnostic simply means *don't know*. Did you know that, Esmeralda?

"Sir, the Church tells us what to believe, so I do not need to think about it."

"That is an incurious attitude."

"I'm *thinking* about the vectors of the Eks ships."

"Oh, haven't you calculated those yet?"

I considered a few quips about expertise and exercises but I nobly refrained.

Anyway, after a while we were closing on the fast-approaching Eks vessels, although not so rapidly this time as before—the rapidity was mainly on their part. We intended to turn more quickly and get on their tails, if a Box can reasonably be said to have a tail rather than, say, a big flat rump. Ahead of us we fired a salvo of matter-disruptor torpedos. I should explain that at velocities such as ours there's no real need to include explosives in a projectile, only powerful fuel. Anything hitting a target will disrupt its matter very destructively. We retained our explosive torpedos for close—or rather, slow—combat, which rarely happens in space.

I guess this bit is for the boys. I imagine that you, Esmeralda, would prefer to learn more about my little ladies and their adventures, but I did promise a space battle.

All of our torpedos appeared to have missed—or rather, they disappeared without visible effect, vanishing even from our radar screens due to their being so small compared with a warship. The vast majority of weapons missing their target isn't at all unusual in a space battle due to extreme distance

and vastness. Twas ever so, indeed. During one engagement
in the Mediterranean Sea during the Eradication of Islam,
out of 2519 shells fired by marine light cruisers (in the sense
of not heavy, rather than the speed of light) only three shells
hit enemy ships, and the combatants were scarcely a few
kilometers apart. Maybe we *were* indeed fortunate that we
wiped out one Box during our earlier fly-by.

As the four Boxes bracketed us at speed, our three holy
naval vessels repeated that broadside. However, this time
both the *Saint Lope de Vega* and the *Saint John of the Cross*
beamed at the selfame Box. Just as well! Somehow the Eks
Boxes were now bobbing up and down rapidly as they
flew—a trick hitherto unknown to us and costing a lot of
fuel, I'm sure, and how those Pak Choi Squids must have
sloshed around. Either us or *Saint John of the Cross*—I
mean to say more grammatically either *we* or *Saint John of
the Cross*—vaporized one corner of the target Box. Speed-
ing away, the Eks ship emitted incandescent debris.

I tire of describing a space battle. The upshot was two
Boxes destroyed, and the *Valiant Crusader* rather badly
damaged, light-cannons fused, ten souls dead (or freed, to
become pure souls), and its Circumvention Drive put out of
action. The other two Boxes fled from the WUM system,
tails between their legs, or rather rumps tucked in tight-
arsedly. Oh I do apologize, edit that out.

Repairs to the *Valiant Crusader*'s Circumvention Drive
would take weeks and require certain rare elements. By
which I don't mean the resistance wires in electric heaters,
if such devices warm your classroom during the winter
when you must wear woolly undergarments rather than thin
cotton briefs, and long serge stockings on your hitherto bare
and breeze-caressed legs until the tan fades to a delicate secret whitness that is both seemingly vulnerable yet at the
same time safeguarded from the casual gaze. I mean sub-
stances such as Ytterbium and Yttrium.

It took a while to assay various asteroids, using a light-
cannon under low power and a spectroscope. Finally we

found a rich enough source of Y & Y, and before long our three ships were in orbit about the world of ocean and islands. Stopovers such as this are few and far between.

No doubt you are visualizing scampering innocently nude across beaches of yellow sand, young friends playing games in the warm azure water. However, first of all we needed to check that no colony of Eks infested that friendly seeming world; for if so, we would have had to destroy them.

Their underwater habitations of boxes piled upon boxes adjoining at all angles would show up clearly enough on penetration radar unless sunken deep. Even so, scanning and mapping the world from orbit occupied several days before our shuttle and *Saint John of the Cross*'s shuttle could fly down with ten crew members aboard each, myself included. *Valiant Crusader*'s shuttle was out of action due to the hangar door being fused shut by Eks beams. No shore leave for the survivors of the battle—there was much work to do putting that vessel to rights.

I admit to pulling privilege to be on the shuttle, for I so yearned to walk with my bare feet on a beach, imprinting my presence at least temporarily upon an alien world. If mishap befell me, José was by now relatively competent—in fact it was José who urged me to avail myself of the opportunity for shore leave—and if a constellation shift occured during my absence, for which he was perhaps hoping (a shift, I mean, rather than my absence!), that wouldn't matter a hoot since we weren't going anywhere.

I debated for quite a while about taking several of my little ladies with me for an outing, a treat, for then I could sunbathe in some private spot out of sight of my fellows, a kind of privacy not vouchsafed aboard ship save in our cabins. Lying flat upon yielding sand, playfully burying part of myself, I could squint at my ladies and pretend that they were distant from me, posing upon the *plage*, which is French for a beach, a naturalistic perspective which I simply couldn't achieve in a cabin. Pleasure is often as much in the forethought and foreplay as in the carrying out. Wise counsel suggested that I ran the risk of losing a precious lady or two. An alien crab might pop out of a hole and grab. Consequently, I foreswore a tableau of ladies and took with me only the lovely Esmeralda.

Ah, Father Morales! I haven't quite yet finished narrating my navigator's tale for the benefit of the children of Earth. So you've been listening while I dictate? My good José, did you broadcast my words by accident? Why are you looking at me like that, José? Why are you and the Chaplain-Confessor nodding at one another?

Captain Hernandez! You're here too? With two armed marines to guard you, when we're between the stars in the midst of nowhere?

I am . . . *what*? Under *arrest*?

For attempted corruption of the morals of minors, equivalent to sorcery? For spiritual deviations and for blasphemy and for being *intolerable*? Surely you jest!

Excuse me! Are you deaf? *Whoops whoops whoops*. A constellation shift has occured.

Don José can attend to that and to all my other duties too? With respect, Captain, have you gone mad?

What, keep the dictating machine—with a new spool in it—and continue with my *confession*? In my cabin, which will now be my cell?

I am sorry to keep repeating your words, but there has to be a record of this for your court martial—for imperiling a ship of the Holy Fleet while under Circumvention Drive.

I wonder if I have been in error. Tell me, Esmeralda, Juanita, Rosa, Francesca, all of you! Enlighten me, little ladies! What have I to confess but flights of fancy? Every man needs something to occupy his mind during these long voyages. Maybe I should not have revealed your importance to my soul. Maybe I should not have exposed myself. Ah, impetuous me, over-generous as ever. Tell me a tale to console me, Juanita. You know the one I like, about you being sold as a slave.

*   *   *

Children of Earth, I am vindicated, utterly exonerated.

Several hours ago, Captain Hernandez and Father Fidel Morales and a sheepish José came to my door.

The constellation shift is an utterly new one. The constellations now correspond exactly to the chart I designed enshrining *my little ladies* in the heavens, which José finally consulted after exhausting all the other charts.

"How do you account for this?" the Captain demanded of me, and for a moment I was hard put to answer. Then I experienced a moment of revelation.

"The simulator," I said, "has obviously been scanning the simulation for an interesting novelty. It has found one which appeals to him, to them, to whatever they are. It has imposed this as reality, at least for a while. Without my knowledge of the stories of my little ladies and how they interlink, I think it's fair to say that navigation will prove rather difficult."

José had to eat humble pie.

"I was worried," he said, "that this might be a new Eks pattern of the constellations."

"Thus allowing the Eks to sneak close to Earth while ships of the Holy Navy are all at sea? Or rather, spaced out—our vessels taking far too long to reach destinations because the flight lines are so unfamiliar?"

Crestfallen, José nodded.

I declared, "The Holy Navy will certainly be spaced out right now—except for ourselves. And the Eks will have no idea how to navigate."

Hernandez said sourly, "Until the next constellation shift restores familiar patterns."

"Whenever that might be, Captain! This new pattern, *de Vega's pattern, mine*, may persist for weeks—and it might recur at any time. We need to get busy right away digitizing my chart of little ladies in the heavens"—I could speak of my ladies unashamedly—"and squirt this by circumvention-communicator to as many ships as we can."

*   *   *

As part of my agreement with the Captain, bindingly witnessed by Father Morales, I did toy with the idea of requiring some penance from José for his plotting against me, but I am not a vindictive person. Indeed, by now, as you may have guessed, children, I'm rather important, since I, Master Lope de Vega, originated an essential new map of the universe. Thanks to my little ladies, we may be on the point of a final push to eradicate the Eks.

In between beginning my narrative and now, my status has changed extraordinarily. There's no doubt in my mind that you'll be listening to these words of mine unedited, intently in your classroom. You have caught me at the cusp of greatness, and every word is precious. I may even be beatified one day. The Holy Navy will probably send me to visit a few schools in person in my braided dress uniform, for there are lessons to be learned from my Navigator's tale. Bless you all.

A DIFFERENT SKY

By Keith Brooke

Nothing had changed, Tom Wharton thought, as he guided his punt along the snaking creek, salt-marsh sprawling all around him. So why this sense of unease?

The birds still fed on the exposed mud, working the London clay by moonlight, their cycles dictated by tide and not by day and night. The blue of the sea lavender was unchanged, so intense in sunlight but a misty drift of pigment at this hour of a September evening. The sea wall ahead of him . . . the salty reek of the marshes . . . all the same.

And yet: the sky. The sky was different.

Wharton stopped rowing and leaned back, almost losing balance as he took in the night sky. He might even have stopped breathing momentarily, for now he gulped at the air as if it were a skill unlearned.

The flat-bottomed boat grounded on a bank of soft mud, and still Wharton leaned back, staring upwards.

He found Orion's Belt. The Great Bear. The garnet speck of Betelgeuse. He recited the names aloud, as if lecturing a guest.

Not different at all.

He leaned on an oar to push the punt back into the channel and then resumed rowing.

*   *   *

Later, at the end of the footway, he grounded the boat again and this time stood and stepped out of the prow onto a springy mattress of sea purslane. He pulled the punt tight to the mud bank and secured it to a post.

The walkway was two planks wide, raised a few inches above the packed mud and vegetation of the salt-marsh. Chicken wire had been tacked to its surface to prevent muddy boots from slipping. He stared at it, as if he had never noticed this before. In places, the loops of wire had been trodden into the grain of the wood, so that the two appeared to merge.

He shook himself, as if suddenly chilled. Slinging his bag over a shoulder, he walked back across the marshes, the stars and the moonlight enough for him to find his way back on a route he had taken so many times before.

The walkway crossed a narrow, deep channel, a gorge carved into the hard mud by the actions of the tide. The water was halfway up it now, its swirling and surging movements recarving the mud structures once more. In subtle ways, this would be a different channel by next low tide.

He shook himself again. He might have been staring at the mud formations for minutes . . . longer even.

Why was he drifting? He had walked back across the marsh oblivious, like a passenger in his own body. And now, why was he so struck by the everyday? He chided himself for this thought: He was an artist, of sorts, an observer.

He tried to analyze his sense of discomfort. Simultaneously he appeared to be both detached and intense. As if he'd been smoking dope, he realized: the floating away juxtaposed with sudden intensities of experience, of sensing. But it was many years since he'd finished his last cube of hash, and he had never gotten around to buying more.

He was almost home, he realized. He could barely recall the walk, although it normally took at least twenty minutes. He'd blotted it out entirely. Some weird kind of out-of-body experience, only he'd gone nowhere—just retreated within. It wasn't even that it was late, although the drawing in of the September nights made it seem much later than it actually was.

He was indoors. He looked back and saw that he had trailed gray mud across the kitchen linoleum. Muttering curses, he returned to the door and kicked his boots into the back porch.

He took a Solo Cuisine from the freezer, pierced the packing with his penknife and put it in the microwave.

He pushed through the door into what had once been a dining room but had for several years been his studio space. Canvases and Daler boards were racked up along one wall, some finished, some not quite there, some merely prepared for future use.

There was a canvas on the easel already, a marshscape with a small group of wigeon peering up above a fringe of samphire, under a sky of subtly textured gray. He put it aside after a brief glance and replaced it with a new canvas four feet across and barely a foot high—he wanted *width*, he wanted *panorama*. He squinted at the bare bulb. He hated artificial light, but this would not wait until morning.

The microwave called him from the kitchen, but he ignored it.

He squeezed onto the palette half a tube of lamp black, then lesser amounts of alizarin crimson and gold ochre. Normally he would meticulously block out his composition in thinned burnt sienna, but tonight, after mixing the color to his satisfaction, he started immediately to apply it thickly with the palette knife.

Later—he had no idea how late it was—he sat back and stared at the canvas with the same mixture of familiarity and discovery with which he had earlier studied the marshland plankway.

It was a starscape, the black of space washed red in places so that it was the color of clotted blood. Stars clustered in thick swathes of yellow, orange, in places blue and green, and at their greatest intensity a white sharper than any white you could squeeze from a tube.

He cursed and swept the canvas onto the floor.

He had no idea where that starscape had come from, but he knew that it was wrong. It was as if he were reaching deep within himself to communicate something that wouldn't quite emerge.

He took another canvas and started again.

He stopped for dawn.

Pink spreading across the flat fields, leaking upward through the sky. The sudden pinprick intensity of the first fragment of sun breaking the horizon. It was as if he had not seen such a spectacle for a long time, even though he was routinely up early.

He didn't remember coming outside to watch but that was where he was when he heard the diesel rumble of an engine in the lane, a farm vehicle, no doubt.

He tore himself away from the developing dawn light and turned to look at the approaching Toyota pick-up. Bill Healey sat at the wheel. What would the teacher be wanting at this time of day? This far down the lane there was only Wharton's bungalow and beyond that the Smithsons' farm.

Wharton rubbed his arms, suddenly aware of the cold. Things weren't *right*. His head—the absences disturbed him. This whole situation—what did Healey want? He shuddered, feeling the chill again.

"Bill," he said, as the pick-up came to a halt. He lowered his hands to his sides, realizing as he did so that it was a wary posture.

Healey looked at him, and it was like the sky last night: familiar and yet not. Blank depths behind a familiar screen.

"Bill?"

"Tom."

He was out of the pick-up now, facing Wharton. Two fifty-something men standing a few feet apart, staring each other out like kids in the playground.

Healey moved and it was instinct that made Wharton

move a split-second later. Healey's hand went to the pocket of his body-warmer.

Everything had slowed right down.

Healey's hand was in his pocket, even as Wharton stepped forward, moving fast despite the apparent slowing of time—but still a fraction late because he had moved in re-action and not anticipation.

But then he was there, reaching across as Healey's hand emerged, something a light-absorbent black in his grip.

Wharton seized his wrist, still moving quickly even as the world around him slowed—a trick of his perception, he had time to wonder? Or some paranormal power that had been lying latent for just the time when a neighbor and passing acquaintance would drive to his home in the early hours of a September morning and try to kill him with an as yet unidentified weapon?

Or something else . . .

Healey grunted, hand stuck halfway out of his pocket. He butted Wharton in the side of the face, then backed his head to strike again.

Wharton had retreated within, but his body continued to react. Moving at snake-strike speed, he twisted and raised his free arm so that when Healey's head came down it was onto the point of his elbow.

Healey cried out in pain, his hand came free from his pocket, and the black object—some kind of gun Wharton felt sure—flew free and landed on the grass verge.

Using another skill he never knew he had, Wharton applied pressure to Healey's jugular for just long enough that he blacked out. Control coming back, he lowered him carefully to the ground and stepped back, then squatted to look at the gun.

It was like no pistol he had seen before, although its smooth lines brought to mind images from nearly four decades earlier.

He lowered a hand to balance himself, countering a sudden bout of dizziness.

He picked up the gun and held it in his palm as it blistered, split apart and then dissolved into a jellied lump. Soon even that had dissolved to nothing.

He turned. Healey was stirring.

He opened his eyes, and Wharton knew that whatever had been there minutes before had now departed.

"What . . . ?"

Wharton offered him a hand and helped him up. "Are you okay, Bill?" he asked. "You blacked out. I was just going to call for help."

"I . . ." Healey was staring at him. He didn't believe Wharton but clearly didn't have an explanation of his own.

"What was it you wanted?" asked Wharton now, wanting to get rid of him and calculating that playing on his bewilderment was the best way.

Healey looked around himself then, as if trying to work out where he was and why he might be here.

"You can hardly have been just passing," Wharton continued. "Only me and the Smithsons down here." He turned then, and said, "If you remember what it was, just let me know. I have work."

He kept the folder in a drawer in the studio. A few faded, brittle newspaper clippings from the late 1960s; the letters his parents had allowed him to see, before they had realized the kind of letters strangers would send to a sixteen year-old who had . . . well, who had, if the papers were to be believed, been abducted and then returned by little green men in a flying saucer.

He looked so young in the pictures. So unworldly—or, perhaps, *other*worldly. You could read what you liked into pictures. He should know: He was adept at the tricks of light and perspective that made his paintings somehow *more than* natural, an extra dimension of life and vitality that made them stand out from the work of his contemporaries. He had often been told that he saw things differently.

He remembered the ridicule at school, and the cranks who

would write to him or, worse, doorstep him at home or wait for him outside school, brandishing their own dossiers of "evidence" and closely spaced handwritten expositions of the UFO cover-up.

He had never talked about flying saucers or little green men. He didn't even believe in UFOs, or not, at least, as anything other than a paranoid mass delusion.

He had just lost some time and a block of memory. There had been a gap of a few days when he had gone missing, which had coincided with a sighting nearby, and the press had made a story out of it. It was hardly as if other teenagers weren't doing strange things at that time.

It had changed his life. That was certain. He had put the change in himself down to the attention, the ridicule, the abrupt education in how he must never trust the reactions and motives of those he encountered. It had cast him as always the outsider, the observer—perhaps it was even why he had ended up as a semisuccessful painter of marshland scenes that tended to sell most reliably to the buggers who would go out shooting the birds he portrayed.

A psychological response, he had always thought: a retreat, a distancing.

He remembered the gun dissolving in his hand, the sleek curves of its design that had brought that time, nearly forty years before, surging to the surface.

At times like this, the memories were so close he could almost touch them. But still, so far.

So: UFO technology in the hands of a neighbor who wanted him dead. He grunted, perversely amused at the line of thought. Again, he felt that something within was trying to expand—an understanding hovering just below the surface of his mind. A seductive presence, just waiting to take over.

He wondered if this was how schizophrenia began. A splitting of thought processes, a sense of chasm within, a paranoid delusion fed by images from the TV. He resisted a sudden impulse to phone Bill Healey and ask if he had really been here at the crack of dawn. He didn't know which answer he wanted to hear. No, you're mad. Yes, the aliens wanted me to kill you.

He put the folder away, and went through to see if it might be possible to rescue last night's microwave meal.

They came for him again, later that morning, and found him asleep in an armchair. He didn't stand a chance.

"Thomas3! Thomas3!" Somehow she managed to squeal girlishly and sound commanding at the same time. He just had to stop and look at her, smile at her. Saffron had donned human form in his honor, and she had chosen the soma she knew he found irresistible. She had a tight blonde bob, sculpted and immovable, held close to her skull like a helmet. She had eyes wide and dark, lashes mascaraed thickly so that even her glossy rosebud lips did not hold your attention over and above those eyes. Her deep-cut tee-shirt did little to restrain perfectly weighted breasts, and her miniskirt revealed long legs without an ounce of excess.

"Saffron," was all he could say. She was a goddess. Or as good as.

She took his arm and, reluctantly, he followed her gaze to the stars. Deep in the bowels of Monopolis, the gallery had been arranged so that three walls and the ceiling were panelled to the exterior, replicating the view that would be afforded anyone who took the trouble to don a suit and step outside. It was as if they were on a viewing platform projecting from the metacolony.

And what a view! The tangled weave and warp of the Monastereal Drift: sheets of stars and star-forming dust clouds, woven together, bunched up here, stretched and tenuous there. Stars like jewels, only more jewels than could ever have existed. It was, many had argued, the finest view in all occupied space.

Thomas3 raised a bulb to the view and drank.

Saffron did likewise, with a bulb she had not had seconds previously. "To your show," she said.

For a few seconds there he had forgotten the purpose of this gathering: a show of his work. His mental castings were nothing to this, he knew. Trivial. And he did not care.

"The show," he said, and drank again.

"We need to talk," Saffron said now. Her touch on his arm was intense, sending waves of pleasure across his sensitised skin.

"Of course," he said.

. . . alone, just the two of them in a mental niche. The exhibition might just as well be on another world, even though to all onlookers the two of them were still there.

"It's your originator," she told him now. He couldn't see her, couldn't see himself—visualization unnecessary, it seemed, for this exchange. The two of them as mental spaces overlapping like this, he had a far greater sense of Saffron as something exotic, nonhuman. He preferred her wearing the soma she had on at the exhibition.

His originator. One of the Onlookers on an insolar planet—one not yet part of occupied space.

Me, he told himself. She's talking about *me*. Or, at least, Thomas3's original self.

"You're in shock—recover."

He felt better, more alert.

"Your originator was brainjacked by a fugitive. He may not have known, but the fugitive was there in his head. It probably intended to hide for a while, hoping it wouldn't be located by us on a nonoccupied planet. The fugitive was wrong, and it was wiped by one of our own hosted operatives."

Brainjacked . . . It could happen. When young Tom Wharton became an Onlooker, he also became vulnerable to this kind of crime. Particularly vulnerable to those most like him. Thomas3 stopped himself speculating, knowing that he was in shared space.

"He's dead?" When they wiped the fugitive, they must have wiped Tom Wharton too.

"Mostly. We'd like your permission to reconstruct him. We have an archived instance of him we could use, and we could splice it together with what is recoverable from the wiped edition and with a swipe of your own early memories. We would like your consent."

Thomas3 knew they didn't have to ask. He was here on sufferance, after all: he was both a soma-copied human and a certified risk to communality. They were within their rights to do whatever they felt necessary.

"Of course," he said

Sensing that his audience was almost over, he quickly added, "But please . . . Can I meet him? When you've reconstructed him?"

They met in a shared mental space—privacy-secured, Thomas3 had ascertained. He asked for visuals and let them be guided by whatever was in his originator's thoughts.

Saltwater marshland. They were in a narrow, flat-bottomed boat, Tom occasionally guiding it with his oars but otherwise letting it follow the gentle flow of the creek. Somewhere a bird sang. A skylark, Thomas3 recalled.

"They came down in the marshes," said Tom Wharton amiably, not put out by the younger soma of himself facing him in the boat. "No flying saucers. All that's balls. They just stepped out of nowhere. Four of them. I knew they weren't going to hurt me, so when they asked me to go with them I went—just stepped into nowhere with them, only it was a nowhere with a sky unlike any sky you'd ever see from here. Normally I don't remember any of that, of course. It'd only make life difficult." He laughed, not too concerned at the edited nature of his memories.

"You're an Onlooker," said Thomas3. "A window into a world unconnected to the wider communality. When you were brought here as a boy they changed you . . . turned you into one who studies. Through your eyes they watch and learn—or rather, *I* do and so our hosts watch and learn through me, in turn. You'll be going back, soon." Thomas3 gestured, encompassing the wide sweep of saltings around them. "Back to this. My other life. You see, you left a part of you out in the stars: you left *me*. I interpret your observations and live here, a human in an alien culture. They study us in so many different ways."

Tom nodded.

Thomas3 watched him, perturbed by his lack of curiosity about what had happened, what was happening. "You were killed, you know," he told him. "Or as good as."

Tom shrugged. "I seem well enough now."

"You were brainjacked: someone hitching a ride in your skull, maybe just hiding, maybe waiting to take over altogether."

Tom seemed to be struggling to recall, but of course those memories from the time of his brainjacking had been suppressed.

"Why?"

Curiosity at last!

"You were just a bystander," Thomas3 said. "Caught up in a story far bigger than you or I will ever grasp. It's like the stars out there." He waved a hand and it was night on the marshes and the sky was filled with the starscape view from Monopolis, the countless billions of stars. "All those stars," he continued. "Each one of them so important to those that depend on it and yet each a mere speck in the firmament. A fleck of color on a vast canvas," he added, struggling for a metaphor that would make it real to his originator self. "What has happened to you is tiny, meaningless in the grand scale. Endless disputes and struggles, some of them lasting longer than our own species has been around. Somewhere out there is another copy of me—of us. Thomas2 didn't have the rebellious elements of his nature expunged. I, on the other hand, am a much more closely edited instance of ourselves. They understood more by the time they cast me. Our rebellious self has joined one of these grand struggles and is

the source of much conflict. The communality would love
the opportunity to reengineer him. Maybe he visited you,
looking for refuge with his originator, looking for safety in
the familiar. Maybe they have, finally, wiped him. That's my
best shot, anyway."

"Why?"

The same question, again. His answer had not been ade-
quate, or it had opened up further uncertainty.

"I don't know. I don't understand. I think they've taken
the rebellious part out of me—or out of the me that I am
now. Just as they've taken parts out of you. They do that. It's
their way of managing things. They want us to be whole and
to fit in. They want us to be content with our roles in the
communality. Me? They could have just given up on our
line after Thomas2 and then I wouldn't be here, but they
persisted. They're very kind. I'm very happy here."

And he was.

He woke, thick stubble on his jaw—more than a day's
worth, he reckoned. He swallowed drily, went through to the
kitchen. Cupping hands beneath a running tap, he drank.

The door to the studio was half open, so he went through.
There were canvases leaning against the wall to dry, another
new one on the easel.

Swirls of violent color daubed across an angry sky, like
something by van Gogh in one of his darkest slumps.

Starscapes.

He didn't remember painting them, but he had clearly
spent many hours working feverishly. No wonder he was
still exhausted, despite what felt to have been a long sleep.
He felt both physically and mentally drained.

He picked one up and held it at arm's length. He wondered what his usual clientele would make of *that*!

The sound of the doorbell interrupted his musing. Visitors? At this hour? Then he realized that he had no idea what
time this was.

A dark thought struck him then, out of nowhere: someone

come to try to kill him again? He shook himself. He'd been watching too much TV.

Or—and again, he did not know where such a thought might originate—what if the person waiting at the door, ringing the bell again now . . . what if it was another me?

THE FULCRUM

By Gwyneth Jones

In the constellation of Orion, and illuminated by the brilliant star N380 Orionis, you will find the reflection nebula NGC 1999, and the "homo sapiens" Bok Globule, famous in astronomical history. This star nursery is the apparent location of the Buonarotti region, to which the 4-space equations give the shape of a notional cross with two-pointed expanding wings, known to Deep Spacers and other romantics as The Fulcrum. To some, this "X marks the spot" is the forbidden gate to Eldorado; to others, it's the source of our consciousness and an oracle of our future, set like Delphi at the navel of space-time . . .

The aliens came back to their cabin to find that they'd been turned over again. Last time, they'd lost their drugs. This time it was the bikes. They sat in the wreckage of scattered belongings, letting the spume of violent and futile emotion shed from them, and feeling scared. Losing the fish-oil stash had been serious, but extreme tourists have to accept that they are rich and they will get ripped off. This was different. No one else on the station had any possible use for the exercise bikes. Their fellow prospectors were almost exclusively Deep Space veterans. A few hours a day of simulated mountain racing wouldn't touch their problem with the gravity well.

In the end, the company of their violated possessions got them down, so they decided to go and see Eddie the Supercargo. They knew he wouldn't do anything, but it's always better to report racial harassment. They put their coats on and bounced gently along the drab corridors—two humanoid aliens, about two meters tall, pale skinned and diffident, each with a crest of stiff red hair. Although they were a heterosexual couple, to human eyes they were as identical as identical twins—but unlike human identical twins, they didn't mind being mistaken for each other. They didn't meet anyone. The Kuiper Belt station did not aspire to the parkland illusions or shopping opportunities of near-Earth orbital hotels. Unless they were preparing for transit, most of the prospectors never left their cabins except to visit the saloon.

There were plans that the Panhandle would become the hub of a Deep Space International City, hence all the empty space in the Pan. For the moment it was simply an asymmetric ceramic fiber dumbbell, spinning in a minimal collision orbit-area of the asteroid reach—the Pan full of prospectors and their support staff, the Knob reserved for the government's business out here, and the Handle an empty, concertina-walled permanent umbilical between. The AIs took care of everything serious. The only actual human authority on board was Eddie. His duties were not onerous. As far as Orlando and Grace could make out, he did nothing when on shift except sit in his office at the Knob end of the Handle and play Freecell. On his off shift he would come down to the saloon and schmooze with assorted ruffians. His squeezesuit and official rank branded him as a dilettante, but he adored the Deep Spacers.

Eddie's gaff was a step or two up from the standard cabins. It had a double skin to keep the cold at bay, and the chairs, desk and cabinets swelling from the walls and floor were designer styled, in a drab, corporate sort of way. There were no personal touches and no visible equipment (besides Eddie), except the desktop screen that he used for his endless solitaire. The Supercargo was a skinny fellow, with wispy dark hair that floated around his shoulders, sad eyes and a taste for extravagant dress. Today he was wearing knee-high platform boots crusted in silver glitter. The bone-preserving pressure suit was concealed by a spiderweb gold silk shirt and black neoprene biker trousers; a copper and silver filigree scarf swayed airily about his throat. The prisoners of knocked-down gravity favored drifty accessories; it was a kind of gallows-humour; and Eddie was a shameless wannabe.

He greeted the aliens with enthusiasm, but he didn't like their complaint.

"Listen," he cut them off, at last, "I'm sorry you lost your bikes, but you know the rules. *There are no rules.* Anything you want, you take. That's the way we live, and you got to breeze it. You can't go all holier-than-thou out here in the Deep."

"We understand *that*," said Orlando, rolling his eyes.

"We'd be *fine* with that," drawled Grace, with a shrug, "If those deadbeats had anything that we *wanted* to steal. It's just unfair that it's all one way."

Eddie beamed, relieved that they hadn't been expecting a police action, and the visit became social. The truth was, passionately as he admired the Deep Spacers, Eddie was frightened of them, and the fact that (theoretically) he could sling them in irons or chuck them off the Panhandle made no difference. It's personality that counts in these back-of-beyond situations. The aliens understood this perfectly: They were pretty much in the same boat. Extreme tourists are always trying to look as if they belong, in situations where only insanely hard-ass nutcases have any real business.

"You know," Eddie confided, "The last Supercargo was knifed in the saloon, over a menu choice. You shouldn't take it personally; the guys are just a wild bunch—"

They knew the story. They thought it was unlikely and

that the prospectors only knifed each other. But they sympathized with Eddie's need to romanticize a shit job: a career in space-exploration that had obviously hit the dregs.

"Thanks," said Grace. "Now we feel much better."

Eddie broke out alcohol bulbs and chocolate from his waistbelt, and the three of them chatted, talking guiltily about the blue planet far away, the overcrowded and annoying dump to which they would soon return—Eddie at the end of his tour, and Grace and Orlando on the next Slingshot—which was to the forgotten heroes of the Deep Space saloon an unattainable paradise. Suddenly the Supercargo went quiet, attending to a summons imperceptible to his visitors. They sat politely, while he stared into the middle distance, wondering if he was receiving an update from the AI machines, or maybe a command from faraway Houston.

"Ooops," he said, "Duty calls. It's time for the alien to be milked."

"You mean the *other* alien," Grace corrected him.

Eddie shook his head, making his hair and his delicate scarf flip about like exotic seaweed in a tank. "Hahaha. C'mon, you two aren't really aliens."

Eddie gave slavish credence to whatever loony resumés the Deep Spacers cared to invent. Wormhole trips? Sentient rocks, diamonds the size of Texas, wow, he lapped it up . . . Orlando and Grace declared their elective cultural identity, which was perfectly acceptable at home, and they were jeered at.

"It's a state of mind," said Orlando.

"Hey," said Eddie shyly. "D'you want to come along? It's against the regs, but I trust you, and you did lose your bikes and all. It'll be okay. You won't get fried."

He stood up, teetering a little because the glitter boots were weighted, and concentrated on stowing his treatpack back on his belt. Grace and Orlando exchanged one swift glance. They knew exactly the terrifying thing that they were going to do.

*   *   *

Eddie did not use keycards, he did not visibly step up to a mark or get bathed in any identifying fields. He simply went up to the blank wall at the end of the umbilical. It opened, and he stood in the gap to let the aliens by. They were through the unbreachable Wall and inside the Knob, a Deep Space Fort Knox, the strongbox which held, according to rumor, the most fabulous treasure in the known universe.

"The Knob recognises you?" said Orlando, suitably impressed. "Or do you have a key or an implant on you, that it recognizes?"

"Nah, it's me. I've got an implant—"

"Yeah. We noticed."

"That's a requirement of the job. But it's my informational profile that's written into the Knob, just for my tour of duty. Bios wouldn't be secure enough."

They were in a miniversion of the Pan, following a spiral corridor divided by greenish, ceramic fiber bulkheads. They noticed at once how clear the air was, free of the dust, shed cells and general effluvia of many human bodies. It was warmer too, and it didn't smell bad. The walls opened for Eddie, he stood and let his companions through like a wise cat inviting guests through the magnetized catflap; the walls closed up behind with spooky finality.

"Is there always air, heat and gravity at this end?" wondered Grace, offhand.

"Always," said Eddie. "Not for the thing, I don't think it uses air. I don't think it *breathes*. It'd be more expensive turning the life support on and off, that's all. The rad protection is shit," he added, "Except in my actual cabin. The AIs are shielded, they don't need it. But half an hour won't fry your nuts."

"What about you?"

Eddie shrugged. "I've got my cabin, and hey, I've finished my family."

The aliens' wiry red hair stood up on end. They felt that, briefly, the Kuiper Belt Station was not rotating aimlessly in place but steaming full ahead. They were sailing *outwards* (the only direction that there is) across the Spanish Main, around Cape Horn, with Franklin to the North West Passage . . . Finally Eddie ushered them into a little room with the same fungoid fittings as his office: desk, chairs, screen and touchpad. One wall was a window, apparently looking into the cabin next door.

"There you go," said the Supercargo, shivering. "Now you can say you've seen it. Oh, no pictures, please. You don't want to get me into trouble."

"We wouldn't dream of it."

Eddie teetered, patting at his wayward hair. The aliens stood like zoo visitors, looking into a naked and featureless cell where something huddled on the floor: a dark, fibrous, purplish lump like a hundred-pound hunk of horsemeat. It was fuzzy in outline, as if not securely fixed in these particular dimensions, and had four blunt extrusions. A convoluted sheet of paler tissue covered some of the main lump, like a skein of fat over a slab of steak.

"Is it really right next door?" asked Grace, casually.

"I suppose," said Eddie. "I never thought about it." His eyes went unfocused as he checked the Knob's internal architecture, and he nodded. "Yeah, actually it is. Shit, I never knew that—" He was shivering more strongly.

"It looks as if it's been skinned alive, filleted, and had its arms and legs and cut off," breathed Orlando.

"And that could be its brain," whispered Grace. "It looks kind of like a cerebral cortex, unfolded out of someone's skull."

"I don't know why you're whispering," said Eddie. He'd started to pace up and down, flexing his long, delicate hands, as if in nervous impatience. "It can't hear you. Hey, you don't know what they're meant to look like. You're anthropomorphizing. It could be a handsome, happy whatsit, for all you know."

"We don't anthropomorphize," objected Grace. "We're aliens."

Eddie groaned a little. "Oh, have it your own way, a different word. You're thinking like it's a person. It isn't."

There's something in every human heart that delights in horrors: Orlando and Grace were not immune. They pored over the creature on the other side of the window, fascinated and seduced. They knew that Eddie was lying for his own comfort. Almost without a doubt, the thing had once been human. Whatever lies the government told, this goose that laid the golden eggs was almost certainly someone who had made a transit, and failed to return intact . . . But from where had it fallen, into this pit? *From where?* Where had it been, the lone voyager to that land of plenty?

"I can't believe they really keep it *here*," muttered Orlando. "I thought that was just Spacer bullshit."

"Where else?" inquired Eddie, sarcastically. "In the Pentagon basement? Give me a break. It's incre-credibly weird and unbelievably d-dangerous."

Now the creature was moving. It had begun to shudder and squirm across the floor of the cell, silently giving every sign of anguish and terror. "That's milking-time behavior," hissed Eddie. "Now you'll see something, watch, this is it—" But he seemed distracted. A flush had gathered around his eyes and nose, he was smiling strangely and breathing hard.

A section of the cell wall slid aside, revealing a recess set with a pair of waldo rings. Then the government arrived, in the form of two heavy-built robotic hands that reached into the chamber. The alien's movement was now clearly an attempt to reach those hands. As soon as it was close, one of the big chunky mitts got a lock on a stubby tentacle, while the other, grotesquely, delved and disappeared into a cleft that had opened in the dark raw flesh. The creature jerked and writhed in pain, shuddering in that rough grip with an awful, sexual-seeming submission. The buried hand reappeared, full of something that squeezed between the fingers like a thick silvery goo, like liquid mercury. The robot arm retracted out of the cell and returned empty to delve again. Orlando and Grace watched this process happen five times, five greedy fistfuls, (with Eddie's breath coming in gasps beside them). Then the robot hands vanished, and the cell wall closed up again.

"Wow, that was *gross*," said Orlando. "Thanks a million, Eddie."

"But it wants to be milked," whispered Eddie, still off on his own track. "It *wants* that to happen. Like the scorpion. It has to obey its nature."

"Was that q-bits?" asked Grace, trying to sound unmoved. "Or the helium?"

"Yeah," said Eddie, blinking and mopping his brow with the filigree scarf. "They get helium, it's half the earth's supply now. An' decoherence resistant particles for building q-bits. It saves pollution, little children get clean water, whoo—"

He pulled himself together. "Shit, I don't know. The goop goes straight back to earth, all automated. I only work here. C'mon. Got to take you back."

The journey out was the same as the journey in, except that Eddie's mood had taken a severe downturn. The aliens were silent too. He parted from them at his office door. "Catch you later," he said, as he slunk into privacy.

They didn't fancy their turned-over cabin, so they made for the saloon.

It was late afternoon by standard time, and the dank, icy bar was quiet, empty except for the hardcore of alcoholics and gamblers who lurked here from happy hour to happy hour. A couple of the support staff were beating up a recalcitrant food machine. The morbidly obese lady in the powerchair, who wore her hair side-parted in a fall of golden waves, was acting as banker at one of the autotables. (The aliens, who were crazy about Hollywood, knew her as Lakey). The tall, gangly bloke with the visor—whom they called Blind Pew—looked up to stare, from the band of gleaming darkness where his eyes had been. He said, "Twist," and returned his attention to the game. The aliens got beer tubes and installed themselves at a table near the games consoles—which nobody played, because they required Earth currency credit, and the Deep Spacers didn't have that kind of money.

"Woooeee," breathed Orlando, finally. "Whaaat?"

"My God!"

"Now I understand why they insist it's an alien."

"The gateway to Eldorado," babbled Grace. "My god, I thought they . . . why don't they . . . You'd think they'd be doing *something*—"

"You mean, why isn't the International Government investigating the thing? Because they daren't, Grace. They're junkies. They're totally dependent. They daren't do anything that might stop the flow."

In the close to four hundred years since spaceflight got started, the human race had never got beyond orbital tourism, government science stations and wretched, hand-to-mouth mining operations in the Belt. The discovery of nonlocal travel had made a huge difference; but the catch was that so far only a conscious human being could make a Buonarotti transit. You could take what you could carry, as long as it didn't contain a processor, and that was all. Hence the Lottery, which had been set up out here, as far from Earth as possible in case of unforseen space-time disasters. The government was handing out cheap survey stakes in the galactic arm to anyone prepared to come to the Kuiper Belt. You got the rights to a portfolio of data (there were programs that would advise you how to make up your package) and the *chance* that your claim would turn up the spectral signature of an Earthtype, good atmosphere, viable planet—the 4-space coordinates of paydirt.

Then you had to check it out: lie down in a Buonarotti couch in the transit lounge, with your little outfit of grave-goods, and go you knew not where.

Prospectors went missing for months; prospectors came back dead, or mutilated, or deathly sick. Just often enough some spacer came back safe, the proud owner of a prime development site: rich enough, even after selling it at a considerable discount, to pay the medical bills and go home to Earth in fabulous style. But once, *once*, back in the early days, someone or something had materialized in the transit lounge bearing not merely information, but *treasure* . . .

Orlando and Grace had come out on the superfast advanced-fusion Slingshot, which made the journey in nine months these days, if the orbital configuration was right. (The harvest from the thing in the Knob traveled faster; it didn't need life-support and could stand a lot more gs.) They'd known they'd be stuck for a year, whether their numbers came up or not, and then face another six months for the homeward trip. They'd known the Lottery was meant for redundant Deep Spacers—kind of a scattergun pension fund for the human debris of the conventional space age. But they had seen a window of bold, dazzling opportunity and decided it was worth the risk.

They'd thought it out. They'd taken a government loan-grant, they'd brought their vitamins, and paid the exorbitant supplement for the freight of the bikes. (They'd done the research, they knew that squeeze-suits were just prosthetic, and you had to do real exercise to save your skeleton.) They weren't crazy. They'd had no intention of risking an actual transit themselves. The plan had been that they would get some good coordinates and sell them to a development consortium (you were allowed to do that, and there were plenty, hovering like vultures). The consortium could hire a deep spacer for the perilous test-trip, and Orlando and Grace would still be taking home a very nice slice. But they'd been on the Kuiper Belt for nine months, watching the survey screens, and their stake had been coming up stone-empty. Nothing but gas giants, hot rocks, cold rocks. The loss of the bikes had been the last straw. Just a couple of hours ago they'd been looking at crawling home from their great adventure three years older, with rotten bones, and in hideous government debt for life.

Now they had something to take to market!

It was big. It was *very* big . . .

"You know," said Orlando, "When we found the bikes gone, I was going to suggest we offer to fuck Eddie's brains out. I mean, he likes us. Maybe he would have twisted the Lottery AI's arm, switched us to a better stake—"

They looked at each other and laughed, eyes bright, slightly hysterical.

The arrival of the tourists hadn't caused a stir. When Jack Solo and Draco Kojima made an entrance, looking mean, the inevitable molls in tow, all the barflies came to attention. The aliens felt the tremor and saw the reason. These were the Panhandle big boys, uncontested top bullies. But Jack and Draco were arch-rivals. They hated each other; what were they doing together? Orlando and Grace hunched down in their seats, lowered their eyes, and wondered who was in trouble. Murderous violence was not at all uncommon, but they didn't have to worry. It was gang warfare, and you were okay as long as you stayed out of the line of fire.

To their horror, Draco and Jack headed straight for the games consoles curve. With one accord, they hauled out the suction chairs facing the aliens and sat down. Jack's scrawny girlfriend, Anni-mah, adopted her habitual bizarre pose, crouched at her boyfriend's feet. Draco's chunky babe, her bosoms projected ahead of her by awesome pecs and fantastic lats, stood at his shoulder, her oversized blue eyes blank, her little mouth pursed in its customary sugar-smile.

When they'd first encounterd the molls, Orlando and Grace had thought they were real people, with strange habits and poor taste in body mods. Of course they were bots, insubstantial software projections. Strictly speaking, they were contraband, because you weren't supposed to use fx generators—or any kind of personal digital devices—on board the Panhandle. But nobody was going to make an issue of it with these two—certainly not Eddie Supercargo.

Jack Solo was a gray-haired, wiry little man, a veteran pilot of the spaceways, who must have fought the damage stubbornly and hard. He showed no signs of Deep Space mutilation, no prosthetic walking frame or deep-vein thrombosis amputations, and he still had normal vision. But then you looked into his eyes, and you knew he hadn't got off lightly. He habitually wore a data glove that had seen better days, and a tube-festooned, battered drysuit—pilot undress, that he sported as a badge of rank. Draco Fujima was something very different—a fleshy, soft-faced young man, with a squeeze suit under his streamlined, expensive, rad-proof jumper. You could tell at once he hadn't been in space for long. Like Grace and Orlando he was just passing through. He was a time-expired UN remote-control peacekeeper, out of the military at sixteen; who had taken the free Lottery option as part of his severance pay.

This was one tourist the Spacers treated with extreme respect. Though crazy Jack might knife you over a menu choice, he probably counted his kills in single figures. Draco's lethal record was official and seriously off the scale.

No one messes with a playpen soldier.

The big boys stared, with radiant contempt. The aliens attempted to radiate the cynical, relaxed confidence that might get them through this alive.

"You went to see Eddie today," said Jack.

"How d'you know that?" demanded Orlando.

Draco leaned forward. "We have our ways. We don't like you, so we always know where you are. Why did you go to see Eddie?"

"Our bicycles," explained Grace, grinning. "They've been stolen. Do you wise guys happen to know anything about that heist?"

Orlando kicked her under the table: there's such a thing as being too relaxed.

Jack jumped halfway across the table, like a wild-eyed Jack-in-a-Box. "Listen, cunts," he snapped, the dataglove twitching, "Fuck the bicycles, we don't like the relationship. You two and Eddie, we see it and we don't like it. You're going to tell us what the fuck's going on."

"He likes us," said Grace. "Can we help that?"

"It's called empathy," explained Orlando, getting braver.

"It might seem like psychic powers, but it's natural to us. You just don't have the wiring."

Jack grabbed Orlando by the throat and flicked the wrist of his other, gloved hand so that a knife appeared there, a sleek slender blade, gleaming against Orlando's pale throat. Anni-mah whined, "*Oh please don't hurt him.*" Jack kept his eyes fixed on Orlando and his grip on the jumper while he reached down to smack his bot around her virtual chops with the gloved hand that held the knife.

He made the smack look real, with practiced ease.

"*Oh yes, oh, hit me big boy,*" whimpered Anni-mah. "*Oh, harder, please—*"

Draco's babe just stood there; she was the strong, silent type.

"Look," said Grace, coolly, "When you've finished giving yourself the handjob . . . you've got it all wrong. We made friends with Eddie by accident, it doesn't mean anything. We're just aliens abroad."

"Shut up, cunt," said Jack. "You *are not* fucking aliens, that's just a story, and I'm talking to your boyfriend."

Draco laughed. Jack slowly released Orlando, glaring all the time.

"Listen, fuckface," said Orlando, straightening his jumper with dignity. "*We are aliens* in relation to you, you pathetic old-fashioned machismo merchant, because you haven't a cat in hell's chance of understanding where we're coming from. *Now* do you get it? And by the way, *I'm* the cunt, thank you very much."

Anyone in the bar who feared the sight of blood had sneaked out. The hardcore remained, riveted. It was strange, and not totally unpleasant, to be the object of so much attention. They felt as if getting senselessly bullied by Jack and Draco was some kind of initiation ceremony, Maybe now, at last, the tourists would be accepted.

Jack sat back. The knife had a handle bound in fine-grained blond leather, and the aliens knew the story about where this "leather" had come from. He toyed with his weapon, smiling secretly, then brought the point down so that it sank, under gentle pressure, deep into the ceramic tabletop. The aliens thought not so much of their vulnerable flesh as of the thin shell of the Pan, made of the same stuff as the table, and the cold, greedy, airless dark that would rush in—

"You're not Spacers," said Jack, calm and affable. "You don't belong here."

Draco tired of taking the back seat. "In the center of the Knob," he announced, "there is a cell, guarded by fanatical killer AIs. What's in that cell is a cold brutal indictment of the inhumanities perpetrated around the globe by those who claim to be our leaders. We should be listening, we should be feeding on that pain, we should be turning the degraded, ripped and slathered flesh into kills, into respect, the respect that's due to the stand-up guys, good men who have protected humanity. We know, we *know* that we deserve better than this and YOU know where we can get it—"

"Don't listen to *him*," Jack broke in. "He knows fuck. The thing in that cell came from NGC 1999, a star-nursery in the constellation of Orion. Everyone knows that, but I'm the only one who knows it came for *me*. Orion has been sacred to all the world's ancient religions, for tens of thousands of years. Nobody knew why, until the space telescopes found out that the new stars in that Bok Globule are just *one hundred thousand years old*. Now do you get it, fuck face, those stars are the same age as homo sapiens. The thing in that cell is human consciousness, twisted back on itself through the improbability dimension. We keep it in chains, for our torment, but I know. I *know*, you see. Out there, *fifteen* hundred *light* years away, is the source of all thought, all science, and from thence, from that magic explosion of cosmic jizm, my *God* has come to find me, has come for *me*."

The knife went in and out of the tabletop. Anni-mah whimpered "*Don't hit me*," or maybe "*Please hit me;*" but Jack's eyes were calm. The aliens realized, slightly awed, that the old space pilot was perfectly in control. This was his *normal state of mind*.

"Fifteen is *five* times *three*. It's written in the Great Pyramid."

"I h-heard about that," Grace nodded, eagerly. "It's the nebula that looks like a thingy, and the ancient Egyptians believed it was, uh, that Orion was Osiris—"

"The Eygptians knew something, girlie. They knew the cosmos was created out of God's own, lonely lovejuice. But I'm the anointed, I'm the chosen one."

"It's made of anti-information," broke in Draco, deciding to up the ante. "Does *that* satisfy you? Does *that* scare you enough? Why d'you think they keep it here, with scum like these deadbeats, where *I don't belong*? Why d'you think they lured me out here? They say I'm morally ambivalent, fucking shrinks, they'll say anything, you should try what I do next. They want me to feel bad, never get the good stuff, There's a conspiracy behind the conspiracy—"

"So you'll tell us," said Jack. "You'll tell us anything you find out."

"From that limp-wrist, fudge-packing, desk-flying government pansy—"

Orlando, Grace noticed, was nudging her in the ribs. She nodded fractionally, and they slid their chairs. The climax had safely passed; they could escape.

"Of course, of course we will. Er, we have to go now—"

Anni-mah cringed and shivered. Draco's babe went on standing there.

The aliens took refuge on the observation deck, which was empty as usual. Real Deep Spacers had seen enough of this kind of view. They stood and gazed, holding onto the rail that saved them from vertigo, until the shaking had passed.

"I think it was just our turn," said Orlando at last. "They didn't know."

"I hope you're right."

Outside the great clear halfdome the glory of the Orion Nebula was spread before them, the jewel in the sword.

They could easily locate the Trapezium, the four brilliant stars knit by a common gravity in whose embrace you would find that notorious Bok Gobule—the star-birthing gas cloud with a vague resemblance to a set of male human genitalia. Jack's conviction had some basis, though it was laced with delusion. There was indeed a persistent story, which the government had failed to suppress, that that particular star-nursery was the point of origin of the "thing." They hadn't been able to make any sense of Draco's rant; but what could you expect from a basketcase who had *really killed* thousands of real people, by remote control. And he knew it, and he'd been rewarded by big jolts of pleasure, and all before he was fifteen years old.

Grace put her arm around Orlando's shoulders, and they drank deep of the beauty out there, the undiscovered country. As much as they pretended they had come to space to make their fortunes, they had their own craziness.

"The sad thing is that we're no nearer," said Grace, softly.

"We can't ever get there. Deep Space destroys people."

"Deep Space is like living in a fucking underground carpark with rotten food. And non-local transit is going to be like—"

"Getting on the Eurostar at Waterloo, and getting off in Adelaide."

"Only quicker, and some other constellations, instead of the Southern Cross."

"It's not even real," sighed Orlando. "That. It's a TV picture."

"It's *sort of* real. Nitrogen is green, oxygen is blue. The spectral colors mean something. If we were there, our minds would see what we see now."

"You sound like Jack Solo. Let's go back to the shack, and watch a movie."

They tidied the wrecked cabin a little and ate a meager supper. They didn't fancy going back to the saloon, but luckily their emergency rations had not been touched. One of the sleeping-nets turned out to be in reasonable shape, once they'd lined it with their spare cabin rug. The Panhandle entertainment menu was extensive (as rich as the food was poor); and they'd tracked down a wonderful cache of black and whites, so pure in visual and sound quality they must have been mastered from original prints long lost on earth. They put on *Now, Voyager*, and settled themselves, two exiled Scottish sparrows in a strange but cosy nest, a long, long way from the Clyde. Their windfall of information could wait. Sobered by their interview with the big boys, they were afraid it was a bust: stolen goods too hot to be salable.

"So it's come to this," grumbled Orlando. "We came all this way to huddle in an unheated hotel room, watching Bette Davis try to get laid."

"That's extreme tourism for you. Never mind. We *like* Bette Davis."

Bette emerged from her Ugly Duckling chrysalis and set off on the cruise that would change her life. Orlando wondered, mildly, "What would anti-information be, Gracie? I've never heard of that before."

"It would be more information, like, er, minus numbers are still—"

"Not like antimatter? Like, you'd explode if you touched it?"

"The robot hands didn't exp— Hey, we're not going to talk about it." But immediately, with a shudder, she added, "God, I'm scared. Draco talks like a serial killer. He talks like one of those notes that serial killers send to the police."

"He is one. A bulk-buy, government-sponsored, son of Sam."

The movie projection shivered.

A tall, broadshouldered figure wearing scanty combat gear materialized in front of the black and white picture. It was Sara Komensky, Draco's virtual babe.

The aliens stared in horrified amazement. The bot wrapped her arms over her bazookas of breasts, bizarrely like a real live young woman mortified by the excess.

"Hey," she said. "Er, Draco doesn't know I'm here."

The aliens nodded. "Right," croaked Orlando. "Of course."

The warrior girl appeared to look around, her little mouth an *Oh!* of surprise. Draco's quarters were in First Class, and probably a bit smarter.

"We've had burglars," Grace explained. "Usually it's better than this."

"It's cool," said the bot. She shrugged. "I've seen worse bunkers. I've been with Drac a while you know. We . . . we've been in some tough spots. Jungles, bombed out cities, volcanos, icefields of Uzbekistan, polluted oil platforms, all kindsa shit."

"Sure you have."

Sara strode up and down, which didn't take her long, and turned to them again, her strong hands clasped on her bandoliers, the muscles in her forearms tight. "You got to help me. You see . . . Drac . . . He's not good at the joined-up thinking. It's the combat drugs, they wrecked his brain. He doesn't get that this is our last chance. He took the Lottery option because it was imprinted on him. He'll take a risk on some lousy half-viable coordinates and kill himself; that's what's meant to happen. The government don't terminate toy-soldiers direct; it wouldn't look good. They just make shit-ass sure people like Drac don't survive long in the real."

"That's rough," said Orlando. "I'm sure he's a truly good person, deep down. But what can we do? We haven't any viable numbers. Y-you can check."

"He's *not* a good person," said the bot. "But if he goes, I go too."

"Huh?"

Sara's little pearly teeth caught her sweet, pouting underlip, "Listen, assholes, you come from the same place I come from. Are you made of information, or what? Don't you have anyone switching you on or off? Me, I live in the chinks, same as you. Are *you* so fucking free?" Her huge blue eyes snapped with frustration. "Okay, okay, I get that you can't trust me. But you two know something about the Fulcrum."

"We don't know *anything*," protested Grace, hurriedly.

The big babyblues narrowed as far as the graphic algorithm would allow. "Yeah, but you do. I'm with the Panhandle sys-op. We're like *that*." The bot released her bandoliers, and hooked her two index fingers. "I can't get inside your heads but I *know you've been where the sys-op can't go*. All it would take would be one drop of that silver jizm. One nugget of the good stuff, he'd be set for life, and you'd never have to be looking over your shoulders. I haven't told him, I swear. This is between you and me. Now I gotta get back. Think about it, is all I ask. We'll talk again."

She vanished.

Orlando and Grace shot out of the net, scrabbled in their belongings for the spygone (a gadget that had often been useful on extreme tourism trips) and bounced around the room wildly, searching cornices, crevices, the toilet, anywhere. They found nothing. It was uncanny, how could Draco be using his bot like that, wireless, from another deck, without a receiver in here? Unnoticed, the movie had continued to play. "The projector!" howled Orlando. They flew to disable the entertainment centre, dumped it outside in the corridor; switched off the lights and the doorlock for good measure. Switching off the air and gravity would not, they decided, improve the situation: even if they knew how. Finally they collapsed on the floor. Grace dragged their gravegoods whisky flask out of the litter.

"What can we do?"

"We are fucked," gabbled Orlando, grabbing the precious reserve of Highland Park from her and knocking it back. "We are fucked to all shit! We have the stolen suitcase full of cocaine, the one that belongs to the Mob."

"No it doesn't! It belongs to *us*!"

"N-no it doesn't! Suitcases full of cocaine, dollar bills, anti-information, they always belong to the Mob. And they're onto us. There's nothing we can do except dump the goods in a shallow grave and run for our fucking lives."

"But we can't run. We can't get off here until the Slingshot."

"We c-could try and gone-in-sixty one of the Deep Spacers' asteroid hoppers?"

"Except we don't know how, and if we did, they aren't equipped to get back to Earth. We'd just die more slowly."

The Panhandle was not supplied with lifeboats. Most of the prospectors and all of the support staff were totally dependent on the Slingshot, which was not due for three months. There had to be a lifepod for the Supercargo, keyed to his identity . . . but forget it. That would be a single ticket. Grace saw a faint hope. "Maybe . . . Maybe Draco *doesn't* know? Maybe the bot was telling the truth?"

"Get a grip. That was an interactive videogram, Gracie. That was *Draco* we were *talking* to, for fuck's sake! What did you think?"

"Are you sure? I hear you, but I don't know, it just didn't—"

Someone knocked on the door. They went dead still, forgot to breathe, and stared at each other. Grace got up, quietly, and keyed the lights.

"Come in," said Orlando.

The door opened, and Lakey the fat lady appeared, in her power chair.

"Your lock's broken," she told them. "You should complain to Eddie."

"It isn't broken," said Grace. "We switched it off."

Lakey looked around, the Veronica Lake fall of gold hair swinging. She didn't seem as surprised to see the state the place was in as Sara the bot had been.

"Can we help you?" inquired Grace.

"I'm here because we want to talk to you."

"Everybody wants to talk to us," said Orlando. "Is your chair in this?"

"My chair has the brains of a hamster. I mean, some of us." The chair hissed. Lakey leaned from it to peer at drifted socks. "You two disappeared this morning. You left the sys-op screen. We think Eddie took you through the Wall, and now you know something that will cost you your sweet little tourist skins, unless you get some help."

"What is the Fulcrum?" asked Grace.

Lakey's body was a wreck, but she still had the remains of tough, old-fashioned natural beauty in her dropsical face and in the way she smiled.

"You just spilled all the noughts and ones, little lady."

"I truly don't know what you mean."

"Give me a place to stand," said Lakey, "and I will move the world."

"What are you talking about?"

"To me the Fulcrum means nothing. To you, it means life or death. You guys had a nerve, coming out to the Pan. Do you even care what non-local has done to our culture, to our heroes? This our fucking patch, the only one we have left. There's a maintenance bay, one junction centerwards of the observation deck, where the food machines go to get pulled apart when they die. You better be there, at oh-four-hundred hours standard, or else. Do you know what *burial at sea* means?"

Burial at sea meant when Deep Spacers chuck some miscreant out of an airlock, naked into hard vacuum.

"Okay," said Grace. "We'll talk. But we want our bicycles back."

Lakey grinned in appreciation. "I'll see what I can do."

Six hours later, the Panhandle was deep in its night cycle. Dim nodes of minimum light glowed along the dark corridors, each node surrounded by a halo of micro-debris. The air exchangers sighed, the aliens bounced toward the rendezvous with barely a sound. As they hit the last junction, Orlando touched Grace's arm. She nodded. They had both heard the crisp tread of velcro soles. Some adept of the spaceways was sneaking up behind them, and it definitely wasn't Lakey. Without a word they jumped up, utilizing

their low-gravity gymnastics practice, kicked off from the
wall, flew, and kicked again.

Not daring to grab at anything, they tumbled into the bay,
narrowly avoided collison with the hefty carcase of a meat
synthesizer; and hit the industrial carpet behind it. The crisp
footsteps came on, like booted feet walking lightly on fresh
snow. They tried not to breathe. The maintenance bay was
pitch dark, but it did not feel safe. They were surrounded by
the shadow operators, disregarded life support, as if by a
dumb and blind and suffering malevolence. Then something
shrieked. Something fell, and a human voice started up, a series of short, horrible, choking groans—

"That's Lakey!" gasped Grace, mouth against Orlando's
ear.

Silence followed. They crept forward until they could see,
in the dim light from the junction, the fat lady's power chair
upended and crippled. Lakey was lying beside it, her golden
hair adrift, her great body as if crushed at last by the
knocked-down gravity that had ruined her bones and
swamped her lymphatic system.

"Lakey?" whispered Grace helplessly. "Hey, er, are you
okay?"

Something whimpered. Jack Solo's bot was crouching
beside the body, like a painted shadow on the darkness,
wearing her usual grubby nightdress. "*Jack didn't do it,*"
whined Anni-mah. She rubbed her bare arms and cringed
from a blow that existed only in the virtual world. "*It wasn't
Jack! He wasn't here! Oh, hit me harder, yes—*"

The legendary pilot's wrist knife was on the floor, covered in blood. Orlando and Grace went over to the strange
tableau. Lakey'd been stabbed, many times. Blood pooled
around her, in swollen globules that stood on the carpet like
grotesque black bubbles. Their eyes met. The madman must
be very near, and in a highly dissociated state. He was certainly still armed. Jack Solo didn't carry just the one knife.

"Anni?" whispered Grace, trying to make it gentle.
"Where's poor Jack?"

"Jack is right here," said a voice they didn't know.

They spun around. White lights came up. Out from among the defunct service machines loomed the gangling man, with the visor and the crooked bones of many fractures, whom they had called Blind Pew. The popeyed fellow they had nicknamed *Joe Cairo* was beside him, supporting his arm. Other figures joined them: one-armed Dirty Harry, a swollen-headed woman they'd called Jean Harlow for her rags of platinum-blonde hair; and two support staff in their drab coveralls. Right now they were supporting Jack Solo. The pilot stared vaguely at the aliens, as if hardly aware of his surroundings, and muttered, "*Jack didn't do it.*"

"Did he kill Lakey?" asked Grace. "We heard a struggle."

"Lakey?"

"The lady in the chair."

The tall man nodded, indifferent. "It looks like it."

"We were supposed to meet her here. She said she could get our bikes back."

"Ah, the *bicycles*. Come along. Leave that." He jerked his chin at the corpse, "The robotics will clear it away. Her name was Lana. She was my wife," he added, casually, as he led the way toward the observation deck, leaning on Joe Cairo's arm. "For many years, when I was a pilot. But we had grown apart."

The halfdome was still filled by the vast, silent majesty of the nebula, studded with its glorious young stars. The other prospectors and the two support staff grouped themselves around the tall man. Jack Solo was still muttering to himself.

Anni-mah hovered in the background, like a troubled ghost.

The tall man turned his back on the astronomy and propped his gangling form against the rail, his visored face seeking the aliens. "My name . . . is immaterial. They call me L'Hibou, which means the owl. I was Franco-Canadian, long ago. These good folk have made me their spokesperson. We have to talk to you, about the information you have concerning the Fulcrum and what you plan to do with it."

"Lake—Lana used that term. We don't know what it means," said Grace.

"A fulcrum, my young friends, is the fixed point on which a lever moves. The unmoving mover one might say. But *reculons-nous, pour mieux sauter*. Eight hundred years ago, explorers set out across uncharted seas, and the mighty civilization that still commands the human world was born. Four hundred years ago, man achieved space flight. What happened?"

Orlando and Grace wondered what to say.

L'Hibou provided his own answer. "*Nothing*," he said, with infinite disgust. "Flags and footprints in the dead dust! Eventually, yes, a few fools managed to scrape a living in the deep. But the gravity well defeated us. We could not become a new world. There was nothing to prime the pump, no spices, no gold: no new markets, never enough materials worth the freight."

The spacers muttered, in bitter assent.

"Buonarotti science has changed everything," continued L'Hibou, "It makes our whole endeavor look like Leonardo da Vinci's futile attempts to fly. Touching, useless precosity. Pitifully wrongheaded! But what will non-local transit, of itself, give to the human race? *Prison planets*, my young friends. Sinks for earth's surplus population, despatched out there with a pick and shovel and a bag of seed apiece. That's what the International Government intends. And so be it, that's none of our concern. But something happened, out here on the Kuiper Belt station fifteen years ago. In one of the first Buonarotti experiments, a dimensional gate was opened, and something came back that was not of this universe. There were deaths, human and AI. Records were erased. No witnesses survived, no similar experiment has ever been attempted, non-local exploration has been restricted to the commonplace. But we have pieced together the story. They were very afraid. They ejected the thing from the Hub, wrapped in the forcefield that still contains it. The Knob was built around that field and connected to the Pan, so that the jailer would have some relief and some means of escape. And there it stays, weeping its precious tears."

"Thanks," said Orlando. "We've read the guidebook."

"It is the scorpion," hissed the popeyed little man. "The scorpion that stings because that is its nature, the scorpion that will fell the mighty hunter."

The tall man smiled wryly. "My friend Slender Johnny is as crazy as Jack. He's convinced that the silver tears will ruin the world below, the way Mexican gold felled the might of Spain. It seems to be a slow acting poison."

"Hahaha. When the gods mean to destroy us, they give us what we desire."

"Be quiet, Johnny." The little man subsided. "The *real* significance of the tears is that they came *through*. What happens in a Buonarotti transit, my tourist friends? Come, you've read the guidebook."

"Nothing moves," said Grace. "The traveler's body and the gravegoods—I mean the survival outfit—disappear, because of local point phase conservation. At the, er, target location, base elements plentiful everywhere accrete to the information and an identical body and, er, outfit, will appear. Coming back it happens the same in reverse. The survey data is never enough, it can only show the trip is feasible, not whether all the trace elements are there. But when the test-pilot comes back—"

The deep spacers drew a concerted breath of fury.

"She meant dumb puppet," said Orlando hurriedly. "Monkey, whatever—"

"Quite so," agreed the tall man, coldly. "But the point is made. Nothing material travels, but the silver tears *are* material. They are the proof, the validation, the gateway to the empire that should have been *ours*, and that is why the government will never, never investigate. *Ships*, my young friends. If we had a sample of those tears, we would be on our way to building ships that could weave through—"

"I'm sure you're right," said Grace. "But, what do you want from us?"

"We know you have the key to the Fulcrum's prison cell."
The aliens looked at each other, dry-mouthed.

"Say you were right," said Grace, "What use is the combination of the safe, when you have no chance of making a getaway?"

"Agreed. But a madman might be persuaded. A dangerous lunatic."

The aliens looked at Jack Solo, still hanging there in the arms of the support staff. The Kuiper Belt patches on the two men's coveralls glowed a little in the dim light. Jack was in never-never land, whispering to the bot, who crouched at his feet in her soiled pink nightie. L'Hibou held up a hand.

"Oh, no. Jack is ours. We look after our own."

"Draco Fujima has *lettres de cachet*," whispered Slender Johnny, and shivered.

"*Lettres de cachet?*" repeated Grace. "What's that?"

"The term is mine," said L'Hibou. "Suffice to say the bastard has contacts, and each of us here has offended him in some way. He's threatening to have us sent down the gravity well."

"We know he'll do it," said Dirty Harry grimly. "Unless we can buy him off."

"Only it has to be the big prize," put in Jean, tossing her head. "Nothing less."

Death by violence had no horror for the deep spacers. To be forcibly returned to Earth, not rich but in helpless poverty, to die in lingering humiliation in some public hospital, that was something like the ultimate damnation.

"We'd want our bikes back," said Grace. "And some useful numbers."

"Deal with the playpen soldier for us, and we will look after you."

The aliens retired to their cabin, very shaken, and put their heads together, figuratively and also literally, for greater security. They had to do this deal, but they'd rather have dealt with Jack Solo, who seemed to them like only a minor bad guy . . . in spite of the knife work. A softbot sex-toy (and this was why the bots had been only a passing phase on earth) inevitably reflects the owner's secret identity. You could *sympathize* with crazy Jack, dragging his whiney Anni-mah around like a flag of failure and defeat. Draco's image of himself as a hefty sugarbabe just turned their stomachs. But it wasn't Anni-mah who could deal with sys-op.

"We have no choice," said Grace, at last. "We know what we have to do. You have to risk your life, playing footsie with the toy soldier."

Orlando nodded. "And you have to fuck Eddie's brains out."

Days passed. "Lakey" was just *gone*. There would be no investigation: The rule is, there are no rules. An obscure spacer with a poor stake, whose chances had seemed remote, made a successful trip. Another prospector sold some good numbers to the developers, several long term "travelers" were posted officially missing. The remote control conversion work that was adapting the Kuiper Belt station for mass rapid transit—turning the place into a latter-day Ellis Island—continued apace. The plans included moving the goose that laid the golden eggs to an even more secure and isolated location, but no one in deep space knew about that, not even Eddie. The Slingshot was on course and growing closer, but still weeks away from dock.

One slow, chill standard noon there was a chime at Eddie's door, and in came Grace. She sat in one of his chanterelle-shaped designer chairs, and they chatted. Jack Solo was behaving as though nothing had happened, but where would he strike next?

Eddie knew it was tactless but he could tell she was hurting, so in the end he asked her straight. "Where's Orlando?"

Grace shrugged. "I don't really care. I know who he's with, though."

"Uh, who? I mean, if you want to talk about it."

"Draco Fujima," confessed Grace, miserably.

Eddie blinked. He accessed sys-op in his head and reviewed the passenger list: which was easy enough to do, and it sometimes gave him guilty entertainment. He couldn't get moving pictures, but he could find out who was in the wrong cabin, so to speak, at any time. Alas, Grace was perfectly correct. Orlando was with Draco.

"Oh, Grace, I'm sorry."

"Don't be. We're an open couple. It's just . . . I just wish it wasn't Draco."

"Is there anything I can do?"

The alien wiped her leaky eyes. "Eddie, you're so *nice*." She smiled bravely. "Well, since you mention it . . . Eddie Supercargo, could we go to your place?"

"You mean right now?"

"If you're allowed, yeah. Right now."

Eddie knew he was "being used." He didn't mind at all. What are friends for?

The aliens played safe for a few days, but Draco was watching them, and he knew when the operation was coming off. He caught one of the pair alone on the observation deck and made his move. Nominally, he and Jack Solo were partners, but fuck that. Jack was a liability, and Draco deserved some luck.

"It's like this," he explained, when he'd marched the alien to his First Class cabin, and knocked him around a little. "I hurt you, you talk. If I don't like what you say, I hurt you more. Clear?"

"You c-can't do this," protested Orlando, "I'm n-not a spacer. I'm a European citizen. If . . . if anything happens to me, you won't get away with it!"

"Hey, don't count on it. We're a long way from home, and I'm a damaged vet. I get temporary insanity. No one's going to take me to court."

In a combat situation, Draco Fujima still had all his noughts and ones.

To save time, he showed the tourist the sidearm he had smuggled on board, and that made Orlando (or maybe it was Grace—he didn't know and he didn't care) very cooperative. In the country of the blind, the one-eyed man is king. This applies best if the one eye is the dark little hole at the end of a gun.

"Now I'll tell you what's going on," said Draco. "You and your partner have implants. You were supposed to ditch them, but you took a chance because you didn't plan on making a Buonarotti transit, and you didn't want to lose your technology. You thought no one would check up, and you were right. Deep spacers have too much brain damage for an implant to function by the time they end up here. When Eddie let you through the Wall that day, you took another chance and mugged his frequency. You have the code in your head that will get us to the cell and activate the harvesting robotics. Now tell me how it works."

Sara Komensky stood at Draco's shoulder, and smiled.

"All right, all right," gasped Orlando. "The government couldn't trust control of what goes on in there to the AIs. They wouldn't dare have it handled by remote commands that could be intercepted by terrorists or rogue states. Eddie is the key. He makes out he's just here for decoration, but he's the walking key."

"And you have him, the noughts and ones of Eddie, copied into your head."

"H-how did you—?"

"Let's just say, computer systems can be hacked in many different ways, and you two have loose mouths. Now I'm guessing your partner is with Eddie right now, and you are waiting for a signal from her to tell you to go ahead."

"No! I'm not going to tell you!"

"They have to be running a diversion, Draco," said Sara. "We don't know what it is they're doing with Eddie, but they're doing something. We didn't get that part."

"It'd better be a good trick," said Draco. "For your sake, asshole."

Orlando reckoned he'd held out long enough to be plausible. "All right, okay, I'll give you the code. I can download, just show me your input device."

Draco grinned. "Oh, no. Sorry, asshole, that's not going to work. The military took my chip when they discharged me. *You're* going to take me in there."

Grace and Orlando knew what Eddie had done, to deal with the horrible burden he had been given. Maybe it was grotesque in human terms, but they were experts on the twisted paths of pleasure, and they could understand. Eddie could not bear what happened to the thing in the cell, he couldn't bear the part he had to play, as the code trigger to that brutal harvest. So he'd rerouted the experience. He had plugged all the helpless guilt and powerless compassion he felt into his libido. When the alien got milked, poor softhearted Eddie got his rocks off.

It wasn't Eddie who designed the human brain, and he wasn't the first to make use of the paradoxical contiguity between sexual excitement and other violent arousal. Actually, she felt bad about deceiving him. But she knew Eddie would forgive her. The rule is, there are no rules. But now what? Where's the way to Eddie's heart? It *couldn't* be that his only pleasure came from watching a flayed, truncated human being get fisted by a robot. Eddie wasn't really like that.

"Won't you sit down?" said Eddie, shyly.

She looked around. The cabin was lovely, even with its boring decor. Everything was exquisite, and delicate, and—*oooh, this figures*—distinctly sexless. Orlando and Grace genuinely did empathy rather well; it was part of the augmentation they had chosen when they got themselves fixed up as near-twins. Her glance lit on a convoluted shelf unit that held, protected from the vagaries of gravity failure, a very pretty tea set, in shades of dark blue and rust.

"Could we have tea?"

Eddie's cheeks turned pink, his eyes shone. "Oh, yes! Indian, or China, or I have some Earl Grey, or would you prefer a fruit, or herbal blend?"

"I would *love* to try your Earl Grey," she told him, very warmly. "Oh, wow, Eddie. Can that be—is that early Wedgwood?"

Nice Eddie's lips parted in unfeigned delight. His breathing quickened.

Draco walked Orlando to the Wall, Sara Komensky on point, a few paces behind. Draco had his hands in the hip pockets of his padded jumper. Every so often he nudged Orlando in the small of his back with the muzzle of the plastic shooter.

"Go ahead, Orlando. You're the one with the key."

"I can't, I daren't," protested Orlando, feebly resistant. "The AIs will spot us, this was never meant to happen this way." The muzzle of the firearm dug into his back. "Okay! Okay!" He summoned virtual Eddie to the forefront of his mind. The Wall opened and Orlando and Draco and the bot passed through. They reached the antechamber with the window looking into the cell next door.

Draco stared hungrily at the horror squirming there.

"Now what?"

"That's milking behavior," said Orlando. Beads of sweat were trickling down his face, and he didn't dare to wipe them. He had no need to pretend to be terrified. "Th-that means G-Grace . . . it means she's on target. Now we have to go next door. The alien is milked once a day. Eddie is . . . his brainstate is linked to the robotics. The copy of Eddie I have on my implant is a reduced instruction set, enough to get us in here, but now I have to patch through to the real Eddie, and he has to be in kind of a particular state of mind. Do you remember, Draco, when you were a little boy? The military recruited you because you had the wiring they could use, and they tweaked your brain further out of neurotypic, so you would feel killing all those people as just a big rush of pleasure, pleasure, pleasure?"

"Shut the *fuck* up," said Draco. "Take me to the robotics chamber."

So Orlando, with the real Eddie riding him like a tremulous, quivering psychic parasite, took Draco around to the robotics chamber. The wiry red hairs were standing up on the back of his neck, because if things didn't go totally, completely according to plan in the next few minutes, he— Orlando—was going to be at the very sharp end of Draco's distorted pleasure principle. And he didn't want to die. But for some reason he looked behind him, over Draco's shoulder. His terrified glance met the bot's big blue eyes, and though he knew "she" was only a virtual sextoy, she seemed to be saying, *hang tough, we can do this.*

"What's with this anti-information, Draco?" he asked, for something to say. "That's a weird concept. Isn't all information the same?"

"The thing from NGC 1999 came through from another universe," said Draco. "Where it comes from, everything is flipped the other way round, in terms of what is real and what is virtual. That's what the fucking science says."

"You mean, the exotic material they harvest here started out, over there, *non*-material, like, pure code without a medium, or unreal ideas?"

"What the fuck. That's just shit-for-brains talk. It's treasure now."

The robotics chamber opened up, and the wall sealed up again behind them. Orlando felt waves of sweet, moist, sensual happiness flooding through him, making a very weird cocktail with the fear of imminent death. It crossed his mind to wonder what Grace was actually *doing* to make Supercargo feel so nice. But they were an open couple, and he didn't mind.

"There you go," he said, standing back. "The sealed unit will drop into that chute. You have to grab it on the way, like pulling luggage off a band."

There wasn't much to see. The waldo-hands hands stuff was happening inside a smooth box on the wall. The harvested material would be delivered, in a small, heavily shielded container, onto a belt beneath this unit, and the belt would convey it to a chute and thence, through a totally automated process, to its secret destination on Earth. On a CCTV screen, you could see the inside of the cell in monochrome. The milking process had begun. Draco put the gun away in his jumper pocket. He opened a compartment on his gadget belt and took out a coil of fine jagged wire.

"What are you doing? Hey, you don't *open* it. Just grab the box!"

The playpen soldier ignored Orlando. He continued to fit together a power saw designed for the toughest cover operations in the world. Just because he'd done his real work by remote didn't mean he hadn't had access to training materials.

"Oh shit, Draco, are you insane!"

"Asshole. Did you think I was going to be satisfied with a few drops of the juice, when I can get the motherlode? That's a gateway. I'm going in."

The saw whined like a mosquito. The thing in the cell shuddered in monochrome, and around it every dimension of real space-time fell apart.

"Sara!" cried Orlando, in panic, his legs giving way with terror. He slipped down against the wall, crying, "Stop him! Oh God, he'll kill us!"

The bot just smiled her sugar smile: and vanished.

If anyone on Earth was watching this, there was nothing they could do. Earth was far away. Draco Fujima sliced his way through the ceramic fiber, and the machinery took no notice. Eddie Supercargo was touching bliss; that was all the machines needed to know . . . Sara Komensky flew through the code that knit the Panhandle's computer systems together and materialized in Jack Solo's cabin. The pilot was sleeping, because somebody in the saloon had dosed his liquor to make sure he was out of commission on this fateful afternoon. Anni-mah crouched on the cold, hard floor in a corner, wearing the *soiled nightie* outfit that Jack liked best. She was dozing like her master, whimpering fitfully in her sleep. "*Jack didn't do it, poor Jack, oh, hit me harder big boy, yes, yes—*"

"Hey," said Sara. "Hey, Tinkerbelle, wake up."

Anni opened her bleary eyes and cringed automatically from the blow she was programmed to crave, with a pleasureless itch.

"Huh?"

"Look, I ain't got much time babe. I don't even know why I'm fucking doing this, but you look to me like you could do with a change and so, if there is anything autonomous going on in there, *come on*. Take my hand."

The bot looked at Jack and then at the dataglove that held the fx generator where her code was stored, permanently turned on. She looked at Sara.

"Jack is very fucked up," she whispered. "He can't help it."

"That's his problem. Will you take my hand, or what?"

Anni reached out her scrawny, skinny virtual hand and flowed into the warrior girl; and they flew back, through the systems, to where Sara's generator was.

Draco had cut through the wall and encountered a massive resistance from the forcefield, but it wasn't deterring him. He was crawling, pushing on his hands and knees, toward that pain-wracked, agonized, hundred-pound lump of meat. The air of the cell shook wildly, virtual lightnings played. "Draco, no!" howled Orlando, splayed against the wall in the robotics chamber, one arm shielding his face. "Don't do it! Don't touch it!" In the four dimensions of the material plane nothing was happening; he had air to breathe, he had gravity. But he was being torn apart, hauled with Draco toward some weird event horizon, somehow contained in that little cell.

"The gateway to Eldorado," croaked Draco Fujima.

There was a crack like a huge electrical discharge, a

blinding flash. For a fleeting, imaginary instant, Orlando thought he *saw* the world ripped open, and two figures that were not human, that had never been human, walking away from him . . . into another world, into the opposite place.

He would never know what that vision had meant.

In the real world he blacked out and regained consciousness in the robotics cell. He couldn't move. He just lay there, barely breathing, until Eddie and Grace arrived.

"Oh my God," gasped Eddie. "Oh, you madcaps, what have you done?"

But there was no damage, apart from a hole in the wall that was going to need some explaining. No one had touched the container that Draco should have stolen; and the lump of agonized meat was where it should be. Perhaps a little *bigger* than before, but no one ever tried to get Orlando to explain why.

Eddie Supercargo forgave Orlando and Grace instantly. He was proud of them for their lawless behavior, and he'd never taken tea with such pleasure in his life. He hit on the brilliant solution that the penetration of the chamber had been a planned but secret security exercise. The AIs were easily convinced to go along with this. Few organizations like to admit they've been successfully hacked, and the International Government was no exception to this rule. If they ever suspected the truth, they didn't let on. The harvesting of exotic material continued without interuption. Draco Fujima was just gone . . . vanished. Which was more or less the fate the government had planned for him, so there would be no repercussions there. No one even wondered what had happened to Draco's bot or to Jack Solo's Annimah, who, it turned out, had terminally ceased to function on that same afternoon. The bots were contraband, and the government couldn't be responsible for strange collateral damage, aboard a station where Buonarotti transits regularly played hell with local point phase.

Jack was inconsolable, but perhaps he was better off that way.

Orlando and Grace got their bikes back, and some useful numbers, which they sold through sys-op for a reasonable return on their investment. They spent most of the rest of their stay in their cabin, watching movies, setting themselves mountain race targets and trying to keep from bouncing off the walls. They didn't visit the saloon much, and they never went near the transit lounge. Shortly before they left on the Slingshot, they made a last excursion to the observation deck.

And there are the stars of Orion. Red Betelgeuse, brilliant blue Rigel, Bellatrix and Saiph; Mintaka, Alnilam and Alniak in the hunter's belt. At this exposure the jewel in the sword was not prominent, and it took a practiced eye to make out V380 Orionis . . . and the reflection nebula where you could find the birth-material called a Bok Globule, "a jet black cloud resembling a T lying on its side," that allegedly held stars so young they were barely the age of homo sapiens.

"We won't be that much further away from them," said Orlando.

They heard limping steps behind them, and L'Hibou joined them at the guard rail. "Not in entire nakedness," he said. "But trailing clouds of glory do we come. If stars are born, my young friends, do they have a life before birth, and after death?"

"I'm sorry it didn't work out," said Orlando. "I suppose you won't get your light ships. But I didn't know he would do that."

Grace shook her head. "I can't figure it," she said. "Light years, gravity equations, time and probability, non-location science . . . I can't think on that scale. I turn it into fantasies, the moment I start."

"All of science can do no more. And here in deep space,

we just live out the same soap operas as you in the world below."

"Maybe it's for the best," suggested Orlando, "Maybe it's better if the gate stays closed, and the empires are contained on separate planets, in the old style."

"Tuh. It won't last. The lightships will come— Hm." The visor that hid L'Hibou's ruined eyes was fixed on the view; but they knew he was working up to one of those confessions that can only be made on the brink of a departure.

"When your partner gets killed," he remarked at last, "you're supposed to do something. Lana and I were together for a long time. In some ways I didn't like her much, but she was still my partner. Solo wasn't the murderer, not in my opinion. It was Draco who told Jack you were meeting Lana in the maintenance bay that night and that she was going to get you your bikes back. Draco knew that would make poor Jack crazy—Jack hated those damned bikes. And I knew Draco would try to go through the gate if he got the chance. I wanted the murderer to suffer. Well, that's all."

The Deep Spacer turned, and limped back into the drab corridors.

Orlando and Grace spared a shudder for the fate of Draco Fujima. But if the rule is that there are no rules, then Drac had nothing to complain about.

"One day," said Orlando, "We'll make the transition nobody can avoid."

"Yeah. And then maybe we'll walk where the stars are born."

And who can tell?

THE METEOR PARTY

By James Lovegrove

Bill yanked open the front door.

"Hope you've brought some decent fucking wine. Trev and Jennifer came with Liebfraumilch. Can you bloody believe it? Liebfraumilch! I thought they were taking the piss."

"But instead they were just giving it," I said.

Bill guffawed.

"Will this do?" Caroline held up our own offering, and Bill's face relaxed into an expression of almost beatific relief.

"Veuve Clicquot. You god and goddess. I could kiss you. In fact, I will."

He enveloped Caroline in a hug—petite her, huge him, engulfing. Then my turn: he planted a big wet smacker on my cheek.

"You big homo," I said, crunching my face up and scrubbing at the slobbered-on spot.

"You wish," Bill leered, and ushered us in.

Deirdra, an Irish cyclone, whirled toward us in the kitchen. "Caroline! Jon! I'm going to murder that bloody husband of mine."

Bill rolled his eyes at me.

"Why, what's he done?" Caroline asked.

"What *hasn't* he done's the problem more like. I sent him down to Sainsbury's this evening to buy some veggieburgers for you because he'd forgotten to, and I told him not to get the TVP ones you hate, and so what did he get? Only the damn TVP ones. The man's an arse, and I'm so terribly sorry, and when this evening's over you get second stab with the carving knife."

From the shopping bag I was carrying, rabbit out of hat, I produced the correct brand of veggieburgers. "Ta-daa."

Deirdra clasped her hands together. "Saints be praised," she said in her best Sister O'Leary voice, adding, "But the useless focker still has to die."

"You just try it, you Erse bint," Bill growled, shouldering past us, unwiring the champagne cork as he went.

"Sure and that's the last time you call me *that* again," Deirdra fired back.

"Erse bint."

"Great beardy gobshite."

It seemed like banter. The trouble with those two was, you could never tell for sure.

Trev and Jennifer, purveyors of bad wine, were out on the patio, enjoying the sunset. Trev I got on well with; Jennifer I had always found hard to take. I didn't dislike her, and she had never been anything other than civil toward me. I just got the impression that at home, behind closed doors, she made Trev's life a misery—an impression reinforced by hints Trev dropped now and then. I was under wifely orders, however, to be nice to her tonight, and not simply because it was the polite and proper thing to do. Jennifer had recently suffered a miscarriage. A terrible thing to happen to anyone, but all the worse for her and Trev because they had been trying for children for four years, and this was the nearest they had come to success.

"Going to be a clear night," Trev said. "The weathergirl said so. Perfect conditions for it."

"Tenner on it pissing down by nine p.m.," I replied.

"You ever see a meteor shower before?"

"Not that I recall."

"Me either. Don't know why. I mean, this lot comes round every year, doesn't it? Maybe the time and the weather's just not been right before."

"I did see that comet that passed by a couple of years back. Wasn't all that impressive, though. Just sort of a murky pale spot in the sky."

"I hope it *doesn't* rain," said Jennifer. Brave face, wounded eyes.

"Ah, it won't," Trev said. "Jon's just a born pessimist."

"Not born, thank you. I worked very hard at becoming one." Jennifer turned to Caroline. "And how are the kids?"

I had to hand it to her; she'd had the guts to broach the subject of children herself, so that the rest of us wouldn't have to pussyfoot around it all evening.

"They're well," Caroline replied.

"And giving the babysitter hell, I hope," I chimed in. "Making sure she earns every penny of her extortionate rate."

Bill arrived with the opened champagne and distributed it. Then he asked if any of us knew how to get a barbecue going. Trev and I both volunteered the benefit of our expertise, and Caroline said, "Men and fires. What is it about men and fires?"

"It's a Y-chromosome thing, dear," I told her. "You wouldn't understand."

It took the pair of us, Trev and I, the best part of quarter of an hour, and half a pack of firelighters, to get the charcoal alight. It took another ten minutes of assiduous blowing to nurture a decent glowing heat. Then Bill, resplendent in a spatter-proof comedy "naked man" apron, began laying slabs of marinaded meat on the grill. The sizzle and smell were gorgeous.

"I trust you've not caught veggie off the missus, Jon."

"Not going to happen," I said, reveling in the smoke. "Not in a million years."

The final couple of guests arrived: Steve and Elaine. I'd

known them both since college. Elaine I'd gone out with for
a while. Steve had been the dweeb in our year but had since
blossomed into a successful computer entrepreneur. Still a
dweeb, but a dweeb with a Mercedes S-class and a holiday
home on the Cap d'Antibes.

Elaine's kiss on the cheek evoked a tantalizing combination of nostalgia and might-have-been. It made me twenty
again and got me wondering, not for the first time, how
things would have turned out if I hadn't been so callous and
cavalier as to dump her just six months into our relationship.
In Elaine's beautiful gray eyes I always saw, or thought I
saw, recrimination and a flint-spark of hope. I still felt that
there was a chance for us. Which was a bad way to be when
both of us were married to other people.

"I finished your new book the other day, Jon," she said. "I
liked it."

"You and none of the critics."

"Oh, what do *they* know?"

"They know how to dismiss two years' work in two hundred words."

"And the next novel's due to be delivered when? Should
be soon, shouldn't it?"

"It's on its way," I said, with a cheery grin.

On its way into the crapper. I had, just that week, aban-
doned my latest opus a hundred and fifty pages in. It was
rubbish. I knew that, and my agent, having read the unfin-
ished manuscript, agreed, although his evaluation of its bad-
ness was somewhat more delicate. "I just don't 'get' it, Jon,"
was what he said. "Your stuff usually works for me right
from the start, but this time . . ."

This time, I had created something that simply didn't *live*,
and the shame of failure throbbed hard inside me.

"What's it about?" Elaine asked.

Caroline came to my rescue. "Jon doesn't talk about his
books while he's writing them. It jinxes them if he does."

"Ah."

A quick crackle of rivalry between them. Caroline

demonstrating how much better she knew me than Elaine. Elaine, with a lowering of her eyes, gracefully conceding.

Not bad for the old male ego, that. Two women getting into a territory-marking contest over you.

Deirdra circulated with some more booze. The dusk deepened, with a few fuchsia clouds loitering innocently on the horizon. No portent of rain. Not even a likelihood of the sky being overcast. The clear night we had been promised.

The meat was charring nicely, and Bill announced an ETD—Estimated Time of Dining—of five minutes from now. Deirdra laid out a huge bowl of salad, some corn on the cob, coleslaw, potato salad, cherry tomatoes, French bread . . . The garden table groaned.

We lavished more booze on ourselves. Everyone lived more or less within walking distance of Deirdra and Bill's, so no need for drink-driver self-restraint. Only Jennifer refused to have her glass refilled, but then she was famously incapable of letting go and enjoying herself.

Finally, food. We heaped plates and then, in various chairs across the dampening lawn, unheaped them. Bill, Trev and I discussed the all-too-likely prospect of a war. The West had got it in for yet another "rogue state," and the politicians were busy banging the tom-toms.

"It's a fucking business decision," Bill said. "Always is. The stock market's slumped, and the best thing to give the economy a boost is to pick on some hapless little nowhere nation and bomb it to buggery."

"Also, the president's in trouble," Trev said. "Congress is gunning for him on account of those dodgy share deals he did a while back. Anything that deflects attention from that."

"You can't criticize your leader while there's a war on," I said, nodding.

"What really pisses me off is the way our leaders go along with it," said Bill. "Every time. Whatever the American government does, ours does. Just on principle I'd like the prime minister to turn round one time and say, 'Actually, no, I think that's a terrible idea, Mr President, sod off.'"

"He's a spineless tosser, isn't he. Did you vote for him, Trev?"

"I voted for his party, not for him. What about you?"

"I voted for the local MP. For what he said he could do for the area, not for his politics."

"And you believe he'll really do what he says he will?"

"Oh, no. But you've got to have faith."

"I never vote," Bill observed. "Absolute waste of time."

Night came. The early, brighter stars scintillated overhead. Deirdra produced garden flares for illumination and citronella candles to keep the mosquitoes at bay.

More booze. Bill had pointedly used up all the guests' offerings except Trev and Jennifer's, then delved into his own cellar, leaving the Liebfraumilch sitting lonely and unopened on the kitchen sideboard. He had a talent for choosing good wines and, better yet, was not miserly with them. Soon, all the stars were out, steady and brilliant, and we were as pissed as farts.

I found myself in a bower-like corner of the garden with Elaine.

"Orion," she said, pointing upward.

"Everyone can do Orion. Cassiopeia. That five-star zigzag there. See it?"

"The woman in the chair."

"Correct. And the mother of Andromeda. Who's just . . . there. To Cassiopeia's left."

"You're *so* clever."

"I know. And that's Hercules. The one that looks a bit like a stick man jitterbugging. Or a swastika. And he's with Boötes, the ploughman."

"Which one's Boötes?"

"On Hercules's right. Sort of, I don't know, shaped like a lightbulb. And listen, if you want *really* clever, I even know the name for a group of stars within a constellation."

"Go on."

"An asterism."

"Nice word."

"Isn't it? Like 'asterisk' but with, you know, an '-ism'."

"What it must be to have a brain full of this sort of information."

"Yeah. I'm special."

"Special as in 'special needs'."

"Ha ha ha."

Elaine smiled, and trained her gaze upward again. "You've always been into astronomy, haven't you."

"Not so much astronomy. I like the constellations. I like the idea that they're so random, just accidents of distribution, and yet all throughout civilization people have recognized them as distinct shapes. The Ancient Greeks, and before them the Phoenicians, and before them the Semites, and before them the Egyptians, and before them the Sumerians—they all looked up and saw the patterns and gave them names and worked them into their mythologies. Like the patterns were waiting there, just needing identification. Like somehow they were meant to be what we made of them."

"But it's just perception. Just our viewpoint down here on Earth."

"Yeah. The individual stars don't bear any relation to one another except the relation we've given them. What it comes down to is humankind's remarkable knack for finding order in chaos. For making sense of things which we know, rationally, are senseless. That's what I like."

She moved closer to me, only a matter of millimeters, nothing that you'd notice—unless you were standing right by her. I cast a guilty glance over in Caroline's direction. She was deep in conversation with Jennifer, her head down, her body inclined toward Jennifer. Compassion. Commiseration.

"We're screwed, d'you know that?" Elaine said.

I frowned at her. "What?"

"Steve and me. Financially. I shouldn't really be telling you this, but . . . It's to do with the tech bubble bursting. I'd thought our money was safe, but Steve had done some stuff he hadn't seen fit to tell me about, some shenanigans.

Backed a few of the wrong horses. Too much faith in his own profession, if you ask me. We're going to have to give up the place in Antibes."

"I thought you owned that outright."

"Nope, nope, just a mortgage job. There's some equity in it, and that'll help redress the balance. And Steve's still got the business, of course, though that's been struggling a bit lately. But I'd thought we were comfortably off, secure, and we're not. Not in the way I'd thought. Not *secure* secure. Our savings are pretty much wiped out, and we're going to have to build them up all over again from scratch."

"Ah, well," I said, "that's what you get for marrying someone who's flash with the cash. You should have gone for someone who wouldn't raise your expectations like that. An impoverished author, for instance."

No sooner were the words out of my mouth than I realized how spectacularly blundersome they were. I was too drunk, however, to do anything about it except hope that somehow, miraculously, Elaine had been stuck stone deaf in the last twelve seconds.

"Jon," she said, with aching coolness. "We made our choices. You made yours. I made mine. Nothing can change that. We are what we are now. We're as fixed in place as that lot up there." She nodded to the heavens. "We're a constellation. No, we're asterisms within the constellation. Me and Steve, you and Caroline. We're safe and solid, we're not moving from where we are, and it's hopeless to hope otherwise."

I nodded, chastened. All at once I remembered the look on her face when I broke up with her. She hadn't been upset. She had been—far worse—disappointed. As if she'd expected better of me than this.

Bill's voice boomed across the garden. "All right. It should be starting soon. Places, everyone."

He and Deirdra had spread out groundsheets in the middle of the lawn, with blankets and cushions on top. The eight of us lay on our backs, human dominoes at odd angles to one another. Caroline was next to me, her head by my stomach. My head was close to Trev's shoes and Deirdra's shoulder. A prerolled joint was passed around, with Jennifer, predictably, the sole abstainer. Each of us, in turn, sweetly fumed the sky.

"OK," said Trev, addressing the universe. "Go ahead. Impress us."

Several minutes passed. Nothing.

"Any time," said Steve. "Whenever you're ready."

Several more minutes.

"What's that?" said Jennifer. "Is that one?"

Everyone peered.

"That moving light?" said Bill.

"Yes."

"Like one of the stars has gone wandering?"

"Yes."

"Satellite."

"Oh."

Another minute. Two.

Trev started fake-snoring. We all chuckled.

"Apparently some of them are as small as a grain of sand," said Deirdra.

"I heard as small as a fist," said Caroline.

"I heard the size of Wembley Stadium," said Bill.

"Christ, I hope not," I said. "Otherwise it's goodbye human race."

Another minute.

"Anybody else here thinking of *Day of the Triffids*?"

"No, just you, Jon," Bill sighed.

"Why *Day of the Triffids*?" Jennifer asked.

"Have you read it?"

"No."

"At the beginning, there's a meteor shower and everybody goes blind."

"Oh, thanks a lot," groaned Trev. "I was looking forward to this, and now I'm not. Well done."

Caroline none too gently whacked my thigh.

"I thought *Day of the Triffids* was about monster plants," said Jennifer. "Isn't it?"

"No," I said. Mischief-making got the better of me. "The Triffids are the meteors. That's their name. Like the Leonids. And the Perseids."

"Really?"

"Yes. What happens is—"

A streak of brilliance shot across the black. There was a sharp, collective intake of breath. Then:

"Whoo!"

"Did you see that?"

"Fuck!"

"Jesus!"

"So bright!"

"Amazing!"

"That was so bloody cool!"

We were still jabbering about the meteor when the next meteor blazed overhead. A line of instant whiteness, there then gone, lingering only as a blue retinal blur.

Again, we gasped and yelped and went "Wha-hey!" and "Fuck!"

Long, eager seconds passed.

"Was that it? Tell me that wasn't it."

More time, then more.

Suddenly, two meteors in quick succession.

We all, quite spontaneously, broke into applause. It felt like a private display, a theater of the universe that had traveled to this spot, our town, this garden, to put on a show solely for us. Bill and Deirdra's trees were our proscenium, the cosmos our diorama, the meteors the actors, we the wowed audience in our lawn auditorium.

And on the meteors came, more and more of them, at intervals of two to three minutes, each performing its brief, dazzling turn, darting from east to west, scorching the ionosphere, little one-shot wonders that had, it seemed, waited all theirs lives for this moment.

It was Bill who came up with idea of throwing out our troubles to them.

"There!" he cried as the next meteor flashed by. "There goes the president and the prime minister and their fucking war."

Trev cheered. I cheered.

"And there!" Bill yelled to its successor. "There goes the wrong type of veggieburgers."

"There!" I joined in, as another meteor flared across the firmament. "There goes men with beards who kiss other men."

"There!" said Bill. "There goes repressed closet cases."

"There!" said Deirdra. "There goes eejit husbands."

"There!" said Bill. "There goes wives who don't appreciate how lucky they are."

"Lucky my arse," Deirdra muttered, but not without affection.

It was a long wait till the next meteor, and everyone wondered who was going to pipe up this time.

It was Elaine.

"There!" she said to the sharp scar of brightness. "There goes bad investments."

I felt Steve nearby writhe with discomfort. But then he said, softly: "Yes. There they go."

For a while we were silent. I had no idea who else had been aware of Steve and Elaine's financial woes. Anyone who hadn't been certainly was now.

Another meteor came and went.

"There," said Caroline, quietly. "There goes regret. And feelings of compromise."

That one was for me. I groped for her hand across the blanket. I found it and clasped it, and at first the pressure wasn't returned, but then, blessedly, it was.

Patient, we lay.

Another meteor came.

"There," I said. "There goes books that don't work out."

I expected everyone to murmur in surprise at my confession, but no one did, and it came to me that what I'd felt was so important, a dark stillborn weight within me, wasn't so important after all. Failures happened. There would be other books.

The moments to the next meteor simmered.

It came. Went.

No one spoke for a while. There was one person present who hadn't yet taken a grievance and hooked it to a shooting star and watched it soar into invisibility. We hoped, and didn't hope, that she would say something.

Finally, she did.

"There," said Jennifer, in a frail, small voice.

That was all.

Just: "There."

WRITTEN IN THE STARS

By Ian McDonald

Two gobbets of undigested yesterday were in Banbek
Shaunt's mind as he stepped out of Ordinatio Apartments on
to the rain-wet street. One was the announcement by his
daughter, Persene, over dinner potatoes, that she wasn't
going to marry Le. Bellis Prunty because she didn't like
him. They had nothing to talk about. They had nothing in
common.

"Nonsense nonsense nonsense," Merionedd Shaunt had
said, bustling around with oven gloves and intimidatingly
hot plates and steaming dishes to give no room to dissent.
"You say that now, but in a few years time, you'll see how
right you are for each other. The stars are never wrong. Ask
your father. He should know. Anyway, it's all been arranged
since the moment you were born. It's all paid for."

But Persene had upped and stormed and the plate of
mashy champ had gone upended, all over the floor. Banbek
Shaunt had sighed.

*A junior family member will have a temperamental turn
involving ceramics. Unlucky root vegetable: potato.*

Two gobbets: one behind, one before. Today the report
would go to Anjers Ree. The report would say that no immediate solution had been found to the distribution problem,

that underfunding in the 'scope-runner network meant keeping them on long after their best and that complaints of vital morning 'scopes not being delivered until midday would continue for the foreseeable future. Anjers Ree would not accept this. He would demand answers by the end of the week. Banbek Shaunt had read it so in his own 'scope, popped promptly into the in-dock of the house *pneumatique*, no aged 'scope-runners on creaking bicycles there.

A superior will have reason to be dissatisfied with your work. Expect pressure increasing until Saturn leaves your trine house on Friday.

And now it was raining. And his head was full of pre-ordained worries. And his umbrella was threatening to blow inside out, so he kept it down, a shield, a battering ram against the morning. And that was how, though his feet knew the quickstep on to the beltway from a thousand mornings, this morning they missed it, stumbled, slipped on the ridged metal and sent Banbek Shaunt reeling, umbrella flying, into the Tall Dark Stranger.

"Oof!" cried the TDS (as every one of Glasthry's twelve districts nicknamed its local Tall Dark Stranger), going down in a flap of coattails and tall hat. "Watch yourself now."

"Sorry sorry sorry." Banbek Shaunt went groping among the bustling heels and trouser cuffs for his umbrella and case, the official red briefcase (hard to come by), embossed with the twelve-pointed wheel of the Astrocratic Service. He helped the disheveled TDS to his feet, wiped off the more obvious dirt from his sable attire, tried to mop up water stains with his handkerchief, then froze, hankie half-way to the Tall Dark Stranger's lapel. "I'm sorry," Banbek Shaunt muttered, snatching up his stuff and hurrying away. "Shouldn't have happened. Shouldn't have happened."

As the beltway chuffed him down to the *radiolare* halt, Banbek Shaunt's sense of gnawing horror rose and rose like bile after a family feast. It wasn't supposed to happen. It wasn't supposed to happen. It was not written. There had been no word in the daily 'scope that Banbek Shaunt would meet a Tall Dark Stranger, let alone knock him flying. And *talk* to him . . . But it had happened, and to an EO1 in the Distributions and Deliveries department of the Astrocratic Service. He should report himself.

By the time he reached the tram stop, the horror had begun to subside. Those two nuggets of discomfort, behind and before him, remained. Banbek Shaunt clutched his red case to him. Inside, the report that would fail. The thudding donkey-engine that powered both the beltways redoubled the gloom with its pall of catching coal-smoke and mist of steam. He glanced up at the Horologica Horoscopyx, the vast astrological clock on its spire at the centre of Glasthry that was visible from any point of the city's twelve Houses. At night arc-lamps lit the slow turning discs of stars and moons and planets and constellations, telling out the times and fates of Glasthry's twelve million souls. Despite the delay, the tram was more than its scheduled four minutes late. He would miss the connection on to the eight thirty-four midlevel *circulare*. He sneaked a glimpse at his 'scope. The cheap yellow paper blotched and curled in the rain. Nothing in it about being late. Perhaps he was back on track. Peering down the track, he could see the tram pulling away from Fifth and Aries. The cable tautened in the groove, a tight singing as the car winched itself up the incline. Banbek Shaunt puffed out his cheeks and looked up at the low vile clouds tearing on the Gothic gingerbread finials of the Horologica Horoscopyx and bleeding sour rain. It was in this moment of small but pleasing melancholy that he noticed the impatient woman. She stood by the ticket barrier, fretting, breathing noisily through her teeth, shifting from foot to foot, looking this that way upway down, every part of her declaring impatience.

"Excuse me, Cap." He read the Sign on her forehead. "By any chance are you looking for someone? A Tall Dark Stranger, perhaps?"

"I am indeed, I'm supposed to meet him."

"Ah, well, he might be a little delayed. There was an unforeseen incident."

"Unforeseen, Aer.?" She in turn had read his House, tattooed on his wrinkled brow.

"A small incident, but you will find him on the beltway on the corner of 12th Aries and 10th. Really. Trust me."

The woman's face brightened.

"Ah, now I understand. *A Ram helps with a small delay.* Thank you so much, Aer., thank you, thank you." And she pushed through the turnstile past the ticket clerk and trotted down the wet iron stairs to the rattling beltway as the tram heaved itself into 10th and Aries station.

There had been a delay on the Median Line *circulare*, all trains running ten minutes late because of signaling the problem. The Dragon seventy-five pulled in ten minutes late and Banbek Shaunt stepped out in a cloud of steam at 5th and Libra only six minutes down. Most of the Libra House's midlevels were given over to the headquarters of the Astrocratic Service. Libra was an auspicious sign for bureaucracy. Trine Tower was a monstrous pile of glass and dark iron, wearing its gubbins on its skin in a web of staircases and transport shafts and elevator racks and *pneumatique* tubes, thus folding its true nature in on itself and concealing by appearing. Banbek Shaunt could well believe those tales of strange and troglodytic tribes who infested the vast heating ducts, generations of pale, inbred things with no language and pale, bulbous eyes, who fed on pastries and bourbons stolen from unattended tea trolleys. It was the fortune of an E01 to have an outside office, a privilege upon which Banbek Shaunt reflected as the slanting elevator ratcheted him up the dripping girder work through vents of steam from the boilers and blue flashes from the poorly maintained power web. It was a view that never ceased to thrill and inspire, even on the dismalest of days. There was a particular moment he saved himself for every day, as the elevator crossed the coal conveyor delivering pulverized fuel to the twentieth level steam engine, the vista would open and fully half of Glasthry would be spread before him. He would close his eyes just after the level eighteen halt and wait for the rattle of the coal belt so he could open his eyes and have it new and glorious every day.

And lo. Glasthry curved before him, a gently sloping disc of apartment blocks and malls and manufactories and radial streets, rising geometrically to the central spine where the highest offices of the Ruling Houses and the Houses Ascendant and Descendant oversaw the well-being of their twelve million charges and, on the highest high, the Horologica Horoscopyx, humanity's connection with the cosmic, ordaining forces of the stars. The three *circulares*: Least, Median and High-Line, inscribed three hoops of steam and smoke around the curved ziggurat of Great Glasthry. He looked down over the sweeping red pantiles of the Libra Sector; across the dark slash of the *radiolare*, the ornately carved wooden steeples of West Scorpio, gaudy with painted allegorical figures. Merionedd was a Scorpio, his Zodiacal Antipode, a Declination as opposed to his Ascendant, which is why she came to live in East Aries slate-roofed tenement blocks. Banbek Shaunt often regretted that. He would have liked to live in bright, aggressive Scorpio, among color and ornament. A few seconds early or late . . . A futile fantasy. One was born when one was born. The stars were fixed, their energies and trajectories measured and counted. On earth as it is in the heavens . . .

On the greatest mornings Banbek Shaunt glimpsed a zeppelin descending through the cloudbase towards the docking needles up on the High, but, as the morning 'scope in the breast pocket of his long civil servant's jacket had ordained, this was not to be a great morning. A sole shaft of light burned through the gloom, picking out a mote of red far to the east in Sagittarius. Against all prediction and horoscopy, Banbek Shaunt felt a tear of pride start in his right eye, his emotional eye. The Astrocratic State was the finest system yet devised for human happiness, order and self-fulfilment and he was proud, damned proud to be part of it. Even if his bicycle boys were not getting the prime agencies of that state, the daily 'scopes, to their recipients until their futures were history.

It was not good with Anjers Ree, but it had been worse before and would be worse again, and it was over soon enough. In his superiors smoked-glass office, cocooned in black girders up on level forty, Banbek Shaunt could not rid himself of the impression that both men were merely playing out what was written in their horoscopes.

The morning worked through its ordained frustrations. The network that distributed twelve million horoscopes twice daily was huge and complex and not liable to simple managerial solutions. Not exactly. The solution was simple. Pay your delivery boys more, and they will not defect to shops and printers and railway companies and potato collectives. Banbek Shaunt looked out at the cloud clearing over the wet rooftops of the city he served and the glossy green fringe of the potato fields beyond and wondered if even in the Age of Uncertainty there had been a bureaucracy that ever had the money to govern effectively. He took his luncheon at his desk, and as he folded his napkin, the *pneumatique* chimed and delivered his afternoon 'scope to its slot. He unrolled it from its cylinder, perused it cursorily— Banbek Shaunt generally only paid attention to workday 'scopes if he had a presentation or a meeting scheduled— and returned once more to the unfathoming lines and nets and nodes that the 'scope-runner delivery network drew glowingly on his televisor. At Monkey-fifteen he pushed the magnifier away from him with a blink and a sigh, for he had heard the jingle of the tea lady's trolley.

"No custard creams again, I suppose?"

"Why, not at all, Aer. Shaunt," said Refreshment Operative Minette Haddo, who every day so far that week had offered a fresh excuse for why something was missing from the standard menu, including theft by ventilation-system troglodytes. "Today we have everything." She presented her plate of custard creams. Marveling, Banbek Shaunt took one. He held it up to his desk lamp. He sniffed it. He examined its waffled surface and thin, soft yellow cream sandwich interior, he traced his fingers over the legend:

Astrocratic Service Refreshment Model 4f. When the tea bell had jingled into inaudibility, he hurried out his afternoon 'scope. As he had glimpsed: *Pluto in your Squared House indicates a possible sweetmeat or cheesy snack frustration.* He bit into the biscuit. The layers were crisp and buttery, the filling soft with a hint of almond and none of the hint of the chemical factory that marred the model 4e.

Banbek Shaunt looked again at his horoscope, then the clock, then the teleprompter on his comptator, then his bakelite phone box.

When Saturn transits the Hour of the Goat, expect troubling news from a spouse or loved one. It was already Monkey-sixty.

He keyed the section secretary Scor. Shondra Mute.

"Any calls for me?"

She had a habit of drawing prominent vowels out into long hoots, flutes and hisses.

"Noooo. Are you expecting any?"

"Just thought my wife might have called. Nothing from her, anyone in my family?"

"Juuuust checking. Nooo. Definitely nothing Aer. Shaunt."

"Okay thank you, very good."

He sat at his desk tapping his fingers together in tense perplexity until the clock on the wall read twenty to Rooster, when he could bear it no longer and keyed a call through Shondra Mute to his home.

"Hello my light."

A slight pause, then: "Hello sweetiebuns."

"Is, um, everything all right?"

Again, the pause. "Er, yes. Everything is fine. I'm just putting the potatoes on."

Banbek Shaunt grimaced. Some day he wished he might find the courage to tell his wife how philosophically sick he was of potatoes, their floury mealy softness, the unpleasant bloating they pressed against his waistband, the watery, rooty smell they invaded into his house so that it no longer seemed his, that he was a lodger amongst a family of tubers.

"And Persene, how is she? Is everything all right with her?"

"Yes yes yes. Everything is all right with everyone. Talpan is back from school and sitting at the table doing his trigonometry homework and we are all fine and happy and everything is exactly as it should be. How are you? Is everything all right with you?"

"Yes, fine, great, grand. Just . . . wondering. Goodbye, thank you. Love you, See you soon."

He listened to the purr of the dead line some seconds before hanging up, then again unrolled his 'scope.

The subsequent entry of Saturn into the baleful family influence of Pluto spells discords arguments and recriminations before Dog. Beware! You will be able to do nothing right.

He glanced down the scroll, printed in the traditional black-letter Gothic of the Astrocratic Service.

A father will provide solace and paternal comfort. He is expecting a reward of fruit or wine. Do not disappoint, or relationships will be muddied until the end of the week.

His father had died five years ago, on the twelfth floor on the South Capricorn Sector Hospital, a sunny place with views of green parks, high above the coal smog, where they put the people who had smoked so much they had to breathe through tubes up their noses. A devout crossword solver, he had been going for a personal best on the *Daily Planets'* cryptic when his son had called into see him. With much frustrated finger clicking and pointing, he had asked Banbek Shaunt to nip out to get the dictionary from the day room to check the exact spelling of *usufruct*, and when he nipped back, his father had gone in a huge welter of poisoned phlegm.

Forecast House had been informed. The funeral had been surprisingly well attended but marred by heavy rain, causing the funeral tram to slip as it winched itself up the incline to the Union With the Stars crematorium.

Panicked now, Banbek Shaunt checked his 'scope. The issue number and embossed seal were authentic. The name, the sign, the address, the National Astrological Identity Number were all correct. Time of Birth. The time of birth. He maneuvred the sheet of paper behind his screen magnifier, brought the tiny script up into sharp magnification. Aries 28th, Rat thirteen and fifty five seconds. His time of birth was Aries 28th, Rat fourteen and twenty five seconds.

This horoscope was thirty seconds early.

He was reading another person's horoscope.

Banbek Shaunt's heart quivered in horror. He wanted to stuff the lying thing back into its cylinder, *pneumatique* it anywhere, to anyone else. He felt dirty, prying, a voyeur. He found his hands had half-acted out his emotions; they held the rolled sheet in a palsied grip. Civil service training saw him through. A mistake had been made. A ghastly, embarrassing, unthinkable mistake, and to an EO1. If any should see, if any should ever hear . . . But it could be solved simply, root and branch. Firm decisive action was the order.

A quick decision will have far-reaching consequences. The treacherous horoscope was the last thing Banbek Shaunt swept from his desk as he hurried out with coat and bag and hat and umbrella.

The building's official title was the Outer Capricorn Comptator and Print Center, but no one in the Astrocratic Service, and many beyond, ever knew the cavernous glass-roofed construction where the daily horoscopes were calculated and printed as anything other than Clackett Hall. Delays on the Median Line kept Banbek Shaunt fretting in a crowded carriage of chattering schoolgirls while *radiolare* tramcars slid overhead on cast iron viaducts.

"No calls for the rest of the day, thank you," he had told Shondra Mute as he swept through the reception area, leaving his secretary open mouthed and round eyed underneath her bakelite dictafon headset. Banbek Shaunt taking an early afternoon? Whatever could it say in his 'scope for today?

Change at South Central Sagittarius and then use the Astrocratic Service pass to get onto the narrow-gauge slotway, a rickety little wooden car wedged between daisychains of coal cars for the power plant and the print cylinders that took away the monstrous rolls of horoscopes to the despatch warehouses. Clackett Hall rose out of volcanoes of damply steaming coal, wreathed in smoky vapors from the turbine plants, dwarfing even those mountains of nutty slack though half of its volume was underground.

"Ah, Aer. Shaunt, fine day fine day fine day."

Comptroller General Finzi Steen came striding through the rubber-baffled double doors into the reception lobby, all woodpaneling and cracked green leather. A brief wave of sound followed him, a shard of the eternal din of the Comptators, rotor arms spinning across electrical connections, calculating, sending data up the swags of quivering rubber cables to the rows upon row of tractor-feed printers, hammering away day and night, telling the future for Glasthry. On his appointment as a JCO in the Astrocratical Service, Banbek Shaunt had been given a brief tour of the Comptation and Print Center. His ears had rung for the better part of a day afterward. The nightmares had lingered all week. The smell of black-soot printer's ink and vaporized gear oil brought him back. Banbek Shaunt thanked his guiding stars for his little glass cubby on the twenty-second floor.

"Not often we see one of you Trine Tower people down here," Finzi Steen said. He was a small, stout, vigorous man, a coronary about to happen. "Here. Health and Safety." He handed Banbek Shaunt a padded headset and a stick-microphone, plugged him into a unit at his waist with a coiled lead. "Don't be wandering off too far, you'll unplug yourself. Press to talk, see? Easy."

He marched back across the lobby and swung the double doors wide. Banbek Shaunt scurried after him. Even with the hearing protectors the din as they stepped into the comptator hall was an assault. They stood on a wrought iron walkway halfway up an immense chamber. Fifty meters above Banbek Shaunt's bald patch steel lotus-flower cantilevers held aloft a tremendous glass vault. Fifty meters below, Comptator Engineers in diarrhea-colored boiler suits moved purposefully along oily gangways. Between them rose the thundering metal cylinders of the comptators, quivering gently on their thick felt vibration pads. Banbek Shaunt could feel the tremble through his worn leather soles. The spaces between were filled with hurtling belts of punched input tapes and arcing output cables. "Bloody magnificent, what? Usual caveat," Finzi Steen crackled into his microphone as he led Banbek Shaunt along the walkway within centimeters of a whizzing punchtape. "Head down, hands in. You don't know the meaning of the words paper cut until you've copped one from one of those. Now, Aer. Shaunt, how can we help Trine Tower?"

Finzi Steen's frown deepened as Banbek Shaunt explained, the microphone quivering on its spring mounts as he bellowed to be heard over the roar of astrological calculation. The frown became thunder as he studied the damning paper.

"A thundering disgrace, Aer. Shaunt. This is most serious. Serious indeed." He studied the header and authentication seal. "Let's see. Aries is printer bank 8. At the moment that's being fed by the number twenty-seven server—like to keep 'em moving around, the armatures can get grooved if you keep them rotating in the same stator ring. Like as not, that's your problem; time register's slipping. Who's up there today?" He flipped out a clipboard. "Ah! Gwillard!" He stabbed the sheet with a stubby forefinger, then uncoiled a second lead from his intercom belt and thrust the copper plug into one of a hundred bakelite sockets on a board marked with faded numbered labels in neat fountain pen. "Gwillard!"

Down on the engine floor a brown figure straightened up from where it was intent upon a bank of dials, scanned the high walkway, hand over eyes to shade out the sharp sunlight falling through the glass roof.

"Stop dicking about down there and get up and check the timer ring on twenty seven! She's slipping."

The figure gave an emphatic thumbs up, ran to a hooped-in ladder on the side of the adjacent comptator and began to climb.

"There you are," Finzi Steen said. "You'll have no more problems with that, I think."

"Just one more little thing. Could we run an identity check on this 'scope?"

Finzi Steen frowned again, then realization spread like dawn through an early smog. He tapped his thick finger to the side of his nose and unplugged Engineer Gwillard.

"Ah, get you Aer.! Keep it among ourselves, eh? No reason for anyone else to find out our little professional slip. Come into my parlor and I'll have a wee look at what I can do."

Finzi Steen's parlor was a wood and glass eyrie on the main partition between the comptator hall and the print room. Double-baffled doors shut out the din of Clackett Hall with such efficacy that Banbek Shaunt feared momentarily he had gone deaf. Finzi Steen tore off his headset and flung it across the desk to his pert receptionist and fell to scratching at his ears and scalp "Good to have that bloody thing off. I'll swear it gives me industrial dermatitis. Come on through." He beckoned Banbek Shaunt into his office, wide, low roofed, glassed on either side, wainscoted at the ends. The floor was a maze of slumped piles of yellowing papers—horoscopes, Banbek Shaunt discovered as he navigated towards Finzi Steen's desk, some decades old.

"Got the T.O.B. there?" Finzi Steen clicked his fingers as he pulled the magnifier down over the televisor screen. From the rasping whine Banbek Shaunt reckoned his image disc needed replacing. He slid the false horoscope across the desk; Finzi Steen stabbed in the Time of Birth. "Come on, come on . . ."

Banbek Shaunt occupied himself by looking at the print hall. Unlike the clear geometry of the comptator hall, the print room was jammed floor to glass ceiling with level upon level of machinery. The best way to understand it,

Banbek Shaunt concluded, was to follow the cables in from where they emerged from the comptator and then take one strand up to the junction box and see how it split into separate flexes, each connected to a teletyper ranked in a long row. He followed the rolls of paper from the overhead feed spindles inch down through the printheads to emerge dark, impure, stained with the official black letter Gothic that was so needlessly difficult to read. He tried to imagine the hammers, beating out predestinations, day and night, one for every man woman and child in great Glasthry. 'Prentices fed the beasts, rushing up and down the narrow aisles with long-spouted cans of ink. Their canvas aprons were stained and splotched; they never stopped moving. Banbek Shaunt reached out a hand to touch the triple glazing. He could feel a distinct vibration.

"Aha!" Finzi Steen smacked a hand off his leather-topped desk. "Here's your man." He swiveled the televisor for Banbek Shaunt to read. He rapped his knuckles emphatically off the magnifier.

Aer. Glevin Thrawn. Andromeda Spires. Central Aries, on the innermost circle: a high liver. Banbek Shaunt had been that high, ten years ago when he had been been promoted to EO1. He had taken Merionedd, and they had strolled arm in arm along tree-y Cuspic Way, him pointing out over the parapets the sights and shapes of Glasthry, most proudly, his own window-glinty corner of Trine Tower far below. He had thought he might rise higher then. He had dreams of rising all the way to the Ruling House itself.

His psychic twin's address was in Ranves, part of the Universuum district. A man of learning, perhaps even a Praecox. Banbek Shaunt could not remember if the rules prescribing celibacy for Academicals were still in force. That troubling news would not have been from a spouse then but from a loved one, a sister, he imagined, a mother, perhaps a clandestine lover. It would certainly have come out of the blue, unforeseen, unprepared for. Had there been a refreshment disappointment, even an early, enigmatic encounter with whatever Tall Dark Strangers haunted the closes and arching bridges of the High City? Suddenly he had to see this man whose troubled, niggling day he had stolen. He felt he owed a double apology, for the prying intimacy of knowing what had gone on in the privacy of his rooms, his cloister, and for the deception into which his misdelivered 'scope had lulled him.

"I'll just take a note of that if you don't mind." Banbek Shaunt rummaged for pencil and pad.

"Here." Finzi Steen thrust a sheet fresh from the printer at him. Banbek Shaunt folded the paper very small and slipped it into his inside pocket.

"Of course, we weren't that surprised, really," Finzi Steen said as he fitted Banbek Shaunt with his ear protectors and showed him back through the baffled doors into the assault of Clackett Hall. He jabbed another printout at Banbek Steen. *A bureaucratic mix-up may call for unexpected guests and a grease-job.*

"Whose is this?"

The scope had no Naino, no T.O.B. nothing to identify its subject's House or sign.

"Nobody's and everybody's," Finzi Steen bellowed into his microphone. He turned to include the ranked comptators in an expansive arm gesture. "We always keep one of the units back to monitor the output from the others, a sort of horoscope for the horoscope makers. It usually gets what the others miss, though it can be a bit gnomical. Mind your head there."

He ducked under a shrieking band of razor-edged punched tape.

That thought of a metahoroscope that foresaw the futures of all the others much occupied Banbek Shaunt's thoughts as the funicular climbed the almost vertical rack and pinion between the close-pressing towers of Andromeda Spires. Futures within futures, the smaller within the greater, the fallible within the infallible. The houses turned in their course, and those course in turn were graved upon a greater wheel. And that wheel within another; up there, within the vast clockwork of the Horologica Horoscopyx, was there a program that churned out the ultimate horoscope, the one that contained all others? It is a true prediction that that prediction is false? His head swam from infinite regress and late afternoon hypoglycemia.

He should have been at home, reinforcing his blood sugar with starchy potato mash. The thought made him quail. It needed no horoscope to predict what he would find there: Persene sullen, her silence erupting in bright flares of temper; Merionedd ponderous and uxorious and wishing everything would just be right and happy, or at least in time for *The Pullein Family* on the audiophone. Few people needed their futures shown to them; they existed straightly enough in the day to day.

These were no thoughts for an EO1 of the Astrocratic Service. Resolved gripped Banbek Shaunt as the funicular slid into its docking slot. He would give this Glevin Thrawn the 'scope he should have had, and all this headachey nonsense would end. There was one world, one future for every man and woman.

Evening quickly welled up among the towers and spires of this Universuum District, and Banbek Shaunt was reduced to peering painfully at the carved waystones. Andromeda Spires seemed to be a cluster of domed towers at the center of a district of high-gabled, turreted housing, but it took him half an hour tracking, backtracking and retracking through Ranves' precipitous—and treacherous under the heavy evening dew—cobbled alleys to reach them. As he rang the bell, a clockwork grating sound disturbed him, and he looked up to the dome above him split in half and open into a slit. When he looked back, the door was open, and a square, squat man in Academical dress smiled out at him.

"Can I help you?" His voice was bell-like and musical.

"Aer. Glevin Thrawn?"

"Indeed so, sir. And you are?"

"Banbek Shaunt, Executive Officer First Class, Astrocratic Service. May I come in?"

Any member of Astrocratic Service of Grade 6 or higher had a statutory right of entry, but Banbek Shaunt thought it only manners not to press it.

"Oh?" said Glevin Thrawn, who in every way was nothing like Banbek Shaunt had expected. "Well of course. You'd better come in then."

The hall held a tall coatstand well infested with umbrellas. Banbek Shaunt noticed a large number of unopened *pneumatique* cylinders lying by the in-slot. He was shown into a large, curved room beyond. Banbek Shaunt saw big leather-topped desks, the blotters edged with worn gold leaf, green-shaded lamps, a compt terminal shedding a blue suffusion through its magnifier panel. The flat wall held a row of bookcases, floor to ceiling. Many of the volumes were bound in official Universuum Press metal covers. The curved wall was papered in a mosaic of maps. Star maps. Maps of the heavens, sparkles of white on deepest indigo.

"Ah, it seems you may already have an inkling of what I'm calling about," Banbek Shaunt said, thinking, *I would love a room like this, a room I would withdraw to and live in for days or weeks without disturbance.*

"Sorry? What? No, not remotely. You must forgive me Aer. Shaunt, I've just had a most unpleasant argument with my sister, over a will. Distasteful things, wills. Now, what was this about?"

"That distasteful argument. On behalf of the Astrocratic Service, I apologize for your . . . discomfiture. Your horoscope . . ."

"Oh I never look at those."

Banbek Shaunt now knew what a boggle, a thing he had only read of in children's books, felt like.

"I beg your pardon, Aer.?"

"I presume that's what this is about; you're here to recommend me for some therapy or reeducation or something."

"Aer., the Astrocratic Service no longer advocates a policy of reeducation. Positive Mentoring is the current term, and that's only for the most recalcitrant deniers. After all, it's true whether you believe it or not. No, concerning your afternoon 'scope. You, er, got the wrong one. But I'm amazed, Aer. Surely these?"

He nodded to the star-speckled band of mapping. Glevin Thrawn rolled his eyes up in exasperation

"Oh, for heavens' sake. Look, it's not just astrologers use star charts. I am an astronomer. Lo. Ger. No. Mer. Hear that difference?"

"Astronomer, Aer.? Never heard of it, I'm afraid. What do they do then?"

"They look at stars, Aer. Shaunt. Real stars in the real sky. They chart their positions and movements and changes and births and deaths. Yes, deaths, Aer. Because stars die. In fact, that's my field, novae and supernovae. Do you know what those are, Aer. Shaunt?"

"Can't say as I do, Aer."

Glevin Thrawn banged his meaty hands on his desk. The low-level lighting lent him a perhaps intentional sinister aspect. Banbek Shaunt's fingers closed on the false 'scope in his pocket; this man's 'scope, this man's true future and destiny, whether he willed it or not, whether he took it out of its tube piled in the hall or left it unopened. In one of those tubes was the prediction of how this meeting would turn out for Banbek Shaunt. He wished very much to see that paper. He felt naked and unready without it. Banbek Shaunt wished very much that the Astrocratic Service had not rescinded its Reeducation Section and disbanded its silver-uniformed and black-booted Star Guard. But Glevin Thrawn was looking up and smiling now, an expression that put Banbek Shaunt at slightly less dis-ease.

"Well, come on up then and learn something."

The evening had transmuted into full night, and Banbek Shaunt followed a weaving beam of torchlight up the shallow spiral staircase that wound around the interior of the tower. Observatory, he told himself. That was the word. A place for watching stars. Why anyone would design a special building for such a pointless and tedious exercise was a bafflement to him. The stars were fixed, their courses set and unchanging, their interactions calculated and predicted by Mathematical Astrologers. Watching them was of the same interest as observing the workings of a pocket watch.

Banbek Shaunt shivered as an eddy of cold High Aries night air swirled through the slot in the open roof. It passed down into his pith as Glevin Thrawn threw the light switch and soft sodium glow lit the interior of the observatory. The ribbed wooden dome arched over Banbek Shaunt, split by a thin dark rectangle from perimeter to apex. He imagined it was filled with stars. He marveled at the gear trains and motors that opened the dome, but his awe was reserved for the device at the center of the circular room, the telescope itself, an intricate cylinder of brass and glass suspended in a complex cradle of gimbals, pivots and pistons, aimed as squarely at the sky as a cannon. Or a vast message cylinder, Banbek Shaunt thought. He followed the intention of the great optical machine down through the lens mountings and focusing rings and gear wheels to the cracked leather chair on its mount beneath the eyepiece. All the brightness of the sky beamed on to that point, into that eye. All that truth and order. Such intricacy and expense for such a waste of energies.

"We don't use it that much these days," Glevin Thrawn said, seeing the tack of Banbek Shaunt's eye. He patted a comptator televisor on a large desk. "And we work like this."

The darkness was so sudden and complete Banbek Shaunt felt as if a meniscus on the night had been pierced and it had all poured drowning and soft through the slit in the sky to fill up the dome. He felt high up in an alien place, filled with strange night thoughts. Then his eyes adjusted and he saw Glevin Thrawn's face lit blue by the glow of the televisor screen.

"Come and see," he said. Banbek Shaunt heard a soft

whirring and sensed motion against the nape of his civil-service haircut. He could not see it, but he knew the telescope, together with its narrow window on the window, were turning to new targets. "Look," Glevin Thrawn urged. "Our sign, our House world. Ares." Banbek Shaunt leaned toward the red circle on the screen. This was no speck in the heavens, no guiding light. Here was a world of dark and shade, of ice at its poles, of discernable pattern and climate.

"I can watch the seasons move across her face," Glevin Thrawn said, softly, gently for such a wide, ursine man. "I have seen the ice recede in summer and advance in winter, I have watched great storms of red dust blanket her for weeks at a time, and you try to tell me the face of the heavens is the face of perfectly maintained clock?"

"Her," Banbek Shaunt said, "You called it 'her.'"

"This is the bringer of war? The epitome of the masculine virtues? Tel me what you see? Spare, serene beauty. Once you've seen her true face, you will always think of Ares as a woman. Look at this."

The red world swam out of focus; the screen blanked as Banbek Shaunt heard the telescope hunt for a new target. He gave an involuntary gasp as a new world swam into view: a storm world, banded by stripes of curdled, streaming cloud. But most startling, most dazzling, this world was hooped by bright rings. Banbek Shaunt felt himself exhale in wonder.

"Kronos, the Bringer of Old Age? Father Time? A gross slander. Here. There is a universe-full."

Then Banbek Shaunt was swept away into a whirl of planets and stars, spiral galaxies and glowing nebulae in the shapes of horse's heads and dumbbells. He was taken into the constellations that spelled his destiny and that of every citizen of Glasthry. The lines that drew those rams and archers and water carriers and scorpions were unhooked, and their constituents assumed their proper dimensions and fled to their proper places as worlds and stars and galaxy clusters so distant the light that shone on Banbek Shaunt's face had left it ten million years before. Then Glevin Thrawn pulled him back from the stars, and as the telescope returned to its night's observation, he turned up the lights and took down the bound metal books and opened them to show pages of gall-ink calculations acid-etched into the paper and precise steel-nib orbits and triangulations and parallax calculations and illuminated minutes of astronomers—at least Banbek Shaunt assumed they must be astronomers—in archaic costumes turning spyglasses to the heavens or pointing from crenellated towers at brightly colored comets.

"Wonderful wonderful yes wonderful," said Banbek Shaunt, head reeling, made mindful by the cold seeping through his office suit that it was well past potato dinner hour. "Marvelous indeed, the symmetry, the mechanisms and forces that tie it all together, and them to us."

Glevin Thrawn slammed the open tome shut with such vehemence that Banbek Shaunt's finger, had it been tracing down the spidery text, would have been burst like a mouse hit by a coal shovel.

"After all I've shown you, and you still don't understand."

Potato dinner seemed hot and floury and welcoming next to the Praecox's hot passion in this high cold tower.

"Aer. Thrawn, I merely called with you as representative of the Astrocratic Service to clear up a bureaucratic bungle; not to be converted to some . . . religious faith. And perhaps I should remind you that I am a representative of the Astrocratic Service, of managerial rank."

Glevin Thrawn clutched his hands in remorse. He spread them: Banbek Shaunt knew a difficult explanation would follow.

"Sorry, sorry. I apologize if I became evangelical. It's just . . . When you study the sky, as I have, you see that it is so much more than we take it for; it is so much more than just a blind clock, dragging us along behind its hands. It's a changing, evolving, organic thing; it's unpredictable. That's what's written in those records; not just constellations changing over the centuries, but stars being born, stars actually dying. That's what we're studying at the moment, a distant star in Aries—our own constellation indeed. We have reason to believe that it is about to go nova—flare up, burn out in a spectacular burst of light, and then ebb into darkness and die. There are signs—a change in the spectrum of light, the luminosity curve. It will be soon. Part of our sign, gone. With all due respect to your station, Aer. Shaunt, but if anything is written in the stars, it is that nothing is fixed and known. Everything is change. Would you like to see it? The telescope is just lining up . . ."

"No, no thank you, I must be going, my wife . . ." Banbek Shaunt had always hated men who used their wives as an excuse, but at that moment there was nothing he wanted more than to be away from this strange, intense, heretical man with his jagged ideas and dangerous philosophy. Again, his hand closed on the paper in his deep official pocket. "Your 'scope?" he slid it across the table, an invitation to straighten up and live right. Glevin Thrawn waved it away.

As Banbek Shaunt slipped away down through the twining alleys of Ranves, he imagined he could feel the lens of the great telescope cold against his back, looking into him, taking apart the lines and contours of his life. The funicular took him down through the tiered towers of Glasthry, between ranks of lighted windows, under lamp-lit overpasses. The hour was late indeed, of a tardiness that other men's wives would have stormed and rowed at. Merionedd would smile and hang his coat up and rack his umbrella and take his plate from the warming oven and set his dinner, dried and crusty at the edges, on the table before him. She would chitter away at him about her day and her friends and the small things they had hoped for and achieved and never once would she ask him where he had been or what he had done or whom he had done it with, and he found himself wishing, wishing so hard it hurt, that for once, once, she would row, accuse, overturn his plate on to the floor like Persene raging against her ordained marriage. Show some anger. Show some passion. Show some of the compatability that had marked them out, her for him, him for her, from the moment their birth charts were computed.

A lone, condensation-wet balloon and flower seller stubbornly held her pitch outside Fifth and Aries Station. Banbek Shaunt bought a prim nosegay and a helium filled inflatable lobster for his wife. Every time he passed the stand the thought crossed him that balloons and flowers were not the most felicitous combination. But it was written in her stars.

Merionedd tied the lobster to the towel handle of her oven.

On Sun Days Banbek and Merionedd Shaunt went to the park. This weekly outing had been ordained years before and had become such a habit that they no longer checked in their 'scopes to make sure it was still prescribed for them. Truth was, they did not know what they would do if it were not. Banbek traditionally wore his candy-striped blazer, Merionedd her buckled shoes and floral hat in her lucky color of purple. She would wear a small spray of her lucky lilacs. They would walk in the sun down one graveled walk, sit by the podium where an ensemble would play short pieces and then walk up another graveled path to buy ice creams, lick them flat and ride home on the tram. No cloud or rain ever made them frown. The Pisco-Arien Pleasure Gardens were domed over by a glass canopy, lit and warmed by gas cressets suspended like little sunbursts from the arches. The air was always blazer-and-blouse-sleeve comfortable.

Today a small ensemble of kithara, zymoxyl, boo, harmonic cannon and cloud-chamber bowls was performing a set of relaxation pieces: *Womb Variations, Order in the Milky Way* and the old favorite *Water Over Round Rocks*. Banbek Shaunt sat back on the slatted bench and squinted up at the rain beyond the coal-gas sun glow. It always seemed to be raining now, he thought. It must be hard to be an observer, a what had he called it? an astro*nomer*, watching for a dying star.

He felt Merionedd move against him, smelled her Sun Day perfume. It was familiar and painful to him. In a free world, would he have married her? It was not perfect, but then he no longer believed in perfect marriages. They worked. Then was his marriage with Merionedd the most painless he was capable of? Would every other possibility, even a woman he married for love, have turned out worse?

If he looked through the moving figures of the musicians at their variations, Banbek Shaunt could see Persene and her affianced Bellis strolling by the bright flowers. Tapping his feet to the tuneful melodies, he watched how they walked, how they moved, how they noticed or did not notice things the other pointed out. He observed the closenesses and the distances, their unspoken language. He did not see the looks and reassurances, he did not see the gentle touchings by which he would steer Merionedd to a particular flower or a bird singing, he did not see them fall into unconscious rhythm with each other where two separate people can see the same thing and think the same thought. He watched with a swelling sense of horror that, if his daughter were to marry that man, it would be a mistake that would ruin her life.

"Dearest," he said idly, a word or two thrown in between the tinkling and chiming of the music. "Do you really think it would be so very awful if Persene were not to marry Bellis?"

He felt Merionedd's soft ampleness stiffen against him.

"What are you saying? Not marry Bellis? How can she not? It has all been worked out, right down to the Auspicious Day. I have been buying her little bits of green since she was eight for her bottom drawer. No no no no no. It is done and dusted."

"Yes yes, my dear, but you know how Persene has been giving us no rest about how they have nothing in common and no chat, and I was just wondering if perhaps in this marriage thing, Persene knows her own mind better."

Merionedd let out a loud pffffing sighing disapproving sound that Banbek Shaunt had heard only rarely in his life but nonetheless had learned to fear.

"Know her own mind best? And you a civil servant and everything? None of us knows best. That's everything we stand on as a society. We're all full of emotions and illusions and fears and dreads and contradictions, and none of us knows our own minds, and we are hopelessly confused, but the stars are true. They never vary in their courses; it's all mapped out there, if only we are clever enough to read it."

"Yes yes. It's just, well, look at her. Look at our daughter. Does she look full of nuptial joy to you? Does she look happy?"

"What's happy got to do with any of this? I'm beginning to worry about you, Banbek Shaunt. I think you've been working too hard. You've been out all hours; the other night you weren't back until twenty past Rat. Not happy? How couldn't she be happy? Next you'll be saying that we aren't happy, that maybe we aren't perfect for each other. It's just natural adjustment. She'll fall in love in time. That's why they give it so long, so it'll have time to develop. Now enough of that sort of talk and buy me my ice cream."

For horoscopical reasons the woman on her ice-cream tricycle only had mint this Sun Day. Banbek Shaunt licked his cone and listened to the band as his daughter and her affianced wandered far and separate along the graveled paths. When he looked up, he could see the rain running in wide ribbons down the soot-grimed glass.

With every ratchet up the inclined cogway, Banbek Shaunt felt the guilt click down another notch. The half-empty funicular car slid up between the light-studded walls of the great Upper Mid-Aries apartmentariums; through the glass roof he could see the spires of the great universuum gleam wetly in the light reflected from the floodlit faces of the Horologica Horoscopyx. At some point—his sense of order guessed it must halfway up the track—the guilt toppled over into thrill, which increased with every turn of the wormscrew toward the observatories of Ranves.

It was thrill to be climbing into an unfamiliar landscape on a Sun Day evening, with work the next morning.

It was a greater thrill yet to have slipped out, unannounced, without a word as to where he might be going, leaving wife, son and daughter round-mouthed at the dinner table.

It was the greatest thrill to have no idea what he was headed into, what might happen. Banbek Shaunt was riding blind. There was no afternoon 'scope folded in his raincoat pocket. He had not looked at his horoscope. Not one reassuring glance. He had no idea where he was going.

The afternoon's rain clouds ripped on the crenellations and Gothic spires of the great astrological clock, as a rising wind from out off the land that he could feel gusting through the tramcar's poor window seals tore them apart and whipped them away. The tramcar swiveled on its gimbals as its ascent approached the vertical, and Banbek Shaunt's eyes moistened in awe as he climbed out of the close-pressing High Arien tower blocks and he saw his city spread beneath him like a many-jeweled kilt. He read the warp and the weft of its boulevards and railways, the soft glowing masses of the summer parks, the knots of shopping malls and residential districts, the dark nodes of office arcologies shut for the national day off. He saw the yellowish streaks from the smokestacks and the glowing soft aurora of the cooling towers and the deep red lava fire of the coking plants and felt a sudden, harsh joy. He had seen into this city of light, seen to the bottom, seen to the glass beneath and the endless light below that shone up through it, of which all Glasthry's machinations and technocracy were stolen glimmers.

The way of it in Arien Ranves of a Sun Day was for the academics to go walking upon the Preview, hands folded in their heavy cuffs. They nodded and smiled and wished a pleasant evening and a peaceful night to Banbek Shaunt as he slipped up through the weaving alleys and echoing closes and steep staircases, still treacherous with recent rain. The stars came out above him, and for the first time they were not eyes. He was on his own. Alone.

Glevin Thrawn came grumpily to his door and his mood was not relieved when he saw that the person who hand banged him out of his work was an EO1 of the Astrocratic Service. The same EO1 that had visited himself upon him the day before with his insistent trivialities.

"Look, I told you, I don't go for the horoscopical nonsense—no offence." He indicated the pile of message cylinders in his hallway. "If you can find it you're more than welcome to it."

"Oh, no no no," hastened Banbek Shaunt. He struggled for the form of words. "There is a question I have to ask you. No no no, nothing official." He had seen Glevin Thrawn's suspicious look. "Just this, you're an astronomer, a watcher of the skies. Just answer this and I'll trouble you no more. Are you happy to be an astronomer, and if you weren't an astronomer, what would you want to be?"

Banbek Shaunt saw Glevin Thrawn wonder if his was the kind of answer that could politely keep a visitor on a cool night waiting on the doorstep on a high-level observatory. He also saw him decide that this was the kind of visitor who would remain on that doorstep on a cold, clear night until his question was answered. The astronomer bowed and invited Banbek Shaunt over the threshold.

"That's a question with many parts," he said as he led his visitor up the spiral to the dome above. "We like questions with many parts because they are the kind the universe asks of us, and they are the most likely to have interesting answers."

The dome was in customary observational darkness, save for the light of the monitor screen. It illuminated an open logbook; neat copperplate figures recorded an exponentially increasing set of numbers. Glevin Thrawn tapped commands into the comptator. Banbek Shaunt felt the great telescope stir and move behind him.

"You'll excuse me; thing are at a crucial juncture. Light curves are maximizing; we could see full nova within hours. Now, the first part of your question. Do I seem to you a man who is happy in his calling?"

"I see a man who is busy, who has great things to occupy him, who has a role and a purpose but I don't know if that man is happy with that or whether he has accepted it because it is his allotted station in life."

Glevin Thrawn adjusted verniers, and a star swam into view on the comptator magnifier, one star among thousands, unexceptional but for the cross-hairs focused on it.

"Are there any of us can say that there is not an alternative life where we might be happier?"

The stars were flat, the night was flat, with no sense of depth or distance in the darkness. They might have been flecks of luminous paint on a plywood dome.

"That is my second question, Aer."

Glevin Thrawn stood upright from his minute manipulations.

"You are a very forward man."

"I apologize, Aer. Thrawn, but in this chamber are questions that go to the very bottom of what I believe and know."

"There was a time when I though I might like to grow things. Plants. Crops. Yes, I think I might like to have been a potato farmer, or raise some more exotic form of root veg. Where I grew up in Low Aries, I had a garden, a small plot up on the roof and I would grow, not flowers, not trees, but vegetables. There is a subtle beauty in a firm, young carrot; the infolding of a lettuce is strangely similar to that of our entire universe. From there I could see all the way to the fields, and I thought how good it would to be out there among them, not here in this dirty, cramped city. But then I was taken away to the Astronomer's Hall, and for ten years I did not look out, but up, into the sky. I did not look at the land once. I studied for ten years in a strange and obscure discipline that no one values any more because it was written in my stars. Thirty seconds earlier, it would have been you up at that eyepiece, focusing on the rings of Kronos. Thirty seconds later, and I would be the civil servant in the bowels of the astrological machine. Why is it so important that we love it, when it is all we can do? In neither of them am I a farmer of root vegetables."

"If you were free, if there were no Astrocracy, if the stars are just what you say they are; would you leave this?"

Glevin Thrawn made to speak, but the words, the thought, the moment, the intent were all blown away by the sudden blinding white light that filled the dome. Every book, every chart, every item on the desk, every cog and vernier and crank and gurney wheel on the brass telescope, every embossing on every book, every wrinkle on every chart, every pin on the desk, every scratch or dimple of casting flaw on every god and vernier and crank and gurney, was lit up by the light from the screen. Banbek Shaunt threw up his hands before his eyes but it was too late. Purple unseeingness danced before his eyes. He was sure he could smell his eyebrows singeing or perhaps, from the sound of Glevin Thrawn's yell and lunge and the creak of multipoise springs, the magnifier was blistering in the intense light. He could see the blood vessels in his shut eyelids. Then there was a pop of electricity being abruptly disconnected; he heard the televisor disc spin down to rest. Clankings, furious mutterings, creakings, the astronomer was doing something with the telescope. How could he see? Banbek Shaunt blinked his way through the pulsing purple, feeling a course along the edge of the desk. Of course. Glevin Thrawn was a man well accustomed to working blind. Too much light is the same as too much dark. Banbek Shaunt blinked his eyes open. It was painful and disorienting, but he though that through the swirl he could see Glevin Thrawn standing pointing and a light brighter than the full of the moon pouring in a silver shaft through the slot in the dome.

"Look; oh look!" Glevin Thrawn cried and Banbek Shaunt peered up into where he was pointing and there was a star, a silver star, brighter than any star of the morning, or of legend, or of any of the dreams or legends of the Houses Major and Minor. A star, hundreds of years in the past, burning itself out. A star, dying for them all.

"Come with me!" Glevin Thrawn called and led Banbek Shaunt up a rusty ladder through a stiff hatch and out on to a none-too-trustworthy gantry. Banbek Shaunt gripped the rail. He felt no cold, no vertigo, no guilt at being out and about without horoscopical authority. He felt only wonder. The Aries nova burned in the east, outshining every other star in the heavens. Beneath it, great Glasthry lay under silver. Silver roofs, silvers strips of streets and gleaming beltways, silver railways and factory chimneys and tenements and towers, falling away beneath him, tier upon tier, to the dim gray inconclusiveness of the potato fields beyond. The front of a great swell of voices reached his ears; the Academicals and learneds of Ranves, hands out of their folded cuffs, gesticulating, asking each other what was it, what could it mean? That wave of questioning breaking like a wave down through the districts and projects of all the Twelve House of Glasthry, people looking up, asking each other, that light, what is that light, leaving their sofas and their wirelesses and their reading tables and their dining tables and pouring out on to the streets to see the new star. Room by room, building by building, street by streets, district by district, the lights were going out.

Banbek Shaunt did not know how long he stood there on the balcony, one of twelve million gapers; long enough for the damp metal to chill through to his finger bones, long enough for him to imagine the light was dimming, the shadows lengthening in the streets, the stars beginning to shine through.

"Is it?" he asked fearfully.

"Dimming. Yes," the astronomer answered. "A shame. I thought it might have burned longer. But then I never imagined it so bright."

"And what will happen . . ."

"When it is gone? It will burn itself out and collapse in on itself and go to nothing. There will be a star missing from the constellation of Aries tomorrow, and forever."

A hole in Aries. The order of the universe was spoiled. A hole in their futures, here on this High Aries parapet; a hole in all Ariens' futures: a hole in the future of every soul of the

Astrocratic Society, woven together by the interactions and interrelations of the stars.

"I suppose it'll be the potatoes then," said Banbek Shaunt. Glevin Thrawn frowned, perplexed by the seeming *non sequitur*. "I mean, that's what you would have done if the Astrocratic Service hadn't made you an astronomer. Be a farmer, grow root vegetables. You're free to do that now, if you want."

"I always was free," Glevin Thrawn said, face upturned to the dimming heat of the dying star. "Just before the star blew, you asked me if I would leave all this. No. I do love what I do, Aer. Shaunt. We can come to love everything in time. So even though it was chosen for me, I have made my choice. What about you?"

"What do you mean?" Banbek Shaunt asked, but he knew what Glevin Thrawn meant, and he did not want to hear the astronomer's soft accusations of a life wasted, of an intelligent man who had sold that intelligence to a stupid system that cracked at the first challenge, who had married and raised a son and daughter and followed a career in cheerful ignorance because he had never imagined there could be an alternative. What about him? What about Banbek Shaunt? What choices had he ever made? What choices did he face now?

He knew one choice and knowing that, he understood that it had been in front of him for years and that it was only now that he could look at it and give it a name. He knew what he wanted to do.

Banbek Shaunt seized Glevin Thrawn's hand, shook it vigorously, evangelically.

"Thank you! Thank you Aer."

If his had been the type of physique and manner of life that readily ran, he would have run from the observatory. He clenched and unclenched his fists in joy. His breath steamed in the night streets, and it seemed like revelation. Yes, he would walk away from them. Yes, he would get up from that table, steamy and rooty-smelling, and tell them all he was leaving, that he was going away, going away forever, he didn't know where, he didn't know to what. No; he would never even return to that table, that crowded apartment, the morning stride along the beltway to the station, head buzzing with the ordinations for the day, the daily choice of Astrocratic Service Official refreshments. He would turn left where he should turn right, he would go up where he should go down, he would take this train rather than that train; he would head on, unpredicted and unpredictable, and the stars above him would just be gas,

Banbek Shaunt almost skipped through the graying alleys of Ranves, now emptying of Academicals and marvelers.

Then he thought of Talpan, sitting at his homework, staring at anything else, legs kicking. He thought of Persene. Who would guide her out of her liaison with Bellis? Who would reassure her in her freedom? Without him across the breakfast table she would cling all the more strongly to what certainty remained. They would go walking arm in arm through the graveled park paths every Sun Day. He saw Merionedd's face, and it stopped him, panting and agonized, on the cold street. What of her? He tried to imagine that face the morning he did not come back, the morning after he did not come back, the week after, the year after, ten years after. He thought of her hat and floral bonnet on a Sun Day afternoon. He thought of her smiling, ladling out soft potatoes. His heart ached. She deserved more, so vastly much more. He had been trapped, but she was shackled. He could help her be all the things he had seen in her on their rainy wedding day.

He loved her. The astronomer had been true: You can come to love anything in time.

Two ways faced him. A staircase led up, twining between walls of heavy black masonry, into the high places. A plaza led to a short flight of steps down to the funicular, advancing toward him through the fast-fading nova-light.

Free to choose, Banbek Shaunt.

He ran down through the streets, toward the funicular, and

as he did the clanking of the gears and winding engines called to mind the racket of Clackett Hall and its towering comptators, churning out star calculations and prophecies. He remembered Comptator General Finzi Steen showing him the horoscope of horoscopes, the metascope generated by the comptator that watched over all the others. Patterns within patterns. A star died in the heavens and the smaller gyre was disturbed, but within the greater gyre, this was written. Had been written hundreds of years before. Within the greater pattern, there was order and predictability and prediction. Banbek Shaunt smiled. A great steely weight of freedom that had been threatening to unbalance his heart was lifted. His freedom was part of a greater ordination. The nova star burned out over Glasthry, and the streets fell dark. A hole was punched in the heart of Aries, but there were potatoes still for tea.

THE ORDER OF THINGS

By Adam Roberts

The starry heavens above me and the moral law within me.

Kant

1

"You know how it can be with teenagers," said Strong-in-the-Lord.

"Teenagers," The-Unerring-Word replied, nodding.

Strong-in-the-Lord adopted a higher, more nasal voice to speak the part of his son: "But *why* Dad, what's *wrong* with nostrils? God made them—didn't God make them?" He shook his head, and resumed in his usual tone. "And so on. Just wouldn't leave it alone. I said to him, God may have made them, but that's no reason to flaunt them around. God made other holes in the body—if you see what I mean. Mouths. Ani. Urethral holes. You wouldn't go about displaying those for everybody to see."

"Which, surely, convinced him."

"But that's what I'm *saying*," said Strong-in-the-Lord. He slid a finger underneath his faceveil to scratch an itch on his lower lip. "Teenagers. They're slippery as—I don't know what. Oh, he didn't agree with me. He carried on arguing. He said *there's your eyeholes, Da, you don't think* they're *obscene?*"

"I know," said The-Unerring-Word, "you don't really believe in it, but if I were you I'd hit him. Sometimes you can't reason with kids like this. I mean, we love our kids, all that, but, hey—spoil the rod. You know?"

"*Spare* the rod, Un?"

The-Undying-Word considered. "Yeah. That. Not what I said. But whatever. The point is that you *can't reason* with *teenagers.*"

"But reason *is* the point," whined Strong-in-the-Lord, as if trying to convince himself. "Isn't it? Why deny the rational thing? God's there, in the sky, in the arrangement of the stars, in the moral soul inside. I said to him: Be logical, that's all I'm asking. Be logical. We cover ourselves for modesty, not for arbitrary reasons. If a hole produces feces, that's not nice—you can't pretend it's nice. So we cover it up, modestly. It's the same with the nostrils, unless you think," he coughed discreetly, added in a lower tone, "excuse me Un, but," and carried on, "*snot* is a pleasant thing? I don't think so. The same with mouths, unless you think somebody else's *saliva* is wholesome? Your eyes are *different*. God has plugged them already, veiled them we might say. With the eyeballs. It follows logically that we do not need to pursue modesty to the extreme of covering the eyes—they're covered already. Your mother for instance, I said to him. *Her* eyes are blue, and they're prettier than any faceveil I've ever seen in a shop. So he started whining, and I'm afraid I lost my temper. *I don't see why God would be upset if we showed our nostrils and People always used to do it* and all sorts of nonsense. I told him to shut up—I used those words. I told him people used to do many things. People used to worship pagan devils and sacrifice children, and that didn't mean they were good things to do."

"He's not arguing, not really, Stron," The-Unerring-Word

told his friend. "He's not interested in the reasonable case, the logical thing. He's just arguing to be difficult. Teenagers."

"Which is exactly what I'm saying. Exactly."

The two of them sat in silence for a while on their bench. They had finished their coffees, and each had wiped his straws with a sanctissue, and now they just sat. They were sitting out the remainder of their break.

The work was continuing day and night, and theirs was a night shift. Below them, at the foot of the hill, the machines were roaring and grinding under floodlights, cranes swinging like giant robot metronomes, diggers creeping forward on the crystalline reel-to-reel of their tracks. Out at sea the many ships sparkled with their various glinting lights, stern and aft white, port and starboard green and red, boathouse lights creamily visible against the black water in a random, messily scribbled array of dots and gleams. But lift the eye upward, and the splendor and the glory of the heavens were displayed. On this cloudless night, through this still air, all the stars could be seen: rank and rank, row and row, the perfectly regular and uniform spread of white stars. You could read their pattern in terms of verticals and horizontals, or you could let your eye detune the image a little, and it would become a diamond-shaped pattern of diagonals intersecting diagonals, on and on, patterning the whole sky. How glorious it was, how glorious.

Strong-in-the-Lord sighed a holy sigh and brushed his gloves absently against the thighs of his pants. He stood up. "Back to work, Un," he said. "Back to the great work."

Strong-in-the-Lord had decided early in his life that he wanted to be a coastal engineer. Well, to be strictly accurate about it, at first he'd wanted to be a coastal architect, but a few words with his teachers had disabused him of that ambition. The architects had dull jobs, he was told. After all, coastal re-designing hardly required architects to shape it!—or, rather, *mathematics* was the true architect. The *Divine order* was the architect. Take a crinkled, wobbly coastline on a map and

redraw it as a straight line or as a smooth arc; redraw this knob-
bly promontory as a circle. A child could do it. But the *engineers* (the teacher put awe in his voice)—oh, the engineers!
They do the *actual* work! They supervise the diggers, they
scour the land, or fill in the bays, or reclaim land from the sea.
Work with a thousand challenges and a thousand rewards! And
all the time (the teacher's voice acquiring a misty, awestruck
tone) making God's harmony and perfection prevail. "So," the
teacher had concluded, slapping his hips with both his hands
simultaneously and afterward rubbing them together. "So
which is it to be? Architect or Engineer?"

"Oh, Engineer! Engineer!" he had squealed. "I want to be
a Engineer!"

After seven more years of school, and four years of spe-
cialist study, and fifteen years of work, he had come to realize that the architects' lot was not so dull as the teacher had
said. Their work was much more than simply drawing a line
on a map. They had to consult geological surveys, to work
out the path of least engineering resistance. It was their job,
not Strong-'s, that provided a thousand challenges; turn this
messy, scuffed up stretch of coastline into one of the desig-
nated pure mathematical shapes—how to do it? Thesis: We
should erase this. Counterthesis: But it's largely granite and
will take years and billions of dollars! Solution: Very well,
redesign the map, and fill *around* the granite with broken
sandstone taken from across the sea. More cost effective!
The Elegant Solution!

Engineers, on the other hand, had much less imaginative
jobs. They did what their supervisors told them. They
blasted, dug, moved, loaded trucks, loaded barges, laid
down rubble, piled up rubble, shoved rubble aside, and just
when they had a sense of achievement, just when they'd
made a smooth and perfect vista out of the fallen mess of nature—why, then they had to move on. It was frustrating, but
Strong-in-the-Lord had learned not to let his frustration poison him. He was working for a higher goal after all. They
were all working toward a higher goal.

His brother, Courageous-in-the-Lord, had had different ideas. "I want to be an astronomer," he had told the family one Sunday when they were both still kids.

It was a rather odd thing to say. None of Ma and Da's friends were astronomers. Strong- didn't know anybody else who wanted to be an astronomer. He thought back: When they had all studied astronomy at school, the class had not ended—as almost every other class ended—with a recruitment talk about the career possibilities. And come to think of it, what would an "astronomer" actually *do*? The stars were there—everybody could see them. The State didn't need to employ special people to look at the stars. Anybody could so that. Row and row, rank and rank. Scientists had already listed every star, named each of them, looked at them with special machines to determine their spectronomy, their chemical composition, their physical composition, how many light years distant they were, their respective sizes, all those sorts of things. What else was there to do?

As a child, he had been unable to express his incomprehension at his brother's choice except in mockery. "Astronomy? That's the most stupid thing I ever heard. Isn't that the most stupid thing you ever heard, Ma? Isn't it, though, Da?"

"Now," Ma had said, "don't bait your brother."

The family was eating: a large steaming Masson-in-slaw, with luscious looking plentrails, green and shiny with butter. It was a Sunday dinner. All four sat at table in the dining room, the tallest, the most elegant room in the house. Precisely seven darkwood boards to each wall. Four curtains drawn across four windows, each in the exact middle of each wall. The faint odor of burnt sandalwood, mixing with the smells of the meal.

"Sorry, Ma," said Strong-in-the-Lord.

For a little while Strong- ate his food. Courageous- was a quieter boy than he was himself, contemplative, inward. He scored highly at school in the meditation classes and poorly in the practical work. Because Strong-'s own results were exactly the other way around, he found it hard to take his brother's mooniness seriously. Couldn't the dolt see that practical work was so much better than sitting around thinking and praying? Nobody remade the world by *meditating*.

After a while, Courageous- spoke, his voice calm but with a worrying, subversive edge to it, as if he were practicing some obscure, wicked little practical joke of his own. "It's no more stupid than wanting to be a coastal engineer," he said, his face angled down towards the plate from which he was eating.

"What?" snapped Strong-.

"The whole Coastal Engineering project is crazy."

"You can't say that!" Strong- chimed. "Ma, tell him!"

"All that effort?" Cor insisted. "It'll be hundreds of years before it's done, and why? Smoothing out the coastlines. We could only see the results if we was in space. What's the point in that?"

"—if we *were* in space, Cor—" Da corrected, holding his fork up like a wand. "The subjunctive is used for unfulfilled wish or condition."

The boys knew better than to challenge this. "If we *were* in space," Cor adjusted his sentence. "But what's the point in it?"

"That's not true," said Strong-. "About only being able to see the results in space. There'll be maps, as well. And high places, like mountains."

"But I don't see what the *point* is," Cor repeated.

"Da," said Strong-. "Ma. *Tell* him."

"We're making the world a better place," said Da. "More harmonious, neater. Maybe you can't see that from the dining room, but God can certainly see it."

"But God made the countries and the continents the way they are," said Cor in his quietly insistent voice. "How is it right to meddle with that?"

"Meddling," said Da, with a hint of severity, "as you dismissively call it, is what God put us here to do. Every person is born with an animal nature every bit as ragged and rough-at-the-edges as the coastline of a continent. But God expects us to smooth our natures down, to control and tame them, to bring them into proportionate and harmonious relation with His will. The Great Project is an expression of the same impulse. Look at the sky and what do you see? The heavens, the perfect order and regularity of the stars. Look down on earth, and do you see the same order? Alas, no. You see disorder and chaos and irregularity. Accordingly, mankind is *saving* this world, making it orderly. That's what the coastline project is about."

"I was in the library," said Cor, "and I looked up some books. They said it's the most expensive thing humanity has ever done."

"Expensive?" repeated Ma.

"In money terms, in terms of man-hours, the labor, the machinery. Do you know, fourteen hundred people died last year in industrial accidents working on coastline projects around the world?"

A distinct chill had settled on the dinner table now. "So when you go before God," Da said, his voice now very stern indeed, "will you say to Him, I'm sorry I did not perfect my soul, it was too *expensive*? Do you think He will be convinced by that argument? Do you think He cares for dollars and cents?"

"What," Ma chipped in, "would you rather we spend the money on, if not on making the world more perfect?"

Still looking at his plate, Cor said, "Sorry."

There was an awkward silence.

"I'm disappointed in you, Cor," said Ma, in a withering tone.

"Sorry," said the boy again.

Strong-in-the-Lord could only feel grateful that he wasn't the one suffering under the parental displeasure. He finished his Masson with a quiet, selfish glee. But later that night, in their shared bedroom, after the lights had been put out, he started baiting his brother again.

"You want to go to the window and look at the stars?" he whispered. "If we do it together we'd *both* be astronomers." He sniggered.

"Don't be stupid," said Cor. "You need to do more than that to be an astronomer."

"Oh, there's *no* such job," Strong- insisted. "Why should the State pay for people to stand and look up? That's just crazy."

To Strong-'s disappointment, Cor didn't rise to the chiding. Instead he spoke in a hushed, careful voice. "I was in the library," he said, as he had done at dinner, "and I looked up some books. Did you know the stars didn't used to be so orderly in the sky?"

"What you talking about?"

"Long ago," said Cor, "they were scattered as randomly as if I threw a handful of sugar from my hand, and the grains landed higgled-piggled on the floor."

Strong- snorted a little laugh and ducked his head under the blanket. "That's just crazy."

"It's a myth, you see," said Cor. "The myth is that God arranged the stars, and then the Devil came and mussed them up, and so God rearranged them for us. It's clever of him, because the stars are not all the same distance from us, they're all different distances, and great distances, like billions and quadrillions of miles away, so to get them all lined up so that they appear neat and in rows from earth is clever."

"Of course God is clever," said Strong-, still under the blanket.

"I'd just like to know more about them," said Cor. "That's why I want to be an astronomer."

The brothers took their different paths through life. Strong- went to college and studied two years of basic engineering, and two years of coastline speciality. He graduated in the top thirty percent of his class. He was found a wife, and he had two children of his own, one girl, one boy, their names shifting *in* to *of* after the tradition of the Northern European congregation to which he belonged: Beauty-of-the-Lord and Wisdom-of-the-Lord. He was promoted. He worked for several years on the two great tapering lines that were reshaping South America, working the machines and afterward supervising the workers on the machines as rubble was channeled and shoveled from inland to block out the underwater reefs that would later be built up and up. He did his work so well that he was transferred back to Europe, and his family could leave the sweltering heat of the tropics for the decent chill of Scandinavia. Promoted again. Here he worked for many years on the more difficult job of filling in fjords. The ground was hard, mostly unyielding granite, and the fjords were deep; it was several years work to fill in one of the smaller inlets. But the work was day to day. Fruition was many centuries away. He was part of a larger whole.

It was in Scandinavia that he became friendly with The-Unerring-Word. Another devout man, church on Sundays and Wednesdays, with a family of two himself. But a more old fashioned man than Strong-. He beat his children on Tuesday nights, whether they had committed specific infractions or not, simply for the discipline of it. On fast-days he starved himself not only from dawn to dusk, as was common, but from midnight to midnight; it made him grumpy and unpredictable at work, but he insisted upon the observance and mocked others for not being so exact. In fact, fasting or not, his temper was usually short with the people working under him.

Then there was the question of clothing. At work both -Unerring- and Strong- wore the company tunic, the plain blue buttonless shift, the blue strides and black engineering boots, matching blue faceveil and gloves. But out of work, Strong- liked to dress up a little. After he got home after work, he would wash the necessary three times and then put on a pale green shift with a single silver cross printed on the chest. He had a favorite faceveil too, with gold thread worked into an olive-green ground. And he wore red silk gloves with black finger-tips.

-Unerring- did not conceal his disdain for these fripperies. In work or out of it, his clothes were always plain. "It's vanity," he might say, as Strong- and he sat in a bar sipping a glass of red wine and cranberry together. "It's nothing else but vanity. You know what I reckon about it. Hey."

"You're probably right," Strong- would concede. "I guess it is."

"But, hey," said -Unerring-. "Forgive, that's part of God's plan too. Yeah?"

"Yeah."

"Yeah," -Unerring- would say, contemplating the concept. "For*give*."

And they would finish their drinks, wipe their straws with sanctissues and throw them away. Walking back through Utoholm in the early morning, taking the main street toward the Engineering camp, they would often laugh together. Slap one another on the shoulder. The citizens of Utoholm, on their way to day work, briefcases like paving slabs in their arms and hats pulled down over their heads tight as a drumskin—the ordinary people of the town would give these two burly men a wide berth.

"Hey," -Unerring- might yell at one of them. "Mouse! You take care! God's wrath, you know! We're making the world a purer place, you know!" It was funny. The mouse would duck, almost doubling over his suitcase, his coat flapping around his body as he scurried and hurried away from these huge men, these shouting, laughing men. Because, you see, they were doing something more important than sitting in an office, sitting in a school or a hospital, counting beans or pushing paper. They were physically remaking the world—with their actual hands, with their own muscles, with their will-to-goodness. Making the world more like the heavens, making it purer and more godly. And that thought made you feel good. Strong- enjoyed the sense of *altitude* he experienced, coming home after a shift, a glass of half wine half juice in his belly, his comrade-in-work beside him, laughing and joking. "You know what we should do?" -Unerring- said, linking his beefy arm with Strong-'s as they strode together towards the Engineering compound.

"What should we do?"

"We should all go holiday together! Yeah! You and me, your family and my family! We should holiday—somewhere in South America, say. You can show me the work you did on that coastline. They got resorts down there, don't they? One on a mountain, with a good view of the reformed coast."

"You want to be cooped up a fortnight with my kids?" Strong- asked, laughing. "You want my teenage son chewing your ear off for a fortnight," slipping his voice into comical-nasal, "*But Dad, why? And why this? And why that?*"

"Sure!" bellowed -Unerring-, and guffawed. "He'd learn soon enough not to bother me with that nonsense!"

And this, for some reason, struck Strong- as simply hilarious. He laughed and laughed. "Hey!" -Unerring- shouted at somebody on the far side of the street, some old woman, or old man, it was difficult to tell. "What you looking at? Mind your own! You want the Lord's wrath, in the shape of my fist, come visit you?" And the figure ducked down and scurried away.

They laughed and laughed, and they strode through the gates to the compound arm in arm as the morning sun dissolved the last of the stars in its lemon-colored dawn light.

2

Strong-in-the-Lord discussed the holiday plans with his wife and found himself coming round to the idea. Maybe it would be fun! -Unerring- could be a little stiff-backed about religious observance, a little overstrict, but he was a good guy, salt of the earth.

Because of this it was a particular discomfort to him that it was -Unerring- who first saw the naked man. Seeing a naked man running around the workplace was bad enough; but for that naked man to turn out to be his own brother, to be Courageous-in-the-Lord, was almost unbearable. "Hey!" -Unerring- shouted. "Hey, who is that guy? He's *naked*, for cry-out-loud!"

"You're right!" Strong- said.

They were at a shafthead, midnight. The shafts were being run into the steep wall of the fjord and would eventually be primed with explosive and blown free so that the rubble would avalanche down into the deep black water below. The two of them had been at the cutting face, inside the mine, inspecting the work. They had just backed a truck along the mineshaft and had emptied its load of rubble down the scree face into the water. Now they were standing beside the truck's cabin, debating whether to take their break now or later.

The road, cut alongside the line of the water and lit with fierce arc-lights at twenty-meter intervals, led back to the main camp. But here was a naked man, hurrying up the road, bold as you like. As he came closer, Strong- said, "Hey, he looks like," and then, "oh, I don't *believe* it."

"What?" -Unerring- asked. "What?"

"It's my brother. Believe that? Oh, would you *look* at that?"

"Oh, man," said -Unerring-. "That's disgusting! Look at that!"

The naked man approached. He was wearing odd, raggedy green trousers. On closer inspection the flaps and fringes revealed themselves to be pockets, but a messier, more disreputable-looking pair of pants it was hard to imagine. There was a dark sweater of some kind, but his hands and his face were completely naked.

"Cor?" Strong- yelled. "Courageous-in-the-Lord?"

By the time he arrived, the newcomer was panting. "Brother," he said, nodding his head in greeting.

"In the name of God!" said Strong-. "Cover yourself up, man!"

For a long moment Cor said nothing, but looked calmly into Strong-'s face. "I got to talk with you, brother. I got to talk with you now."

"You're *naked*, man," shouted -Unerring-.

Cor ignored him. "Can we talk now? Is there somewhere we can go?"

"You heard what I *said*, man?" yelled -Unerring-.

"I don't want to talk with *you*," said Cor to -Unerring-, without looking at him. "I got nothing to say to you. You should get on your way."

"I'll tell you *what*," said -Unerring-, fiercely. "No naked man is going to run around my site. You got permission to be here? No way. You got permission to be *anywhere* naked like that? Oh no. I'm taking you in—you're coming back down the road with me until the police can deal with you."

He brought his huge hands up in front of him and took a step towards Cor.

"Stop," said Cor.

And -Unerring- froze. Cor was holding a gun, a bulky handgun of struts and sharp doublebacks, like an anglepoise-lamp. Clearly a gun. Military issue.

When -Unerring- spoke his voice was much softer. "Where you get that, man?"

"Go," said Cor. "Just head off. Go back to the camp. I got to talk to my brother." He lifted the gun.

"That's military, isn't it?" -Unerring- said. Then, abruptly, he had turned face-about and was trotting down the road. His figure swiftly dwindled to a smudge of dark, trotting from one patch of lit ground to the next. Above him the stars, ranked in awful sublimity, gave the illusion of hundreds of receding dark roads, each one lit by lamps all along its length, shrinking toward the horizon that was also -Unerring-'s destination.

Cor watched him go.

"What are you *doing*?" Strong-in-the-Lord cried. "Are you insane? You'll go to prison—is that what you want?"

"What I want," said Courageous-in-the-Lord, folding his gun away and pushing it back into one of the pockets in his ridiculous pants, "is somewhere warmer where we can talk. Warmer than this freezing night. How about the cabin of this truck?"

*   *   *

They clambered inside, pulled the doors shut. Cor turned on the heating. For a while he simply sat until he had warmed up a little. Strong- sat in silence during this time; he offered up an unspoken prayer, tried to calm himself. Eventually he turned to face his brother.

"So," he said. "So. I haven't heard from you in five years, and now you turn up like this. Five years!"

"You're doing the same thing now as you were then."

"*Then*," said Strong-, "I was in South America."

"It's all the same thing," said Courageous-.

There was a pause.

"You will," said Strong-, trying to sound compassionate, "go to prison for this. You do know that, don't you?"

Courageous- laughed. "I've been dodging prison for most of those five years, you know," he said. "It's been one long chase for me."

Strong- could not help staring at his brother's naked face. He just couldn't help himself. He ought, perhaps, to have looked away, but he found himself staring. The myriad tiny strands of black hair, curling a few millimeters out of the chin and cheeks, like pubic hair—revolting. The snickering, serpentine curling and uncurling of those pink lips, moistened from time to time by his tongue. His tongue! Glimpses of that pink muscle, that lewd contorting thing; its penile probing and movement, soft-hard, stippled with hundreds of miniature nipples along its upper surface. Strong- couldn't stop staring at it. As his brother spoke, he found himself hypnotized by the movement of lips, the flashes of tongue, the lurid gaping of the nostrils with their own hideous stuffing of pubic hair. He could hear that his brother was saying something, but he could not make sense of the words. It was all blotted out by the spectacular, obscene image of the naked face.

"Ugh!" he called out. He looked away. "You could at least cover up."

"You weren't listening to me," said Courageous-. He sighed. "It's the same. You're the same as you were. I'd hoped you were different, I hoped—Jesus, I don't know what I hoped."

"Oh," said Strong-, still looking carefully at the darkened windscreen. "So, it's swearing now, as well, is it?"

"I didn't know where else to go," said Courageous-, in a more subdued voice. "I guess that's it."

There was silence.

"What happened to you, man?" Strong- asked the darkened windscreen. He could see his brother's naked face reflected, smokily, in the glass, but that wasn't as bad. "How did you get like this? You were a devout kid. Devout enough, anyhow."

"Listen to me, brother," said Courageous-. "I've seen the truth, yeah? Once you've seen the truth, and understood the truth, things can never be the same."

Strong- took a deep breath. He exhaled, carefully. "The-Unerring-Word," he said. "That's my co-worker, the man you terrorized with the gun. He'll inform the police as soon as he gets to the compound. They'll come up here. They'll come up armed, probably. You should give yourself up, right now."

Courageous- sighed again. "You know what I wanted to be when I was a kid, brother?"

"Of course," said Strong-.

"Remember?"

"You wanted to be an astronomer."

At this memory, Courageous- laughed quietly; and at the sound of his laughter Strong- laughed a little too. Suddenly the whole encounter took on a comical, unreal edge.

"It was crazy of me," admitted Cor.

"Man, it was, though? Wasn't it?"

"I told the teachers at school, and I got caned, got whacked—you remember that? They thought I was being disrespectful even by asking after it!"

The two of them laughed together.

"You were full of crazy thoughts in those days," said Strong-, kindly.

"When you came here," Cor said, "you used to write to me. *Come stay with the family, come see Scandinavia!*"

"That's right!" said Strong-. "I did that. Of course," he said, the laughter still burbling along between the words, "I didn't think you'd come see me *naked*. Or, or," and here, for some reason the laughter dribbled away, "or carrying a gun. Or carrying a gun." There was a pause.

They weren't laughing any more.

"I did become an astronomer, in the end," said Cor, leaning forward in the cab. He pressed the blade of his hand against the glass and peered through the shadow at the world outside. "In a manner of speaking. Do you ever think it's odd that the stars are arranged in the sky in so orderly a pattern?"

"Odd?"

"The constellations—you know what that word means?"

"Something to do with stars?"

"Constellations are the patterns made by the stars. But there's only one pattern of course. This grid."

"Do I think it's odd?" said Strong- loudly, as if waking from a snooze. "No, I don't. Why should I? God declares His majesty and order in the heavens."

"And if," said his brother, in a low voice, "there is no order in the heavens? If the stars were arranged in a chaotic spread?"

"That's a nonsense question," said Strong-. "A nonsense, and a hypothetical question."

"Okay," said Courageous-. He yawned, egregiously, his mouth opening wider and wider. Strong- could see every detail reflected in the glass; the teeth, arrayed like stars, the pulsing mass of pink flesh that was the tongue, the open funnel of throat, tonsils dangling at the very back like glistening, miniature testicles. Strong- had to lift his hand to his eyes to block out the image. He could not tear his eyes away. He had actually to lift his hand to block the image out.

"Sorry," said Courageous-. "Sorry about that. I'm just really tired. I haven't slept in ages."

"If you'd been wearing a veil," said Strong- faintly, "it would not have been so bad."

"Yeah, veil, yeah," said Courageous-. "Except that once you discover the truth of things, it seems pretty hypocritical to wear the veil."

"The truth of things?" snapped Strong-, trying to achieve the same tone of withering sternness that their father had managed so effortlessly. "I thought that's where all this was leading—to irreligion and atheism and terrible things. Don't! Don't, that's all I say. Truth? Do you say truth? Truth—there's a word that means two things, isn't it? It means *not in error*, but it also means *properly placed*—we talk of a line in a drawing being true, don't we? When we say God is Truth, we mean not only that he cannot lie, we mean that everything about him is properly placed, orderly, harmonious. That's the point of the stars—that's what they show us. The rank on rank of them."

"I think I just ran out of steam," said Courageous-, wearily, as if to himself.

But Strong- wasn't to be interrupted. "No, no, the lines of stars in the sky are *true* lines. That's why the coastline project is so important—the line of the coastline of Scandinavia does not, at the moment, run true. Do you see? We must make it true. For the sake of God!" He stopped. Was there, he wondered, any point in haranguing Cor in this way?

"You know about the sky-net?" his brother asked.

"What's that got to do with anything?" Strong- snapped.

"All those satellites up in earth-orbit? What are they for?"

"What are you talking about now? How's this relevant? They prevent asteroid strikes, you know that. Asteroids and comets and, uh, nebulas and things. Without them, we'd be vulnerable to . . ."

"Do we really need so many of them?" Courageous- asked.

Strong- turned his head and stared straight at his brother, disregarding his nakedness. "What," he said, "are you *talking* about?"

"Nothing," said Courageous-. "Only, could you take this?" He was holding a folded square of paper, half a meter along each side. Strong- looked at it. It was folded several times. Unfolded, it would be a fairly big thing, like a wall-chart or something.

"What is it?"

"You can look at it," said Courageous-. "When you get home. Just take it, please. Please?"

"Tell me what it is."

"Just dots on a page. Random dots. Randomly generated pattern. Or, rather, lack-of-pattern. That's harmless, surely? Well, you and I might think it harmless, though the Government doesn't think so. Obvious the government thinks it's dangerous; it's why they're after me. But how can it be dangerous? It's only dots on a piece of paper. I'm asking you as a brother to take it for me. Please."

"I don't know, Cor," said Strong-.

"If you take the paper," said Courageous-, "then I promise I'll hand myself over to the police."

"Is it contraband?" Strong- asked. But he took the paper.

"Tuck it away inside your tunic," Courageous- advised. "I wouldn't let the police know you have it. Just take it away and look at it at home. Then you can do what you like. There are some numbers along the bottom margin you can call if you want. Or you can just chuck it away if you like."

"What's going on, Cor?" said Strong-. He felt a wobbly sense of uncertainty, and he didn't like that feeling. "What are you doing?"

Courageous-in-the-Lord was settling himself back against the seat of the cab, folding his arms. "Waiting for the police," he said.

"They'll put you in jail."

"Are you advising me to run away, brother? Surely you'd prefer me to face justice?"

"Well yes, only," said Strong-. "Look, I don't understand."

"It's all right," said Courageous-. "I don't really know

why I picked you, brother. If I'd thought about it, I should have known you could not have changed. I've been in the company of so many people over the last few years who *have* changed, you see, people who had once been devout like you and now aren't any more. When you're in that sort of company over a long period of time, it's easy to forget that most people haven't reached that place yet. You still believe in the coastal engineering project, don't you?"

"This again? Always knocking it. I might almost be cross with you, brother," said Strong-. But he wasn't cross. He couldn't shake the grumbling, fluttery sensation of uncertainty in his gut. "It's mankind's noblest project."

"Mankind's most pointless, certainly."

"It's *not* pointless." He meant to sound assertive, but he sounded petulant as a child.

"You don't think there are better avenues for man's energies? When you were in South America—you know that thirty percent of the population there are malnourished? You must have seen it. That many thousands die each year of starvation."

"The soil there is bad," said Strong-.

"Couldn't we put our energies into making it better, instead of redrawing coastlines? Christ alive."

"Please don't swear."

Courageous- had sat up again. "You really don't see beyond it, do you? How many coastal cities have you bulldozed?"

"Most of them are already ruins," Strong- said, grumpily. "After the war, there were many ruins."

"Most, but not all. And a deal of poisoned soil, too. Which means people tend to starve; pushed out of their homes, they go beggarly. Even though the war was more'n a hundred years ago, now. And after the war we had strong government, Church-and-Government. Order and a better life. All that," he threw his left hand up, dismissively. "All that."

"Why do you have to be so—cynical?" Strong- asked. His voice was almost tearful.

"I'm sorry, brother," said Courageous-, sounding weary again. "I just don't believe it. I think the whole thing is like prisoners working a treadmill. I think it soaks up people's energies, and people's money, and stops them questioning the Government—stops them, heaven forbid, from challenging, or changing, or—hell—overthrowing the Government."

"And why," said Strong-, baffled, upset, "would anybody want to do anything like that?"

"Quite right," said Courageous-, grimacing. "The Government governs according to the principles of truth, doesn't it? Of course it does. That speech you gave me five minutes ago, I can't remember all the details of it, but it was all about truth, wasn't it."

"God is truth," said Strong-, agreeing, and at the exact moment he said the words there came a sharp tap against the glass of the truck's windscreen. Strong- started, pressed his face against the glass to peer at the crowd that had gathered outside. He opened the door and clambered down.

The-Unerring-Word was standing there, along with four policemen. Two of the policemen were carrying weapons—long-barreled police-guns, aimed at the cabin. "Sir?" said one of the policeman.

"*He*'s alright," said -Unerring-, gruffly. "This is my work colleague. It's the other guy—in the cab."

Strong-, feeling foolish, stood, superfluous, as the police dragged his brother—naked—out of the cabin. They cuffed him, searched him and removed from him the gun he had (presumably) stolen from somewhere. They dragged him over and strapped him into the back of their Law-wagon. Afterward Strong- accompanied -Unerring- to the police depot, and they swore statements, and agreed witness dates, and answered questions, and gave details, until the whole thing had taken up almost the entire night's shift. All through it Strong- kept thinking that maybe he would wake from the experience, as if from a dream—everybody has that sort of dream, don't they? You've had it, surely? The dream where you are walking down Main Street, stark-

naked, *entirely* naked from forehead to neck, and people are
looking and staring, and you become more and more embarrassed. The experience felt something like that for
Strong-, except that it was Strong-'s brother who had been
naked rather than Strong- himself. But the whole thing had
that terrible dream-like quality to it.

It was almost dawn by the time Strong- got home.

He slipped the key in his lock and stepped inside quietly,
trying not to wake his wife, his two children. He needed to
sit, to think. He went through to the kitchen and made himself a beaker of hot milk.

He placed the folded square of paper on the table in front
of him.

He couldn't make sense of any of it. What was it Cor had
been saying? None of it made any sense. Why had he said
that thing about the sky-net satellites—everybody knew that
they were essential for global defense, all of them. Every
single one. Sure there were lots of them, but what of that?
What had Cor been going on about? What had gotten into
his head?

Strong- tried to imagine what image was printed on the
paper in front of him. Random dots, Cor had said. What
could that possibly mean? It sounded harmless, and yet
Strong- felt a strange intertia, a profound disinclination to
open up the sheet of paper and look at what was printed
there. It would be—he felt intuitively—*upsetting* to him.

Upsetting.

He took hold of one corner with his thumb and pushed it.
Paper slid against paper, hissing like silk. But the sheet was
opening up now, he was swinging the panels out and smoothing the whole thing down against the table. And there it was.
A purple square, a yard by two-thirds, pocked and marked all
over with white dots of various sizes, spattered everywhere
but coagulating in a mass marking a diagonal spread from
corner to corner. There was something terrible about it; the
randomness of these dots. The horrible prolific mass of them,
like bacteria spreading and spreading uncontrollably across

its medium. He recalled the line in the Bible about the veil of the temple being rent across. God's temple rent and split diagonally across, splashes and dabs of ichor, like God's white blood, spattered over creation, falling with appalling randomness. There were some words printed along the margin of this abstract image, but Strong- didn't read them. Didn't read them yet. He couldn't stop looking at the terrible, terrifying mess of everything that this picture represented. The long night. The indifferent stars.

His hand was resting on the table, his fingers playing with one corner of the open sheet, folding it up, smoothing it down, folding it up. Above his head, upstairs, he could hear his wife moving around, oblivious, performing her habitual morning ablutions. The triple-flush of the toilet. The squeak and gushing flow of the bath-tap. Her voice humming a tune to herself as she prepared for her day.

THE LITTLE BEAR

By Justina Robson

Be it the northern or the southern sky, the constellations on a dark night look as they do from only one point in the universe; from Earth. Being adrift in the universe isn't like being lost at sea, or in the desert, where knowing their patterns can set you on the right path. Constellations are stories, convenient memory markers existing purely in our minds so we don't have to experience the truth of our position in a great and indifferent space.

Violette thought this as she looked up into the night, searching against the setting gleam of Venus for the white engine-track of a returning craft. She felt without a shadow of doubt that the expanse of outer space was a bagatelle kind of nothing, compared with the space she'd become aware of as it grew inside her mind: the distance between herself and her husband Guy.

Someone had once told her that she might try to imagine infinity thus: picture a steel ball the size of the Earth. A fly lands on it once in a million years. When the friction caused by the fly's feet has worn the steel ball away to nothing, infinity has not even begun.

Space is Time, Time is Space. She had written that as the last line in her thesis. The constellations above her had traveled with her since then, apparently much unchanged by either aspect of the continuum, as far as she was aware. But she was much changed by time. It had grooved her face and bleached her hair and was close to swallowing her whole. As for space . . .

She touched the eternity ring she had bought for herself on finishing her studies—a circle, naturally, because she had hoped, against her logical conclusions, that spacetime was a doughnut shape and, as a sugar-mote on its surface, her life lay safely perpetual there, always to be returned to, always repeated as space progressed along the doughnut's roundel of time, although she could not experience it that way. The ring had a diamond, a small one, and two flanking stones like tiny gateposts. Her finger counted them as she watched Venus decline in the west. Slowly she let out the breath she'd been holding.

The spinnaker of her small boat billowed with freshening wind and rode the swell with a drunken swagger quickly smoothing into a surf. She released the ring and took hold of the helm again, reassuring herself by the feel of the boat's lively passage resonating in the wheel. Above her Orion was sinking, and his dogs were quick on his heels. Dawn was coming, and already the glow of the sun had begun to erase the clarity of the stars in the eastern sky. Soon the single planet would be her only guide.

Time is space wasn't news even then. Einstein had said it decades ago. But in Violette's interpretation of the physical laws it had to be re-stated. Time was a space of no volume. Hence one could not go back to a point in it, navigating one's way by the look of past and future worlds, constellations there of people and actions, of objects in their exact array and bearings tuned by the flavor, smell and zest of a single instant viewed from all directions. Time was a cusp, the wave's crest, a moment of perpetual immanence. Guy was lost in space, since his mission failed to return all those years ago. But she didn't believe him dead. She considered him dislocated in time. Although this might make no difference to the facts, it made her feel less alone. In one part of the continuum, Guy was still there.

She reached into the inner pocket of her oilskin and removed a laminated photograph. Looking at Guy's picture—it seemed only an instant ago that he'd gone. How could that be so far away that she could never get there? Of course, if they allowed her to work the machine, she might try to get there, which is why it was shut off in its bunker, never to be used again. They thought Guy's mission a sufficient loss, in the wake of all the events after the machine's first use, and no doubt that was the wisest way. Teleportation remained a dream, even though Violette knew first hand that it was not.

A wave recklessly covered the deck and fell to nothing, draining in the sluices and drenching her feet. It splashed the photo and she wiped it clean as she put it away before turning a degree to the south. She'd built the boat— Arrowflight—herself, learning via several false starts and many hard hours as she went along, determined to attempt a full circumnavigation of the world by star and sun before she died. She'd left Les Sables a week ago and hadn't switched on her radio since. On the third day she'd become aware that direction didn't matter.

Wherever she went Guy would never be. The trail of a spacecraft that should have come in a long time ago was only in her mind's eye, a nervous tic of hopeful longing. She reasoned that there had been a miscalculation on board, and the moment of return had failed to find Earth where it should have been in space, materializing behind or in front by a critical margin to discover . . . to do nothing in fact, for to miss utterly was to cease to exist in a timely manner, at least in this universe.

Violette did not believe in discontinuity, where objects could dot in and out, not there one minute but there the next, skipping time steps like a child over chalked hopscotch lines. Guy had gone out to test their theories in the only safe place they could think of, and he was lost.

*   *   *

Guy took a seat in a café bar near Montmartre. It was the time of evening when his father had liked to light a cigar and ask his mother to provide him with a glass of fino. Guy liked neither but ordered the sherry anyway and when it came, tasted its woodiness and dryness with a hidden grimace. He only had to wait for a few minutes and then Rafaella appeared, slinking like a cat out of the shadows. Her face was contorted with the pressure she was feeling. It spoiled her beauty, made her look older and more disappointed than he'd hoped.

She slumped in her seat and crossed her legs, kicking the loose sole of her cheap flip-flop against her foot. He regarded her with a fondness he felt correct for a father to feel toward his daughter. The lamplight coming from the bar's interior made her look more like Violette than ever.

Rafaella batted a moth away with a flick of her hand and crossed her legs the other way. A waiter appeared as though summoned by majesty, and she ordered wine without rewarding him with a single glance. She caught Guy's look of amusement at this naked display of feminine power,

"Don't look at me like that."

"You remind me of her."

"And don't say that."

"What? I have to say something. It's the reason we're here."

"I hate anniversaries. It's pointless nostalgia." She raked her gaze over the other people on the street and, finding nothing in them to grip her attention, looked up at heaven for patience.

"Then why did you come?"

She snorted, "To humor you, of course. You think she meant to come back."

"You don't."

"If she'd meant to then she would have—duh!" Rafaella took her wineglass from the offered tray and took a big swallow, bigger than she intended. A line of red ran down her mouth and dripped onto the boho chicness of her outfit. She swore and ignored it.

Guy said, "The solicitor thinks it's time to ask the court to declare her legally dead."

Rafaella focused her emotion on the distant stars and didn't look at him. Her flip-flop counted away a minute, and she glanced at her watch.

"Plane to catch?" He cursed his own sarcasm even as he said it.

"I'm meeting Paul," she said and then heaved herself around as if it was a Herculean effort. "If we do this, what does it do?"

"It means that her will can be executed," he replied, the words and their meaning a simple skim on the surface of his mind, not allowed to disturb what lay beneath. "You'll get some money. I will. The house . . ."

"Is not going to be sold," she declared, taking a swallow of wine.

"Be reasonable," he began, but she cut him off.

"It's the only place she knows. What if she comes back and we're not there? What if she goes there and nobody knows who she is? What if it's all she recognizes?"

Guy sighed and watched a young couple walk by, their arms entwined, nothing in the span of their regard except each other. He and Violette had walked like that once. He wanted to believe they would again. Perhaps they were doing so even now, in some other time and space that he could not find. He didn't know how to explain to Rafaella that her mother might be missing on another Earth. He didn't want to believe it himself.

The house in question was far away in rural Yorkshire, but he could feel its presence as though a lodestone in the walls pulled at him twenty-four seven. He could feel its emptiness and the chilly transparent dome of its roof, above which the Great Bear pawed the northern sky and pointed helplessly at the single unmoving mote of Polaris, the north star, with her tail.

Rafaella believed her mother had suffered a stroke causing a kind of amnesia and had simply wandered off. Or that

she had had an affair and created a clever story to cover her
absence. It had been years, and although she'd left home by
then anyway, the idea of Violette's abandonment of her was
too hard. Guy knew that the moment hadn't been anything
so mundane. There was a chance Rafaella was right and that
the house and its coordinates were the only points in the universe where Violette might return.

"Little Bear," he said fondly to Rafaella, hardly realizing
he spoke aloud.

She shot him a cold look but could not sustain it and returned to watching the people pass by.

If universes intersect one another at all, then they must do
so at at least one point. However those points are mapped, a
moment and a space or both are shared. This could be used
as the focus of all maps that serve to describe those separate
worlds, no matter how giant or how fleeting.

Why shouldn't this be a house, or a heart?

The machine towered over them, humming with power—
so strange to think that such a small wattage could achieve
so much—as Guy and Violette watched their chosen test object vanish from sight. The telephone rang in the outer office. Violette answered,

"Oui?"

There was a breathless pause.

"Vraiment?"

Another beat, another mark that nailed down each moment to its position without ambiguity.

"Guy!" she shouted, the phone raised high like a staff of
power. "He has the bottle! Alain has the bottle! In Greece!
Right now!"

But at the time they'd never thought about where the
bottle might have been when it was neither with them, in
Paris, nor with Alain, in Athens. Between one second
and the next, how much space could there be? And for his
part Alain never mentioned, thinking it bad luck, that the

old Chateauneuf du Pape was foul and corked beyond drinking.

Violette searched the sky again for the one unchanging constant, following the blunted end of Thor's Hammer. The North Star was faint as she angled the boat away from it. A fresh update on the monitor revealed that none of the satellites heard anything of Guy's scout mission, and why should they? He was full fifty years lost, and the machine in its laboratory was thick with dust, guarded by young soldiers who didn't even know what it was for and thought maybe it was an old cold war thing.

Alain had texted her—*OK ld grl*?

She hadn't replied yet, she thought, although she fancied that she was replying, had already replied—OK.

After the first few attempts they'd given up trying to calculate how many fresh universes had peeled away from their one original with each repeated use of the machine. Violette had no idea whether or not there were many of her sharing this space right now; others turning about, others reckoning the sky, others at home, far away, watching old movies with Guy and Rafaella in the house below the hill.

In her mind *that* Violette in the house was the real one. Somehow she had become one of the pale copies instead, her consciousness slipping away from its true course and into this unsatisfactory illusion. She took comfort from the knowledge that it was only a shard in time that separated her from this perfect life, even though crossing back into it might be impossible. Other Violettes may make it. And other Guys may never have left with the astronauts to verify the fracture by viewing it from the outside—traveling into a sister reality.

The wind was as strong in any other world. The boat made a tortured banging sound as it drove into the waves. The bowsprit surfaced to point up at the three Norns, and Violette switched on the autopilot, exhausted, and went below.

*   *   *

Rafaella uncorked the bottle of wine and stood on the balcony in the humid night heat, the stone of the terrace barely cool against her feet. She could hear Alain playing Chopin on the piano. Its notes were bell-like in their melancholy patterns, picking out the essence of her emotion without her having to articulate it. How like him to know what to play at an hour like this, she thought, and how like her father to wander off to the bottom of the garden, a white shape in the gloom like a ghost.

In the dining room the legal documents lay crisp below the stare of another wine bottle—this one in a protective glass case. The original Chateauneuf of the first experiment was fragile enough to break these days, without much encouragement from anyone. It was the thinning of its walls which had first suggested danger in the method. Not only had it lost something during its travel to Athens that night, years ago, but with every subsequent use of the machine another integral layer had been peeled from its substance. Its label was unreadable, the printing ink flayed off. The glass itself was, at a microscopic level, pitted with holes until it resembled a peculiar bone, the fossil of an ancient time. Since the wine itself had gone down the sink in Athens, nobody knew what had happened to that.

Rafaella thought of the papers there, awaiting her signature. Guy's was still drying on the page. He was convinced Violette must be dead or never coming back. Rafaella felt she ought to sign, if only to end the suspension of his life, to allow him to move on, but a more bitter, stubborn piece of her wouldn't let her. The bottle's problem was that it had moved unpredictably through space because of its predictability in time. Violette was the opposite. Rafaella was sure she was alive somewhen soon, and they did not, as Guy insisted, live in a Universe which had allowed her to vanish from it absolutely. Matter could not disappear like that from all coordinates of the continuum; ergo, her mother was out there somewhere, and she was not going to sign away the one point of contact they might have.

When is it?

Rafaella set the corkscrew on the terrace wall, started pouring a libation down the stones, then let all the wine run there, each rivulet of darkness winding its own way over the rough and porous surfaces. *Where* is the crossing where all these worlds collide?

Guy said it was at Ago, at the first use of the machine. They couldn't get back there, because they'd already been.

But what if it was in the future? What if there was a universe in which the machine never worked? *That* universe couldn't possibly intersect with this one in the past. In fact there must be an infinity of worlds in which the machine did not exist or had never been used and an infinity of crossroads from this world in which it did, presenting chances to jump over. But Guy would only laugh at this reasoning of hers.

In the garden her father's white form walked toward her. He looked up as he came into the terrace lights.

"There's always another possibility," he said as the final chord sounded from the piano. "That she might have stepped out of existence only for a *certain length* of time. In which case, she hasn't moved in space at all."

Rafaella stared down at him, brushing a moth away from her hair. "What?"

"But even if she did," he continued, "the world has moved on. Literally. In space. The planet has moved. The galaxy has moved. Nothing is where it used to be. Even positions that seem to be fixed have altered beyond recognition."

The moth returned, blundered against her cheek, corrected itself and fled up into the brilliance of the terrace light. Dust from its wings powdered the air. She listened to it battling against the glass, beating itself to death with the force of its determination to reach what it had mistaken for the moon.

Alain checked the set up for the eighth time. In fact there was nothing to check, but he smoothed the tablecloth over the cold marble top one more time and walked around the invisible perimeter of the three beacons, noting their alignment. According to theory the bottle should arrive two millimeters above the cloth. He didn't know what would happen if it came in any lower, but then again he didn't know what would happen to the air it displaced on its arrival either. He put his goggles on and moved back to the safe distance of his cane chair.

Beyond the shuttered windows the low growl of traffic persisted, overshot with the bright, sudden notes of the calls of birds that were gathering to roost in the eaves of his hotel. They weren't swallows, he knew that, but birds weren't his thing, navigation was his interest. Migrations from one continent to another over vast distances had intrigued him since his boyhood. Geese had been the first animals he'd studied for his dissertation, and then the wandering albatross. A curious mixture of the Earth's magnetism, the stars and the sun traced their paths for them. The turning year and the flares of solar agitation or tropical storms could cast them far beyond their routes. The memory of routes also passed on from generation to generation, even when conditions at the destinations altered, became less desirable. How curious he'd been to discover that instinct was so powerful, even when its drive took you in the wrong direction. He wasn't sure himself if this position he was in was less desirable. He didn't like the idea of the machine and hoped it would fail.

His watch, in regular contact with an atomic clock, counted the moments to midnight. The church at the end of the street chimed in early, its hand-rung bell marking the hours, the end of the day, the start of something. Bathed in the moment, suspended between past and future, Alain wished for nothing.

There was a sharp bang, like a muted gunshot, and a softer thud.

Wings beat suddenly against the shutters, a flurry, and were still.

A bottle of wine stood on the table, the meniscus just visible beneath the collar label, quivering.

He was surprised it didn't startle him. He mustered enthusiasm, rang Paris as he moved forward to inspect it, briefly wondering why they hadn't bothered to wipe the dust off it before they sent it over. Violette's delight was so infectious he found himself starting to laugh, to smile. When he rang off he was grinning as he took out his keys from his pocket, undid his corkscrew from the Swiss army knife and opened the bottle.

The cork came out easily and with it a soft, resiny odor quickly turning sour. He poured it and took a sniff. Pure vinegar. The cork in his fingers was slimy. What a bad omen, he thought then, his smile fading. He resolved never to mention it to the others but quickly watched the bottleful splash its way down the plughole. Probably he should have saved it for testing, but the glass would be enough.

He suddenly remembered that in all the excitement he'd forgotten to turn off the recording equipment. It only took a few minutes to roll back the tapes and erase what he'd done.

"He's not coming back," Rafaella said, her voice almost drowned out by the cries of the children, fighting over a toy. She sounded weary rather than irritated to Violette, who cradled the receiver against her chin as she guided the boat back to its mooring.

"I know," she said. "But I like to look."

"When are you coming home?"

"Soon," Violette assured her. "The estate agent says the house is sold. I have to pack it up—that will take a while—and then I'll be coming. I'm selling most of the furniture, unless there's something you particularly want."

"No," Rafaella said, pausing to administer some kind of hasty discipline. Violette heard her saying, "We'll get another, Little Bear, don't worry about it," and then Martine's voice whined, "Don't want another. Want *that* one." She came back on the line, "But if you find anything personal of Dad's . . ."

"It'll all come back with me," Violette said. "You can look through it yourself. Did you get Alain's card?"

"He still signs himself off 'A Friend of Your Father's' as if I didn't know who he was," Rafaella sighed. "Yes. And a hundred Euros, even though I'm thirty-five and earn more than his pension."

"He feels responsible," Violette said. "I have to go, the wind is changing." She hung up and brought the vessel about just in time to make it safely around the harbor buoy. Gulls circled the mast lazily, giving her the once over, not even bothering to call out from their frozen postures in the air.

A week later, kneeling in the attic on the Rue St Denis, she dragged over a wooden packing case from the very back. It wasn't the last to be cleared out, but nearly the last, and it must have been there since the day they moved in, she reckoned—a strip of 1989 *Le Monde* hung from its slats. She brushed filthy gray dust from it and sneezed, pausing to wipe her face with a tissue and seeing black marks stripe it as she put it away again. In the light of the single weak bulb she wondered if she could be bothered to check it, or whether she should simply leave it here for the new owners to find. Whatever was in it hadn't interested her for forty years, so why should she want it now?

She opened the lid anyway and looked at the unexpected top of a bottle of wine, her heart thudding suddenly loud in her chest. It had been for Guy's return of course, she thought, to celebrate, and then, unable to throw it away, she'd put it away. The bottle itself was clean and new looking, but she couldn't help thinking it must have gone bad after living through so many hot summers up here. She couldn't bring herself to read the label or hold it in her hands, thinking of the time it ought to have been uncorked and the emotions she'd hoped to feel.

A pigeon, perched on the tiles above her, burbled its ridiculous love-warble. She heard its claws tacking and the sudden muffled clapping of winged escape.

That settled it. She pushed the case back into the darkest shadow and backed up on her hands and knees along the grimy length of carpet until her foot found the top rung of the ladder again.

Alain walked the last mile to Guy's house in the dale. It took him an hour and many pauses, resting against walls, sitting on his shooting stick, stumbling over the rocks on the back road. He was tired when he got there, but it was worth it. For every mile he'd covered since Paris the weight of the bag had become lighter, and now he could hardly feel it in his hand.

Rafaella was there, looking thin and irritable. She let him in. The place was warm but smelled of damp nonetheless. They should have let it go, moved somewhere with a more temperate climate, Alain thought. England had its beauties but he would have traded them for the comfort of the Avignon villa. But it hadn't been up to him. The girl had never stopped hoping that Violette would come back here, and Guy hadn't had the heart to stifle her hope. It was a pity, because now Rafaella was getting too old for children and too bitter for marriage, and Guy was, like himself, simply a relic awaiting destruction.

He said as much as they sat down to a whiskey.

Rafaella was taken aback by his bluntness.

"There's not much time for games," Alain shrugged. He pushed at the bag with his foot. "Open it."

She did so and unwrapped the bottle from a swatch of heavy velvet curtain. Her glance at him was quizzical, "Why now?"

"It's my fault she got lost," Alain said. "I never told you that the wine in that bottle was rancid. Something was wrong with the whole thing. I could have said so, but it didn't seem that important at the time. I thought it was a coincidence."

"You couldn't have known," Guy began, trying to brush Alain's grimness aside.

"No, but I could have guessed. We said before that what's known in space must be uncertain in time if it leaves the continuum here at all. And if time was certain, then space would be the opposite. She was gone for five minutes, and in that time we forgot that we would have MOVED, Guy. Moved forty thousand bloody miles . . . and when she came back it's us who wasn't there. Nothing was there."

Rafaella was staring into nothing. She said, into the silence that followed, "I wonder if it's the same bottle. Is there any way of proving that?"

Her father took his glass from his mouth halfway into a sip and swiped a line of whiskey from his lip. Alain's face grew even more bleak. She could tell they hadn't considered this, as she hadn't, until now. The bottle's decay had stopped, which they had taken to mean that the universes had ceased to peel away from one another or, if that theory was entirely wrong, that at least whatever dimension had leeched its substance away was now stabilized, all reactions come to their natural conclusions. She hadn't been a part of the science, barely understood any of it, but she said now, "I mean, was there any way of telling it to be the bottle you sent, Dad? Or could it be from a different continuum? Maybe we switched bottles with someone else's universe, and they didn't get one in return. Maybe this bottle is trying to get back to its own space and time."

They stared at the offended item and then, with a single, swift movement Rafaella lunged forward and sent it hurtling against the wall. It smashed instantly and the shards of glass scattered, tinkling on the floor with a sound like stars ringing in an empty heaven.

"No more uncertainty," she said, sitting back, withdrawing her hand carefully as though it were a snake that might strike again. "I can't stand it any more."

Guy crossed over to her and put his arm around her shoulders.

Alain looked at the shining splinters. "See," he said, his

voice cracking as he pointed a shaking finger at the patterns they made on the floor. "It's Andromeda, and Leo."

A smile moved from one to the other of them beginning with Guy and passing to Rafaella, and then to Alain before it faded away. Alain tried to look at the glass and see no pattern in it, but, no matter how hard he tried, he saw more and more familiar shapes as the minutes passed until he had to look away.

"Do you remember her?" Rafaella said. "Because I can't. Only little things. Her smell. The shape of her chin. The way her eyes looked when she smiled. But not all at once. I can't see her anymore. I always thought that's how you lived forever, in people's minds, but it can't be true, because we can't remember like that. If she walked in here now, I sometimes think I wouldn't know her."

Guy stood up and began to pick up the pieces, gathering them in his hand.

Alain got up to go.

There was a knock at the door.

They glanced at each other, eyes wide, and saw hope in the others' faces, impossible to extinguish but already beginning to twist with resigned disappointment. Nobody moved to answer it.

KINGS

By Colin Greenland

1

The Hunter

Soon, surely, we must come to the oasis, and the Ruby City. "Tomorrow," the guides murmur. "Tomorrow, certainly, Masters. . . ."

We make a strange trio. Balthus is taciturn and tall, like all his people, weighty and loose-limbed in his crumpled suit and brown boots. Malachi is stocky, swarthy, with thick crinkly hair the color of burnt pastry. He is much given to hearty, incomprehensible jests and sudden belligerence. One night when the water for his feet was too hot, I saw him knock the man clear across the tent.

It is a chronic infection he has, some kind of fungus that withstands the desert air. His people bathe his feet morning and evening and slather them with ointment. When they come with their bowls and towels and bottles, I withdraw.

"Hoo, Caspar," Malachi laughs. "That's it, you keep clear! You don't want to catch my rot!"

Broad yellow teeth flash within his beard.

He is provoking, Malachi, but he means no harm. He is

weary, as we all are—sick of the endless empty levels, the sand in everything. He too longs for home.

We do not travel by any direct way. We have been East, then South, then West again, by my reckoning. Already my feet are callused and cracked as a deerherd's. Every day after breakfast and again before dinner, the boy Finn rubs them with oil. He is dutiful still, and patient of all hardships.

Every day, too, I look at my photographs of Natalia and the children and continue the letter I am writing to them.

The sky by day is blue, solid blue as a painted dome over our heads. A cloud is an event; an anomaly, rarely seen and soon dispersed, as if the Creator notices His mistake and erases it. There has been no rain here for a thousand years, a hundred thousand. The kites that circle all day overhead caw derisively, as if they know something we don't.

This morning while I was writing, Malachi banged the gong that hangs outside my tent, and before I could answer, he came in: alone, unaccompanied. This is his way: informal, impatient. "What the devil are you scribbling there, Caspar?" he barked. "Your will?"

Before I could reply, he set one hand on his heart and began to declaim. "I, Caspar the Forty-Third of Uqbar, hereby bequeath my tie to my mistress Bandylegs, whom I adore, and my shoelaces to the dog, who is even better."

By now his rudeness is familiar. Almost, it is welcome. It is a diversion, here where any diversion is welcome.

"It's a letter," I told him.

"Letter?" he echoed, as if such a thing were preposterous. "Who to, this letter?"

He knows, of course. "To my wife," I said.

He laughed at that, and said, "No good writing to wives. Wives can't read."

He was boasting. In his country literacy is forbidden to

women. It is a precaution, as I understand it, against organized resistance.

"Stupid sows," said Malachi. I whispered a prayer, that his offense might be overlooked. Malachi chuckled. His faith is casual, robust. It admits of no argument, no theology. It is simply *there*, like the rock under your bed.

2

The Old Goat

We met, Malachi and I, at Aleppo, where people of all nations make common cause. In the square before the hotel I saw Moors bargaining noisily with Lascars. In the lobby a lone northerner, his skin and hair pale as milk, shared a pipe with tattooed Saracens.

A page led me to a suite on an upper floor. The rooms were scented with jasmine and rosewater. In silent slippers, my escort led me to one where a corpulent man reclined, sipping pink fizz through a straw. Servants came darting to receive me, slaves, I surmised, with long eyelashes and automatic smiles. They filled a chair with so many cushions it scarcely left me room to sit.

I saluted Malachi of Saba, and asked the Lord to preserve him.

"Caspar!" roared Malachi of Saba. "Now we're all here!" His voice was rich and merry. He slurped noisily at his drink. "This disgusting stuff! I don't know why I love it so. Here, you try!"

Unnerved, I declined the offer. He laughed and, as if I to applaud my decision, clapped his hands on the belly that bulged, broad and bare, from his tiny waistcoat. "Fetch the man a decent drink," he commanded, and barefoot maidens scurried to obey.

I asked for tea, and they brought it flavored with almonds, in a delicate china bowl. It was delicious. As I sipped it, we spoke of Saba, its checkered towers and resinous wines. In my youth, before I came into my inheritance, I traveled widely in the east and saw many great cities. I mentioned Persepolis, with her palaces of gold and ivory, the stone lions of Ecbatan. "But Çirwah I shall never forget," I said. "The most beautiful of them all."

Malachi smiled and waved a chubby hand of many rings. I presumed he was beckoning me nearer; yet he would not suffer me to rise. Instead, four brawny slaves were directed to lift my chair and bring it, with me in it, to stand beside his own. This they did with great ease and gentleness.

"Tell me about Çirwah," their master bade me, in a soft rumble. "What did you do in Çirwah?"

I recalled for him how I had strolled in her public gardens and climbed the belltower where, it is said, the thirty-two winds dwell, each in a niche adorned with its portrait carved in porphyry; and how I had endured the spectacle of the *Gdaj*, that old and brutal race. From dawn, when the city gates were barred, we had stood in our thousands waiting in the streets, shoulder to shoulder in the baking heat, without food or water except what we could win from householders who had set out temporary stalls, many just a tray on a windowsill, piled with dates and pistachios. For a handful wrapped in a paper poke they asked a villainous price. Noon had come and gone, the white sun declining from its pitiless zenith, before the horses themselves appeared: ferocious sinewy beasts with yellow eyes, each bearing the colors of its owner's tribe. Through the streets they ran, pounding uphill and hurtling down at frightening speed.

"The dust!" I said. "Enough to choke an army."

"You should have come to the palace and made yourself known!" Malachi assured me, long before my reminiscence was complete. He clapped me on the shoulder and signaled for my cup to be refilled. "Watch the whole thing in comfort, eh? A jug of wine in one hand and a girl of your choice in the other."

He rubbed his lips then, surveying his docile entourage, as if to guess which of them might suit my taste; but before he could speak, I saw Balthus of the Teutons standing over by the wall. He had come in unannounced, unattended, in a collarless shirt and a hempen suit, yet I knew him at once, so perfectly did his appearance match his reputation. My Uncle Yareb always recalled how at his wedding Balthus uttered not a word but sat the whole week apart, refusing in the chilliest manner every drink, every dance. I was a babe in arms then, but Balthus did not seem to have changed. I do not know how long he had been there silently listening, a sardonic smile on his blue jowls. Malachi, noticing where I was looking, swore mightily, laughed a harsh loud laugh and offered him too a glass of pink fizz. Jovially as he spoke, there was a certain contempt in it, quite audible. They had been traveling some weeks together already.

Balthus ignored him, gazing at me as if expecting me to do him obeisance, which I resisted, though he is my senior by many years. Then he bowed his head to me, saluting me in my own tongue, shaming me.

3

The Cup-Bearer

Now it is night. The tents glow softly. Smells waft in and out: kif, camels, leather, roasted lamb. Huge moths come to the lamp, crawl on the glass, their great furry antennae erect and trembling.

Finn, on his mat by the door, is a still small bundle beneath a sheet. The back of his head is the only part of him visible. He still wears his purple cap. He is so proud of that cap.

I call his name. "Finn." He does not move.

I rise from my couch, ungirdled, and cross to where he lies, the sand beneath the carpet shifting. I call him again, stoop and put my hand to his shoulder.

He blinks, squints as if the dim light blinds him. "Master . . . ?" His confusion is comical. I keep my face stern.

Without our customs, what are we? Moths, only, captive to any flame.

"Time to pray."

He rises, tracing a reverence in the air. He opens the shrine; lights incense. I read the text; he recites the responses. This is how we always pray: quietly, alone. From across the camp comes the sound of Malachi at his devotions, which are loud and public, with bells and the continual farting blasts of a sheep's-horn trumpet. Finn was most alarmed and offended the first time it shattered our peace. "Master!" he cried. "Is God deaf?"

Balthus prays to no one, so far as one can tell. His reverence is reserved for the stars, in whose silver trace across the sky all things are written.

Finn is of the hill tribes of the northeast, a chieftain's son from the high sierra. I took him some years ago to secure a truce, though it was an act of mercy too. His mother is dead, he told me later, relinquishing her own life in giving birth to him. I was fond of him already: his sensitive eyes, his pale fawn skin. I will have no one else near me when I sleep.

Our prayers done, Finn closes up the shrine. Malachi is still boasting and bellowing in his own language. "Lord be merciful to Thy servant a sinner! Turn not away Thy face . . ."

Finn bows to me, then raises his eyes expectantly. I dismiss him to sleep, with my blessing.

Unable to rest, I take the small lamp and step outside. The guards touch their foreheads. I nod, blessing them too, and walk out a little way beyond the camp. It occupies a natural amphitheatre, a shallow dry basin among the dunes. In the east floats the Maiden's Star, the moon hung beneath it like a silver hook to draw us on. I take pen and paper, and write.

> *Finn is a quick and faithful follower. He is more sensitive than anyone, even our guides, to the hidden life of the desert. He is always the first to spot the bird in*

*the sky, the minute flecks of green among the brown
that signal water near at hand.*

Among the tents of the Sabeans a drowsy windchime tin-
kles. A wakeful camel coughs and groans, at which all the
other camels cough and groan one after another. The sound
is like a monstrous organ played by devils.

Later I sleep and dream of Natalia and her women spreading freshly washed linen on the bushes. The billows of white
cloth conceal something in my dream, something I badly
need to find. I run urgently from bush to bush, the laughter
of women in my ears. I think I am a child again, innocent
and indulged; and I wake to daylight, the smells of baking
bread and brewing coffee.

4

The Fish

Despite the maps, we are still not arrived at the oasis. The
guides blame the sand, the wind, the sun—anything but their
own incompetence.

The overseer grovels. His face is like a mule's. "Tomorrow, Masters. Tomorrow."

Malachi shouts. He makes to strike the man with his
whip. I stay his hand. He turns away, grinding his teeth.
"Jackals, eh? Festering, flea-chewed jackals."

The overseer pulls at the corners of his mouth with finger
and thumb. "A thousand apologies, Masters . . ."

I say the word to dismiss them before he can begin to in-
sinuate another of his wheedling pleas for more pay.

Malachi cuffs me on the arm, spending the blow he meant
for the overseer. "Flog the lot of them." I fear he might if
this goes on much longer. His temper is worsening, and
Malachi is the type that must relieve his own feelings,
though it lead to mutiny or worse.

Balthus, all this while, stands with his arms folded,

gazing up at the Star. Dark glasses mask his face. A scarf is tied about his head. His only attendant is the astrologer, an ancient weasel with a long plaited beard, whom he keeps close at all hours. The astrologer, likewise, is never seen without his books, huge great volumes broad as doorsteps. They travel on their own special cart, pulled by a mute. I have often wished their space might have been given over to more provisions. Oranges, perhaps. Oranges I miss particularly. Melons. Peaches. The cart gets stuck continually in the sand and has to be dug out. On days of frustration and fatigue, like today, that seems a kind of symbol for our whole enterprise.

Gripping his long staff with both hands, Balthus speaks of a vision vouchsafed him in the desert. An hour after dawn, ranging out among the dunes, he came upon a hollow where it seemed to him there lay a lake of rainbows, fed by a waterfall.

"Above the fall," he says, "a willow tree, all green." His voice is dry, his fair skin burned and peeling. "The branches of the tree hung down into the water. In the water, two fish, one silver, one gold, swimming in circles around each other." He speaks as if to commission a painting from me. "The fish swam in among the trailing branches. As I watched, they turned into birds. And the birds flew in a great circle, up into the air, then down again into the water, where they turned back into fish."

There he stops, regarding me like a schoolmaster. It is my turn to speak.

This is how all conversations are conducted with Balthus. It is most disobliging. It ties my tongue.

I, in any case, count least in our lopsided triumvirate. It is apparent at all our discussions. Balthus itemizes the omens, interpreting each passing lizard, each bleached bone, providing chapter and verse. "*And Rizpah the daughter of Aiah took sackcloth, and spread it for her upon the rock, from the beginning of harvest until water dropped upon them out of heaven . . .*" Malachi interrupts without restraint, thumping the table, thrusting back his chair to pace about. He swears vilely. "Urchin-snouted excrement-grubbing maggot-pie!" He has the force of his personality, Balthus conviction enough for twenty. I sit all the while like a dummy, waiting to be asked my opinion. I am too used, I think, to hearing debate, to handing down judgements based on representations from all sides of a question. Their eyes turn to me at last. "Caspar? What do you say?"

Then I say yes, or no, or stay, or go, whatever seems least likely to embattle them again.

I am the youngest, the least seasoned by experience. I have trudged fewer miles, faced fewer dangers. I did not have to cross the sea to come here, as Balthus did, or endure the mountains, like Malachi. My bond, my commitment, therefore, must be less than theirs. This, I am sure, is what Balthus believes, why he patronizes me.

But sometimes, as now, Malachi rescues me. "Sunstroke," he says, ostensibly to me, though loud enough for all to hear.

Does he mean to offend? To imperil the alliance? I wonder sometimes if he is altogether trustworthy. Perhaps he keeps something from Balthus and me, knowledge of some special grace or power to be won by the first to see this visitation.

Balthus nods. He is above offense, or above showing it. "The Great Lord Sun too is a star," he says, blandly. His eyes remain invisible behind his sunglasses.

"Mirage," says Malachi then, more conciliatorily. Those we see daily: pools of clear water where beckoning women swim. If you ride toward them, they evaporate, leaving only sand, sand, sand.

"The tree is the World Tree," says Balthus, prompting me. With his staff he traces a pattern in the sand. "If the golden fish is the Star, what is the silver fish?"

I know his belief that at the end of time our earthly selves will be reunited with their heavenly counterparts, who watch over us from the sky. I dislike being catechized, yet I respond.

"The Maiden?"

He gives a nod of satisfaction. "The Maiden," he repeats. We are all, ultimately, stars.

Some miles south of Osq my companions were set upon by brigands! Presumably they mistook them for an embassy or even a common trade caravan. How surprised they must have been to discover the party well armed and perfectly able to repel them. Three of the ruffians, they say, were unfortunate enough to lose their lives in the encounter, while not one of the guards received so much as a scratch. Since then, my dearest darlings, nothing so dramatic has happened, I do assure you. One day is much like another.

Returning to my tent I see Finn sitting at the door with his chin in his hands, gazing out at the emptiness of the land, drinking in the infinity of it. I pause, unwilling to disturb him. The wind toys with his hair.

5

The Sheep

The road is long, straight and empty but for a straggling procession of rusty oil drums and wrecked cars. Aluminium cans, scoured of all content and design by sand and wind, blow rattling across the tarmac, alarming the dogs and making them bark. The din of the Ruby City reaches a long way. It sounds like a storm, crashing and crying.

Gradually the ground inclines. Ahead, the Sabeans start down the slope. My people follow. I attempt to slow my malodorous mount, which plods on oblivious as ever to the reins, my heels, my voice. It knows I am a foreigner, ignorant, negligible.

In the lanes of the city there are people everywhere, derelicts, scavengers. The children, filthy, howl at us, holding

out their hands for *baksheesh*. Whole families with their animals and servants throng the streets and clamor at the wells.
Mounted police rope and drive them here and there in herds.
In the stockyards and along the river camps have been
thrown up of hardboard and corrugated iron. Behind the
wire old men in filthy pajamas clutch bundles to their chests.
Disease is already rife.

Up in the painted council chamber platters of delicate
pastries circulate, bonbons and little iced biscuits proffered
by beautiful, tall young women in gauzy dresses of pink and
green. "The best we can do, I'm afraid." The mayor, a portly
individual with oiled hair and a pink, perspiring face, offers
us sweet wine in tiny jeweled glasses. "Under the circumstances," he says, in diplomatic English.

I smile my approval. I thank him, and praise his hospitality. He thanks me for my generosity. "You see," he keeps
saying. "You understand."

Balthus sips a glass of water. He is fasting now. No food
may pass his lips until the quest is over. The shoulders of his
suit are dusty with flakes of dead white skin.

Malachi is in his element. Stuffing petit fours into his
mouth, he gazes down into the streets. Night is falling, swift
and unequivocal at this latitude. In every alley, fires smol-
der. Over the stockyards arc lights blaze. More than ever the
sprawl resembles some jaundiced, metallic hell. What sins
must its inmates have committed to deserve this?

Malachi toasts the mayor and gestures with his glass at
the arc lights. He seems impressed. "How long have you had
the electricity?"

The mayor beams and blots his brow with a large white
kerchief. "It was the first priority of the new administration . . ."

Malachi laughs knowingly, as if the whole thing were a
splendid trick played on a worthy opponent. "Nowhere to
hide, eh?"

Below, a demonstration is in progress. Makeshift banners
wave, slogans are chanted, incomprehensible above the

general hubbub. Malachi points out the armored plow pushing through the crowd toward the place. "Oho!"

"The police," confides the mayor. Missiles go sailing through the air, stones and lumps of dung. Malachi chortles. He crams in another marshmallow and holds out his glass to the nearest waitress.

"People everywhere," he says, indistinctly. "All the same. Eh? Don't know when they're well off."

Below, the plow reaches the dissenters. Cries of pain mingle with the cries of anger. A donkey brays hysterically, over and over again.

The mayor bustles us away from the window. "We are so proud of our police!" he tells us. "They are so strong, and so cheerful always, even in the most arduous conditions."

Outside the batons rise and fall in the chromium light.

"Nothing is too much trouble for them!" smiles the mayor of Ruby City.

6

The Harness Bull

The hotel is named, for some reason, after Sinbad the Sailor. It has proper beds, with mosquito nets, and a "health spa" where you can purify your body. The balcony juts out over the river. Here we sit late into the night, discussing the next step, while lines of barges go by with their cargoes of bicycles and yams, shrink-wrapped jugs of water and crates of M-249s.

"You don't want to underestimate these provincial officials," Malachi keeps saying. "They know more than you think. They know more than *they* think, very often, eh?"

"This one thinks he knows a good deal," says Balthus. His voice is distant, a small croak. The sand blows black out of the desert, swirling tirelessly in the air, coating everything that it touches. The astrologer opens another scroll.

"If I see that guide again I'll carve my name in his guts,"

vows Malachi. He shifts on the couch. "The tall one, with the funny eye. Cockroach-munching son of a pox-ridden mare."

He is agog for bloodshed tonight. The riot has given him the taste. A slave girl strokes his thigh.

Balthus is not listening. He paces the balcony, fingering a favorite device of his, a sort of horoscopic sextant, seemingly, made of brass. My Lord of the Teutons is uncomfortable here in the city. The lights blot out the Star.

I take up my pen once more.

After the silence of the desert, the oasis is quite a shock. Suddenly, there are flourishing groves of dates, oranges, apricots. Lakes fringed with reeds where wild duck swim, men working in the fields, donkeys turning waterwheels. Their houses are low, built of mud but painted gaily with patterns of ochre, pink and yellow. The men wear rings in their noses and eyebrows; the women veil their faces as you pass.

Today we have at last reached Ruby City. We were warmly welcomed by the mayor, a very jolly man.

"Master?"

It is Finn, come all the way from the camp to find me. He takes off his cap. "Master, Eli and Omar were talking."

Malachi chuckles with disdain. "Who are *Eli* and *Omar*?"

I bid Finn come closer. I draw him to me. More gently, I ask him who Eli and Omar are. Two of the bearers, it appears. They speak a harsh dialect that Finn understands. He has overheard them planning a mass desertion. "Tonight, Master . . ."

"Good riddance, then," grunts Malachi.

A policeman is summoned. In a sweat-stained white uniform strapped and studded and bedecked with equipment, he salutes, identifying himself as the chief of the local force. He is a squat man with broad shoulders, hairy as a djinn. Black hair protrudes from the neck of his shirt. Balthus complains at length and in detail about the untrustworthiness of the local inhabitants. Malachi gives him brandy, questions him closely about firearms. I hardly listen. The decision is already made. The guides will be dismissed, the camels, if there are any left, sold. The policeman smiles obsequiously, ingratiatingly. He is only too willing to procure vehicles for us.

Balthus stands up, tugging at his jacket. The astrologer gathers up his materials. Malachi is occupied with his slave girl. Embarrassed for the policeman, I address him, complimenting him on his control of a difficult situation. "The refugees," I say. "One's heart goes out to them."

He seems not to understand me. Then he laughs. "Refugees? No, no." He hitches up his trousers. "Forgive, my lord, you make mistake. It is the census. The census only."

7

The Twins

The ferryman has only one arm, the right. Use has enlarged it. His biceps is as thick as my waist. He rows standing up, dressed only in a couple of rags, one about his head, the other about his loins. He carries our party across to a tall white house, four stories, with stained glass in the windows and lamps of pierced brass in the porch.

The porter wears a black robe. He greets the policeman with exaggerated respect, though the sounds he makes are the unpleasant ones of a man who has lost his tongue. I wonder then if everyone in Ruby City is maimed in some way.

We are conducted into a parlor full of old-fashioned European furniture: mahogany tables, dark oils in gilt frames; sofas of uncut moquette. There is an upright piano, and a gilt birdcage on a stand. Seated at the piano is a young woman dressed only in a chemise and black stockings. Her hair hangs loose about her shoulders. When we enter, she is play-

ing a wistful melody, but on sighting us her companions—
all women, none fully dressed—call out to her, and she
changes to an ironic march.

"Captain!" One of the women, a fat brunette in salmon-
pink underwear, rises and embraces Malachi. They kiss
busily, like lovers long separated. I try not to watch. Malachi
is chortling, calling for alcohol.

Another denizen of the place ventures to greet me. She is
more demure, though scarcely better clad. I accept a chair
but will not let her on my lap. The woman at the piano plays
a boisterous, bouncing song. There is lewdness in every note
and in every corner of the room, wherever I avert my eyes.
They are divesting the policeman of his uniform. Discom-
fited, I look at the bird in its cage. It is a budgerigar, a blue
one.

I can never see a budgerigar in a cage without thinking of
one we had when I was very young. Kili lived in the solar-
ium. I remember the strangeness of his yellow face, dusty as
the center of a daisy, the lavender nostrils above his tough
little beak. My sister and I took turns to feed him, wedges of
cuttlefish and spikes of millet poked carefully between the
bars. Once in a long while Mother would let him out to fly
around the room or bathe in a soup-bowl of water, which he
did with much flapping and splashing. At liberty, Kili might
perch on your head or hand. I remember his claws, sharp as
pins. Father could bear them; I could not.

Kili grew a hump on his back, a mass the size and shape
of a thimble. It was brown and bloody where he kept peck-
ing at it. When he died, I wept. Mother tried to comfort me,
but Father said, "Let the child cry. He must learn the facts of
death."

The woman who sought to debauch me watches me
steadily from across the room. She is very young, little more
than a child. She toys with the pianist's hair. I realize then
they must be sisters. They have the same huge eyes, the
same slight figure. Bored with music and my refusal, they
begin to caress each other. Malachi roars, his entourage

squeal as they drag him upstairs. *"Blast your eyes, Caspar, is there blood in your veins?"* The fat woman's face is between the policeman's thighs. I wonder how this house and its occupants will appear in his census.

The relentless glare of day, the smoking lamps of night. My eyes are sore. I rub them. Behind my eyelids images gleam, cavorting, like the women, languidly. The gold sister, the silver one. I pray fervently to the Lord, and to his Heavenly Daughter. *Let me come safe home to Natalia and the children.*

When I open my eyes, I see a boy, a Teuton in leather shorts and a little cocked hat. He glances around in curiosity, then amazement, at the scene. Idle women coo and rush to pet him. At my call he straightens himself and approaches, bowing and craving pardon from everyone.

The message is from Balthus. The Star has come to rest.

8

The Crab

The name of the village is Rac. In the language of the place, Malachi remarks from the front seat of the half-track, it is the word for *crab*.

"A strange name," I observe, "so far inland."

Malachi doesn't reply. I glance at Balthus. He sits beside me, a statue in silhouette. He is not interested in anything I might have to say. The interpretation of signs is his preserve, not mine.

The driver takes us to the middle of the village, where a low fire burns, tended by old women with sticks. The reek of charred dung fills the air.

The guardians of the fire stare at us resentfully. Balthus opens his bag of instruments. The astrologer licks his thumb and turns a page. The rustle of dry paper sounds loud in the darkness. Still no one speaks. The boy Finn sits wrapped in a whore's coat. The night is cold, and he was thinly clad.

My throat is thick with dust. Clearing it discreetly, I get to my feet. "Blessings on this place," I say. "We are pilgrims from distant lands. We follow the Star." I point where it blazes white over our heads, much the brightest thing in the heavens.

People have begun to appear, peeping or emerging from their huts, clutching rags about them. They look not at the Star but at my hand, as if they do not understand the convention of the outstretched finger. Feeling a trifle foolish, I sit down again.

Balthus orders the passenger door to be opened. He plants his staff, takes a few steps away, and with many obeisances kneels in the dust.

Now the villagers murmur nervously. They look unhealthy, malnourished. The firelight glimmers on swollen bellies, deformed limbs.

Gathering his robes, his cumbersome tablets, the astrologer has climbed out too. Deprived of his cart and its mournful operator, he shuffles awkwardly, sideways, to join his master. Balthus, still kneeling, is making sightings. Fearful of the strange man, the spectators have fallen silent again. The only sound is the muffled popping of the flames—that and a hollow ringing in my ears. Finn is half asleep. I do not wish to wake him.

A quality of improbability begins to radiate from the whole locality, as if we have stumbled into the middle of an illusion, an artificial place such as might be built for the making of films. I look around the low, mean buildings, the diseased inhabitants, the reeking fire. I wonder how I shall describe it in my letters. Seeking a good complexion to put on it, I begin to imagine a Creator who might choose this rude, plain corner of the world for His revelation. Perhaps in the Eyes of the Most Exalted its very lowliness commends it.

Balthus is now on his feet again, and deep in consultation with the astrologer. Nothing seems to be happening. To the back of Malachi's head I murmur, "Well, it's not exactly what I'd expected . . ."

Malachi sits still as stone, brooding. Ever since we left the mansion of depravity, he has been subdued. Perhaps the imminence of our grail chastens him. Perhaps he grows mindful of his sins. He breaks wind, and chuckles coarsely. Annoyed, I cough. Finn stirs.

Balthus returns, shaking his head. "Further on," he says.

All at once I am furious. "How *much* further?"

Finn starts awake. Malachi turns in his seat, grinning. He likes to see me lose my temper.

Balthus is rolling up a chart. "Not far," he says. "Come." I stare stonily at him, unwilling to be commanded. "We proceed on foot," he explains. The astrologer nods weightily.

Malachi gets out of the vehicle. He stands stretching and scratching himself. I am so tired my head is like a stone. I climb out too, and Finn scrambles after me.

"The boy stays here," Balthus says.

This is intolerable. I look pointedly at the old man with his arms full of books. "The boy comes with me."

9

The Mountain Lion

The track winds from the village, through the valley, passing between squat mesas. Outcrops protrude from the ground. In the dark they look like giant hands signaling to one another. In the distance another clutch of buildings appears, smaller still than Rac. A single smallholding, perhaps.

Balthus strides confidently ahead, at each stride thrusting his staff into the sand and jerking it free. I know so little about him still, or about his homeland. I imagine cold hills, rock chasms, caves where ice lingers. Along the hills tall trees grow gnarled and harsh, bowed sideways by the gales of an eternal winter. Among them stalk tall men with large heads, large hands and feet. They wear furs. They are great hunters, tracking their prey for miles before bringing it down in a sudden roaring ambush of knives and blood.

I do not know from where this idea comes. Conversations with Malachi, perhaps, about our companion from the North. Or perhaps it is a dream I had, once, long ago.

Behind Balthus Malachi waddles suspiciously through the sand. He sniffs the air and glowers. I need not speak to him to know he shares my gloom. How many false dawns has the Teuton lord declared since we left Aleppo? In how many circles has he led us? This place, whatever it is, will be no different. I am quite sure of that.

The buildings look sturdier than the hovels of Rac. They are built from crude blocks of pink mud, square against the wind. Around the buildings the sand lies in great scooped drifts. It must be a ceaseless task to shovel it back, lest it flood everything altogether. This sudden insight into the cares of the poor startles me, as if my mind had been invaded by another's thoughts. I shiver. Finn turns to me at once. "Master?" I shake my head and signal him onward.

Through a gatehouse we enter a central plot of rough grass where a few thin animals lie, sheep or goats, looking more dead than asleep. There is a long interval of communications, negotiations, translations. The master of the place is gone, it seems, and taken all his family. They are in the city, of course, along with everyone else. Balthus speaks to one who remains, a wrinkled old man in a shepherd's smock. The astrologer points at the Star. The shepherd nods sagely. He knows what we have come to see.

Suddenly I wonder if this, finally, can actually be the place. I too look at the Star. It seems no different now from when we saw it an hour ago, at Rac. Together we start forward, moving at a stately pace behind the old shepherd, through another gateway, and across a yard to a large wooden building.

"This is a stable," says Malachi, as we step inside. He sounds perplexed. So it must have been once, with stalls for beasts and troughs for food and water. Now it is only a store for old barrels, old planks of timber, old tarpaulins rolled and tied with twine. Farm implements and disused furniture stand in piles. A peculiar stink lingers in the place, of long-dried sweat and manure, dust and tar. Finn covers his mouth and nose with his shirt.

The shepherd speaks a word, a single gruff monosyllable. He directs us to one corner that seems to have been left clear of rubbish. Something stands there: a pole a yard long, upright, supporting something small.

My heart beats faster. Malachi whispers a prayer. Balthus, very active now and busy, strides around, calling for lights.

I consider the shepherd. His face, his whole body, shows wariness, mistrust. I give Finn a silver coin for him.

"Tell him we are pleased," I say. "He has done well."

Finn obeys. The shepherd looks at me rheumily. He bites my coin, then touches his forehead, nodding a bow.

The lights are arriving, smoky torches borne aloft. No electricity here.

10

The Maiden

The construction is a stand that supports a short perch, all crudely wrought of thick black iron. Sitting on the perch is a small brown bird. It is about the size of a thrush, or less. It looks dehydrated: mummified even, as if its plumage has shriveled and its skin turned to leather. Nonetheless it stirs, turning nervously toward the light; and as it moves, a dusty train catches the light. A skein of cobweb, ancient and dusty, stretches between the bird and its perch.

Malachi stumbles forward. The torchlight makes him seem to grin, to salivate, almost, as if he wants to eat the thing.

My heart is in my mouth. I wonder what he thinks he sees.

Balthus stands forth, the master of ceremonies. He speaks an incantation: loud, harsh syllables in some unrecognizable tongue. He gestures with his staff.

The bird gives a little shivering twitch, quite as if it were real, which of course it cannot be. It looks like a prune, shiny and puckered. It levers open its wings a little and patters along the perch in our direction. Its eyes are glinting, hard and black as onyx beads.

I think of the budgerigar at the bordello, and of Kili, with his bloody hump. This is some kind of trick. I glance wildly at the others, to see who is grinning. All eyes are fixed on the shriveled bird.

Balthus and his shadow blend together. They swoop upward to the roof. The lion of the mountains is a veritable giant. He looks down at me. He holds out his hand, palm up.

My eyes are adjusting now to the dimness. It is a cunning piece of work: a jointed carving, worked no doubt by strings inside the metal stand. Else, why such a hefty support for such a tiny creature? There is an extension attached to one end of the perch: a cylinder, with what looks like a slot in it, as if to take a coin. I am reminded of mechanical automata, amusements on the promenade. There is some fee, I suppose, confusedly: a tribute to be paid. I open my pouch again.

Finn tugs my sleeve. "Master—" he breathes.

Gently I set him aside and examine what I have. I hear my voice say: "What does it take?"

Among the coins is something that is not one and does not belong with them. It seems to be a small disc of chocolate. It must have got in there somehow at the reception in Ruby City. I pick it out, as if to put it in my mouth or Finn's, but I stop. This, I think, must be what Balthus wants. I hold it out to him, and he takes it. It looks absurdly small in his huge, coarse fingers.

He passes it over the slot, if indeed it is one and not merely a shadow, and gives it to the remarkable bird, which takes it: not daintily, as one might have supposed, given its small size and obvious frailty, but fiercely. It snaps it up, as a lizard might snap up a fly. Then it shakes itself again, vibrating rapidly. It seems no longer pitted but plump.

Stretching out its head, it begins to sing.

11

The Balance

I could not say, then or now or ever, what it was the Maiden sang. Her song made pictures in my mind: waterfalls in great humid forests; strange buildings hundreds of feet high, with thousands of shining windows; trains of painted steel carriages racing between the rooftops; caverns of ancient lava, or marble pink as raspberries, glazed with the perpetual sheen of seeping water.

There were words too, in the song, though not any I could write here. They seemed so obvious, as they emerged from that minute pulsating throat, that there would be no point to trying to remember and reproduce them. They were aspects of the moment, like the stale reek of long-departed horses and cattle; like the dust sparking in the torches; like the wonder in Finn's eyes. They were there and gone; or rather, always there, always here, like the air we breathe, that is inside us and outside us and everywhere around us, but can never be seen.

The tune of Her song, the music of it, was more like laughter than anything I can say: laughter with mischief in it, as if there was a joke indeed, the best joke in Creation— one we all know, every man and woman and child and beast and bird of us. Then again, to put it another way, it was like water trickling into sand; or fire raining from a gunpowder rocket, a shower of stars in the black night, that blazed out of nothing and vanished again into nothing before one could say, *There it is, or there; it is this shape, or that.*

It was madness. I would confess that, certainly. I was aware of that, even while it was upon me. I was in the grip of something, perhaps, like the nonsensical phrases upon which certain monks in the East are said to meditate for years, attaining enlightenment only when they penetrate at last to the sacred heart of them. Balthus came into my sight, his face rapt, with an expression I could not have named,

that I had never seen there before. Meanwhile, Malachi was
laughing once again, deep and low, laughing and laughing
and laughing. Malachi saw the joke. His laughter was the
tune, just as Balthus's staff *was* the willow tree, and the twin
fish that were birds were also women that swam around and
around, gold melting into silver and back again into gold.
There was good but also evil, life but also death. Neither
could exist without the other. Each generated and contained
the other. Each was the other. I wanted to tear off my clothes
and dive into the sun. I wanted to scream, and dance, and
throw knives, and drink hot blood. I wanted to run all the
way home to Natalia and fling my arms around her and tell
her how much I loved her. People were crowding around.
They were coming—where were they coming from? They
were coming between me and the Maiden. I could not see
Her any more. There was the sound of furniture toppling.
Something rolled across the floor. There was a babble of excited voices. I became aware that it had been going on for
some time.

Malachi was in the press, elbowing his way forward. I
reached out to detain him, to tell him it didn't matter: the
bird was saying nothing we didn't know already, which was
everything, everything!

Then it was over. We were gathered, my companions and
I, around a small brown bird on a perch, in a filthy shed.

12

The Scorpion

I am on the floor, for some reason. Finn is gazing down at
me in horror and alarm.

Malachi looks at me blankly, then bursts into laughter
again. Balthus rubs his chin, and turns away.

The shepherd stares at me, then at my companions. Concern flickers on his gnarled face, as if he can't understand
why they aren't helping me out of my undignified position.

He limps forward, extending a grimy hand to me. I ignore it. I'm perfectly capable of rising unaided, and do so.

My neck aches, as if I have been straining it. I must have been standing for the Lord knows how long, in a kind of trance. My face is wet with tears. I have the boy wipe it. He is crying too. Crying for the little bird.

"Hush," I tell him.

The perch is empty. The bird has gone.

"Where is it?" I demand to know. "Where has it gone?"

No one answers.

I grow agitated. Someone has stolen the bird in the crush. It no longer matters to me whether it was a clever toy or a real bird disfigured by torchlight or disease. I wish to look at it properly, and it has gone.

I pick up the perch. It is even heavier than it looks. Cobweb trails over my hand. I flick it away.

"Who has taken it? Who has hidden it?"

The shepherd speaks to Finn. Finn speaks to me. "He says perhaps it flew away."

That makes me angry. I throw down the perch. It topples over, almost striking the shepherd. "That?" I say, pointing my finger. "That? That thing, *fly*?" My vision narrows to a dim spot. "You must take me for an idiot."

Everyone starts talking at once. I turn over a pile of boxes. They tumble thunderously to the ground. "Pick those up," I order. "Move everything away from here." I wave my arm. I am convinced the bird is still here somewhere, among all the lumber, if only we can find it. I seize hold of the stable wall, trying to pull a plank free from its battens. "Rip all this out. We'll find it!"

As soon as the peasants start to obey, I stop them. "Did you hear that? Who heard that?" There was a noise, I am certain: a fluttering, rustling noise, as of wings against dry wood. "Silence!" I bellow. But there is nothing. "Are you going to shift all this rubbish?" I yell.

They look at me warily. They do not move. I start to sense a disrespect growing among them. Enraged, thinking to

shame them, I wade in among the fallen boxes and seize a
roll of carpet. I fling my arms around it, soiling my clothes.
I cannot budge the thing. I fall back, panting. I kick a tea
chest, splintering the slatted side. A large red scorpion runs
out, darts into the nearest shadow and disappears again.

The old shepherd stands before me, waving his hands pla-
catingly. I seize him by the arms and shake him bodily.
"What have you done with it?"

"My lord—!"

A hand falls on my arm. A fat brown hand cobbled all
over with rings. Malachi.

"Come out of it, Caspar."

The boy Finn weeps still, and trembles. When I put a hand
on his shoulder, he embraces me suddenly, burying his face
in my clothes as if to breathe me in. I am surprised, touched,
consoled. I wait a moment before moving him away.

"It has been a difficult day for all of us," I announce, for-
giving him before he can apologize. From the corner of my
eye I see the astrologer nodding, tracing a complicated gesture in the air before him: a sign of acquiescence, perhaps.

13

The Hunter

Outside, the desert wind cools my brow. The dawn seems no
nearer. We might have been in there an hour listening to that
unearthly song or only a minute. Chief among my tangled
feelings is resentment. I am sure still that some trick has
been played. The whores at the bordello. The hags around
the fire.

I find myself regretting quite keenly the waste of time and
money, the effort and resources we have expended already.
What has been achieved? Nothing.

Balthus emerges now, ducking his head. I watch him take
out a scarf and wipe his scalp and hands. Even now I am unsure what he intends. I fold my arms.

"I hope you're not going to say that was it," I say, as coolly as I can. "In there. That thing."

Balthus shakes his head, seeming not to answer my question so much as dismiss it. He studies the sky, the unspeaking Star.

"We must get on," he says.

BEYOND THE AQUILA RIFT

By Alastair Reynolds

Greta's with me when I pull Suzy out of the surge tank.

"Why her?" Greta asks.

"Because I want her out first," I say, wondering if Greta's jealous. I don't blame her: Suzy's beautiful, but she's also smart. There isn't a better syntax runner in Ashanti Industrial.

"What happened?" Suzy asks, when she's over the grogginess. "Did we make it back?"

I ask her to tell me the last thing she remembered.

"Customs," Suzy says. "Those pricks on Arkangel."

"And after that? Anything else? The runes? Do you remember casting them?"

"No," she says, then picks up something in my voice. The fact that I might not be telling the truth, or telling her all she needs to know. "Thom. I'll ask you again. Did we make it back?"

"Yeah," I say. "We made it back."

Suzy looks back at the starscape, airbrushed across her surge tank in luminous violet and yellow paint. She'd had it customised on Carillon. It was against regs: something about the paint clogging intake filters. Suzy didn't care. She told me it had cost her a week's pay, but it had been worth it

to impose her own personality on the gray company archi-
tecture of the ship.

"*Funny how I feel like I've been in that thing for months.*"

I shrug. "*That's the way it feels sometimes.*"

"*Then nothing went wrong?*"

"*Nothing at all.*"

Suzy looks at Greta. "Then who are you?" she asks.

Greta says nothing. She just looks at me expectantly.
I start shaking, and realize I can't go through with this.
Not yet.

"*End it,*" *I tell Greta.*

Greta steps toward Suzy. Suzy reacts, but she isn't quick
enough. Greta pulls something from her pocket and touches
Suzy on the forearm. Suzy drops like a puppet, out cold. We
put her back into the surge tank, plumb her back in and
close the lid.

"*She won't remember anything,*" *Greta says. "The con-*
versation never left her short term memory."

"*I don't know if I can go through with this,*" *I say.*

Greta touches me with her other hand. "No one ever said
this was going to be easy."

"*I was just trying to ease her into it gently. I didn't want*
to tell her the truth right out."

"*I know,*" *Greta says. "You're a kind man, Thom." Then*
she kisses me.

I remembered Arkangel as well. That was about where it
all started to go wrong. We just didn't know it then.

We missed our first take-off slot when customs found a
discrepancy in our cargo waybill. It wasn't serious, but it
took them a while to realize their mistake. By the time they
did, we knew we were going to be sitting on the ground for
another eight hours, while in-bound control processed a fleet
of bulk carriers.

I told Suzy and Ray the news. Suzy took it pretty well, or
about as well as Suzy ever took that kind of thing. I suggested she use the time to scour the docks for any hot syn-

tax patches. Anything that might shave a day or two off our return trip.

"Company authorized?" she asked.

"I don't care," I said.

"What about Ray?" Suzy asked. "Is he going to sit here drinking tea while I work for my pay?"

I smiled. They had a bickering, love-hate thing going. "No, Ray can do something useful as well. He can take a look at the q-planes."

"Nothing wrong with those planes," Ray said.

I took off my old Ashanti Industrial bib cap, scratched my bald spot and turned to the jib man.

"Right. Then it won't take you long to check them over, will it?"

"Whatever, Skip."

The thing I liked about Ray was that he always knew when he'd lost an argument. He gathered his kit and went out to check over the planes. I watched him climb the jib ladder, tools hanging from his belt. Suzy got her facemask, long black coat and left, vanishing into the vapor haze of the docks, boot heels clicking into the distance long after she'd passed out of sight.

I left the *Blue Goose*, walking in the opposite direction to Suzy. Overhead, the bulk carriers slid in one after the other. You heard them long before you saw them. Mournful, cetacean moans cut down through the piss-yellow clouds over the port. When they emerged, you saw dark hulls scabbed and scarred by the blocky extrusions of syntax patterning, jibs and q-planes retracted for landing and undercarriage clutching down like talons. The carriers stopped over their allocated wells and lowered down on a scream of thrust. Docking gantries closed around them like grasping skeletal fingers. Cargo handling 'saurs plodded out of their holding pens, some of them autonomous, some of them still being ridden by trainers. There was a shocking silence as the engines cut, until the next carrier began to approach through the clouds.

I always like watching ships coming and going, even when they're holding my own ship on the ground. I couldn't read the syntax, but I knew these ships had come in all the way from the Rift. The Aquila Rift is about as far out as anyone ever goes. At median tunnel speeds, it's a year from the center of the Local Bubble.

I've been out that way once in my life. I've seen the view from the near side of the Rift, like a good tourist. It was about far enough for me.

When there was a lull in the landing pattern, I ducked into a bar and found an Aperture Authority booth that took Ashanti credit. I sat in the seat and recorded a thirty-second message to Katerina. I told her I was on my way back but that we were stuck on Arkangel for another few hours. I warned her that the delay might cascade through to our tunnel routing, depending on how busy things were at the Aperture Authority's end. Based on past experience, an eight-hour ground hold might become a two day hold at the surge point. I told her I'd be back, but she shouldn't worry if I was a few days late.

Outside a diplodocus slouched by with a freight container strapped between its legs.

I told Katerina I loved her and couldn't wait to get back home.

While I walked back to the *Blue Goose*, I thought of the message racing ahead of me. Transmitted at lightspeed upsystem, then copied into the memory buffer of the next outgoing ship. Chances were, that particular ship wasn't headed to Barranquilla or anywhere near it. The Aperture Authority would have to relay the message from ship to ship until it reached its destination. I might even reach Barranquilla ahead of it, but in all my years of delays that had only happened once. The system worked all right.

Overhead, a white passenger liner had been slotted in between the bulk carriers. I lifted up my mask to get a better look at it. I got a hit of ozone, fuel, and dinosaur dung. That was Arkangel all right. You couldn't mistake it for any other place in the Bubble. There were four hundred worlds out there, up to a dozen surface ports on every planet, and none of them smelled bad in quite the same way.

"Thom?"

I followed the voice. It was Ray, standing by the dock.

"You finished checking those planes?" I asked.

Ray shook his head. "That's what I wanted to talk to you about. They were a little off-alignment, so—seeing as we're going to be sitting here for eight hours—I decided to run a full recalibration."

I nodded. "That was the idea. So what's the prob?"

"The *prob* is a slot just opened up. Tower says we can lift in thirty minutes."

I shrugged. "Then we'll lift."

"I haven't finished the recal. As it is, things are worse than before I started. Lifting now would not be a good idea."

"You know how the tower works," I said. "Miss two offered slots, you could be on the ground for days."

"No one wants to get back home sooner than I do," Ray said.

"So cheer up."

"She'll be rough in the tunnel. It won't be a smooth ride home."

I shrugged. "Do we care? We'll be asleep."

"Well, it's academic. We can't leave without Suzy."

I heard boot heels clicking toward us. Suzy came out of the fog, tugging her own mask aside.

"No joy with the rune monkeys," she said. "Nothing they were selling I hadn't seen a million times before. Fucking cowboys."

"It doesn't matter," I said. "We're leaving anyway."

Ray swore. I pretended I hadn't heard him.

I was always the last one into a surge tank. I never went under until I was sure we were about to get the green light. It gave me a chance to check things over. Things can always go wrong, no matter how good the crew.

The *Blue Goose* had come to a stop near the AA beacon which marked the surge point. There were a few other ships ahead of us in the queue, plus the usual swarm of AA service craft. Through an observation blister I was able to watch the larger ships depart one by one. Accelerating at maximum power, they seemed to streak toward a completely feature-less part of the sky. Their jibs were spread wide, and the smooth lines of their hulls were gnarled and disfigured with the cryptic alien runes of the routing syntax. At twenty gees it was as if a huge invisible hand snatched them away into the distance. Ninety seconds later, there'd be a pale green flash from a thousand kilometers away.

I twisted around in the blister. There were the foreshort-ened symbols of our routing syntax. Each rune of the script was formed from a matrix of millions of hexagonal platelets. The platelets were on motors so they could be pushed in or out from the hull.

Ask the Aperture Authority and they'll tell you that the syntax is now fully understood. This is true, but only up to a point. After two centuries of study, human machines can now construct and interpret the syntax with an acceptably low failure rate. Given a desired destination, they can as-semble a string of runes which will almost always be ac-cepted by the aperture's own machinery. Furthermore, they can almost always guarantee that the desired routing is the one that the aperture machinery will provide.

In short, you usually get where you want to go.

Take a simple point-to-point transfer, like the Hauraki run. In that case there is no real disadvantage in using auto-matic syntax generators. But for longer trajectories—those that may involve six or seven transits between aperture hubs—machines lose the edge. They find a solution, but usually it isn't the optimum one. That's where syntax run-ners come in. People like Suzy have an intuitive grasp of syntax solutions. They dream in runes. When they see a poorly constructed script, they feel it like a toothache. It *af-fronts* them.

A good syntax runner can shave days off a route. For a company like Ashanti Industrial, that can make a lot of difference.

But I wasn't a syntax runner. I could tell when something had gone wrong with the platelets, but otherwise I had no choice. I had to trust that Suzy had done her job.

But I knew Suzy wouldn't screw things up.

I twisted around and looked back the other way. Now that we were in space, the q-planes had deployed. They were swung out from the hull on triple hundred-meter long jibs, like the arms of a grapple. I checked that they were locked in their fully extended positions and that the status lights were all in the green. The jibs were Ray's area. He'd been checking the alignment of the ski-shaped q-planes when I ordered him to close-up ship and prepare to lift. I couldn't see any visible indication that they were out of alignment, but then again it wouldn't take much to make our trip home bumpier than usual. But as I'd told Ray, who cared? The *Blue Goose* could take a little tunnel turbulence. It was built to.

I checked the surge point again. Only three ships ahead of us.

I went back to the surge tanks and checked that Suzy and Ray were all right. Ray's tank had been customized at the same time that Suzy had had hers done. It was full of images of what Suzy called the BVM: the Blessed Virgin Mary. The BVM was always in a spacesuit, carrying a little spacesuited Jesus. Their helmets were airbrushed gold halos. The artwork had a cheap, hasty look to it. I assumed Ray hadn't spent as much as Suzy.

Quickly I stripped down to my underclothes. I plumbed into my own unpainted surge tank and closed the lid. The buffering gel sloshed in. Within about twenty seconds I was already feeling drowsy. By the time traffic control gave us the green light, I'd be asleep.

I've done it a thousand times. There was no fear, no apprehension. Just a tiny flicker of regret.

I've never seen an aperture. Then again, very few people have.

Witnesses report a doughnut shaped lump of dark chondrite asteroid, about two kilometers across. The entire middle section has been cored out, with the inner part of the ring faced by the quixotic-matter machinery of the aperture itself. They say the q-matter machinery twinkles and moves all the while, like the ticking innards of a very complicated clock. But the monitoring systems of the Aperture Authority detect no movement at all.

It's alien technology. We have no idea how it works, or even who made it. Maybe, in hindsight, it's better not to be able to see it.

It's enough to dream, and then awake, and know that you're somewhere else.

Try a different approach, Greta says. Tell her the truth this time. Maybe she'll take it easier than you think.

"There's no way I can tell her the truth."

Greta leans one hip against the wall, one hand still in her pocket. "Then tell her something half way to it."

We unplumb Suzy and haul her out of the surge tank.

"Where are we?" she asks. Then to Greta: "Who are you?"

I wonder if some of the last conversation did make it out of Suzy's short-term memory after all.

"Greta works here," I say.

"Where's here?"

I remember what Greta told me. "A station in Schedar sector."

"That's not where we're meant to be, Thom."

I nod. "I know. There was a mistake. A routing error."

Suzy's already shaking her head. "There was nothing wrong . . ."

"I know. It wasn't your fault." I help her into her ship clothes. She's still shivering, her muscles reacting to movement after so much time in the tank. "The syntax was good."

"Then what?"

"The system made a mistake, not you."

"Schedar sector . . ." Suzy says. "That would put us about ten days off our schedule, wouldn't it?"

I try to remember what Greta said to me the first time. I ought to know this stuff off by heart, but Suzy's the routing expert, not me. "That sounds about right," I say.

But Suzy shakes her head. "Then we're not in Schedar sector."

I try to sound pleasantly surprised.

"We're not?"

"I've been in that tank for a lot longer than a few days, Thom. I know. I can feel it in every fucking bone in my body. So where are we?"

I turn to Greta. I can't believe this is happening again.

"End it," I say.

Greta steps toward Suzy.

You know that "as soon as I awoke I knew everything was wrong" cliché? You've probably heard it a thousand times, in a thousand bars across the Bubble, wherever ship crews swap tall tales over flat company-subsidized beer. The trouble is that sometimes that's exactly the way it happens. I never felt good after a period in the surge tank. But the only time I had ever come around feeling anywhere near this bad was after that trip I took to the edge of the Bubble.

Mulling this, but knowing there was nothing I could do about it until I was out of the tank, it took me half an hour of painful work to free myself from the connections. Every muscle fiber in my body felt as though it had been shredded. Unfortunately, the sense of wrongness didn't end with the tank. The *Blue Goose* was much too quiet. We should have been heading away from the last exit aperture after our routing. But the distant, comforting rumble of the fusion engines wasn't there at all. That meant we were in free-fall.

Not good.

I floated out of the tank, grabbed a handhold and levered myself around to view the other two tanks. Ray's largest

BVM stared back radiantly from the cowl of his tank. The bio indices were all in the green. Ray was still unconscious, but there was nothing wrong with him. Same story with Suzy. Some automated system had decided I was the only one who needed waking.

A few minutes later I had made my way to the same observation blister I'd used to check the ship before the surge. I pushed my head into the scuffed glass halfdome and looked around.

We'd arrived somewhere. The *Blue Goose* was sitting in a huge zero-gravity parking bay. The chamber was an elongated cylinder, hexagonal in cross-section. The walls were a smear of service machinery: squat modules, snaking umbilical lines, the retracted cradles of unused docking berths. Whichever way I looked I saw other ships locked onto cradles. Every make and class you could think of, every possible configuration of hull design compatible with aperture transitions. Service lights threw a warm golden glow on the scene. Now and then the whole chamber was bathed in the stuttering violet flicker of a cutting torch.

It was a repair facility.

I was just starting to mull on that when I saw something extend itself from the wall of the chamber. It was a telescopic docking tunnel, groping toward our ship. Through the windows in the side of the tunnel I saw figures floating, pulling themselves along hand over hand.

I sighed and started making my way to the airlock.

By the time I reached the lock they were already through the first stage of the cycle. Nothing wrong with that—there was no good reason to prevent foreign parties boarding a vessel—but it *was* just a tiny bit impolite. But perhaps they'd assumed we were all asleep.

The door slid open.

"You're awake," a man said. "Captain Thomas Gundlupet of the *Blue Goose*, isn't it?"

"Guess so," I said.

"Mind if we come in?"

There were about half a dozen of them, and they were already coming in. They all wore slightly timeworn ochre overalls, flashed with too many company sigils. My hackles rose. I really didn'tlike the way they were barging in.

"What's up?" I said. "Where are we?"

"Where do you think?" the man said. He had a face full of stubble, with bad yellow teeth. I was impressed with that. Having bad teeth took a lot of work these days. It was years since I'd seen anyone who had the same dedication to the art.

"I'm really hoping you're not going to tell me we're still stuck in Arkangel system," I said.

"No, you made it through the gate."

"And?"

"There was a screw-up. Routing error. You didn't pop out of the right aperture."

"Oh, Christ." I took off my bib cap. "It never rains. Something went wrong with the insertion, right?"

"Maybe. Maybe not. Who knows how these things happen? All we know is you aren't supposed to be here."

"Right. And where is 'here'?"

"Saumlaki Station. Schedar sector."

He said it as though he was already losing interest, as if this was a routine he went through several times a day.

He might have been losing interest. I wasn't.

I'd never heard of Saumlaki station, but I'd certainly heard of Schedar sector. Schedar was a K supergiant out toward the edge of the Local Bubble. It defined one of the seventy-odd navigational sectors across the whole Bubble.

Did I mention the Bubble already?

You know how the Milky Way galaxy looks; you've seen it a thousand times, in paintings and computer simulations. A bright central bulge at the Galactic core, with lazily curved spiral arms flung out from that hub, each arm composed of hundreds of billions of stars, ranging from the dimmest, slow-burning dwarfs to the hottest supergiants tee-tering on the edge of supernova extinction.

Now zoom in on one arm of the Milky Way. There's the sun, orange-yellow, about two-thirds out from the center of the Galaxy. Lanes and folds of dust swaddle the sun out to distances of tens of thousands of light-years. Yet the sun it-self is sitting right in the middle of a four-hundred-light-year-wide hole in the dust, a bubble in which the density is about a twentieth of its average value.

That's the Local Bubble. It's as if God blew a hole in the dust just for us.

Except, of course, it wasn't God. It was a supernova, about a million years ago.

Look further out, and there are more bubbles, their walls intersecting and merging, forming a vast froth-like structure tens of thousands of light years across. There are the struc-tures of Loop I and Loop II and the Lindblad Ring. There are even super-dense knots where the dust is almost too thick to be seen through at all. Black cauls like the Taurus or Rho-Ophiuchi dark clouds or the Aquila Rift itself.

Lying outside the Local Bubble, the Rift is the furthest point in the galaxy we've ever traveled to. It's not a question of endurance or nerve. There simply isn't a way to get be-yond it, at least not within the faster-than-light network of the aperture links. The rabbit-warren of possible routes just doesn't reach any further. Most destinations—including most of those on the *Blue Goose*'s itinerary—didn't even get you beyond the Local Bubble.

For us, it didn't matter. There's still a lot of commerce you can do within a hundred light-years of Earth. But Schedar was right on the periphery of the Bubble, where dust density began to ramp up to normal galactic levels, two hundred and twenty-eight light-years from Mother Earth.

Again: not good.

"I know this is a shock for you," another voice said. "But it's not as bad as you think it is."

*   *   *

I looked at the woman who had just spoken. Medium height, the kind of face they called "elfin," with slanted ash-gray eyes and a bob of shoulder-length chrome-white hair.

The face hurtingly familiar.

"It isn't?"

"I wouldn't say so, Thom." She smiled. "After all, it's given us the chance to catch up on old times, hasn't it?"

"Greta?" I asked, disbelievingly.

She nodded. "For my sins."

"My God. It is you, isn't it?"

"I wasn't sure you'd recognize me. Especially after all this time."

"You didn't have much trouble recognizing me."

"I didn't have to. The moment you popped out, we picked up your recovery transponder. Told us the name of your ship, who owned her, who was flying it, what you were carrying, where you were supposed to be headed. When I heard it was you, I made sure I was part of the reception team. But don't worry. It's not like you've changed all that much."

"Well, you haven't either," I said.

It wasn't quite true. But who honestly wants to hear that they look about ten years older than the last time you saw them, even if they still don't look all that bad with it? I thought about how she had looked naked, memories that I'd kept buried for a decade spooling into daylight. It shamed me that they were still so vivid, as if some furtive part of my subconscious had been secretly hoarding them through years of marriage and fidelity.

Greta half smiled. It was as if she knew exactly what I was thinking.

"You were never a good liar, Thom."

"Yeah. Guess I need some practice."

There was an awkward silence. Neither of us seemed to know what to say next. While we hesitated, the others floated around us, saying nothing.

"Well," I said. "Who'd have guessed we'd end up meeting like this?"

Greta nodded and offered the palms of her hands in a kind of apology.

"I'm just sorry we aren't meeting under better circumstances," she said. "But if it's any consolation, what happened wasn't at all your fault. We checked your syntax, and there wasn't a mistake. It's just that now and then the system throws a glitch."

"Funny how no one likes to talk about that very much," I said.

"Could have been worse, Thom. I remember what you used to tell me about space travel."

"Yeah? Which particular pearl of wisdom would that have been?"

"If you're in a position to moan about a situation, you've no right to be moaning."

"Christ. Did I actually say that?"

"Mm. And I bet you're regretting it now. But look, it really isn't that bad. You're only twenty days off schedule." Greta nodded toward the man who had the bad teeth. "Kolding says you'll only need a day of damage repair before you can move off again, and then another twenty, twenty-five days before you reach your destination, depending on routing patterns. That's less than six weeks. So you lose the bonus on this one. Big deal. You're all in one shape, and your ship only needs a little work. Why don't you just bite the bullet and sign the repair paperwork?"

"I'm not looking forward to another twenty days in the surge tank. There's something else, as well."

"Which is?"

I was about to tell her about Katerina, how she'd have been expecting me back already.

Instead I said: "I'm worried about the others. Suzy and Ray. They've got families expecting them. They'll be worried."

"I understand," Greta said. "Suzy and Ray. They're still asleep, aren't they? Still in their surge tanks?"

"Yes," I said, guardedly.

"Keep them that way until you're on your way." Greta smiled. "There's no sense worrying them about their families, either. It's kinder."

"If you say so."

"Trust me on this one, Thom. This isn't the first time I've handled this kind of situation. Doubt it'll be the last, either."

I stayed in a hotel overnight, in another part of Saumlaki. The hotel was an echoing multilevel prefab structure, sunk deep into bedrock. It must have had a capacity for hundreds of guests, but at the moment only a handful of the rooms seemed to be occupied. I slept fitfully and got up early. In the atrium, I saw a bib-capped worker in rubber gloves removing diseased carp from a small ornamental pond. Watching him pick out the ailing metallic-orange fish, I had a flash of déjà vu. What was it about dismal hotels and dying carp?

Before breakfast—bleakly alert, even though I didn't really feel as if I'd had a good night's sleep—I visited Kolding and got a fresh update on the repair schedule.

"Two, three days," he said.

"It was a day last night."

Kolding shrugged. "You've got a problem with the service, find someone else to fix your ship."

Then he stuck his little finger into the corner of his mouth and began to dig between his teeth.

"Nice to see someone who really enjoys his work," I said.

I left Kolding before my mood worsened too much, making my way to a different part of the station.

Greta had suggested we meet for breakfast and catch up on old times. She was there when I arrived, sitting at a table in an "outdoor" terrace, under a red-and-white striped canopy, sipping orange juice. Above us was a dome several hundred meters wide, projecting a cloudless holographic sky. It had the hard, enameled blue of midsummer.

"How's the hotel?" she asked after I'd ordered a coffee from the waiter.

"Not bad. No one seems very keen on conversation, though. Is it me or does that place have all the cheery ambience of a sinking ocean liner?"

"It's just this place," Greta said. "Everyone who comes here is pissed off about it. Either they got transferred here and they're pissed off about *that*, or they ended up here by routing error and they're pissed off about that instead. Take your pick."

"No one's happy?"

"Only the ones who know they're getting out of here soon."

"Would that include you?"

"No," she said. "I'm more or less stuck here. But I'm OK about it. I guess I'm the exception that proves the rule."

The waiters were glass mannequins of a kind that had been fashionable in the core worlds about twenty years ago. One of them placed a croissant in front of me, then poured scalding black coffee into my cup.

"Well, it's good to see you," I said.

"You too, Thom." Greta finished her orange juice and then took a corner of my croissant for herself, without asking. "I heard you got married."

"Yes."

"Well? Aren't you going to tell me about her?"

I drank some of my coffee. "Her name's Katerina."

"Nice name."

"She works in the department of bioremediation on Kagawa."

"Kids?" Greta asked.

"Not yet. It wouldn't be easy, the amount of time we both spend away from home."

"Mm." She had a mouthful of croissant. "But one day you might think about it."

"Nothing's ruled out," I said. As flattered as I was that she was taking such an interest in me, the surgical precision of her questions left me slightly uncomfortable. There was no thrust and parry, no fishing for information. That kind of directness unnerved. But at least it allowed me to ask the same questions. "What about you, then?"

"Nothing very exciting. I got married a year or so after I last saw you. A man called Marcel."

"Marcel," I said, ruminatively, as if the name had cosmic significance. "Well, I'm happy for you. I take it he's here too?"

"No. Our work took us in different directions. We're still married, but . . ." Greta left the sentence hanging.

"It can't be easy," I said.

"If it was meant to work, we'd have found a way. Anyway, don't feel too sorry for either of us. We've both got our work. I wouldn't say I was any less happy than the last time we met."

"Well, that's good," I said.

Greta leaned over and touched my hand. Her fingernails were midnight black with a blue sheen.

"Look. This is really presumptuous of me. It's one thing asking to meet up for breakfast. It would have been rude not to. But how would you like to meet again later? It's really nice to eat here in the evening. They turn down the lights. The view through the dome is really something."

I looked up into that endless holographic sky.

"I thought it was faked."

"Oh, it is," she said. "But don't let that spoil it for you."

I settled in front of the camera and started speaking.

"Katerina," I said. "Hello. I hope you're all right. By now I hope someone from the company will have been in touch. If they haven't, I'm pretty sure you'll have made your own enquiries. I'm not sure what they told you, but I promise you that we're safe and sound and that we're coming home. I'm calling from somewhere called Saumlaki station, a repair facility on the edge of Schedar sector. It's not much to look at: just a warren of tunnels and centrifuges dug into a pitch-black D-type asteroid, about half a light year from the nearest star. The only reason it's here at all is because there happens to be an aperture next door. That's how we got here in the first place. Somehow or other *Blue Goose* took a wrong turn in the network, what they call a routing error. The *Goose* came in last night, local time, and I've been in a hotel since then. I didn't call last night because I was too tired and disoriented after coming out of the tank, and I didn't know how long we were going to be here. Seemed better to wait until morning, when we'd have a better idea of the damage to the ship. It's nothing serious—just a few bits and pieces buckled during the transit—but it means we're going to be here for another couple of days. Kolding—he's the repair chief—says three at the most. By the time we get back on course, however, we'll be about forty days behind schedule."

I paused, eyeing the incrementing cost indicator. Before I sat down in the booth, I always had an eloquent and economical speech queued up in my head, one that conveyed exactly what needed to be said, with the measure and grace of a soliloquy. But my mind always dried up as soon as I opened my mouth, and instead of an actor I ended up sounding like a small time thief, concocting some fumbling alibi in the presence of quick-witted interrogators.

I smiled awkwardly and continued: "It kills me to think this message is going to take so long to get to you. But if there's a silver lining, it's that I won't be far behind it. By the time you get this, I should be home in only a couple of days. So don't waste money replying to this, because by the time you get it I'll already have left Saumlaki Station. Just stay where you are, and I promise I'll be home soon."

That was it. There was nothing more I needed to say, other than: "I miss you." Delivered after a moment's pause, I meant it to sound emphatic. But when I replayed the recording it sounded more like an afterthought.

I could have recorded it again, but I doubted that I would have been any happier. Instead I just committed the existing message for transmission and wondered how long it would have to wait before going on its way. Since it seemed unlikely that there was a vast flow of commerce in and out of Saumlaki, our ship might be the first suitable outbound vessel.

I emerged from the booth. For some reason I felt guilty, as if I had been in some way neglectful. It took me a while before I realized what was playing on my mind. I'd told Katerina about Saumlaki station. I'd even told her about Kolding and the damage to the *Blue Goose*. But I hadn't told her about Greta.

It's not working with Suzy.

She's too smart, too well-attuned to the physiological correlatives of surge tank immersion. I can give her all the reassurances in the world, but she knows she's been under too long for this to be anything other than a truly epic screw-up. She knows that we aren't just talking weeks or even months of delay here. Every nerve in her body is screaming that message into her skull.

"I had dreams," she says, when the grogginess fades.

"What kind?"

"Dreams that I kept waking. Dreams that you were pulling me out of the surge tank. You and someone else."

I do my best to smile. I'm alone, but Greta isn't far away. The hypodermic's in my pocket now.

"I always get bad dreams coming out of the tank," I say.

"These felt real. Your story kept changing, but you kept telling me we were somewhere . . . that we'd gone a little off course, but that it was nothing to worry about."

So much for Greta's reassurance that Suzy will remember nothing after our aborted efforts at waking her. Seems that her short-term memory isn't quite as fallible as we'd like.

"It's funny you should say that," I tell her. "Because, actually, we are a little off course."

She's sharper with every breath. Suzy was always the best of us at coming out of the tank.

"Tell me how far, Thom."

"Farther than I'd like."

She balls her fists. I can't tell if it's aggression, or some lingering neuromuscular effect of her time in the tank. "How far? Beyond the Bubble?"

"Beyond the Bubble, yes."

Her voice grows small and childlike.

"Tell me, Thom. Are we out beyond the Rift?"

I can hear the fear. I understand what she's going through. It's the nightmare that all ship crews live with, on every trip. That something will go wrong with the routing, something so severe that they'll end up on the very edge of the network. That they'll end up so far from home that getting back will take years, not months. And that, of course, years will have already passed, even before they begin the return trip.

That loved ones will be years older when they reach home.

If they're still there. If they still remember you, or want to remember. If they're still recognizable, or alive.

Beyond the Aquila Rift. It's shorthand for the trip no one ever hopes to make by accident. The one that will screw up the rest of your life, the one that creates the ghosts you see haunting the shadows of company bars across the whole Bubble. Men and women ripped out of time, cut adrift from families and lovers by an accident of an alien technology we use but barely comprehend.

"Yes," I say. "We're beyond the Rift."

Suzy screams, knitting her face into a mask of anger and denial. My hand is cold around the hypodermic. I consider using it.

A new repair estimate from Kolding. Five, six days.

This time I didn't even argue. I just shrugged and walked out, wondering how long it would be next time.

That evening I sat down at the same table where Greta and I had met over breakfast. The dining area had been well lit before, but now the only illumination came from the table lamps and the subdued lighting panels set into the paving. In the distance, a glass mannequin cycled from empty table to empty table, playing *Asturias* on a glass guitar. There were no other patrons dining tonight.

I didn't have long to wait for Greta.

"I'm sorry I'm late, Thom."

I turned to her as she approached the table. I liked the way she walked in the low gravity of the station, the way the subdued lighting traced the arc of her hips and waist. She eased into her seat and leaned toward me in the manner of a conspirator. The lamp on the table threw red shadows and gold highlights across her face. It took ten years off her age.

"You aren't late," I said. "And anyway, I had the view."

"It's an improvement, isn't it?"

"That wouldn't be saying much," I said with a smile. "But yes, it's definitely an improvement."

"I could sit out here all night and just look at it. In fact sometimes that's exactly what I do. Just me and a bottle of wine."

"I don't blame you."

Instead of the holographic blue, the dome was now full of stars. It was like no kind of view I'd ever seen from another station or ship. There were furious blue-white stars embedded in what looked like sheets of velvet. There were hard gold gems and soft red smears, like finger smears in pastel. There were streams and currents of fainter stars, like a myriad neon fish caught in a snapshot of frozen motion. There were vast billowing backdrops of red and green cloud, veined and flawed by filaments of cool black. There were bluffs and promontories of ochre dust, so rich in three-dimensional structure that they resembled an exuberant impasto of oil colors; contours light-years thick laid on with a trowel. Red or pink stars burned through the dust like lanterns. Orphaned worlds were caught erupting from the towers, little spermlike shapes trailing viscera of dust. Here and there I saw the tiny eyelike knots of birthing solar systems. There were pulsars, flashing on and off like navigation beacons, their differing rhythms seeming to set a stately tempo for the entire scene, like a deathly slow waltz. There seemed too much detail for one view, an overwhelming abundance of richness, and yet no matter which direction I looked, there was yet more to see, as if the dome sensed my attention and concentrated its efforts on the spot where my gaze was directed. For a moment I felt a lurching sense of dizziness, and—though I tried to stop it before I made a fool of myself—I found myself grasping the side of the table, as if to stop myself falling into the infinite depths of the view.

"Yes, it has that effect on people," Greta said.

"It's beautiful," I said.

"Do you mean beautiful, or terrifying?"

I realized I wasn't sure. "It's big," was all I could offer.

"Of course, it's faked," Greta said, her voice soft now that she was leaning closer. "The glass in the dome is smart. It exaggerates the brightness of the stars, so that the human eye registers the differences between them. Otherwise the colors aren't unrealistic. Everything else you see is also pretty accurate, if you accept that certain frequencies have been shifted into the visible band, and the scale of certain structures has been adjusted." She pointed out features for my edification. "That's the edge of the Taurus Dark Cloud, with the Pleiades just poking out. That's a filament of the Local Bubble. You see that open cluster?"

She waited for me to answer. "Yes," I said.

"That's the Hyades. Over there you've got Betelguese and Bellatrix."

"I'm impressed."

"You should be. It cost a lot of money." She leaned back a bit, so that the shadows dropped across her face again. "Are you all right, Thom? You seem a bit distracted."

I sighed.

"I just got another prognosis from your friend Kolding. That's enough to put a dent in anyone's day."

"I'm sorry about that."

"There's something else, too," I said. "Something that's been bothering me since I came out of the tank."

A mannequin came to take our order. I let Greta choose for me.

"You can talk to me, whatever it is," she said, when the mannequin had gone.

"It isn't easy."

"Something personal, then? Is it about Katerina?" She bit her tongue "No, sorry. I shouldn't have said that."

"It's not about Katerina. Not exactly, anyway." But even as I said it, I knew that in a sense it *was* about Katerina, and how long it was going to be before we saw each other again.

"Go on, Thom."

"This is going to sound silly. But I wonder if everyone's being straight with me. It's not just Kolding. It's you as well. When I came out of that tank I felt the same way I felt when I'd been out to the Rift. Worse, if anything. I felt like I'd been in the tank for a long, long time."

"It feels that way sometimes."

"I know the difference, Greta. Trust me on this."

"So what are you saying?"

The problem was that I wasn't really sure. It was one thing to feel a vague sense of unease about how long I'd been in the tank. It was another to come out and accuse my host of lying. Especially when she had been so hospitable.

"Is there any reason you'd lie to me?"

"Come off it, Thom. What kind of a question is that?"

As soon as I had come out with it, it sounded absurd and offensive to me as well. I wished I could reverse time and start again, ignoring my misgivings.

"I'm sorry," I said. "Stupid. Just put it down to messed up biorhythms, or something."

She reached across the table and took my hand, as she had done at breakfast. This time she continued to hold it.

"You really feel wrong, don't you?"

"Kolding's games aren't helping, that's for sure." The waiter brought our wine, setting it down, the bottle chinking against his delicately articulated glass fingers. The mannequin poured two glasses and I sampled mine. "Maybe if I had someone else from my crew to bitch about it all with, I wouldn't feel so bad. I know you said we shouldn't wake Suzy and Ray, but that was before a one-day stopover turned into a week."

Greta shrugged. "If you want to wake them, no one's going to stop you. But don't think about ship business now. Let's not spoil a perfect evening."

I looked up at the stars. It was heightened, with the mad shimmering intensity of a Van Gogh nightscape.

It made one feel drunk and ecstatic just to look at it.

"What could possibly spoil it?" I asked.

What happened is that I drank too much wine and ended up sleeping with Greta. I'm not sure how much of a part the wine played in it for her. If her relationship with Marcel was in as much trouble as she'd made out, then obviously she had less to lose than I did. Yes, that made it all right, didn't it? She the seductress, her own marriage a wreck, me the hapless victim. I'd lapsed, yes, but it wasn't really my fault. I'd been alone, far from home, emotionally fragile, and she had exploited me. She had softened me up with a romantic meal, her trap already sprung.

Except all that was self-justifying bullshit, wasn't it? If my own marriage was in such great shape, why I had I failed to mention Greta when I called home? At the time, I'd justified that omission as an act of kindness toward my wife. Katerina didn't know that Greta and I had ever been a couple. But why worry Katerina by mentioning another woman, even if I pretended that we'd never met before?

Except—now—I could see that I'd failed to mention Greta for another reason entirely. Because in the back of my mind, even then, there had been the possibility that we might end up sleeping together.

I was already covering myself when I called Katerina. Already making sure there wouldn't be any awkward questions when I got home. As if I not only knew what was going to happen but secretly yearned for it.

The only problem was that Greta had something else in mind.

"Thom," Greta said, nudging me toward wakefulness. She was lying naked next to me, leaning on one elbow, with the sheets crumpled down around her hips. The light in her room turned her into an abstraction of milky blue curves and deep violet shadows. With one black-nailed finger she traced a line down my chest and said: "There's something you need to know."

"What?" I asked.

"I lied. Kolding lied. We all lied."

I was too drowsy for her words to have much more than a vaguely troubling effect. All I could say, again, was: "What?"

"You're not in Saumlaki station. You're not in Schedar sector."

I started waking up properly. "Say that again."

"The routing error was more severe than you were led to believe. It took you far beyond the Local Bubble."

I groped for anger, even resentment, but all I felt was a dizzying sensation of falling. "How far out?"

"Further than you thought possible."

The next question was obvious.

"Beyond the Rift?"

"Yes," she said, with the faintest of smiles, as if humoring a game whose rules and objectives she found ultimately demeaning. "Beyond the Aquila Rift. A long, long way beyond it."

"I need to know, Greta."

She pushed herself from the bed, reached for a gown. "Then get dressed. I'll show you."

I followed Greta in a daze.

She took me to the dome again. It was dark, just as it had been the night before, with only the lamp-lit tables to act as beacons. I supposed that the illumination throughout Saumlaki

station (or wherever this was) was at the whim of its occupants and didn't necessarily have to follow any recognizable
diurnal cycle. Nonetheless, it was still unsettling to find it
changed so arbitrarily. Even if Greta had the authority to
turn out the lights when she wanted to, didn't anyone else
object?

But I didn't see anyone else *to* object. There was no one
else around; only a glass mannequin standing to attention
with a napkin over one arm.

She sat us at a table. "Do you want a drink, Thom?"

"No, thanks. For some reason I'm not quite in the mood."

She touched my wrist. "Don't hate me for lying to you. It
was done out of kindness. I couldn't break the truth to you
in one go."

Sharply I withdrew my hand. "Shouldn't I be the judge of
that? So what is the truth, exactly?"

"It's not good, Thom."

"Tell me, then I'll decide."

I didn't see her do anything, but suddenly the dome was
filled with stars again, just as it had been the night before.

The view lurched, zooming outwards. Stars flowed by
from all sides, like white sleet. Nebulae ghosted past in
spectral wisps. The sense of motion was so compelling that
I found myself gripping the table, seized by vertigo.

"Easy, Thom," Greta whispered.

The view lurched, swerved, contracted. A solid wall of
gas slammed past. Now, suddenly, I had the sense that we
were outside something—that we had punched beyond
some containing sphere, defined only in vague arcs and
knots of curdled gas, where the interstellar gas density increased sharply.

Of course. It was obvious. We were beyond the Local
Bubble.

And we were still receding. I watched the Bubble itself
contract, becoming just one member in the larger froth of
voids. Instead of individual stars, I saw only smudges and
motes, aggregations of hundreds of thousands of suns. It

was like pulling back from a close-up view of a forest. I could still see clearings, but the individual trees had vanished into an amorphous mass.

We kept pulling back. Then the expansion slowed and froze. I could still make out the Local Bubble, but only because I had been concentrating on it all the way out. Otherwise, there was nothing to distinguish it from the dozens of surrounding voids.

"Is that how far out we've come?" I asked.

Greta shook her head. "Let me show you something."

Again, she did nothing that I was aware of. But the Bubble I had been looking at was suddenly filled with a skein of red lines, like a child's scribble.

"Aperture connections," I said.

As shocked as I was by the fact that she had lied to me— and as fearful as I was about what the truth might hold—I couldn't turn off the professional part of me, the part that took pride in recognizing such things.

Greta nodded. "Those are the main commerce routes, the well-mapped connections between large colonies and major trading hubs. Now I'll add all mapped connections, including those that have only ever been traversed by accident."

The scribble did not change dramatically. It gained a few more wild loops and hairpins, including one that reached beyond the wall of the Bubble to touch the sunward end of the Aquila Rift. One or two other additions pierced the wall in different directions, but none of them reached as far as the Rift.

"Where are we?"

"We're at one end of one of those connections. You can't see it because it's pointing directly toward you." She smiled slightly. "I needed to establish the scale that we're dealing with. How wide is the Local Bubble, Thom? Four hundred light-years, give or take?"

My patience was wearing thin. But I was still curious.

"About right."

"And while I know that aperture travel times vary from point to point, with factors depending on network topology and syntax optimization, isn't it the case that the average speed is about one thousand times faster than light?"

"Give or take."

"So a journey from one side of the Bubble might take—what, half a year? Say five or six months? A year to the Aquila Rift?"

"You know that already, Greta. We both know it."

"All right. Then consider this." And the view contracted again, the Bubble dwindling, a succession of overlaying structures concealing it, darkness coming into view on either side, and then the familiar spiral swirl of the Milky Way galaxy looming large.

Hundreds of billions of stars, packed together into foaming white lanes of sea spume.

"This is the view," Greta said. "Enhanced of course, brightened and filtered for human consumption—but if you had eyes with near-perfect quantum efficiency, and if they happened to be about a meter wide, this is more or less what you'd see if you stepped outside the station."

"I don't believe you."

What I meant was I didn't *want* to believe her.

"Get used to it, Thom. You're a long way out. The station's orbiting a brown dwarf star in the Large Magellanic Cloud. You're one hundred and fifty thousand light-years from home."

"No," I said, my voice little more than a moan of abject, childlike denial.

"You felt as though you'd spent a long time in the tank. You were dead right. Subjective time? I don't know. Years, easily. Maybe a decade. But objective time—the time that passed back home—is a lot clearer. It took *Blue Goose* one hundred and fifty years to reach us. Even if you turned back now, you'd have been away for three hundred years, Thom."

"Katerina," I said, her name like an invocation.

"Katerina's dead," Greta told me. "She's already been dead a century."

*   *   *

How do you adjust to something like that? The answer is that you can't count on adjusting to it at all. Not everyone does. Greta told me that she had seen just about every possibly reaction in the spectrum, and the one thing she had learned was that it was next to impossible to predict how a given individual would take the news. She had seen people adjust to the revelation with little more than a world-weary shrug, as if this were merely the latest in a line of galling surprises life had thrown at them, no worse in its way than illness or bereavement or any number of personal setbacks. She had seen others walk away and kill themselves half an hour later.

But the majority, she said, did eventually come to some kind of accommodation with the truth, however faltering and painful the process.

"Trust me, Thom," she said. "I know you now. I know you have the emotional strength to get through this. I know you can learn to live with it."

"Why didn't you tell me straight away, as soon as I came out of the tank?"

"Because I didn't know if you were going to be able to take it."

"You waited until after you knew I had a wife."

"No," Greta said. "I waited until after we'd made love. Because then I knew Katerina couldn't mean that much to you."

"Fuck you."

"Fuck me? Yes, you did. That's the point."

I wanted to strike out against her. But what I was angry at was not her insinuation but the cold-hearted truth of it. She was right, and I knew it. I just didn't want to deal with that, any more than I wanted to deal with the here and now.

I waited for the anger to subside.

"You say we're not the first?" I said.

"No. We were the first, I suppose—the ship I came in. Luckily it was well equipped. After the routing error, we had enough supplies to set up a self-sustaining station on the nearest rock. We knew there was no going back, but at least we could make some kind of life for ourselves here."

"And after that?"

"We had enough to do just keeping ourselves alive, the first few years. But then another ship came through the aperture. Damaged, drifting, much like *Blue Goose*. We hauled her in, warmed her crew, broke the news to them."

"How'd they take it?"

"About as well as you'd expect." Greta laughed hollowly to herself. "A couple of them went mad. Another killed herself. But at least a dozen of them are still here. In all honesty, it was good for us that another ship came through. Not just because they had supplies we could use, but because it helped us to help them. Took our minds off our own self-pity. It made us realize how far we'd come and how much help these newcomers needed to make the same transition. That wasn't the last ship, either. We've gone through the same process with eight or nine others, since then." Greta looked at me, her head cocked against her hand. "There's a thought for you, Thom."

"There is?"

She nodded. "It's difficult for you now, I know. And it'll be difficult for you for some time to come. But it can help to have someone else to care about. It can smooth the transition."

"Like who?" I asked.

"Like one of your other crew members," Greta said. "You could try waking one of them, now."

Greta's with me when I pull Suzy out of the surge tank.

"Why her?" Greta asks.

"Because I want her out first," I say, wondering if Greta's jealous. I don't blame her: Suzy's beautiful, but she's also smart. There isn't a better syntax runner in Ashanti Industrial.

"What happened?" Suzy asks, when's she over the grogginess. "Did we make it back?"

I ask her to tell me the last thing she remembered.

"Customs," Suzy says. "Those pricks on Arkangel."

"And after that? Anything else? The runes? Do you remember casting them?"

"No," she says, then picks up something in my voice. *The fact that I might not be telling the truth, or telling her all she needs to know.* *"Thom. I'll ask you again. Did we make it back?"*

A minute later we're putting Suzy back into the tank.

It hasn't worked first time. Maybe next try.

But it kept not working with Suzy. She was always cleverer and quicker than me; she always had been. As soon as she came out of the tank, she knew that we'd come a lot further than Schedar sector. She was always ahead of my lies and excuses.

"It was different when it happened to me," I told Greta, when we were lying next to each other again, days later, with Suzy still in the tank. "I had all the nagging doubts she has, I think. But as soon as I saw you standing there, I forgot all about that stuff."

Greta nodded. Her hair fell across her face in dishevelled, sleep-matted curtains. She had a strand of it between her lips.

"It helped, seeing a friendly face?"

"Took my mind off the problem, that's for sure."

"You'll get there in the end," she said. "Anyway, from Suzy's point of view, aren't you a friendly face as well?"

"Maybe," I said. "But she'd been expecting me. You were the last person in the world I expected to see standing there."

Greta touched her knuckle against the side of my face. Her smooth skin slid against stubble. "It's getting easier for you, isn't it?"

"I don't know," I said.

"You're a strong man, Thom. I knew you'd come through this."

"I haven't come through it yet," I said. I felt like a tightrope walker halfway across Niagara Falls. It was a miracle I'd made it as far as I had. But that didn't mean I was home and dry.

Still, Greta was right. There was hope. I'd felt no crushing spasms of grief over Katerina's death, or enforced absence, or however you wanted to put it. All I felt was a bittersweet regret, the way one might feel about a broken heirloom or long-lost pet. I felt no animosity toward Katerina, and I was sorry that I would never see her again. But I was sorry about not seeing a lot of things. Maybe it would become worse in the days ahead. Maybe I was just postponing a breakdown.

I didn't think so.

In the meantime, I continued trying to find a way to deal with Suzy. She had become a puzzle that I couldn't leave unsolved. I could have just woken her up and let her deal with the news as best as she could, but this seemed cruel and unsatisfactory. Greta had broken it to me gently, giving me the time to settle into my new surroundings and take that necessary step away from Katerina. When she finally broke the news, as shocking as it was, it didn't shatter me. I'd already been primed for it, the sting taken out of the surprise. Sleeping with Greta obviously helped. I couldn't offer Suzy the same solace, but I was sure that there was a way for us to coax Suzy to the same state of near-acceptance.

Time after time we woke her and tried a different approach. Greta said there was a window of a few minutes before the events she was experiencing began to transfer into long-term memory. If we knocked her out, the buffer of memories in short term storage was wiped before it ever crossed the hippocampus into long-term recall. Within that window, we could wake her up as many times as we liked, trying endless permutations of the revival scenario.

At least that was what Greta told me.

"We can't keep doing this indefinitely," I said.

"Why not?"

"Isn't she going to remember *something*?"

Greta shrugged. "Maybe. But I doubt that she'll attach any significance to those memories. Haven't you ever had vague feelings of déjà vu coming out of the surge tank?"

"Sometimes," I admitted.

"Then don't sweat about it. She'll be all right. I promise you."

"Perhaps we should just keep her awake, after all."

"That will be cruel."

"It's cruel to keep waking her up and shutting her down, like a toy doll."

There was a catch in her voice when she answered me.

"Keep at it, Thom. I'm sure you're close to finding a way in the end. It's helping you, focusing on Suzy. I always knew it would."

I started to say something, but Greta pressed a finger to my lips.

Greta was right about Suzy. The challenge helped me, taking my mind off my own predicament. I remembered what Greta had said about dealing with other crews in the same situation, before *Blue Goose* put in. Clearly she had learned many psychological tricks: gambits and shortcuts to assist the transition to mental well-being. I felt slight resentment at being manipulated so effectively. But at the same time I couldn't deny that worrying about another human being had helped me with my own adjustment. When, days later, I stepped back from the immediate problem of Suzy, I realized that something was different. I didn't feel far from home. I felt, in an odd way, privileged. I'd come further than almost anyone in history. I was still alive, and there were still people around to provide love and partnership and a web of social relations. Not just Greta, but all the other unlucky souls who had ended up at the station.

If anything, there appeared more of them than when I had first arrived. The corridors—sparsely populated at first— were increasingly busy, and when we ate under the dome— under the Milky Way—we were not the only diners. I studied their lamp-lit faces, comforted by their vague familiarity, wondering what kinds of stories they had to tell, where they'd come from home, who they had left behind, how they had adjusted to life here. There was time enough to get to know them all. And the place would never become boring, for at any time—as Greta had intimated—we could always expect another lost ship to drop through the aperture. Tragedy for the crew, but fresh challengers, fresh faces, fresh news from home, for us.

All in all, it wasn't really so bad.

Then it clicked.

It was the man cleaning out the fish that did it, in the lobby of the hotel. It wasn't just the familiarity of the process, but the man himself.

I'd seen him before. Another pond full of diseased carp. Another hotel.

Then I remembered Kolding's bad teeth, and recalled how they'd reminded me of another man I'd met long before. Except it wasn't another man at all. Different name, different context, but everything else the same. And when I looked at the other diners, really looked at them, there was no one I couldn't swear I hadn't seen before. No single face that hit me with the force of utter unfamiliarity.

Which left Greta.

I said to her, over wine, under the Milky Way: "Nothing here is real, is it?"

She looked at me with infinite sadness and shook her head.

"What about Suzy?" I asked her.

"Suzy's dead. Ray is dead. They died in their surge tanks."

"How? Why them, and not me?"

"Something about particles of paint blocking intake filters. Not enough to make a difference over short distances, but enough to kill them on the trip out here."

I think some part of me had always suspected. It felt less like shock than brutal disappointment.

"But Suzy seemed so real," I said. "Even the way she had doubts about how long she'd been in the tank . . . even the way she remembered previous attempts to wake her."

The glass mannequin approached our table. Greta waved him away.

"I made her convincing, the way she would have acted."

"You *made* her?"

"You're not really awake, Thom. You're being fed data. This entire station is being simulated."

I sipped my wine. I expected it to taste suddenly thin and synthetic, but it still tasted like pretty good wine.

"Then I'm dead as well?"

"No. You're alive. Still in your surge tank. But I haven't brought you to full consciousness yet."

"All right. The truth this time. I can take it. How much is real? Does the station exist? Are we really as far out as you said?"

"Yes," she said. "The station exists, just as I said it does. It just looks . . . different. And it *is* in the Large Magellanic Cloud, and it is orbiting a brown dwarf star."

"Can you show me the station as it is?"

"I could. But I don't think you're ready for it. I think you'd find it difficult to adjust."

I couldn't help laughing. "Even after what I've already adjusted to?"

"You've only made half the journey, Thom."

"But you made it."

"I did, Thom. But for me it was different." Greta smiled. "For me, everything was different."

Then she made the light show change again. None of the other diners appeared to notice as we began to zoom in toward the Milky Way, crashing toward the spiral, ramming through shoals of outlying stars and gas clouds. The familiar landscape of the Local Bubble loomed large.

The image froze, the Bubble one among many such structures.

Again it filled with the violent red scribble of the aperture network. But now the network wasn't the only one. It was merely one ball of red yarn among many, spaced out across tens of thousands of light-years. None of the scribbles touched each other, yet—in the way they were shaped, in the way they almost abutted against each other—it was possible to imagine that they had once been connected. They were like the shapes of continents on a world with tectonic drift.

"It used to span the galaxy," Greta said. "Then something happened. Something catastrophic, which I still don't understand. A shattering, into vastly smaller domains. Typically a few hundred light-years across."

"Who made it?"

"I don't know. No one knows. They probably aren't around any more. Maybe that was why it shattered, out of neglect."

"But we found it," I said. "The part of it near us still worked."

"All the disconnected elements still function," Greta said. "You can't cross from domain to domain, but otherwise the apertures work as they were designed. Barring, of course, the occasional routing error."

"All right," I said. "If you can't cross from domain to domain, how did *Blue Goose* get this far out? We've come a lot further than a few hundred light-years."

"You're right. But then such a long-distance connection might have been engineered differently from the others. It appears that the links to the Magellanic Clouds were more resilient. When the domains shattered from each other, the connections reaching beyond the galaxy remained intact."

"In which case you *can* cross from domain to domain," I said. "But you have to come all the way out here first."

"The trouble is, not many want to continue the journey at this point. No one comes here deliberately, Thom."

"I still don't get it. What does it matter to me if there are other domains? Those regions of the galaxy are thousands of light-years from Earth, and without the apertures we'd have no way of reaching them. They don't matter. There's no one there to use them."

Greta's smile was coquettish, knowing.

"What makes you so certain?"

"Because if there were, wouldn't there be alien ships popping out of the aperture here? You've told me *Blue Goose* wasn't the first through. But our domain—the one in the Local Bubble—must be outnumbered hundreds to one by all the others. If there are alien cultures out there, each stumbling on their own local domain, why haven't any of them ever come through the aperture, the way we did?"

Again that smile. But this time it chilled my blood.

"What makes you think they haven't, Thom?"

I reached out and took her hand, the way she had taken mine. I took it without force, without malice, but with the assurance that this time I really, sincerely meant what I was about to say.

Her fingers tightened around mine.

"Show me," I said. "I want to see things as they really are. Not just the station. You as well."

Because by then I'd realized. Greta hadn't just lied to me about Suzy and Ray. She'd lied to me about the *Blue Goose* as well. Because we were not the latest human ship to come through.

We were the first.

"You want to see it?" she asked.

"Yes. All of it."

"You won't like it."

"I'll be the judge of that."

"All right, Thom. But understand this. I've been here before. I've done this a million times. I care for all the lost souls. And I know how it works. You won't be able to take the raw reality of what's happened to you. You'll shrivel away from it. You'll go mad, unless I substitute a calming fiction, a happy ending."

"Why tell me that now?"

"Because you don't have to see it. You can stop now, where you are, with an idea of the truth. An inkling. But you don't have to open your eyes."

"Do it," I said.

Greta shrugged. She poured herself another measure of wine, then made sure my own glass was charged.

"You asked for it," she said.

We were still holding hands, two lovers sharing an intimacy. Then everything changed.

It was just a flash, just a glimpse. Like the view of an unfamiliar room if you turn the lights on for an instant. Shapes and forms, relationships between things. I saw caverns, wormed-out and linked, and things moving through those caverns, bustling along with the frantic industry of moles or termites. The things were seldom alike, even in the most superficial sense. Some moved via propulsive waves of multiple clawed limbs. Some wriggled, smooth plaques of carapace grinding against the glassy rock of the tunnels.

The things moved between caves in which lay the hulks of ships, almost all too strange to describe.

And somewhere distant, somewhere near the heart of the rock, in a matriarchal chamber all of its own, something drummed out messages to its companions and helpers, stiffly articulated antlerlike forelimbs beating against stretched tympana of finely veined skin, something that had been waiting here for eternities, something that wanted nothing more than to care for the souls of the lost.

Katerina's with Suzy when they pull me out of the surge tank.

It's bad—one of the worst revivals I've ever gone through. I feel as if every vein in my body has been filled with finely powdered glass. For a moment, a long moment, even the idea of breathing seems insurmountably difficult, too hard, too painful even to contemplate.

But it passes, as it always passes.

After a while I can not only breathe, I can move and talk.

"Where . . ."

"Easy, Skip," Suzy says. She leans over the tank and starts unplugging me. I can't help but smile. Suzy's smart—there isn't a better syntax runner in Ashanti Industrial—but she's also beautiful. It's like being nursed by an angel.

I wonder if Katerina's jealous.

"Where are we?" I try again. "Feels like I was in that thing for an eternity. Did something go wrong?"

"Minor routing error," Suzy says. "We took some damage and they decided to wake me first. But don't sweat about it. At least we're in one piece."

Routing errors. You hear about them, but you hope they're never going to happen to you.

"What kind of delay?"

"Forty days. Sorry, Thom. Bang goes our bonus."

In anger, I hammer the side of the surge tank. But Katerina steps toward me and places a calming hand on my shoulder.

"It's all right," she says. "You're home and dry. That's all that matters."

I look at her and for a moment remember someone else, someone I haven't thought about in years. I almost remember her name, and then the moment passes.

I nod. "Home and dry."

AUTHOR BIOS

Eric Brown was born in Haworth, West Yorkshire, in 1960. He is the author of fifteen science fiction novels, story collections, and books for children, as well as plays and more than eighty short stories, which have appeared in various magazines and anthologies in Britain and the US. His novels include *Penumbra*, and the Virex Trilogy consisting of *New York Nights, New York Blues*, and *New York Dreams*. *Bengal Station*, his most recent novel, is out now in the US.

Years before light pollution was general over England, **Paul McAuley** spent summer nights in a deckchair, watching the skies with a pair of secondhand binoculars. He has worked as a research biologist in various universities, including Oxford and UCLA, and was a lecturer in botany at St. Andrews University before becoming a full-time writer. His first novel, *Four Hundred Billion Stars*, won the Philip K. Dick Memorial Award, and his fifth, *Fairyland*, won the 1995 Arthur C. Clarke and John W. Campbell Awards. His latest books are a novel, *White Devils*, and a short story collection, *Little Machines*. He lives in North London.

Brian W. Aldiss writes, "I'm currently writing a short story every other day. It's very exciting: you never know what will come next. Much like life itself, you might say. My current novel, *Super-State*, is being well-received in Europe. Nearer to home, I'm doing readings round the village, like a poor man's Charles Dickens. With luck—enormous luck—my opera, *Oedipus on Mars*, will be performed sometime soon. Happy days!"

Tony Ballantyne writes, "I'm a relative newcomer to the field of writing: I've had short stories published in *Interzone* and other publications, both SF and mainstream. My first novel, *Recursion*, was published by Tor UK in June 2004, and I am currently hard at work on the follow up."

Stephen Baxter writes, "I was born in Liverpool, England, in 1957. I have degrees in mathematics, from Cambridge University, engineering, from Southampton University, and in business administration, from Henley Management College. I taught maths and physics and worked for several years in information technology. I am a Chartered Engineer. I applied to become a cosmonaut in 1991—aiming for the guest slot on Mir eventually taken by Helen Sharman—but fell at an early hurdle.

"My first professionally published short story was in 1987. I have been a full-time author since 1995. I am a Fellow of the British Interplanetary Society and Vice President of the British Science Fiction Association. My science fiction novels have been published in the UK, the US, and in many other countries including Germany, Japan, and France. My books have won several awards including the Philip K. Dick Award, the John Campbell Memorial Award, the British Science Fiction Association Award, the Kurd Lasswitz Award (Germany) and the Seiun Award (Japan) and have been nominated for several others, including the Arthur C. Clarke Award, the Hugo Award and Locus awards. I have published over 100 SF short stories, several of which have won prizes. My novel *Voyage* was dramatized by

Audio Movies for BBC Radio in 1999. My short story 'Pilot' is currently under development for a feature film."

Roger Levy is the author of the novels *Reckless Sleep* and *Dark Heavens*. He is married with two children and lives and works in London.

British author of some thirty-five novels—the latest being *Mockymen* (Golden Gryphon Press, Fall 2003) and of nine story collections, most recently *The Great Escape* (Golden Gryphon Press Spring 2002)—**Ian Watson** lectured in Literature in Tanzania and Japan, then in Futures Studies in Birmingham, England, before becoming a full-time writer in 1976. Recently he started publishing poetry, resulting in a collection from DNA Publications, *The Lexicographer's Love Song*. A year's work with Stanley Kubrick resulted in screen credit for Screen Story for Steven Spielberg's movie *A.I. Artificial Intelligence*, made by Spielberg after Kubrick's death and released in 2001. Ian lives in a tiny village in rural England with a little black cat called Poppy.

Keith Brooke has had more than fifty short stories and several books published since 1989, including the novels *Keepers of the Peace*, the Expatria series and, most recently, *Lord of Stone* and the collections *Parallax View* (in collaboration with Eric Brown) and *Head Shots*. He launched the web-based SF, fantasy and horror showcase infinity plus (www.infinityplus.co.uk) in 1997, featuring the work of many top genre authors, including Michael Moorcock, Stephen Baxter, Mary Gentle, Lucius Shepard, Ian McDonald, Vonda McIntyre and James Patrick Kelly. He is co-editor with Nick Gevers of anthologies derived from the website and a guest issue of Hugo Award-winning magazine Interzone. Hiding his identity behind the pen-name Nick Gifford, he likes to scare children, with the novel *Piggies* published in January 2003 and another in 2004. You can find out more about Keith and his work at www.keithbrooke.-co.uk and www.nickgifford.co.uk

Gwyneth Jones was born in Manchester, England, studied at a local convent school and then at the University of Sussex, where she took an undergraduate degree in History of Ideas, specializing in seventeenth-century Europe, which gave her a taste for studying the structure of scientific revolutions and societies (scientific and otherwise) in phase transition; this background still resonates in her work. In the eighties she spent two years in gainful employment, writing scripts for a sci-fi tv cartoon series called *The Telebugs*, which now gives her a curious cult status with twenty-something UK fans. Since then, she's been writing, and occasionally teaching creative writing, full time. She's written more than twenty novels for teenagers, mostly using the pseudonym Ann Halam, and several highly regarded science fiction novels for adults, notably the Aleutian Trilogy, "*White Queen*" (co-winner of the James Tiptree Memorial Award); *North Wind* and *Phoenix Café*. *Bold As Love*, the first novel of a sequence tackling pop-culture in the near future, won the Arthur C. Clarke award for 2001. Her teenage novel *The Fearman* (1995) won the Dracula Society's Children of the Night Award. Her short story collection *Seven Tales and a Fable* won two World Fantasy Awards in 1996. Her critical writings and essays (*Deconstructing The Starships*) have been published by the Liverpool University Press. She practices yoga, has done some extreme tourism in her time, likes old movies, and enjoys playing with her websites.
Email: gwyneth.jones@ntlworld.com
Websites: http://www.boldaslove.co.uk
http://homepage.ntlworld.com/gwynethann

James Lovegrove was born on Christmas Eve, 1965, and is the author of *The Hope, Escardy Gap* (with Peter Crowther), *Days, The Foreigners* and most recently *Untied Kingdom*.

He has also published a short story collection, *Imagined Slights*, a novella, *How The Other Half Live*s, and two books for younger readers, *Wings* and *The House of Lazarus*. His next books are the palindromic double-novella *Gig* and a full-blown fantasy novel *Worldstorm*. He lives near the south coast of England with his wife Lou and their newly arrived son Monty and is looking forward to his next good night's sleep sometime in 2010.

Ian McDonald was born in 1960 and has lived in Northern Ireland for most of his life. His first novel was *Desolation Road* in 1988. His most recent are *Ares Express*, a companion to that earlier work a mere fourteen years later, and *River of Gods*, an epic set in India one hundred years after independence. He'd love to do more stories, but the exigencies of a day job in television production keep his mind on more trivial things.

Adam Roberts is the author of the novels *Salt, On, Stone*, and *Polystom* (Gollancz, 2003) and the novellas *Park Polar* (PS Publishing, 2001) and *Jupiter Magnified* (PS Publishing, 2003). He has published short fiction in a variety of places, and has also published various works of literary criticism, including *Science Fiction*. He lives in London, England. He is not yet forty.

Justina Robson is the author of three science fiction novels to date and a few short stories within the SF/F and mainstream genres. Her first two books, *Silver Screen* and *Mappa Mundi* were both shortlisted for the Arthur C. Clarke award in 1999 and 2001 (a record for a new novelist!), and together they won the first amazon.co.uk Writers' Bursary Award in 2000, which resulted in a semester as Writer In Residence at Queen Mary and Westfield College, London. Her third book, *Natural History*, was published in the UK in April 2003 and will see US publication in early 2005. She continues to write from home in West Yorkshire, England, where she lives with her husband and baby son.

In many ways, **Colin Greenland's** early SF and fantasy, especially the novels *Other Voices* and *Harm's Way*, were the precursors for the New Weird and the current British boom, but he's too old and fat and tired to go through that all again. Instead, he's writing strange, evocative slipstream books, like *Finding Helen* and the forthcoming *Losing David*. He lives in Cambridge (the British Cambridge, or one of them) and wastes much of his time at http://www.ttapress.com/discus.

Alastair Reynolds was born in Barry, South Wales, in 1966. Apart from Wales, he has lived in Cornwall, Newcastle and Scotland, and—since 1991—the Netherlands, where he works as a scientist with the European Space Agency. He wrote and published his first science fiction novel when he was five (a limited edition of one) and has never looked back. His short stories have appeared in *Interzone, Asimov's* and *Spectrum SF* and have been widely reprinted and translated. His first proper novel, *Revelation Space*, appeared in 2000 and was nominated for both the British Science Fiction Association and Arthur C. Clarke awards. His second, *Chasm City*, won the BSFA award. Since then he has published *Redemption Ark* and *Absolution Gap*. In his spare time he rides horses, plays pool and inflicts his taste in music (The Fall, mainly) on his very tolerant partner, Josette.

CJ Cherryh
EXPLORER

"Serious space opera at its very best by one of the leading SF writers in the field today." —*Publishers Weekly*

The *Foreigner* novels introduced readers to the epic story of a lost human colony struggling to survive on the hostile world of the alien atevi. In this final installment to the second sequence of the series, diplomat Bren Cameron, trapped in a distant star system, faces a potentially bellicose alien ship, and must try to prevent interspecies war, when the secretive Pilot's Guild won't even cooperate with their own ship.

Be sure to read the first five books in this action-packed series:

0-7564-0131-3

To Order Call: 1-800-788-6262

CJ Cherryh
Classic Series in New Omnibus Editions

THE DREAMING TREE
Contains the complete duology *The Dreamstone* and
The Tree of Swords and Jewels.   0-88677-782-8

THE FADED SUN TRILOGY
Contains the complete novels *Kesrith*, *Shon'jir*, and
Kutath.   0-88677-836-0

THE MORGAINE SAGA
Contains the complete novels *Gate of Ivrel*, *Well of
Shiuan*, and *Fires of Azeroth.*   0-88677-877-8

THE CHANUR SAGA
Contains the complete novels *The Pride of Chanur*,
Chanur's Venture and *The Kif Strike Back.*
0-88677-930-8

ALTERNATE REALITIES
Contains the complete novels *Port Eterntiy*, *Voyager in
Night*, and *Wave Without a Shore*   0-88677-946-4

AT THE EDGE OF SPACE
Contains the complete novels *Brothers of Earth* and
Hunter of Worlds.   0-7564-0160-7

To Order Call: 1-800-788-6262